op lot R^{50}

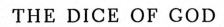

THE DICE OF GOD

THE DICE
OF GOD

HOFFMAN BIRNEY

HENRY HOLT AND COMPANY, NEW YORK

80963-0116
Printed in the United States of America

Again . . .

to Marguerite

CONTENTS

The dice of God are always loaded.

—Emerson: *Essays on Compensation*

THE DICE OF GOD

1 A HANDSOME FILLY

The hotel proprietor did not linger over his coffee. He gulped it hurriedly, murmured that his presence was required in the office, and left the table. The captain watched him cross the dining room, then grinned wryly and gave his attention to the wine the man had ordered. A mild drink, a ladies' drink, but it brought a little life to the whisky he'd had before dinner. *Won't you ever learn sense, Demas Harrod? Are you going to sound off every time you hear the name of Tuthill? He's your commanding officer, remember. Now you'll have to find that hotel man again and apologize for your rudeness. You were rude, goddam it!*

He drew a cigar from his pocket but refrained from lighting it in the presence of the ladies in the dining room. St. Paul was still on the edge of the frontier and the Metropolitan Hotel was a long way from Willard's in Washington, but there were some women here who didn't have to take a back seat to the best of 'em in Washington or New York. Take that one over by the window—a handsome filly if there ever was one. Nice hands and slender wrists—always a sign of small feet and a well-turned ankle. She was married, though. There was a ring on the third finger of her left hand and she chatted gaily with the man who sat across from her. *Not for me! I don't fool with married women—especially in a town that's department head-quarters, like this.*

He pushed back his chair, rose, and walked toward the lobby and the bar on the further side, quite unaware that the eyes of the woman followed him until he was out of sight. He lit his cigar at the gas flame of a torch held by the bronze figure of an Indian maiden at the end of the bar—*whoever made that thing sure hadn't seen many squaws*—and signaled the bartender.

"Yes, sir, Captain, be right with you. 'Tain't often I get a chance to serve two captains, both at once."

Harrod glanced toward the other man on his side of the bar.

"Captain—?" he began hesitantly.

"Yes, sir," the bartender said proudly. "This here is Captain Jonas Whiteman of the packet *Des Moines*. Meet Captain Harrod of the Twentieth Cavalry, Fort Doniphan."

The two shook hands. The packet captain invited the cavalryman to drink and the bartender supplied a glass. The bottle held an old—an unbelievably old—brandy which was Captain Whiteman's especial pride. He had purchased the last dozen bottles to be found in New Orleans, twelve bottles which by some miracle had survived the war, the thirst of the occupation forces, and the chaos of Reconstruction. He had resold them to Davidson, proprietor of the Metropolitan, and now . . .

"Whenever I get to St. Paul he lets me buy some of my own liquor back from him. Drink hearty, Captain, and tell me if any sweeter liquor ever touched your tongue."

The brandy was superb. Harrod would have enjoyed taking it to a side table and there devote himself to the pleasant task of lowering the level in the bottle, but Captain White-man was already maudlin and Harrod had little desire for further acquaintance. He made his excuses—"I'm leaving for Fort Doniphan tomorrow and have an appointment with an officer from the department"—and returned to the lobby. The woman he had noticed in the dining room was seated in a chair beneath one of the artificial palms. She was alone now and when she met his eyes she smiled.

"Good evening, Captain Harrod."

He bowed. His eyes flashed to the hand in her lap. By God, he'd've sworn she'd been wearing a wedding ring in the dining room, but the third finger was bare now.

"Your servant, madam, but——"

"But you don't remember me—is that it?"

"I'm ashamed to confess it, ma'am, but that's the truth."

"I can't blame you, really. It was a long time ago and a lot has happened since—to both of us. You were in St. Louis on the unpleasant duty of inspecting mules and approving their purchase by the army. My father had a contract to deliver several hundred and——"

"Wait a minute!" he interrupted. "Your father is Cyrus Pierce—'Long Cy' Pierce. I dined twice at your home on the Bluff Road. Your name's Louise. I remember now."

"The name's Lulu, but outside of that you're quite right. You left out only one thing—we rode together one Sunday. Have you forgotten that?" She smiled gaily.

"Of course not! That ride is the most pleasant memory I have of St. Louis." He had dined at the Pierce home on Satur-day and after dinner, mellowed by Long Cy's excellent whisky, had remarked that his life followed a rut between his boarding-house and the stockyards. He was a cavalryman, he had said, and he missed his horse. Pierce's daughter had suggested in-stantly that they ride together the next day; her father had several excellent saddle horses which were eating their heads off. She was a skinny youngster, much younger than he, and not particularly attractive. A born horsewoman, though; nice hands, a good seat, and quite fearless at the fences they'd taken when they left the road and struck cross-country. He'd enjoyed every minute of the afternoon and had thanked her sincerely for the pleasure she'd given him. Then, as she clung to his arm, he had turned her face upward and kissed her. Damn if he knew why, but something had told him that she wanted him to. She had returned the kiss—if she'd been a couple of years older he'd have said she was passionate about it—and then had dashed into the house without a word.

"You can't blame me for not recognizing you at first, Miss Pierce. That was some time ago and—well, you've changed."

"You mean I'm fatter!"

"No, no!"

"Well, I am—nearly twenty pounds—and I'm glad of it! It's been more than six years and I was just a skinny girl, as skinny as a plucked jaybird, who was trying to keep house for my father and to entertain his friends. And it's not Miss Pierce now—it's Mrs. Gorton."

"My apologies again. Was that Mr. Gorton I saw you with in the dining room?"

"No, merely an acquaintance who happened to arrive today on the *Des Moines* packet. I'm a widow, Captain, and have been for three years."

"I'm sorry, I didn't know——"

"Of course not, how could you? I'm flattered that you even remembered Cy Pierce's skinny daughter. Do tell me, Captain, what are you doing in St. Paul? Are you stationed here—and if you are why haven't we met?"

"That's my misfortune, Mrs. Gorton. I only reached town this afternoon and am leaving again in the morning. I'm on my way to South City—Fort Andrew Doniphan. I've been assigned to the Twentieth Cavalry."

He heard the quick intake of her breath.

"No!" she exclaimed. "Please tell me you're not going there!"

"The orders were pretty clear, Mrs. Gorton, they said Fort Doniphan and the Twentieth."

"But"—her breast rose and fell quickly—"that means you'll be in the fighting—in the war against the hostiles!"

"Probably so." *What the hell's the matter with her?* "I've heard, quite unofficially, that such a campaign is being planned. It's too late for it this year, though."

When she spoke again she had regained her control.

"I'm sorry," she said lightly. "I hoped you were going to tell me that you were stationed here and that we'd see something of each other. I"—she dropped her hand to his—"I was so glad when I recognized you. I have very few friends in St. Paul and when I saw you leave the dining room, I just made up my mind that I'd wait right here in the lobby until you came back."

"Now I'm the one who's flattered, Mrs. Gorton. We"—Captain Harrod considered for a moment—"it's not at all late. We could return to the dining room and have a cup of coffee, or perhaps a bottle of wine, together."

She shook her head quickly. The jet beads on her bonnet jingled musically.

"No, that wouldn't do. Somebody would be sure to see me and——"

"You can be seen just as easily here in the lobby."

"I know. Light a cigar, Demas—I'm going to call you Demas and I want you to call me Lulu, please. Light a cigar and let me think for just a minute."

He smoked quietly. There was half an inch of ash on his cheroot when she broke the silence.

"I live here in St. Paul now, Demas," she said at last. "It was Mr. Gorton's home and after he died—he was killed in an accident at his factory—I kept right on living here. His people, his mother, and his brothers and their wives resent it. He left his business to me and they think it should have gone to his family—to them. They want me to sell it back to them at a perfectly ridiculous figure. Nothing would please them more than to spread the gossip that I'd been drinking with a man in the Metropolitan."

"That sort of gossip can't hurt you."

"It can—that's where you're wrong. Oh, Demas, I'm lonely here, terribly lonely." Again her restless hand touched his, clutched it quickly, and was withdrawn before he could return the pressure. He dropped his cheroot in the tall brass cuspidor that stood beside his chair.

"Demas?"

"Yes, Lulu."

"You don't gossip, do you? If I suggested something very, very unconventional you wouldn't gossip about it, would you?"

"Of course not, Lulu. I hope——"

"Listen to me. Fourth Avenue and A Street, can you remember that?"

"Of course."

"The third house on A Street north of Fourth Avenue, west side of the street. It's a white house with a porch in front and it sits back from the street a little. There'll be a light in the second floor window but none downstairs. You'll remember all that?" He nodded and she continued hurriedly. "It's a quarter to eight now. Don't hurry. Wait until—oh, until nine o'clock—and then take a hack and tell the driver to take you to Fourth and B. That's a block away and you can walk over. We . . . we won't be disturbed and I can promise you something a lot better than wine. I still have some of father's old Monongahela whisky."

"I remember it well."

"Now walk with me to the door, Demas. I'll tell the porter to call a hack for me, and don't pay any attention to what I say where the desk clerk can hear me."

He walked at her side across the lobby.

"It's been so pleasant to meet you, Captain," she said clearly, "and I'll wish you the best of luck on the expedition next summer. When you write your mother please give her my very best regards."

"It will be a pleasure, Mrs. Gorton. I never expected to meet an old friend in St. Paul—it was a pleasant surprise."

"To us both, Captain. There—the porter has a hack for me."

Captain Harrod turned toward the bar, then recalled that he'd probably find the steamboat captain there and considerably drunker than he'd been half an hour before. The situation seemed to call for a drink, several drinks, but he returned to the chair beneath the straggling palm and informed himself that he'd be goddamned, good and goddamned. *By God, it's been six or seven years and she remembers that one time I kissed her. She wanted me to remember it too—wasn't happy until I let her know I'd never forgotten it. One kiss—Jesus, how many girls have I kissed since then? She's been married —married and widowed for three years. Marriage has sure improved her. She's plumped out where she needed plumping and her hair looks different. What in hell is her game? Wait till nine o'clock, then take a hack to Fourth and B and walk the rest of the way . . . she sure doesn't want anybody to know that she's having a visitor. And she's still got some of Long Cy's old Monongahela whisky. A drink of it would go good right now, but I can wait. I'll just bring along a little extra present, though. Wonder if I can talk the proprietor of this place out of a bottle of that New Orleans brandy? And some champagne to go with it—we'll by God mix 'em. The king's peg!*

He found the hotel proprietor, Davidson, in the rear of the lobby and apologized for his rudeness during dinner.

"Your mention of Colonel Tuthill," he said, "recalled my previous service with the regiment and the fight at Wishbone

Creek. That was a long time ago, but I lost one of my best friends there, Major Harris. Sometimes, you know, things like that come back to a man . . . and they're not always pleasant."

"Think nothing of it, Captain, I beg you. If you'll step in the bar I'll be proud to buy you a drink."

"Many thanks, but I've had plenty for the present. There's one thing I'd sure like to buy from you, though, Mr. Davidson. That's a bottle of that New Orleans brandy of which I had a taste a few minutes ago."

"Captain! You're asking for a quart of my life blood!"

"I know it, but——"

He pleaded mightily and the picture he drew of the loneliness of Fort Doniphan, the horrible quality of the sutler's whisky, and the joy with which his fellow officers would welcome liquor of the matchless quality of that New Orleans brandy finally persuaded Davidson to release a bottle of the precious stuff. The champagne was much easier to obtain. Davidson, after consulting his headwaiter, suggested Ruinart '58, the same brand, Harrod recalled, that he had ordered for the never-to-be-forgotten luncheon with Miss Alice Lowell Peabody. *God, that's barely two weeks ago! One day, lunch with an ex-senator's daughter. The next, or pretty damn nearly the next, and I'm on my way to the frontier! Just like that. How far is it from Washington to St. Paul or should I say from Alice to Lulu? Wonder what the sweet and proper Miss Peabody is doing now, or has she quit thinking about the narrow escape she had from one Demas Harrod? She used to invite me out to the house, too, when she knew nobody would be around, but not like this Lulu did. I don't know your game, Lulu, but if it's what I think it is, I'll sure play it with you.*

2 THE CAPTAIN (1)

Had Captain Demas K. Harrod been asked how he felt about receiving orders to join the Twentieth Cavalry at Fort Doniphan, he would have declared that he was a cavalryman and was damn sick of sitting at a desk in Washington. He wanted active service, and assignment to the Twentieth—actually it was a reassignment—offered that opportunity.

He would have denied emphatically that the decision had been influenced even indirectly by Miss Alice Lowell Peabody, daughter of ex-Senator Amos Somerville Peabody, who was president of the Somerville Knitting Mills, a director of a dozen banks and corporations, and a millionaire several times over. *Jesus Howard Christ, man, I haven't got a sou outside of my army pay—what I make in a year wouldn't pay for the earrings she had on last night.*

All of which would have been quite untrue, but no other explanation was possible for an officer and a gentleman. Harrod considered himself to be both.

His diploma from the United States Military Academy declared him an officer; he was a gentleman by virtue of the traditions of that institution and the mercilessly enforced discipline of upper classmen and cadet officers who corrected a plebe's table manners as swiftly as they did an unfastened button, unshined shoes, or a disordered room. Until he had entered the academy he had not known that a knife was for cutting one's food, not for conveying it to the mouth; that one waited for soup or coffee to cool and did not hasten the process by blowing into a spoon or cup.

Demas Harrod was the only son of an immigrant Englishman who kept a small neighborhood store in the Northern Liberties section of Philadelphia. The father had worked for a time for the Philadelphia & Reading Railroad, then had moved to Kensington and the textile mills there, then back to railroading as a switchman for the Pennsylvania in the freight yards west of the new station at Thirteenth Street. He had lost the toes from one foot in that service and been awarded a pension of twelve-fifty per month. On that and the income from the store on Vineyard Street he supported a family: his wife, his son Demas, and two daughters.

The store had originally been the parlor of the small two-story frame dwelling. Behind it was a dining room and kitchen, above were two bedrooms, one for the elder Harrod and his wife, the other for the two girls. Demas slept on a folding cot in the store. There was a sink and running water in the kitchen, a privy in the back yard.

Demas could not remember a day in his life when he had not hated and despised his home and its environment. Because he held them responsible for that home and its surroundings, he had little affection and certainly no love for either of his parents. He saw older boys in the neighborhood quit school at the eighth grade and find work on the railroads, as apprentices in the locomotive works, in the breweries which were springing up along Girard Avenue and Master Street. When his father suggested that he do the same, he refused.

"I am going to finish high school," he declared. "And afterward—I know I'll have to work my way, but I'll do it somehow —I'm going to go to college."

He led his classes in the lower grades and through the four years he attended the Northern Liberties High School where he told the principal of his determination to obtain a college education.

"In what field, Demas? I mean, what do you want to make of yourself?"

"I don't know. I thought for a while that I'd like to be a doctor, but that takes a long time. I can finish at the engineering school in four years. It seems as though there are new factories going up everywhere and new railroads being built in the West—that might be the best thing."

"Engineering is a tough course, but I have faith in you as far as that's concerned—you're a natural student if there ever was one. College is expensive, too, and I don't imagine that your father will be able to help you to any great extent."

"No," said the boy bluntly. "He wouldn't even if he could. He—he's English, you know, and doesn't see much use in a college education. He's already told me that after high school I'm on my own, even for food and clothes."

"I see. Let me think if over, Demas. Come in and see me again tomorrow."

"Yes, sir—and thank you." The boy was leaving the room when the principal called him back.

"Something just occurred to me. Have you ever thought of going to one of the service schools—to the military academy at West Point or the naval academy at Annapolis? You'll get an education there, as good a one as you can get anywhere, and the government pays all your expenses."

"I—no, sir, I've never thought of it at all. It would be wonderful, though. How could I get to go to one of them?—I honestly don't care which."

"You'd have to get an appointment—and I don't imagine you know your senator or any of the congressmen."

"No, sir. To tell you the truth I don't even know their names."

"Let me see what I can do. I happen to come from Lancaster and Senator Stevens is a neighbor of mine; my family knows him very well. I've never asked him for a favor in my life, but there's got to be a first time for everything—even for Thaddeus Stevens doing something decent."

The long-delayed result of that conversation was an official letter directing Mr. Demas K. Harrod to report to the United States Military Academy, West Point, for physical and mental examinations preliminary to appointment as a cadet.

He had been in his second year at the academy when, on April 12, 1861, the Charleston batteries fired on Fort Sumter and the red tide of war, threatening for years, burst over the land. The four-year course was promptly condensed to three and he and his classmates were "race-horsed" through to their commissions. Demas Harrod was a cadet sergeant and fourth in his class. Under normal conditions he would have been appointed to the Corps of Engineers, but the need for line officers was pressing and he elected and was granted appointment as a second lieutenant of cavalry.

The son of the Northern Liberties storekeeper received far more from West Point than the fundamentals of military science and tactics, electricity and chemistry, mathematics and a smattering of French and German. Those he took in his stride and was the envy of his plodding classmates. Less obvious was his indoctrination with the traditions of the service, the honor of the Corps of Cadets, the significance of the term "officer and gentleman." He who had skillfully lied his way out of a dozen schoolboy scrapes learned that a gentleman did not lie, that an officer's word of honor was never questioned, that a woman's virtue was taken for granted and was sacred.

The bright polish on that shield was somewhat tarnished after three years of war in Virginia, Maryland, and Pennsylvania; a dozen major engagements, two wounds, promotion to first lieutenant and—by brevet—to captain and major; and service under a dozen regimental commanders of varying degrees of ability. Not all of his brothers-in-arms were Rolands and Bayards, nor were the ideals of the service a sacred oriflamme to be followed unswervingly.

Duty to one's country, one's God, and one's fellowman was, at times, a question of personal interpretation as to the precise meaning of that term. In battle one obeyed orders; advanced, deployed, charged, or halted as commanded. At other times, during the long winters when the troopers chafed restlessly and cursed snow and slush and roads belly-deep in slimy mud, orders were carefully studied before execution. Recognition and preferment were often rewards of obeying the spirit of orders while violating the text.

He had learned that promotions came slowly to those who had elected to follow the military profession, and that brevets —the temporary elevation to higher rank—were not always awarded to the most deserving. He had won two brevets, both for gallantry in action, but had seen others advanced for services no more conspicuous than the procurement of supplies or the handling of transportation. Early in '64 he had been hospitalized for six weeks when a ricocheting bullet had slashed through his thigh during a routine patrol above Gay's Ford of the Rapidan. When he was fit for duty again, the corps was in the Shenandoah Valley under Sheridan, and Harrod served the remaining months of the war on staff duty with Hancock's II Corps. While in hospital he became quite friendly with a gray-haired major of field artillery who managed to get drunk at least twice weekly on Medical Corps whisky smuggled to him by a quartermaster sergeant.

"How old are you, Harrod?" the artilleryman asked suddenly.

"Twenty-six, sir." Though their rank was the same, Harrod was still not accustomed to the gold leaves on his shoulder straps.

"This war will be over in another year—you're not too young to quit. That's my advice: get the hell out of the army and make something of yourself."

"I haven't thought of it," said Harrod uncomfortably. "Soldiering is all I know."

"It's all I know, too, but I'm forty-eight and too damn old and stove up for anything else. The sawbones tell me that I'll get the use of my leg again, but that's all. I'll transfer to the Quartermaster Corps and sit at a desk in some damn QM depot until my head is as fat as my ass. What's your permanent rank?"

"First lieutenant."

"Same as mine and I've held it since 'fifty-six. We'll go back to it, you and I, as soon as the fighting's over. If I'm lucky, goddamned lucky, I'll get my two bars before I retire. You married?"

"No."

"You're lucky—or should I say you're lucky so far? Army life is hell on women, as anybody with a brain in his head knows, and the women take it out on the men. If you do marry, though, pick the girl a damn sight more carefully than you'd pick a personal mount. Sound in wind and limb, yes. Well-gaited and answers to bridle, spur, or knee, yes. Meets all standards for color and configuration, yes. There's one other thing to look for. D'you know what it is?"

"Can't say I do, Major, if it's a wife you're talking about."

"I am. Call me cold-blooded but I've seen too many army marriages go on the rocks for the want of it—and that's a bank account. Yours if you've got means outside your pay, hers if you haven't. Trying to keep a wife on army pay is like trying to feed a dog on a Chinaman's leavings. Pick a wife with an income of her own—and the bigger the better so long as she knows that you're boss in your home and your profession. If her father's in politics and knows the right people, fine, but it's the money that counts. It means promotion. It means duty as an aide to the President or assignment to some foreign embassy. It means you can take care of the other fellow—even your commanding officer—when Congress adjourns without making appropriations and the man in uniform goes without pay. If a woman has money you can forget a harelip and cross eyes—you don't notice 'em once the light is out anyway. Take a look at her bank account or her prospects and marry her.

"That's the best goddam advice you'll ever get in the army, Major. Maybe you'll remember it sometime. And if you're ever on the faculty at the academy, recommend that they teach how to live on army pay without going deeper into debt every year. God, what a life!"

Harrod never saw the man after the day he left the hospital to rejoin his regiment. He soon forgot the major's name, but the memory of his bitter advice remained. He had certainly been correct in one thing, at least. Demotions from brevet rank came swiftly after Appomattox, and Harrod replaced his major's leaves with the single bar of his permanent rank. He was unmarried and the reduced pay was less to him than the loss in rank and prestige, but there were moments when he thought of following the artilleryman's advice and resigning his commission. The mood rarely lasted more than a few minutes. He had only to look about him to realize that there were thousands of men, former officers and with records as distinguished as his own, who were looking for work of any kind. He told himself that he could never return to Philadelphia and the shabby store in the Northern Liberties, and he was trained for no profession but that of arms. He shrugged his shoulders, poured himself a drink, and remained in the army.

In the fall of 1866 Congress passed a bill calling for the reorganization of the army. Harrod was promoted to captain, greatly to his surprise, and assigned to the Ninth Cavalry, a Negro regiment. Eighteen months later, when the expedition against the Southern Cheyennes was planned, he was transferred to the Twentieth Cavalry and commanded a company of that regiment in the Battle of Wishbone Creek when Black Eagle and his people were slaughtered and Major Joseph Harris and nineteen troopers died in what came to be called a massacre.

Demas K. Harrod had his own opinion of who was responsible for Harris' death, but he expressed that opinion only to the man himself—to Colonel and Brevet Major General Frederic C. Tuthill, commanding officer, Twentieth U. S. Cavalry. Of what passed between them neither he nor Tuthill ever spoke. After Wishbone Creek, Harrod rode with the regiment in the long pursuit of the fugitive Cheyennes and Arapahos, but within a month after the weary troopers had returned to their home station he received orders which transferred him first to temporary duty with the Quartermaster Corps in St. Louis, then to various posts in the South, and eventually to Washington.

In the capital he recalled, and cold-bloodedly decided to follow, the advice of the wounded artillery major. There he clambered for a brief space to the social peaks and from that eminence looked down upon the promised land of luxury, assured position, and easy promotion which awaited a man who combined a military career and a matrimonial alliance with Miss Alice Peabody, daughter and sole heir of a former senator from Massachusetts. He had met her quite casually at one of the monthly hops given by the officers at Fort Myer, had danced with her four times, and before the evening ended had been invited to call by her aunt and chaperone, Mrs. Lorenzo Hubbard, who was permanently in residence in her widowed brother's Washington mansion.

"I am at home on Tuesdays, Captain Harrod," Mrs. Hubbard had said. "I would be very glad to see you then and to present you to some of my friends—my niece tells me you have been in Washington only a short time."

He donned the resplendent full-dress uniform of his rank. He bowed over Mrs. Hubbard's hand and those of her friends. He met what seemed to be a battalion of young ladies, all of them astoundingly beautiful, who flirted most discreetly and asked astonishingly silly questions about the frontier. And he was acutely aware that Miss Alice Peabody observed the mild flirtations, listened to the chatter, and skillfully intervened when it appeared that one of the maidens might entice him to a more secluded position on the chairs beneath the potted palms which stood in each corner of the room. When he placed his teacup on the grand piano she appeared beside him. She fingered the music on the rack.

"I would like to ask you to play, Miss Peabody, but I'm afraid this is scarcely the time."

"No, and I'm not nearly good enough to play for an audience. I strum a little, that's all, as you'll know when you hear me. Do you play—or sing—Captain?"

"The mouth-harp, Miss Peabody, the soldier's instrument which can be shoved into the pocket or the leg of a boot. And I sing like a crow—in fact, some crows would be ashamed of my voice."

"I don't believe you," she smiled archly. "Your speaking voice is deep and musical and I know you can sing."

"I would gladly prove to you that you are quite wrong, but it would stampede your aunt's guests. Some other time possibly."

There it is, my girl, what do you want to do with it. Pick it up or let it lie!

"I just know you're only teasing me and that you're musical! I—come and sing for me Friday evening, Captain Harrod!"

"I am yours to command, Miss Peabody." He whistled inwardly. She was sure rushing things, asking a man to call so directly and so soon after they had met. Maybe they worked faster in Washington than in the West. Maybe an ex-senator's daughter made her own rules. His eyes had already told him that his surroundings were those of great wealth. He was impressed but not awed by the many evidences of opulence, the delicate china, the silver, the soft-footed English servants, and the formality which prescribed that a footman be summoned for so simple a task as filling a glass from a carafe which stood within inches of Mrs. Hubbard's hand.

He called on Friday evening and found, as he'd expected, that Miss Peabody was alone or nearly so. Her aunt was present but remained well in the background while her niece played simple melodies and they sang—his baritone was quite untrained but true—"Who Is Sylvia?" and "Old Black Joe." The piano occupied about the same space as the tent which sheltered him and his lieutenant and their belongings when the Twentieth was in the field. Her fingers slipped from the keys.

"Why are you laughing, Captain?" she asked quickly. "I know I played that passage correctly and even if I hadn't, you shouldn't have laughed."

"Was I laughing? You were watching your music, not looking at me."

"I could feel it. I'm very sensitive, Captain."

So's a troop horse when he's getting his hoofs trimmed, thought Harrod. Aloud he said:

"It's strange that you should have known I was laughing. I was, but not at you or your playing, I assure you. I laughed to think of the great difference a couple of thousand miles can make, of where I am now and where I have been. It was the ice water, I think."

"The ice water? You speak so strangely, Captain. I'm afraid I don't understand."

"I'm afraid you couldn't, Miss Peabody. That pitcher of clear, cold ice water made me think of the times I've drunk standing water, green and slimy, out of a buffalo wallow and been glad to get it; of times I've eaten horse or mule meat and been glad to get that, too."

She shuddered. The silk scarf had fallen to the floor and her bare white shoulders quivered.

"How horrible! I hope that you'll never have to do things like that again. Surely you can manage to stay in Washington."

"I'm a soldier, Miss Peabody. The War Department, not I, decides where my station will be."

"My father will be here next week or early the week following. He knows everyone and I'll ask him to inquire about you."

He did not reply. A senator, even an ex-senator if he knew the right people, could do a lot for an army officer. Five days later a note was delivered at the rooms he occupied on D Street, behind the State, War, and Navy Building. *Just how in hell did she learn where I live?* Mrs. Hubbard invited him to dine the following Friday at seven.

"Just *en famille*, Captain," she wrote. "My brother arrives from Boston on Wednesday and I know that he will enjoy meeting you. He has always been interested in the army and in conditions in the Indian country."

He replied that he was honored to accept, then consulted another captain, on duty with the Ordnance Department, whom he had known at West Point. Could Captain Barrett recommend a tailor who could supply suitable evening clothes on very short notice?

"I've accepted an invitation to dine next Friday," Harrod told him, "to meet Senator—he's an ex-senator—Peabody from Massachusetts. Nothing was said about dress and I'll be damned if I'm going to show my frontier ignorance by asking."

"A big affair?"

"No, quite the opposite. Just the family—the senator, his sister who runs his house since his wife died, and the daughter, Miss Alice."

The ordnance captain whistled.

"A small affair, all right, but damned fast company, Demas my boy. Peabody's not in Congress any more, but when he tells certain congressmen what to do, they do it. Civilian full dress, by all means. Washington society had enough of uniforms during the war; they're quite *de trop* now except at strictly military affairs. My own tailor—Mueller on Eleventh Street—will fix you up. We'll go 'round there after lunch. I owe him about three months' pay and he'll be delighted to take care of a friend of mine."

"Thank you. I'd thought of Holloman——"

"No, no. Never go to a military tailor for civilian clothes or to a civilian tailor for your uniforms. Mueller's the best in Washington."

"Thanks again. I've been away from the amenities of civilization for a long time. You forget things—just like you and I have forgotten some of the lectures we got at the academy. I hope I don't wipe my knife on my pants leg and stick it down in my boot!"

"Not much chance of that, I imagine," Captain Barrett laughed, "but I know what you mean. It's mighty easy to forget little things, such as how many cards you're supposed to leave and that you're expected to send flowers to your hostess."

Flowers! God, I've never even thought of 'em!

"I've remembered that much, of course," he said quickly. "What I'm not sure about is should I send flowers to both ladies. Mrs. Hubbard is my hostess, but there's Miss Peabody, too."

Captain Barrett cogitated.

"To both, I think. Yes, that's indicated. Go to Legrand on Thirteenth Street and accept his suggestions. Roses are always in good taste."

Christ on a crutch, what terrific decisions you Washington coffee-coolers are called on to make. Shall it be roses or violets or piss-the-bed dandelions? It'd do you good to have to poke those nice pink fingers in a pile of horse dung while you study out *how fresh it is and how close you are to the bunch of hostiles whose ponies dropped it. How many are there and have you got enough men to take care of 'em? Roses or violets —and shall you head for that break in the hills and maybe cut the featherdusters off or shall you follow their trail and maybe run into a neat ambush. Roses . . .*

"Thanks, Lewis, thanks for everything."

He repeated his gratitude with considerably more sincerity later that day in the barroom of Willard's Hotel. Captain Barrett had escorted him to Mueller's shop, he had established the credit of his good friend Captain Harrod, he had selected the material and suggested how it should be cut—"the deep-notched reveres by all means, Demas, and the silk facing should end right there. The full silk collar is definitely *passé*"— and at Galt's had aided in the purchase of studs, cuff links, and smoky pearl buttons for the white vest. "A touch of contrast, you know. Quite in form, too." The least that Captain Harrod could do in appreciation was to suggest dinner at Willard's.

"Don't know what I'd have done without you, Lewis. Didn't really realize until today what a country bumpkin I'd become."

Three brandies-and-soda had made Captain Barrett expansive.

"Happy to have been of service, Demas. Man in your position has to study his campaign, you know, and staff advice helps. From the frontier to Senator Peabody's dining room is quite a hurdle, old fellow. There's plenty of hot competition running against you, from what I hear. Entries from Boston and New York as well as a couple from here in Washington." He took another swallow and laughed. "A million-dollar flame draws a lot of moths. We can't have the army's sole entry left at the post."

"By no means." *A tour of duty at a frontier post would teach you to hold your liquor better, my friend.* "To tell you the truth, Lewis, I haven't been thinking along those lines. The gentleman I'm going to meet might possibly be worth knowing, that's all."

"Precisely. A man is known by his friends in high places. Tuthill must have taught you that a cavalry charge, properly launched, is irresistible. I'm backing the cavalry against the field."

"I'd suggest waiting until there's a race," said Harrod coolly. "At present I'm considering which fork to use and remembering that the waiter won't be a trooper drafted out of C because his fingernails were fairly clean."

His apprehensions were groundless. The Corps of Cadets at the U. S. Military Academy has its own method of teaching the social graces which are as much a part of the equipment of an officer and gentleman as his saber or his spurs. The tutelage is severe but the lessons are never forgotten. Harrod had preconceived Senator Peabody as a pompous windbag who would dominate all conversation with congressional profundities; the man he met was a leathery New Englander with the lean features of a medieval ascetic and an easy graciousness with his guest. He had known Lincoln; he knew Stanton and Steward, the acidulous Thaddeus Stevens, McClellan, Halleck, Meade, and Grant; Jefferson Davis and Robert E. Lee.

"My acquaintance with the last gentleman was from the other side of the fence," said Harrod dryly. "I saw him once, though—at Appomattox Courthouse. We were camped in a field when a group of rebel officers rode past on the road. They were returning to their camp from the surrender. General Lee on his gray horse was in the lead."

"I knew him well," said Peabody. "I was one of those who urged him in 'sixty-one to accept the command of the Union forces in the field, but his conscience dictated that he go as his state went. He was a great military leader and a very great gentleman."

"That's a high tribute, sir, coming from a Northerner. There were plenty who were all out for hanging him after the war."

"There are hotheads and extremists everywhere, young man. Things would be very different in the South today if Mr. Lincoln had lived. He would never have tolerated the policies which Stanton and that miserable Stevens dictated."

No wine appeared with the meal. After the dessert—a lemon ice—Mrs. Hubbard remarked that they would have their coffee in the drawing room. Harrod glanced hopefully at the serving table for brandy or some other liqueur, but there was none. *Temperance household, eh—well, I can stand it—once. Wonder how Alice likes it; I'll swear I saw her at the punchbowl at Fort Myer and what they served there was sighted for a thousand yards, point-blank. Talking's dry work.*

There was no suggestion that Miss Peabody favor them at the piano nor did the senator make any excuse which would enable him and his sister to withdraw and leave the younger couple to themselves. He continued the conversation and skillfully led the captain to talk of the frontier and his service there.

"You mentioned the Colt's revolver, Captain—how about the rifles? Are they the right weapons for warfare against the tribes?"

"They could be better, sir. The regiments on the frontier should have repeating rifles like the Winchester. Nearly all of us have repeaters as our personal hunting rifles and they're entirely satisfactory. The Ordnance people, though, maintain that they're not suitable for military use, that they get out of order easily—which I haven't found to be true—and that both the ball and the powder charge are too light. So they recall the Spencers and give us new model Springfield with a forty-five-caliber ball weighing five hundred grains and seventy grains of powder to push it along.

"What Ordnance doesn't realize is that the targets are Indians on fast ponies. If you miss with the single-shot Springfield, Mr. Indian is over the hill and far away before you can kick out the empty shell, load another cartridge, cock the hammer, and get off a second shot. The Winchester does all that in one motion, like this"—his hand flicked forward and back. "With one of them you've got two or three chances to make a good Indian out of a live one."

He talked well, as do most men who speak of their chosen profession, and the senator prompted him skillfully. Harrod knew that Alice Peabody listened, wide-eyed, to every word. He knew that she was ravishing in apricot-colored silk, that her bodice was cut extremely low, and that her breasts were swelling and firm. He addressed the senator, but he talked to her as young Marco Polo might have talked to the Venetian maidens of Prester John and far Cathay.

He told them of lonely forts in the Indian country, of Laramie, of Phil Kearney—now abandoned and in ruins—where a supremely overconfident and inexperienced officer, Captain and Brevet Lieutenant Colonel William J. Fetterman, had flatly disobeyed orders and led eighty-one men to their deaths in an ambush skillfully planned by the wily Red Cloud. Of Hays and Harker and Riley in the heart of the buffalo country, and of Andrew Doniphan far up the Missouri in Dakota Territory.

He told them of life at those stations where officers and men, underpaid and frequently unpaid, guarded the frontiers of the nation; of inadequate, dilapidated quarters without sinks or closets; of rationed water; of flash floods in the spring, searing heat and withering drought in the summer, and terrible blizzards with snow as dry and as fine as powder and so thick that men could lose their way and die between the mess halls and the picket lines.

And through it all, like a scarlet warp-thread through drab cloth, ran the reason for those posts' existence and the threat to their survival—the Sioux and their allies the Northern Cheyenne, the irreconcilables, the hostiles, the "wild" Indians as distinguished from those tribesmen who had forsaken the warpath and were now huddled miserably on reservations.

"The Indians have been a problem since the earliest days of this nation," said the senator sententiously. "I have asked myself many times if there is any solution to it. What is your personal opinion, Captain?"

"I'm an army man, Senator," said Harrod slowly, "and my opinion is that of an officer who has served on the frontier. Sooner or later we'll have to smash them, smash them completely!"

He was grimly silent for a moment, then continued:

"It will have to be done if the western country is ever to be opened to settlement. We'll have to smash every hostile tribe from the Apaches in Arizona to the Sioux in Dakota. Shoot the ponies, burn the lodges, and kill every warrior who moves a foot over the reservation line. It will cost lives, but not so many as some people think, and it will cost millions of dollars which will set Congress to screaming, but it's the only way. It was General Sheridan who said that the only good Indian was a dead one and no truer words were ever spoken.

"Give me a minute more, sir . . ." the senator had cleared his throat as though to interrupt. Harrod paused a moment. *I've been a damn fool. He's been leading me along all the time and I've sounded off like a second lieutenant criticizing the tactics of Lee and Napoleon and Caesar. He asked for it, though—I'll by God give it to him.*

"I'm only a cavalry captain," he said slowly, "and I should leave matters of policy to my superiors. I'm giving you the opinion of a man who has fought white enemies—in the South for nearly four years—and red ones. There's a big difference, sir. The Indians are savages, utter savages. I saw what they did to Major Harris and his men on Wishbone Creek in 'sixty-eight and to Lieutenant Kidder of the Second a year before that. What was done to those men can't be mentioned in the presence of ladies, and there isn't a newspaper in the country that would print it. Some of those poor fellows were alive when the reds got hold of them."

He paused again and the three who listened heard the slow exhalation of his breath.

"That's what the fuddy-duddies in the Indian Bureau ought to see. They talk about pacifying the Indians—you can no more tame Rain-in-the-Face or Sitting Bull or Crazy Horse than you can tame a rattlesnake. Those Indians are wild and they're as vicious as locoed wolves. There's only one way to handle them and to solve what you call the Indian problem. I've told you what it is."

2

Various and quite unrelated thoughts coursed through Captain Harrod's mind as he walked from the Peabody home toward the lights of downtown Washington. The most important at the moment was that he earnestly desired a drink, several drinks. Hell had no corner sufficiently hot for a man who would serve a guest a dinner without so much as a glass of white wine —not to mention Benedictine or brandy with the coffee—to wash it down. Second thereto, but more assertive after he was seated at a table in Willard's bar, was the cold-blooded realization that he stood high, very high, with Miss Alice Peabody, heiress to textile mills and banks and sundry town and country mansions. She had walked with him to the door after he had taken his leave of her father and aunt and they had stood together for some minutes in the dimly lighted vestibule.

"I will see you again soon, I hope, Captain?" He had bowed over her hand but had retained her slim fingers between his own. She had made no attempt to withdraw them.

"Very soon, Miss Peabody. It was very kind of your aunt— and you, of course—to invite me. I will call to express my appreciation. That call should be paid within a week, shouldn't it?"

The fingers of her left hand plucked at the roses, his roses, which she wore on her breast.

"On Wednesdays," she said slowly. "Aunt Sophie always goes to the church-guild meeting. She expects me to go with her, but I don't feel at all well. In fact, I'm sure that next Wednesday I will be quite indisposed so far as the guild is concerned."

Christ on a crutch! There's an opening wider than the Missouri River. Play it carefully, Demas. She knows what she's doing, all right, but she's not one of Lily Day's girls even though she's fishing with the same sort of bait.

"My deepest sympathy, Miss Peabody, for your future indisposition. I will keep it in mind on Wednesday evening." The situation seemed to call for a wink but he substituted a smile.

"Thank you, Captain." She half turned toward the inner door but he did not release her hand. He raised it deliberately and planted a kiss in the palm. *Take that by way of a promise and do what you want about it.* She pulled her hand free, plucked a rosebud from among those she wore, and dropped the bloom at his feet. She shot a quick glance over her shoulder as she retreated from the vestibule.

You had to see if I picked it up, didn't you. Captain Harrod took the rose from his pocket and tossed it into an areaway as he turned the corner of K Street. *On Wednesday, my dear, I'll assure you that a certain withered rose is the most precious of my possessions.*

Before the month was out he had decided to marry Miss Alice Peabody. He was not in love with her but she had demonstrated—and no man could ask for clearer demonstration—that he had supplanted all other men she had ever known. *And just what in the hell you see in an impecunious captain of cavalry—pay proper $95 per month—I'd sure like to know!* He would not resign his commission but neither would he return to frontier duties. There were other assignments, plenty of them. Senator Peabody had remarked, quite casually, of course, that thought was being given to the assignment of a military attaché to the embassy in Paris. A job like that called for a field-grade officer. He'd worn a captain's two bars only since January of '67 and in the normal course of military promotions a majority lay far, far, in the future . . . but all things were possible to the son-in-law of a millionaire ex-senator who strolled in and out of the White House as though it were Willard's bar.

He had not yet approached the senator, as convention required, and requested permission to pay formal attention to Miss Alice. Time enough for that. After all, less than two months had passed since that hop at Fort Myer, of which the senator would be sure to remind him. The proper tactic was to scout the position and then to overwhelm it with a charge. Never mind such secondary fortifications as the senator and Aunt Sophie. Once the citadel was subdued, the outposts would be compelled to surrender.

His behavior had been impeccable as far as Miss Alice's elders were concerned. Damn good word, impeccable. It meant "without sin," and God He knew that Demas K. Harrod had done no sinning, not even when the blonde heiress had indicated, oh, so coyly, that a slightly sinful approach would not be rebuffed. He had entertained her and her aunt at Willard's for afternoon tea; twice the senator had been his luncheon guest at the Army and Navy Club. The banker and mill owner was a curious combination of political astuteness and stuffy righteousness. On their first visit to the club a poker game was in progress in a corner of the lounge and Harrod had spoken to an officer he recognized. The senator's eyes had rested briefly on the cards and chips.

"Gambling!" he had snorted after they were in the dining room. "It's the curse of the army, Captain."

"There's not much else to do in the evenings at a frontier post, Senator."

"Gambling and drink," the senator had repeated. "The ruination of young men—and older ones, too. I trust, Captain, that you resist the many temptations of military life."

Wouldn't I like to tell you, you old bastard!

"I'm not quite so virtuous, Senator. You'd have to live at a frontier post to appreciate how lonely it is. Whist I enjoy—it's a game of skill, while poker has nothing to recommend it except the gambling element. I have always made it a rule, though, never to play for stakes higher than I can afford."

Is that sanctimonious enough for you? Small wonder that Alice is ready to jump the fence if that's the sort of pap she's fed at home.

They were already on an "Alice" and "Demas" footing when they were alone, which was more frequently than her father or aunt realized. A note, discreetly unsigned and innocently worded, delivered at his rooms or at his desk in the War Department, advised him that she would be alone at home that evening. The characters "W—2" on a scrap of paper in a sealed envelope would send him at two o'clock to Willard's Hotel where he would be properly surprised and delighted to encounter her in the lobby. She was bold in making those clandestine appointments, timid in keeping them. She ended their meetings at Willard's within ten or fifteen minutes; he stayed considerably longer on those occasions when he called at her home where, she admitted, she had bribed the servants to say nothing of his presence, but she was tense whenever hoofs clattered on the cobblestones outside. None of which was particularly pleasing to Demas Harrod who, although he pressed his lips ardently to her hand when they parted, had only once been granted the fleeting surrender of her lips.

"No, no. Demas. Not again. We're not even engaged. Aunt Sophie said that a girl should never think of kissing a man until they were engaged."

I'll bet she did. I'll bet that on her wedding night she ob-

served all the proprieties and that she put out all the lights be-
fore she even touched the top button of her gown. You'll learn,
my little hard-frozen New England turnip, you'll learn.

"You're quite right, my dear girl. Please sit at the other end
of the sofa so I won't be tempted. Tell me, Alice, have you
ever visited the Golden Fox?"

"I never heard of it. What is it?"

"An old inn—dates back to Colonial times—about five miles
from Alexandria. During the war it was used as a hospital,
but as soon as the shooting stopped the family that owned it
came back, dug up the silver they'd buried, and opened up
again. It's a beautiful old place, very quaint and completely
unspoiled, and the best food this side of New York. We could
drive there in a little over an hour—but of course you'd have
to manage to escape from Aunt Sophie for all afternoon."

Miss Peabody deliberated.

"Maybe . . . it sounds most attractive, Demas. Are you
quite sure it's respectable?"

"Of course! Do you think that I——"

"No, of course you wouldn't. Let me think. Nellie Fortner
has been begging me to visit her, but Baltimore's too far.
There's Grace Jeffers—no, she would be sure to gossip. Oh,
Demas, I know just the one—Helen Begley. Her father's Admiral Begley and they live in Georgetown. Helen just adores a
romantic situation. She'd help me, I know."

3

Captain Harrod knew that a successful campaign was planned
well in advance of actual operations. He waited patiently until
Miss Peabody advised him that she had talked with her friend
Miss Begley and that assistance in every detail had been promised. With the date fixed, he borrowed a mount from a friend
at Fort Myer, rode to the Golden Fox, and there impressed the
innkeeper with his rank and his insistence that nothing less

than perfection would be acceptable in the entertainment of a captain of cavalry and his lady.

He discussed every item of food and its preparation. He studied the wine list and selected a glass of sherry to be at each place when they entered the private dining room he had reserved; then a dry sauterne with the fish, and champagne—vintage of '58—with the meat.

That's enough to start on, my girl. Your white-ribbon relatives believe that you're spending the night with the Begley wench, who probably has her own ideas about where you're going and how long you'll be gone.

He rented the shiniest high-wheeled trap that was obtainable in the city of Washington, and inspected the horses and their harness with the eye of a cavalryman who could detect an unpolished fitting or a misplaced buckle while riding at the gallop. He was proud of his team, his preparations, and himself when he met Miss Peabody a block away from the old brick mansion where she was supposed to be spending a day or two with Admiral Begley's daughter.

Miss Peabody could have been little more excited had she and the captain been departing on their honeymoon. She had selected a gown of plum-covered velvet with a deeply ruffled skirt and the latest and most snugly fitting bodice. Miss Begley believed that it really called for a large hat with a drooping plume but Alice overruled her. A large hat, she said, might be in the way, quickly adding "in the carriage, I mean." She sat quite close to Captain Harrod and clutched his arm tightly.

"I've never done a thing like this in all my life, Demas," she whispered. "I mean going away with a man, alone, for nearly all afternoon. I feel as though I was positively brazen."

"Not at all, my dear girl, not at all. You couldn't be brazen, even if you tried, and, besides, what is there wrong with you and me having lunch together?"

"You put things very nicely, Demas, but all the same I certainly hope that we don't meet anyone I know."

"Scarcely likely." *Shall I tell her I've reserved a private room? No, she'll find out soon enough.*

An attentive stableboy took the horses and assured the captain that they'd be allowed to cool before being watered and fed. The proprietor of the inn met them at the door, announced that all was ready, and led them to the room. A huge bowl of garden flowers decorated the table; the afternoon sunlight touched the blooms and the russet-brown wine in the glasses.

"It's lovely, Demas, just lovely."

Miss Alice Peabody saw only the flowers, the snowy linen, and the silver. She had almost reached the table and the chair which the innkeeper held for her before she noticed the wine —a full glass at either place, beside it two others, empty now, but waiting for the sauterne and the champagne. She froze where she stood.

"De—Captain Harrod, what is this?"

"Sherry, my dear." The chill in her voice did not reach Harrod immediately. "After a long drive, you know——why, what's wrong?"

"You dared—you dared to put strong drink before me! You dared to bring me out here, miles into the country, to ply me with wine! Oh, you cad, you unspeakable cad!"

She turned toward the door. As she passed she withdrew her skirt lest it touch Harrod's boots. Protestingly he touched her arm.

"Alice! My God, what's the matter with you? After all, a mere glass of wine——"

"I do not wish to hear your apologies, Captain. My regret is that I am an only child. If I had a brother he would horse-whip you!" Her blue eyes, as chill now as glacial ice, shifted to the bewildered innkeeper.

"I will wish to see you, sir, and arrange for a—a vehicle to take me to Washington."

"Alice——"
The door closed behind her.

4

Captain Harrod never learned whether or not Miss Peabody
had told her father of how closely she had approached drunkenness and seduction. He never knew whether or not she had
given a whispered account of her escape to her friend Miss
Begley. The only thing of which he was quite sure was that
three days after the incident at the Golden Fox an orderly approached his desk and laid before him orders which directed
him to proceed immediately to Fort Andrew Doniphan, Dakota
Territory, and report to the commanding officer, Twentieth
Cavalry, for duty.

The night before he left Washington he met his friend Barrett in the bar of Shoemaker's Tavern.

"I saw the orders, Demas," the Ordnance captain commiserated. "So you're on your way to Doniphan. Pretty sudden,
wasn't it?"

"Very," said Harrod grimly. "Out of the blue, so to speak."
He hesitated a moment, then blurted: "It appears that I was
guilty of a tactical error, Lewis. A certain race you were interested in—you remember."

"Yes, indeed. Don't tell me——"

"Exactly that. I was policed at the first jump—no, not the
first jump. Since we're in a bar and names aren't mentioned,
let's just say that a certain party drinks only water. I was so
presumptuous as to suggest sherry at lunch, followed by sauterne and champagne."

Captain Barrett whistled.

"My God, Demas, and you never knew?"

"Apparently not. What was I supposed to know?"

"The mother was one of the founders of the New England

Society for Total Abstinence and a certain gentleman whom you invited to the club contributes more money to that cause in a month than you and I draw in a year. The entire family is absolutely fanatical on the subject. I could have told you, but I didn't! My God, Demas, it's too late now to tell you it's my fault."

"Forget it, Lewis. If I'd known it and had played the game according to their rules, I'd have been the damnedest hypocrite since—since Benedict Arnold. Let's have a drink."

3 THE CAPTAIN (2)

It was a long and excessively hot day's journey from Washington to Pittsburgh. The train rattled and jerked around the numberless curves by which the Baltimore & Ohio negotiated the mountains. Coal dust and cinders accompanied the puffing ascent of the long grades. Captain Harrod endured the heat and the cinders and the irritable children and commiserated mightily with himself in his misfortune. A glass of sherry—one glass—had sent him back to the frontier instead of to Paris, Berlin, or the Court of St. James. He would never be the same again. He was through, absolutely and eternally through, with women.

In Pittsburgh, between trains, he had an opportunity to wash and to don fresh linen in the station washroom. He also had a long drink, cool and cooling, in the station bar. The drab skies assumed a faintly roseate hue that deepened when he found that he was seated directly across the aisle from a most attractive young woman. True, she was married and announced that she was counting the minutes which separated her from the husband who would meet her in Fort Wayne, Indiana, but she was quite willing to make those minutes pass more swiftly in conversation with a gentleman so considerate as Captain Harrod.

She was properly impressed to learn that he was an officer in a famous cavalry regiment, that he had fought Indians and was on his way to fight them again; and she asked all the usual silly questions about the frontier and conditions there.

"Are you married, Captain? That's a very personal question, I know, but I was thinking of how terribly hard that country must be on a woman."

"No, Mrs. Keith, I'm not married, I never have been married, and I'm not likely to be until I can offer a woman considerably more than the pay and allowances of a cavalry captain."

"But——"

"There aren't any 'buts,' Mrs. Keith. A post like Doniphan or Laramie or Harker is no place for a woman. I've seen too much of it and I feel very strongly on the matter."

He did not tell her of the months he had spent in Washington or that a broken heart beat painfully in his breast. He was genuinely sorry when, late that night, she left the train.

He lay over in Chicago to make connections with a train which would reach St. Paul late the following afternoon. In the bar of the Palmer House he recognized Carruthers, an 18th Infantry major whom he had known for some years.

"Ha, Harrod. Glad to see you. Sit down and order a drink."

"Thanks, Clay. I've got to kill time until midnight tonight."

"On your way, eh? We might meet in the field, but I doubt it. They're not likely to call on the infantry to chase Sitting Bull and his playmates. It'll be you yellowlegs who see the fun."

"There'll be fighting, you think?"

"Assuredly. Haven't you heard?"

"Nothing definite." Harrod was cautious. "I've been on Washington duty for some time. Then—very suddenly—I got orders to rejoin the Twentieth immediately. I was so glad to get away from a desk job that I didn't run around asking questions."

"You'll hear it soon enough in St. Paul, at Department Headquarters, or after you reach Doniphan. Simple fact is that Grant has finally got his bellyful of the way the church crowd is handling the Indian question. He's going to throw them out, lock, stock, and barrel, and give the problem to the army—and about time, most of us will say."

"Amen to that." Harrod was sincere. "It will mean a fight, sure."

"A big one. We've been playing around with those hostiles too long—too damned long, I'd say. Now we throw everything into it, smash 'em and keep 'em smashed."

"Good. While in Washington I was asked by a senator, an ex-senator to be accurate, my opinion on the solution of the Indian problem. I used the very words you've just said: 'smash 'em!' Now I know why my orders came so suddenly."

He raised his glass.

"Well, here's to a good fight, whenever and wherever it comes."

They drank.

"A good fight," Carruthers repeated. "Maybe the last one. With the Sioux licked there'll be no place for a man except sitting on his tail in Washington. I think I'll transfer to coast artillery and Fortress Monroe."

"There'll be a few Indians left—such as Apaches in Arizona and New Mexico."

"That's right. Well, luck to you, Demas, wherever you go."

"Thanks, Clay."

2

In St. Paul, Captain Harrod descended from the Chicago train
and went directly to the Metropolitan Hotel where he bathed
and changed his clothes. For a moment or two he considered
making an official call at the headquarters of the Department
of Dakota at Fourth and Wabasha streets, but dismissed the
notion. Why be a stickler for etiquette? His orders were to report to Fort Doniphan; if they'd been changed during the
hours he had been traveling from Washington, an orderly or
an adjutant would have met him at the train.

Fort Doniphan! Was there, he wondered, a more God-
forsaken spot in the entire country? He'd heard plenty about
it from men who looked on a month's leave from Doniphan as
a convicted man would regard a reprieve from the gallows.
From November to April it was the devil's icebox. The guard
was mounted in buffalo coats and overshoes so bulky that a
man could scarcely get his feet into the stirrups. Even the Indians didn't stir abroad in such weather. And in summer it was
worse, if possible. Tuthill had transplanted cottonwood seed-
lings from the Missouri bottoms and was struggling to persuade them to grow where they would shade the officers'
quarters, but the battle was a losing one against sun and wind
and cutting dust and grasshoppers. The dust swirled and
eddied all day long, and when the wind died the mosquitoes
swept up from the river and the stagnant pools along its banks.
Swarms of them and they could bite through a boot. The
women wore heavy veils and gloves and wrapped newspapers
about their ankles beneath their stockings.

South City was four miles away, across the river. It was the
railhead of the Northern Pacific and offered all the tawdry at-
tractions to be expected of an end-of-the-line town. You could
gamble there and you could find women and you could drink.

In winter you drank to keep from freezing to death; in summer —if there was no fighting—whisky offered the only surcease from hopeless boredom.

Which reminded him—his friends in the regiment would appreciate a drink of liquor superior to that obtainable in South City. He descended to the barroom and bought three quarts of twenty-year-old Greenriver and a box of cigars.

"You're stopping here, sir?"

"Yes, Room three-eighteen. Harrod's the name. Captain Harrod."

"I'll have a boy take the bundle up to your room. Would you care for a drink, sir?"

"Thanks. Don't care if I do."

He had a drink on the house, then bought another before he went to the dining room. While he was eating, the proprietor of the hotel approached the table and introduced himself.

"Davidson is the name, Captain. Glad to have you at the Metropolitan. Won't you join me in a drink?"

"Gladly, if you'll sit down and have supper with me."

"I've already had my supper, thank you. A cup of coffee, though——"

He raised his finger to a passing waiter and ordered coffee and a bottle of white wine.

"An army man, I take it, Captain?" The hotel man raised his glass.

"Yes. Twentieth Cavalry, Fort Doniphan."

"Indeed, sir. I'm proud to make your acquaintance and it's odd I haven't met you before. I know your commanding officer, General Tuthill, quite well. He and his charming wife have stopped here many times."

Why the devil does the mere mention of that name always make me see red?

"His actual rank is that of colonel," Harrod corrected stiffly.

"Yes, yes, of course. Still, you must admit that he has made the Twentieth into as fine a regiment as there is in the service."

"There's none finer, but it takes more than one officer to make a regiment—considerably more."

Harrod bit his lips against further comment as the hotel man prattled on. He'd done the same in Washington—bitten back the angry words which would express his personal opinion of the "Hero of Wishbone Creek." When he had first joined the Twentieth, the acting regimental commander was a young, a very young, major named Harris who was struggling to make soldiers and cavalrymen out of five hundred sullen, dissatisfied men, poorly equipped, poorly mounted, ill-housed in torn tents and dilapidated barracks, and miserably fed. Harrod had formed an instant liking for young Harris, and the feeling had intensified during the weeks they had fought their own rebellious men, the lackadaisical attitude of departmental authorities who ignored or postponed action on every request, and the thinly veiled hostility of other officers of the regiment who seemed to delight in deprecating every act of theirs and in praising the absent colonel. *Christ on a crutch, Tuthill had made a good record during the war as a hell-for-leather commander of a cavalry brigade and then a division, but he sure hadn't proved himself as an Indian fighter. Look at the complete failure of the campaign of '67 and the court-martial he'd received. Why the hell was it that some men followed Tuthill with the same blind sort of adoration that the goddam apostles had followed Jesus Christ?*

Early in October, Tuthill had rejoined the regiment and assumed command. As a soldier, Harrod had to admire the energy with which the tall, red-haired man had thrown himself into the task of making soldiers out of the hobbledehoy assortment with which Harris had struggled. Sheridan, Phil Sheridan, the stocky, goateed cavalry leader, was behind him. When Tuthill demanded anything, Sheridan lashed the department into action. New horses replaced the old crow-baits and were so distributed that each company had mounts of the same color. Tuthill junked every old, shot-out rifle in the command and obtained new ones—Spencers—as swiftly as they could be shipped from the warehouses in which they had lain for months. Overloaded escort wagons delivered ammunition by the case and the men spent day after day on the target ranges. Tuthill broke noncommissioned officers and made new ones. His biting tongue lashed officers and men alike and within a matter of weeks the mob had become soldiers.

Of all the officers he had ever met, Harrod thought, Tuthill stood alone. He was a cavalryman from his dragging spurs to the broad-brimmed white hat, which he constantly wore in defiance of uniform regulations. He had been promoted—every man in the army knew the story—from first lieutenant to brevet brigadier general of volunteers. He was then twenty-three years old. Some three weeks later, at Gettysburg, he had led a single company of cavalry in a pell-mell charge against Wade Hampton's cavalry division. The hard-bitten men in gray had blasted the company to pieces. Its captain had been killed along with half the troopers, Tuthill's horse had been shot from under him, and only a few yards separated him from capture when a sergeant had pistoled the nearest Confederate. Tuthill had vaulted behind the man's saddle and returned, unscratched, to the Union lines.

That was Tuthill in '63 and that was he when Demas Harrod had first encountered him—courageous beyond all question, utterly tireless, as merciless to himself as to all under him, dashing, flamboyant, as arrogant as when he had ridden at the head of a division, and as vain as a peacock. Harrod had paid the customary formal call on Tuthill in his quarters, had answered a few casual questions as to his own military service, and then had listened for two hours to the regimental commander's high-pitched, staccato voice as Tuthill rattled on about his own deeds as a brigade and division commander, of the commendations he had received and the honors he had won. It was I, I, I, from seven o'clock until after nine. Such vainglory was unnecessary and, in Harrod's opinion, rather offensive, but he came to admire the man for what he had done with the regiment and he was intensely proud of the company he commanded when the Twentieth took the field in November.

At the end of that march had been Wishbone Creek. They had ridden through a blinding snowstorm that obliterated all landmarks so effectively that the white scouts who accompanied the column admitted frankly that they were lost. Tuthill laughed shrilly when he heard the same confession from the eleven Osage Indians who had been hired as trackers.

"Can't expect 'em to track where there aren't any tracks," he exclaimed. "Follow me."

His confidence was supreme as he led them through a blank white world to sheltering timber and a camping place. Two days later they reached the Canadian where Major Harris, scouting with three companies, reported that he had found an Indian trail. They rode through that day and the night which followed. Tuthill was like a hound on a hot trail. He would not rest nor would he grant rest to the weary men who rode behind him. It was after midnight when they halted near the summit of a ridge above a watercourse known as Wishbone Creek. Beneath them, half a gunshot away, was the village of Black Eagle. Tuthill did not know whose village or what village lay in that dark valley. It was enough for him that there were Indians within reach. He promptly divided his command so as to surround the village and laid the plans for the attack.

They struck at dawn. Eleven companies of cavalry and a platoon of selected sharpshooters under Lieutenant Clagett. They charged into the very shadow of the lodges and shot down the Indians, men and women, as they staggered out into the gray light. Some ran for their ponies, farther down the valley. Others saw a gap between two of the attacking battalions and streamed through that opening. Major Harris struck spurs to his mount.

"Here goes for a brevet or a coffin," he shouted. "Let's get those Indians. Follow me!"

Eighteen troopers and the regimental sergeant major galloped after him.

So far, good, thought Harrod. That was the way a cavalryman was supposed to fight. There was only one tactic for cavalry, the charge. If you didn't charge the enemy, you might as well get off your horse and trudge through the mud like a doughboy. He and his company remained with the regiment. They killed every Indian who showed himself. They burned the lodges and the buffalo robes and the food which was stored for the winter's needs. Some eight hundred ponies were in the valley. Tuthill ordered them shot, every one, and the order was obeyed. An officer who led a detail in rounding up the Indians' herds mentioned that he had heard firing from farther down the river. Major Harris, he observed, had ridden in that direction. Tuthill ignored the remark.

"Did you see any Indians?" he demanded. "Any other villages?"

That faraway firing continued. Harrod heard it repeatedly when he drew away from the slaughter of the Indian ponies, a slaughter in which the regimental commander participated enthusiastically. Once he suggested to Tuthill that he lead F company in that direction, that Harris and the men who rode with him might be in trouble.

"Harris is all right," said Tuthill brusquely. "Other men have been fighting down that way—they'd have reported it if Harris was in trouble."

Night had fallen when they rode away from the smoldering lodges, the dead Indians, and the hundreds of dead ponies. They rode swiftly, as though every warrior of the southern Plains was on their trail. The major portion of the regiment was permitted to halt at two in the morning; four companies were sent on with orders to find the wagon train and bring it to where the regiment waited. That juncture effected, the regiment pushed on to Camp Supply where Sheridan congratulated the Twentieth and its commander on their victory.

Some two weeks later Tuthill had proudly guided Sheridan to the scene of that triumph. They found Harris, the sergeant major, and fourteen of the eighteen men who had joined in the charge for a brevet or a coffin. All were stripped naked and the bodies mutilated in ghastly fashion. Four men were not found. Harrod had never permitted himself to think of the slow deaths that were theirs if they had been captured alive by the vengeful Cheyennes.

That had been Wishbone Creek. That had been how Harris and nineteen good men had died—could he tell that story to a damned hero-worshiping hotelkeeper?

4 CY PIERCE'S DAUGHTER

Harrod dismissed the cab at the corner of Fourth and B
streets and waited in the shadow until the vehicle was headed
downtown. Around the corner, third house, west side of the
street—and a light burned dimly in the second-story window
just as she had promised. He walked quietly across the porch
and fumbled for the bell pull. The door opened before he
could find the knob and a soft voice spoke from the darkness.

"I was watching for you, Demas. Come in. I'll close the
door and then I'll light the lamp."

He sensed that she was moving to the left, and faced in that
direction. She scratched a match, held it until the stinking
sulfur broke into flame, then touched it to the wick of a tall
lamp with a deep yellow shade.

"I'm glad to see you, Demas. Welcome." She extended both
hands and he juggled the bottles under his arm and bowed

until his lips brushed her fingers. She'd changed her clothes and looked even better than she had in the hotel lobby. She was wearing a dress—damn if he could remember ever seeing one like it. It sure wasn't a house wrapper and yet it looked like one. A woman would call it a robe, he guessed. It was golden-yellow in color and it fitted her closer than a coat of paint. It was meant to do just that, to show her white throat and breast, the line of her waist and the smooth, flat stomach, the round thigh. She looked good, by God. Slim she was, but she'd lost every bit of the angular scrawniness he remembered in Cy Pierce's daughter. And she wasn't bulged out in front and behind with a haversack-load of padding and ruffles. None of those damned false hoops or bustles or crinolines or whatever it was the women called the things that built out their backsides like a blanket roll slipped back over a horse's rump. There wasn't any padding—nor much of anything else—under that yellow robe. It was cut low and square in the front and what it showed wasn't anything for her to be ashamed of.

"Can't you say anything, Demas, or are you just going to stand there and stare at me?"

"I think," he said slowly, "that I'm just going to stand here and stare. You look wonderful, Lulu."

"In this old thing? You nice man."

He placed the heavy package in her hand. She tore off the wrapping.

"Just in case we run short of the Monongahela you were talking about."

"We're not likely to; there were six or eight cases the last time I checked on them. This is wonderful, Demas, old brandy and what I used to call bubble-water before I learned what it was."

"We'll try mixing them, Lulu. A big slug of brandy in a tall glass with plenty of ice. Fill it up with champagne. It goes down as smooth as grease and then—look out! It has what the artillerymen call a delayed-action fuse."

"We'll start on the Monongahela," she declared. "I promised you some, you know. I'll light the lamp in the kitchen; there's ice there."

He followed her, watching the smooth movement of her hips beneath the clinging gown. The kitchen lamp was in a wall bracket and, as she reached for the chimney, she rested one knee on a chair. The motion raised the tight skirt and showed a tiny foot in a black slipper, a slim ankle, and a lovely, a truly lovely leg in a yellow silk stocking that was a shade lighter than the gown. Almost to the knee . . . either she didn't know what she was showing or she didn't care. One hand held the lamp chimney, the other the match. The position drew the gown tightly about her body. *Christ on a crutch! I wonder if you've got even as much as a shimmy-shirt on underneath that thing. There's no corset or petticoat, on that I'll bet a month's pay. Don't get overanxious, Demas. The whole night's ahead of you.*

"A new bottle, Demas. Pull the cork while I'm getting the glasses."

"You'll have one, of course."

"Of course, and I won't say just to keep you company, either. I like it."

She placed bottle, glasses, and a bowl of ice on a tray and carried them to the parlor and a table which stood in front of a sofa where there was room, but not too much room, for two people. Harrod filled the glasses.

"Have you got a toast, Demas?"

"To you, Lulu. To the good luck which brought about our meeting and to our much better acquaintance."

He tossed down his drink. By God, he'd wanted that. Time had dulled the exhilaration of the brandy he'd had after dinner. This woke it up, stirred it around a bit, and he looked with appreciation at his companion. She sipped lightly at her whisky and after each swallow ran her tongue over her lips. Her eyes were bright, moist. *Damn it, this was the kind of woman a man ought to have. She wasn't a millionaire's daughter, but she had blood in her veins, not ice water out of Massachusetts Bay. If he reached over now and gave her a friendly slap on the rump, she'd probably laugh and slap him one in return. Wonder what in the hell Miss Alice Lowell Peabody, of Bahston and Washington, would do if anybody ever slapped her on the rump? Wonder if Miss Alice Peabody would ever, in all her life, receive a friendly slap on the rump? And he'd really thought about marrying her! Hell, all he'd really had in his mind was her money—her father's money. Hell of a time you'd have unless there was something else. Taking a checkbook to bed didn't promise any excitement.*

A tightly stuffed plush pillow was on the sofa between them. He tossed it to the nearest chair. Lulu moved an inch, perhaps two, toward him and Harrod closed the gap. He refilled the glasses—she had sipped perhaps half of hers—then let his arm fall across the back of the sofa. His fingers touched her neck, lightly, beneath the coiled mass of dark hair.

"It's your turn to give a toast, Lulu."

"You want one?"

"Sure. Don't tantalize me when I'm dying of thirst."

She raised her glass.

"This is one that Joe, my husband, taught me," she said. " 'Here's to it and to it again. If you ever get to it and don't do it, may you never get to it or do it again!' "

He pounded his thigh.

"By God, that's good!" he roared.

"Shssh, Demas, not so loud."

"Sorry, I forgot."

"Don't forget again, please. Not all the cats in this neighborhood are walking on the back fences. And we're going to make this drink last us a little while. You drink like a soldier—toss it down and reach for another. Sip it slowly and then when you begin to feel it you feel it all over . . . ummmm. It's been a long time, Demas Harrod—are you married?"

"No, ma'am! Not married and not likely to be. I'm cavalry and it's likely now that I'll be on the frontier until I retire or get snagged by some scalp-hunting Injun. The frontier posts like Doniphan and Harker and Hays and Laramie are no place for a woman."

"Some women go there with their husbands."

"Yes, and it's a hell of a life for them. I'm not swearing, Lulu, that's what it is: a hell of a life."

"After I left you at the hotel I got to wondering if maybe you hadn't married since I saw you in St. Louis. It's been a long time, Demas. Lots of things could've happened."

"Lots of things have happened, but getting married wasn't one of them."

"I've been married, Demas."

"So you told me—and that you'd been a widow for more than three years."

"Yes." She swirled the whisky in her glass, sniffed its aroma, and sipped. "I'm a lot different from the girl you met in St. Louis. She was just a long-legged, gawky thing, and—and as ignorant about life as anybody could be."

"It's done you a lot of good; being married, I mean. When you spoke to me there in the lobby I could hardly remember what Cy Pierce's daughter looked like. Now, well, I'll always remember you now."

"I'm being serious. Just for a minute, then we'll finish our drink and be silly if we want to." She rose and turned down the lamp until a mere rim of yellow flame showed above the blue. "That's better. I want to talk to you, Demas, and it's somehow easier when the lamp is turned down." She hesitated a moment, then blurted: "Would you be horrified if I told you that I never loved—really and truly loved—my husband?"

"That was your business, I guess," he said uncomfortably.

"It—it's just a little bit your business, too, Demas. I was just a girl there in St. Louis but I fell in love with you, madly in love."

"You—I never——"

"I know you didn't, but I fell in love with you just the same. Don't ask me why. No woman can ever give a reason why she falls in love. I'd met a few men, but not very many. The boys I knew—boys I'd gone to school with—well, I just couldn't seem to get even the littlest bit interested in them. Other men, men that Father invited to the house just like he invited you, they were just men, that's all.

"Then you came along. You were different or at least I thought you were. You didn't treat me as though I was a little girl who ought to be playing with her dolls instead of sitting at the table with grown people. And when we rode together that Sunday—do you remember that, Demas?"

"Of course I do. I told you——"

She continued as though there had been neither question nor answer.

"—you kissed me. Some of the boys had tried to kiss me before, but not many. I didn't want them to, but you I did. All the time I was hoping you would and wondering what I could do that would make you want to. And then you did. Don't tell me you remember that kiss—men don't. They might remember kissing, but not the kiss. There's a difference, Demas. I never forgot it, and when you went away from St. Louis I thought my heart was broken. I sat in my room and cried because I didn't have anything to remember you by and I wondered whether a girl—a Protestant girl, that is—could ever become a nun. That was awfully silly and I know it now, and that's the way I felt.

"And then"—she drew a deep breath—"the next spring I made a trip with Father to Cincinnati and Pittsburgh and on the way back, on the Ohio River steamer, we met Joseph Gorton and about six months later we were married.

"I knew I wasn't in love with him the way a girl ought to love her husband, but I married him. I told myself that being married to him would make me forget you, but it didn't. We went to the Planters' Hotel on our wedding night and when he put out the light and came across the room and got into bed with me and put his arms around me, I just said, 'It's Demas. It's Demas,' over and over. It was you I was kissing, not him. It was you that I was—giving myself to, every time."

"By God Almighty, girl!" Harrod downed his drink and poured another. "You didn't tell him that, did you?"

"Of course not! I knew I didn't love him, not the way I loved you, but I certainly didn't want to hurt him. I wouldn't have hurt him for the world. It was just my secret, my very own, and I kept it to myself. I think I was a better wife to him because of it."

Harrod mopped his brow. *By the bones of St. Crispin, this situation certainly wasn't covered in any textbook of tactics!*

"I—I'm glad you were," he stammered.

"I was, really," she said seriously. "We had lots of fun together. He was older than I was, eight years older, and he'd— well, he'd been around a lot and while I was the first woman he'd ever married, I wasn't the first he'd ever—ever slept with. I knew that and it kind of made things even for my loving you. He taught me how to drink, how to sip my whisky just a little at a time and really get the most out of it, and he taught me how to kiss, really kiss, and . . . shall I stop there or tell you some more?"

"I—Lord God, you've told me just about everything you could!"

"I had to say it. I had to tell you everything. I thought of all that while we were talking in the hotel. If you'd told me that you were going to be stationed here in St. Paul, well, we wouldn't be sitting here tonight. I'd have waited—it seems as though women always have to wait—and let you find things out for yourself. And then you said you were going to be here only this one night, tomorrow you'd be on your way to Fort Doniphan and the Indian fighting. My heart stopped, Demas. Don't laugh, please, it stopped. All I could think of was that you might be killed and that you'd never, never know. That was when I made up my mind to ask you to come out here and then to tell you everything."

"You—you certainly have done that, Lulu," he said slowly.

"I had to. Then we'd start, if it was a start, all fair and honest."

"Not many women are like you, Lulu. You're so damned straightforward."

"I'm me, Demas. I can't change me and I don't think I will ever want to. Now"—he heard distinctly the long expiration of her breath—"now let's forget how serious we've been. Let's open that bottle of brandy you brought and try it with the champagne."

She drank the king's peg as she had her whisky, in quick birdlike sips.

"It's good, Demas, awful good!" She wrinkled her nose delightedly. "We're not going to be serious any more, are we?"

"Not a bit. As the chairman would say: 'Formal business being concluded, we will proceed to the social features that have been planned for the evening.'"

"That's right." She snuggled into the curve of his arm and he drew her closer. He'd been right, dead right, about the absence of a corset. Her body was soft, as a woman's body should be, but it wasn't flabby. The swelling flesh framed in the square yoke of her gown was firm, like the proud muscles of a stallion's arched neck, but he didn't make the comparison aloud. She rested her head on his shoulder and he caressed the lobe of her ear and ran his fingers lightly around her throat.

"I like that, Demas. It makes me feel good—do it some more. We're having a good time, aren't we?"

"Just the best."

"I'm going to spike my drink a little. Should I use the brandy or the bubbly?"

"Whichever you want." He chuckled. "They both work, if that's what you want."

She moved to the edge of the sofa and reached for the brandy bottle. The front of her robe fell away from her breasts, but she laughed as she straightened slowly.

"Naughty! Mustn't peek—but it was my fault. I ought to be careful about things like that but I never seem to remember until it's too late."

"Don't be careful on my account, Lulu. How about filling my glass for me?"

She looked at him levelly, then deliberately leaned far over the table again as she placed ice in his glass and added the brandy and champagne.

"There!" She pushed the straps of the robe into place on her shoulders. "I deviled you a little, didn't I—but you wanted me to."

"Yep. I'd have been disappointed if you hadn't. 'Here's to it and to it again.' "

" 'And if you don't, may you never.' I'm a brazen hussy, Demas."

"I'm glad. I like it a lot better than——"

"Than what?"

"—than the way a girl I knew in Washington—I've just come from there—always acted. She was so persnickety-nice about everything that it must have hurt her."

"Did you like her?" She sensed the hint of disappointment in his voice.

"No," he said quickly. "Oh, for a while I wondered if maybe I liked her, but she—her father, that is—had all sorts of money and I haven't got a dime in the world outside of my army pay. And then, well, I learned she was a red-hot total abstainer. Do you want to know how I found out?"

"Uh-huh."

"I invited her to have lunch with me at an inn near Washington. I thought I'd do things right, you know, so I went out there first and ordered the lunch and told 'em what wines to serve and to have a glass of sherry at each place when we arrived. She saw it and, by God, Lulu, she walked out on me! Gave me the frozen stare for daring to do such a thing and told the proprietor of the place to call a carriage to take her back to Washington. When I tried to explain, she walked past me with her nose a mile in the air and slammed the door in my face."

"And what did you do?"

"What could I do? I wasn't going to open the door she'd slammed and tell her she could go to—you know——"

"Hell. You can say it, Demas."

"—hell. So I drank the sherry myself and ate the lunch I'd ordered."

"You didn't see her again or write her and apologize?"

"I didn't see her and I didn't want to. And I certainly didn't apologize. I had a colonel during the war, Lulu; he'd been a lieutenant under Scott in Mexico in 'forty-six. Once I told him I was sorry for something and I've never forgotten his reply. 'Never apologize, Mr. Harrod,' he said. 'Ninety-nine times out of a hundred an apology is a confession of weakness.' "

"I'm glad you didn't, awfully glad. I'd hate to think of you as weak."

She nestled closer and his arm tightened about her shoulders. Her face was pressed against his chest. He turned it, his hand beneath her chin, and her lips parted hungrily to meet his. Her hands caressed his throat.

"Lulu——"

"No, no. Kiss me, Demas. Kiss me a lot."

She writhed in his arms and swung her gold-stockinged legs so that they rested across his knees. Their lips met. Daintily, then boldly, her tongue flashed restlessly in and out. His free hand touched her bare shoulder and she seized it and pressed his palm against her breast. Slowly, as passion slaked for the greater joy of its renewal, he lifted his face.

"I'm so happy," she whispered. "This is what I've dreamed of for years. Oh, Demas, I love you so much."

"And I love you, Lulu." *A man had to say that, he had to. Christ on a crutch, how many things might have prevented that meeting in the Metropolitan lobby! He might have reported at Department Headquarters and been invited to dinner by some crabbed major with nothing on his mind but army gossip. He might have gone to another hotel. If that steamboat captain hadn't been half-drunk, he might have spent the entire evening in the bar. He might—oh, Lord!*

"Kiss me again, Lulu, like you did before."

Again the hot lips, the questing tongue, the little gasps and sighs.

"I'm shameless, Demas, and you might as well know it. When I'm with you, I want to be whatever you want me to be. Fill my glass—just to there. The brandy, not the whisky—and then I'm going to tell you something.

"This is the last one, the last for a little while. When this is gone—don't you want one, too?—when this is gone we're going upstairs where I can show you how much I really love you."

4

He'd been right about one thing. Beneath the golden silk robe there was only white flesh, softly shadowed, fragrant, compliant. He hadn't been drunk then and neither had she. That came later, after the initial passion had been satisfied and they had lain in the dark bedroom and finished off the brandy and champagne. That mixture had sure hit them both and hit them hard. One minute they'd be drunk as fiddlers' bitches and playing tag all over the house in the dark. He'd fall over furniture and Lulu would giggle from the closet where she hid. Seemed like she'd forgotten the neighbors and their keen ears because she'd squeal like a little pig when his hands closed on her.

And then, a little later, she'd be lying close against him and asking questions about the frontier, about Laramie and Doniphan and Hays and Riley, and did he think that wild country beyond the Yellowstone would ever be settled. Sure it would be. It had to be. Grant had quit listening to the Christers and was going to give the army a chance next summer. Three months was all it would take—oh, well, maybe four. Two months for the campaign and two for herding the scattered bands back to the reservations.

He told her of Tuthill—the Murat of the American Army— and his hatred for the man who had permitted Joe Harris to die while he practiced marksmanship on Cheyenne ponies. He told her of his fellow officers and of the wives who followed some of them to the lonely posts of the Indian country, of their petty jealousies, of the autocratic manner in which the post commander's wife dominated their lives and even their thinking.

"Talking makes me thirsty, Lulu. Let's have another drink— we're back on the whisky now—and then you sing that song again, the one about 'the little ball of yarn.' "

Lulu had obliged.

That was what made her so wonderful, she always obliged. She wasn't like so damn many women, willing enough maybe, but wanting things done their way, always. Don't light the lamp. Don't say words like that, it's swearing. Don't do this, don't do that. Don't take another drink. Don't play poker and neglect me. Women who talked too much or—sometimes worse —not at all. Women who lied. Women who eternally hinted about marriage, even while they lay in your arms like Lulu was lying now.

Not Lulu. Sure, she'd played around a little first but right from the beginning—right from the minute she'd told him to wait until nine o'clock and then to come out here—this was

*what she'd been heading for, this was what she wanted. By
God, he could do a lot worse than marry her. Suppose he had
known what she was like before the preacher gave them the
word? What difference did that make? A man would be a lot
happier married to her than to some mewling, simpering, female like—yes, like Alice Peabody: "Please, Demas, I know
we're married but that doesn't mean you should forget yourself."*

*Give Lulu one summer at a cavalry post and she'd be riding
and shooting like a trooper. Cursing and drinking like one,
too. She wouldn't put her fingers in her ears when a gun
went off and she wouldn't faint at the sight of deer or antelope
blood on a man's hands or boots. She'd kill her own meat if
the need arose and, what's more, she'd have enough sense to
act like a lady at the garrison parties. By God, he'd like to see
her crooking her little finger as she sipped tea and listened
to Mrs. Tuthill's gushing inanities and her eternal chatter
about "the General."*

*"We think your bride is charming, Captain Harrod. Do tell
me, where did you meet her?"*

*"In St. Paul, ma'am. She invited me out to her home and I
slept with her that night and proposed to her the next morning. She'd much prefer a glass of good whisky to that tea-table
slop."*

*He'd never say anything like that, but he liked to think of
the expression on their faces if he did say it. He liked to think
of Lulu at Laramie or Doniphan on New Year's Eve when the
ladies partook—that was the word they used—of a glass of wine.
Lulu, junior bride on the post. Lulu, demure and decorous
except when her eyes met his and showed him the lurking
devil behind the mask of innocence. "Give us a toast, Mrs.
Harrod." "Certainly." And they'd stand about the long table
waiting for something like "To the New Year; may it bring
happiness and promotions to us all!" That's what they'd wait
for, but they none of them knew Lulu. She'd hop on her*

chair, put one foot on the table, and give them, "Here's to it and to it again. If you ever get to it and don't do it, may you never get to it or do it again."

She wouldn't, of course. She'd have too much sense for that. She'd know that such conduct on the part of an officer's wife would throw him out of the service quicker than a court-martial could. "Hmmm, I think you know why I have called you to my office, captain . . . Hmmm. Hrrmph . . . There are many opportunities in civil life for a man of your quali-fications, sir . . . Hrrmph . . . I am quite confident that your resignation, if tendered immediately, will be accepted."

Lulu wouldn't let a man in for anything like that. She'd save it all until they got to their own quarters. There, with a drink of neat whisky in her hand, she'd recite the toast she might have given and show him how she'd have given it—foot on the table, skirts pulled up clear to here, by God. She was a mixture of woman and devil and strumpet and lover, but she wasn't a fool.

Before he slept he made Lulu promise that she'd waken him so that he could reach his hotel in time to pack his bags and pay his bill before the departure of the Northern Pacific train. Then they'd collapsed on the bed, tightly wrapped in one another's arms. She'd roused him long before the first hint of daylight paled the eastern stars.

"Demas!"

"Yeah." He rolled over, sat up, blinked in the lamplight, and groped for his clothes. His watch was in the pocket of his flowered vest.

"God!" he remarked. "It's only a couple of minutes after four."

"I know, and my head's just as big as yours and I want to sleep just as much as you do. I hated to wake you, but you've got to leave before daylight. Some of the neighbors are early risers."

"Tell 'em what they can do!" he growled.

"I'd like to—but they won't do it."

He knotted his tie and she walked with him to the door.

"I'm sobering up a little," he said. "Enough sober to kiss you good-by and tell you I hate to go. I sure do, Lulu."

She returned his kiss ardently but her eyes were grave.

"And you don't hate me, Demas?"

"Hate you? My God, no, why should I?"

"For what I did—you know."

"Of course not. I—I love you for it, Lulu."

"Say it again, Demas, please."

"I love you, Lulu."

"You . . ." she stared into his eyes. "Yes, I think you really mean it, or you think you do, which is just about the same thing."

"I do mean it. Lulu——"

She kissed the words from his lips.

"And now you must go, Demas, you really must. Remember how much I love you, and think of me sometimes. Don't let any of those wild Indians scalp you."

"I won't."

He closed the gate carefully behind him and walked, far from steadily, toward the downtown section of St. Paul. *Jesus, what a head I've got! She's wonderful. Man could go further and do a hell of a lot worse than marrying a girl like Lulu.*

5 THE TROOPERS (1)

Corporal James Gregory, D company, Twentieth Cavalry, had slept less than three hours, but he told himself that he missed his slumber not at all and that he was proud of himself. Why shouldn't he be? Take how he had handled the five recruits for the Twentieth who had been placed in his charge in Chicago. He had remained sober all the way to St. Paul and had kept the recruits sober too. He'd found quarters for them in the enlisted detachment barracks at Department Headquarters, and had obtained the solemn promise of the corporal there that the men would not be turned loose to visit downtown St. Paul and encounter its temptations. Not until then had Gregory considered himself free to follow his own inclinations as to how the evening should be spent. These led him swiftly to an area of glowing red lights and jangling pianos south of the Northern Pacific Depot.

Even there, at Katy Kelly's place, the corporal remained sober. Liquor and women, in his opinion, did not mix; too much of the first spoiled your appreciation and enjoyment of the second, even though a hell of a lot of fellows thought different. All the way from Chicago, he'd been thinking of a lively little brunette named Claire who had delighted him when he passed through St. Paul on his way east. *If she's gone from Katy's place or if she's not working tonight, I by God will get drunk.* She was at Katy's, and working, and she remembered him or succeeded in convincing him that she did, which was equally satisfactory, and the corporal had remained sober and had had himself a time, a real honest-to-God time that he could remember all the way to South City and Fort Doniphan.

Nor was that all. Claire had urged him to stay and get a little bit more sleep and had reminded him that Miss Katy's nigger-girl, Millie, always served breakfast in the room when a gentleman had stayed all night, but Gregory hadn't been tempted. *They'll nail me to the cross if I don't show up to collect them recruits. I'll find some place where I can get a cup of coffee and then grab a horsecar out to the barracks.*

It was still dark, pitch dark, when he passed the Metropolitan Hotel but the gas lamps on either side of the entrance had revealed a gentleman—drunker than a twice-boiled owl he was—struggling vainly to open the door. Gregory had crossed the sidewalk to aid him, and had steered the unknown to the desk and had heard him ask for the key to Room 318. The sleepy clerk had flipped it toward Gregory's hand.

"Are you going to take him up? Harrod's his name, Captain Harrod of the Twentieth Cavalry."

Enlisted men just weren't supposed to be lucky, but luck fell on them once in a while. Like when they got a chance to help a captain up to his room, see that he got his clothes off before he fell into bed, and listen to him talk—fool talk, most of it—about a sweet little girl named Lulu who sure must have been something. Captain Harrod had said that if he was bound for any place in God's green world other than Fort Andrew Doniphan, Dakota Territory, he'd by God marry Lulu and take her with him and tell the old grannies—and he meant those who wore spurs as well as those in skirts—to go jump in the Missouri.

"I'm not doing it, though, Corporal," the captain declared. "Frontier post is no place for women and only a damn fool tries to mix fighting and love-making. Look at your own colonel, Old Eagle-beak Tuthill. It was before your time with the regiment—before mine, too—but there's still some around that remember it. He left his command strung out to hell-and-gone after an all-night march and he took off and rode to Fort Campbell where his wife was. They say she heard his spurs rattle on the porch and came to the door to meet him. He shoved her inside the quarters and that was the last anybody saw either one of them for the rest of the day. Folks who were at Campbell say that the pair of 'em were worn to frazzle."

The corporal, being somewhat frazzled himself, said, "Yes, sir." *I sure wish to hell he'd flop down and go to sleep. If I hadn't told him I was a corporal in the Twentieth and that I'd take care of him, I could walk out on him. Now I've got to listen until he runs down.* The captain continued with no sign of running down.

"What did it get him? A court-martial, that's what. He was officially reprimanded and suspended from rank and pay for a year. He'd have served that suspension, too, except that they needed a fightin' man to get the Southern Cheyennes in line and he was their huckleberry. Now there's another good fight coming, one hell of a good fight, the last one of all; and then the hostiles will be herded up on the reservations and we'll turn the country over to the grangers. That's what I'm coming back for . . . one hell of a good fight, just like at Wishbone Creek."

He had talked clearly up to about that point. The corporal had tried twice to turn down the lamp and leave the room, but the captain had ordered him to remain. The corporal hadn't been with the Twentieth at Wishbone Creek but he should know what had happened there.

"I've heard about it, sir, plenty of times. That was where the regiment smashed Black Eagle."

"Barracks still talkin' about it, eh? Old shoulders—soldiers, I mean—tellin' th' recruits all about it. Did they ever tell you about Major Harris, Corp'ral? Did they tell you what happened to him and nineteen men?"

"Yes, sir. The Indians killed them, all of them."

"Is that what they tell you? Lissen t' me, Corp'ral, they were murdered, tha's what. Murdered by Colonel and Brevet Major General Eagle-beak Tuthill who could have saved 'em but didn't bother. He was havin' too good a time killin' th' ponies. Eight hundred ponies—it was sickenin'. Shootin' ponies while good men died and after they were dead bein' cut to pieces by the goddam Indians. Tuthill did that. That's one reason why I'm coming back for one big fight with him in it. Him and me. Not this year but nex' summer for sure."

The corporal had turned down the lamp. The sky beyond the window was gray. The captain's head was on the pillow.

"I put the basin right here on the floor, sir, in case you might feel sick."

"Huh? Yesh. Yes, I said. Thank you, Corp'ral. Damn good man. Deserve to be sergeant and I'll tell your company commander so."

"Thank you, sir. Good night."

"Good night, Corp'ral. I'm 'bliged, much 'bliged."

Gregory walked from the hotel into the silvery dawn. Thank God, he thought, there was still time to get out to the barracks and pick up those five Johns. Reckon he'd better take care of getting Captain Harrod to the train too.

2

The blue uniforms were uncomfortable and so new as to proclaim loudly that the five men who wore them were the rawest of recruits. None of the jackets or stiff trousers fitted, nor had the flat forage caps achieved individuality of wrinkle or angle to indicate that the men were accustomed to the headgear. The sharp creases at midthigh of the trousers and across the shoulders of the jackets were the folds of the quartermaster's shelves, not the softer wrinkles by which a garment shows that it has adjusted itself to its wearer. The black shoes were polished, but they were as new as the coats and trousers and creaked loudly with every step.

The final touch was the revolver on each man's hip, a .44-caliber percussion Colt of the Civil War pattern. Many months were to pass before the army's cavalry regiments would be equipped with the new .45-caliber weapon which fired fixed ammunition. None of the five was accustomed to carrying a sidearm. They wore the belts too high and too tightly drawn about their waists, and they held their right arms stiffly away from the gleaming new holsters which had never known saddle soap or the softening—and darkening—touch of neat's-foot oil. From time to time one of the men would finger the black leather cartridge box on his left hip or allow his hand to rest briefly on the revolver's square walnut butt. The gestures were supremely self-conscious.

The corporal stood a little apart. He was in uniform now but he wore no pistol, and his blouse and trousers, unlike those of the recruits, were faded by exposure to sun and rain. Moveover, they fitted him. The post tailor at Fort Andrew Doniphan had shortened the sleeves and taken in the trousers until they clung to Gregory's lean flanks as a cavalryman's trousers should. The seat was molded snugly to his backside; it did not droop or protrude, angular and uncompromising, as did those of the recruits. The corporal wore his cap cocked jauntily over one eye, and from time to time his glance flickered toward his charges to see if any of them had dared imitate the devil-may-care attitude of an old soldier, a man who'd seen the Rocky Mountains and had traded shots with hostile Indians. If they did, he'd tell 'em off proper. Johns like them were supposed to wear their caps square on their heads. There'd be plenty of time for them to get rooty after they'd learned to stay on a troop horse or had chased some hell-raisin' Injuns over the dry hills.

All in all, the corporal thought, he'd done a good job. A damn good job. He'd dry-nursed them recruits from Chicago to St. Paul, he'd bedded 'em down last night, and now he had 'em all right side up and sober at the Northern Pacific depot. He'd done as much for the new captain, Harrod, too. It had taken some lively jumping around, and he'd had to leave the recruits in the hotel lobby and trust to God that they wouldn't head for the bar, but he'd seen to it that the captain was up and dressed, that his valises were packed, and that he and they were loaded into a cab and dispatched to the depot. Gregory and the recruits had walked, of course. Cabs were not for enlisted men. He'd marched them and their carpetbags and their shabby telescopes to the depot and had decided that they were a sorry lot indeed. The army was sure going to hell fast if these Johns were sample soldiers. All that the army got nowadays were farm boys who'd fallen for a recruiting sergeant's glib talk and wanted to go West and kill Injuns, or maybe fellows who'd picked the army in preference to jail. Some magistrates gave vagrants and drunks that choice. Other recruits—some of these for all he knew—were just looking for a warm bed and a roof over their heads and three meals a day until they encountered an opportunity or an inducement to desert. These Johns, if that were the kind they were, sure didn't know what they were in for when they joined up with the Twentieth. Old Eagle-beak would make soldiers of 'em.

"Corporal?"

That was the oldest of the recruits. He looked old enough to have known what he was doing. Why the hell hadn't he signed up for coast artillery and comfortable brick barracks and easy duty instead of for a cavalry regiment on the frontier? A tall, lean character with a cold and sardonically humorous gray eye. He'd make either a damn good man or a rebel and it wouldn't take long to find out which.

"Whadda you want?"

"The train's still out in the yards. We got ha'f an hour yet. I got the price of a drink f'r you and me."

"Can't do it." The corporal permitted his righteousness to register, then added: "Captain Harrod—he's a new officer—is in the waitin' room now an' takin' the same train we are. Wouldn't do f'r him to see me drinkin' on duty, 'specially with a recruit. It's a damn long ride to South City, though. If you wanted to buy a bottle for drinkin' on the train——"

"Mebbe I will." The man turned to join his companions. The corporal raised his voice slightly.

"Hey, your name's Crane, isn't it?"

"Yep. Eli Crane." The man added "sir" as though by after-thought.

"You don't say 'sir' except to officers, and then don't ever forget it. I'm puttin' you in charge of these fellows, Crane, while I go speak to the captain. Keep 'em together. No wan-derin' 'round an' no drinkin'."

He turned at the door of the station and saw that Crane had seated his charges on the iron benches which faced the tracks. Captain Harrod was in the waiting room. He touched his hat brim with one finger when the corporal halted at the regu-lation six paces and saluted.

"Reporting, sir. Train won't be backed in for maybe half an hour. I have five recruits with me, sir, and I'll see that the captain's trunks are in the baggage car and his bags in the seat with him. Would there be anything else, sir?"

"No, not that I can think of. What's your name, Corporal? Somehow I can't remember."

The corporal was too experienced a soldier to smile.

"Gregory, sir. James Gregory. D company."

"Yes, sure. I was pretty drunk last night, wasn't I, Corporal?"

"No, sir. Not that I noticed, sir."

"Corporal, you're a goddam liar, as every good noncommissioned officer should be on occasion. Since I was sober, as you said, I don't imagine you heard me say anything about how I liked going to Fort Doniphan or about the Twentieth Cavalry or its commanding officer?"

"Not a word, sir."

"You're probably lying again. Thanks, Corporal. Here are my luggage checks. That'll be all."

"Yes, sir. There's just one other thing if the captain will excuse me."

"What is it?"

"I paid the cab driver last night, sir. A dollar and a half. I don't like to mention it, but——"

"Was I in a cab? God Almighty, I must have been drunk. I'd 've sworn I walked all the way. You didn't ask the driver where he brought me from, did you?"

Silver clinked in the captain's hand.

"No, sir, I didn't think——"

"That's right. Never think in the army. Do what you're told and keep your nose clean—that goes for all ranks. Here you are, Gregory. Buy yourself a cigar with the change."

"Thank you, sir."

Over a cup of coffee and a bun in the station restaurant, Corporal Gregory pondered on some of the things the captain had said. Sure, he'd been drunker than a coot, but he knew what he was talking about. Only thing the liquor did was take the brakes off his tongue—like when he talked to an enlisted man about the big fight that was in the making. Damn trouble with officers was that they never thought that enlisted men heard anything or could figure things out for themselves. He'd heard that big-fight talk before he left Doniphan. Heard it again in Chicago—about how Grant was set to toss the Christers out on their tails and run the Indian Bureau the way he'd run the Army of the Potomac. Harrod sure must have had himself a time, if he didn't know whether he'd come to the hotel in a hack or had rolled down there. He'd bought himself a time just like Corporal James Gregory had, a big old wing-ding to celebrate leaving for Doniphan and the frontier. Only difference was that he mixed women and liquor, th' damn fool. Him and his Lulu! Fancy stuff. Officers only—but she was just as much a hooker, he'd bet, as the dollar-smash girls in Bessie Rivers' place.

He paid for the coffee and rejoined his recruits. The man Crane nodded and let his eyes flicker to the carpetbag at his feet.

"I got a pint, Corporal. Like you said, it's a long ride—a pint sure ain't lastin' us all the way."

"Maybe there'll be more along the line. Free, too . . . I'll show you how. You didn't join up with any milishy outfit, Crane. I'll show you how the Twentieth does its foragin'." A whistle sounded and he spoke sharply to the five. "Get your possibles together, men—your possibles—your warbags—them grips of yours. God, what dumb bastards you are, not knowin' a possible sack! Git 'em together. You, what's your name?"

"Gentry, Corporal."

"Get 'em on the train, Gentry, all of 'em. You others come with me. There's Captain Harrod's stuff to be got aboard, too."

3

In the '70s, as it does today, the Northern Pacific Railroad ran northwesterly from St. Paul in a long diagonal across the state of Minnesota and entered Dakota Territory at Fargo on the Red River. South City, slightly more than halfway across what is now North Dakota, was the railroad's end, the head of easy land travel from the East, the frontier of the Indian country which extended without a single white settlement far into Wyoming and Montana. Buffalo could still be hunted there, although the herds were but pathetic remnants of those which once roamed from the Arkansas to far beyond the Canadian border. Deer and antelope were abundant, there were bighorn and elk in the distant mountains, and the streams were alive with trout. To all of those things, except the trout, the Sioux clung as their last hope of survival as an independent people. For half a century—the first treaty with the Sioux on the Missouri was signed in 1825—they had been lied to and defrauded and had done their own full share of lying. They had fought the white man in the East and in the South, along the Platte, and had lost. They had fought him in the North, in the country drained by the Yellowsone and its tributaries, and had won. Gloriously, from the Sioux point of view, for among other victories they had wiped out Captain Fetterman and eighty-one men of the Eighteenth Infantry and Second Cavalry and had forced the closing of the Bozeman Road from Fort Laramie to the Montana settlements and the abandonment of the forts—Reno, Phil Kearney, and C. F. Smith—which had been built to defend that road and those who traveled it.

The Sioux now held what they chose to call their ancient hunting grounds—they had themselves invaded and conquered the area early in the century—all of the country between the North Platte and the Missouri, although they had but little interest in the lands which lay beyond the Yellowstone. They held indisputably the valleys of the Little Missouri, of the lower Yellowstone, and of the Powder, the Tongue, the Rosebud, and the Big Horn. Greatest of the prizes in the long struggle, the Sioux and their allies the Northern Cheyennes held Pa-sappa, the Black Hills. The white men had accepted the name and believed firmly that it was the Sioux's own as was that of Inyan Kara, the great peak which stands as the northern bastion of the range. Both names represent Cheyenne adaptations of the original Crow terms, and the letter R is not among the Siouan vocables.

A few white men had approached the Hills; a very few had actually entered them and ridden beside clear streams over meadows gay with wild flowers. From those rare stolen visits, legend sprang. Many men believed firmly that gold could be found in Pa-sappa by labor no greater than that required to pull up a clod of grass and beat out the bright nuggets that clung to the roots. None was so valiant as to risk his life by entering the Hills to test that conviction.

Some of those things the corporal, dozing in his seat as the train got under way, knew. Half of his first enlistment had been spent at Fort Laramie. He knew of the Sioux's contempt for their agents and of their grudging respect for the soldiers upon whom those agents called when trouble threatened. He knew there had been many treaties and that all had been broken, remade, and broken again. He knew that of all the Sioux there were only a few old men who urged peace with the whites and that for each of them there were a dozen chieftains who hated the whites with a venom equaled only by white hatred for the red men. The hostile leaders were revered and obeyed by every warrior and every young hothead who had yet to count *coup* or take his first scalp.

The corporal believed firmly that every Indian agent was a thief who was rapidly becoming wealthy by cheating the government on trade goods and food which were supposed to be issued to the Indians but actually were sold by the agent. The Indian Bureau, he believed, hated the army from Lieutenant General William T. Sherman down to the newest recruit in the ranks and was deliberately arming the Indians with the most modern repeating rifles and cartridges beyond all count-

ing. There was some element of justification for all his be-
liefs save that which he most cherished: that the Twentieth
Cavalry under Frederic C. Tuthill could whip any force of
hostiles which might be brought together on the Plains.

4

The engine whistle wailed from its brass dome and the train
halted jerkily. The sign NAWISSA beside the track told the corporal that St. Paul was one hundred twenty-six miles behind
them. A few men appeared and began, lazily, to transfer billets
of pine from piles beside the track to the tender. In sight were
two empty flatcars on a side track, seven or eight cabins, a platform, and, across a rutted area which might be called a street,
an unpainted frame structure with a sign that announced it a
saloon. The corporal stirred suddenly.

"Hey, you fellows!"

"All present, Corporal," drawled the lanky Crane. "What's
wrong? This ain't Fargo yet."

"No, it ain't." Time enough later to tell this fresh John to
refrain from comments until they were invited. "This here's
the place where we get our liquor—free liquor—and enough
of it to last us through to South City if it's worked right. Lissen close, now. Git them holsters off your belts and shove the
pistols in the waistband of your pants. Pull your coats down
over 'em so they won't show . . . that's right. Now, hustle
over to that saloon and buy a drink—just one drink, no more.
Don't show no loose money. There's five of you and you got to
make the bartender think that the price of one drink is all the
money you got between you. Got that?"

"Yep." Crane pulled a plug of tobacco and bit off a chew.
"Then what, Corp?"

"Ask him how much for a quart. Tell him you're going clear
through to the end of the line and you'd sure like to have a
bottle. You ain't got no money, though, not a cent. Then one

of you—it'd best be you, Crane—git th' bartender to one side and tell him maybe you can make a trade. Show him the gun under your coat. Ask him if that ain't a fair swap: one good govvamint Colt against a quart of good whisky. The rest of you Johns play your cards along with Crane's. Git th' liquor and then come back here on the high lope. I'll handle the rest of the deal."

"Right." Crane's eyes were dancing. "Come on, you fellers. Train ain't gonna wait here all day."

Three of the men—Gentry, Morelli, and Dugan—followed him to the platform. The fourth lingered.

"Git along with the others. What's holdin' you?" snapped Gregory.

"I—is that an order, Corporal?" He was a slender lad who probably lacked by six months the twenty-one years he'd sworn to on enlistment. He was doubtful, hesitant, but his timidity was bolstered by a sturdy inner assurance. The corporal bit off, half spoken, his sharp affirmative.

"No," he corrected. "It ain't any military order, if that's what you mean. What's eatin' you, kid? Git along after them others, on the double. We got a long ride ahead of us and some good drinkin' liquor will make it a lot shorter. Don't you want your share?"

"No, sir, I mean Corporal. I don't drink. Besides, this"— he touched the scabbarded revolver—"this is charged to me. The quartermaster sergeant said so. I don't want to start out in the army by getting myself in trouble."

"Is that so?" When all other verbal ammunition is exhausted, irony remains for the military man. "A barracks lawyer already and you ain't been in the army long enough to know which's your left foot. What's your name? I ain't got you fellows straightened out yet. You ain't Dugan, are you?"

"No, I'm Hale. Private Martin Hale."

"Ain't that nice? And where do you come from?"

"Ohio. Burnsville, Ohio."

"And I guess you gave your right name to the recruiting sergeant because you know it's wrong to tell a lie, and now you're going out West and start right in killin' Injuns, ain't you?"

"I——"

"Let me tell you something, Private Martin Hale. You got a hell of a lot to learn in the army—a whole hell of a lot—and it's going to be me and fellows like me that'll learn it to you. You'll find that arguin' with a noncommissioned officer don't . . ." he craned his neck through the open window as a clanging bell interrupted him. The whistle tooted four shrill blasts. Crane and his fellows emerged from the saloon and walked briskly toward their car. Their jackets bulged suspiciously.

"Y' git it all right?" the corporal met the first man at the door.

"Sure did," the man grinned. "Five quarts. Crane talked the feller out of an extra. You should've heard him!"

"Never mind that. Git in your seats, all of you, and hide that stuff. You don't know nothin', see, none of you. Hale, if you open your big mouth to anybody I'll beat it shut with a gun butt!"

The conductor stood by the steps, watch in hand.

"This is just a wood stop, soldier," he warned, "and we're pulling out in a couple of minutes. You should've got your drink when the others did."

"I ain't drinkin'. That fellow over there robbed my men. Robbed 'em of govvamint property. I gotta get it back, and you'd better wait f'r me."

He ran toward the barroom, hurdling the ruts and puddles. Within the building a man in a soiled shirt was mopping the unpainted bar. Two men sat on packing boxes by the wall. One was whittling and the white slivers of pine littered the dirt floor and clung to his muddy boots. The revolvers were not in sight.

"You the boss here?" the corporal addressed the man behind the bar.

"I reckon. What'll you have?"

"I'll have them guns you cheated my men out of, that's what, and no monkeyin' about it. The train's leaving."

"And you'd best leave on it. I don't know——"

"Don't give me that talk!" The corporal rapped his knuckles sharply on the bar. His cause was righteous and his strength mighty. "You thought you could get away with somethin'—thought that train would be clear to Fargo b'fore anybody found out what you'd done. Well, you guessed wrong, mister. Them guns 're govvamint property. They're marked so. And I've got"—he slapped his breast pocket—"I've got a list of their numbers."

"Listen, bub . . ." The man hesitated. The whittling loafer chuckled and spat among the chips at his feet. "Listen, how 'bout my liquor. Five quarts of good rye they traded me out of, claimin' the guns were theirs to do what they wanted with."

"That's none of my business." The corporal was all virtue. "You knew damn well they was govvamint guns. I want 'em, and I want 'em right now. You c'n take your choice between handin' 'em over to me or to Cap'n Harrod of the Twentieth. He's on the train right now and I'm tellin' you for your own good he made the rounds in St. Paul last night and he's in no mood f'r foolin' or argufyin'. Take your choice, mister, and take it fast."

"I'll have that train held and searched!" the man blustered. "I'm gonna get my liquor back."

"You can settle that with th' Northern P'cific Railroad—it's their train. Th' guns!"

The saloonkeeper grumbled, protested, and swore, but produced the revolvers. The corporal unbuttoned his blouse and by some mysterious legerdemain disposed of three of the weapons in the waistband of his trousers. The fourth was in his hand when a tall man in civilian dress strode into the room.

"What's the matter here? What's the matter?" The words rattled from his lips like volley fire. He was tall, lacking only a fraction of an inch of six feet, but his broad shoulders, tapering body, and lean horseman's flanks made him appear taller. He was bareheaded and a mop of red-gold hair curled over the velvet collar of a coat which New York would have declared a full four years out of style. His eyes were blue, piercing, his mouth hidden by a huge mustache that was redder by many shades than his hair.

"What's the matter here?" he repeated. "Corporal, you're Gregory of D, aren't you. What's the matter?"

The corporal stood rigidly at salute. His face was white but he managed to hold the fourth revolver so that its bulk was hidden. He dropped his hand from his cap when the man in civilian dress acknowledged the salute.

"Nothing at all, sir. Nothing except a little argument a couple of recruits had about—about what they were charged for a drink. It's all right now. I didn't want to bother Captain Harrod about it."

"Captain Harrod? I heard he'd been assigned to the Twentieth. Where is he?"

"On the train, sir. He's on his way to Doniphan to report for duty."

"Present my compliments to him. Tell him that my wife and I are in the last car—a special car which the president of the line put at our disposal. And"—the ice-blue eyes froze the corporal—"keep your men out of boozing dens like this! Understand?"

"Yes, sir." The noncom's hand remained at his cap visor until the door had slammed. Then he relaxed and wiped from his forehead the sweat which had gathered there.

"Partner," he said earnestly to the bartender, "maybe you don't know it but right now you're the luckiest goddam man west of the Mississippi River. If you hadn't give up them guns peaceable, like you done, Old Eagle-beak would've taken this place apart one board at a time, and you with it."

"Mebbe I'd have had somethin' t' say 'bout that." The saloon man was shaken but he tried to speak with confidence. "Who is this Old Eagle-beak—that captain you were talkin' about?"

"Hell, no!" The corporal dropped a half-dollar on the bar. "Give me a drink, a big one. I need it."

The whittling loafer spoke.

"I'll tell ye, Lem," he cackled. "That was him that was in here just now. Last time I seen him he was ridin' hell f'r leather at the head of a whole division of cavalry. Thet there was Gen'ral Tuthill—Old Eagle-beak!"

6 THE TROOPERS (2)

The recruits had obtained good whisky, surprisingly good whisky, at the fueling stop at Nawissa, but Corporal Gregory had lost any eagerness for drinking. He hastily stacked four of the five bottles beneath the seat of the coach and hid them behind a valise and a carpetbag. He passed the remaining bottle from one man to another. When it was returned to him he took a quick swallow, then wedged the bottle between his body and the side of the car.

"There's plenty more, Corporal," expostulated Crane. "No need to——"

"The hell there ain't!" Gregory was emphatic. "I'm telling you we'll do damn little drinking 'tween here and South City. You fellers—and it goes for me too—have got t' be cold sober when we git to Fargo and all the rest of the way. You don't know who's ridin' in the last car on this train . . . I do."

He paused. They had turned one seat and Gentry, Morelli, and Dugan were wedged into it, riding backward. Crane sat beside the corporal. The remaining recruit, Hale, as though conscious of Gregory's disfavor, occupied the seat across the aisle. Crane broke the silence.

"All right, Corp. I'll bite. Who is it in the last car?"

"It's the old man, that's who! Old Eagle-beak himself, Gen'ral Tuthill. Christ! He come in that saloon just after I'd run the bluff on the bartender that if he didn't turn loose of them guns I'd call Captain Harrod. 'What's the matter here?' he says. There I was—three guns under my coat and tryin' to hide the fourth one behind me—and I sure had to talk fast."

"What did you tell him?" Crane's eyes twinkled.

"Told him nothing was wrong, just a little argument you fellers had had over the price of a drink. He swallowed it, and the barkeep kept his mouth shut, thank God. Then he walked out after telling me to keep my men out of places like that. That was a close one!"

"He—he's the boss-man, eh?" Morelli asked. His voice was sharply accented.

"He sure is, and I'm tellin' every last one of you that when you git to the fort you'd better not f'rget it."

"Tough guy?" the Italian persisted.

"They don't come any tougher. Floggin' ain't been allowed in the army since 'sixty-two, but you try buckin' Old Eagle-beak and he'll make you wish you could take something light, like twenty lashes."

Gregory glanced quickly toward the door at the rear of the car, then produced the bottle for another round.

"You got good whisky back there," he remarked. "It's a sight better than the gut varnish the bootleggers sell on payday."

"Loggers' liquor." Crane jerked his thumb in the general direction of Nawissa. "Them fellers was lumbermen. I've seen plenty of them. P'ticular as all hell, loggers is, 'bout their eatin' an' drinkin'. Soldiers an' sailors, they'll drink anything that'll pour, but not loggers. P'ticular as all hell." He chewed for a few moments, then added: "It ought t' be good—look what we paid f'r it."

The corporal laughed for the first time since his encounter with the Twentieth's commander. Dugan and Gentry laughed with him. Morelli stared from one man to another, then added his cackling to theirs.

"You one smart feller, Corporal, I bet me."

"Yeah. Call me corporal good and loud. I come so damn close to losin' these stripes I'm still shakin'. What's your first name, Morelli?"

"Giovanni. John, you say it."

"That's a big mouthful; you'd better call yourself John. Dago, eh?"

"Yep. Italiano," the man corrected with no trace of rancor. "Eight mont' dis country, dat's all. I talk English pretty good, eh?"

"Eight months since you got off the boat and you're in the army already. What made you hold up your hand, Johnny?"

"I don' un'erstan'—my han'——"

"What made you join the army?"

"Oh." The little Italian shrugged. "My brud', he live New York an' I work there. Dig in sewer. Mooch work, not much mon'—dolla day. Then got laid off. Man come and says, 'You come wit' me. Good job in Penn—Penn—' I can't say eet."

"Pennsylvania?"

"Yeah, dat's him. 'Work in coal mine,' he say. 'Good job, two dolla day.' Me, I no want to work in mine, un'ergroun', in dark; I like work in light. I walk aroun' and talk with 'nudder man, a soldier this one. I tell him I fight in Italy, with Garibaldi. He say, 'Good. We needa fighting man, needa good man to kill Injuns. Tha's good job too. Good place to sleep in bed by self, not wit' two-three udder mans. Good grub t'ree times day. T'irteen dolla month'. I say 'Good. When I go?' An' here I am."

The others laughed.

"Maybe you'll get your chance to kill Injuns, Johnny. You won't find any dagos in the Twentieth, though. All Americans there."

"Dat's me, American. No Italiano no more. American—American soldier."

"I guess that's right too. Maybe you come to the right place after all. Have another drink, Johnny."

The Italian drank. His eyes were bright with a fire that was not kindled by the whisky.

"American now, I bet me," he said ecstatically.

"Tell 'em that, Johnny. The first guy that calls you a dago, punch him in the nose." Gregory turned to Dugan, a heavy-set youngster with a puffy ear. His movements were quick, shifting. "By the name you're Irish—are you an immygrant like Johnny here?"

"Not me. I was born and raised on Avenue A—that's New York."

"You join up to kill Injuns?"

"Christ, no!" Dugan spat out the window. "I don't care if I never see one. Y' eat reg'lar in the army, I've heard, and that's more'n I've been doin' under the damn Republicans. My old man says Republican is just another name for hard times."

"Uh-huh. Me, I'm a soldier which means I don't know a damn thing 'bout politics and care less. What d'you say, Gentry?"

The third man faced him slowly. He was considerably older than Morelli or Dugan; as old, Gregory decided, as Crane although his reddish hair was untouched with gray. Both of them had probably lied five or ten years off their ages when they enlisted.

"You're askin' me why I joined up?"

"Sure." Gregory felt suddenly uncomfortable under the other's steady eyes. There flashed through his mind the recollection of a night in South City, a pay night, when he'd told a civilian to get the hell away from the bar and let a soldier drink. He'd learned some sulfurous seconds later that the man was an artillery major.

"There'll be plenty will ask you why you joined up," he remarked. "It's what they ask every rookie."

"And I'm a rookie." The man's voice was flat. "I'll tell 'em all the same thing I'm tellin' you. I had my reasons for joining and what those reasons are is none of their goddamned business. That ought t' be enough for 'em."

"It's enough to get you invited down beyond the picket line, rookie. You might have to prove on somebody's front teeth that something wasn't his business."

The man shrugged.

"They're free to make anything they want out of it."

"They will, all right." Gregory was glad when Crane's nasal voice interrupted.

"Me," he said deliberately, "I had a mother-in-law—something you younkers have been spared. She talked too much, and most of it was about how good-f'r-nothin' a son-in-law she'd drawed. I wasn't half-bad durin' the war when I was makin' good money at Colt's in New Haven, but when work slacked off and I was down to doin' odd jobs, then I got on the skunk list. When my wife started agreein' with her mother I walked out—took a coupla dollars outa th' sugar jug in the cupboard an' walked out. I went to New York and then to Philadelphia. It was there I got kinda drunk. It'd been a hell of a long time since I could take a drink without two wimmen sniffin' me when I come home, an' somehow 'r other enlistin' seemed like a good idee."

"That winds it up," said Gregory. "No, it don't. Damn if I hadn't forgotten the Ohio kid. Hey, Private Martin Hale, what 've you got to say?"

The boy laughed nervously and blushed to the roots of his fair hair.

"I didn't want to get married—that's why I'm in the army."

"Whatever you might mean by that." The corporal scowled but Crane, seated at his side, chuckled.

"I'll lay I can call that shot pretty close," the Yankee observed. "What was it, one of these here shotgun weddings, son, and you run out on it 'fore there was any trigger-pullin'?"

Young Hale nodded, and blushed again.

"I—half the fellows in town had been with her. More than once too. I knew that when she came along while I was fishing in Bushy Creek, and started smartin' up to me. You know how it is?"

Crane leaned in front of the corporal and spat from the open window.

"We know how it is, son. Leastways, I reckon most of us do."

"Well, only six weeks or so after that, her father and a brother of hers came to the house. They had guns and they talked pretty hard about how she was going to have a baby and I'd have to marry her. She was waiting at the end of the lane in the buggy, they said, and we'd go to the preacher's right now—the license could wait till tomorrow."

Crane whistled.

"They didn't care how they crowded y'. Whut did y' do?"

"I didn't argue; there wasn't any use. It was a Wednesday night and my father and mother had gone to prayer meeting. I invited the two of them in and told them to have a seat in the parlor while I put on my good suit instead of the work clothes I was wearing. All I took time to do was to grab twenty-seven dollars I had in my bureau drawer, then I went out the back window and down over the shed roof. By morning I'd covered twelve miles and then a fellow gave me a ride to Youngstown, eight miles further on. I got a train from there to Cincinnati and enlisted."

"Under your right name?" Gregory asked quickly.

Hale nodded.

"The sergeant told me——"

"I know what the sergeant told you—all about false enlistment. Hell, boy, half the men in the army if you ask them their name they got t' stop and think."

"You played it smart," Crane interjected. "Only thing is, your folks ought to know where you are."

"They do. I wrote them from Cincinnati and gave the letter to another recruit who was being sent to the Quartermaster Depot in Philadelphia. I told them everything except what regiment I was being sent to. I didn't know that."

Gregory nodded approval.

"Like he said, you played it smart. Even if they find out you enlisted, they won't take time to run you down—they need a son-in-law too bad for that.

"You'll make a trooper, kid. By God, you will. When you didn't want to help in getting that liquor I put you down as a sis, but I take it back. There's a fellow comes and goes from the fort—you'll meet him, Sol Rogers. 'Solitary,' they call him, 'cause he always goes it alone, never takes a partner with him. He's the best scout and hunter there is in the West and I sure want to see his face when I tell him how you invited them fellers to have a seat while you put on your Sunday suit. That's the kind of trick he admires. He'll say, 'That shines!' "

2

From the moment that Captain Harrod had read the orders assigning him to the Twentieth Cavalry he had known that sooner or later he would have to face that regiment's commander. Behind them both were memories of the Battle of Wishbone Creek. To Tuthill that dawn conflict had been a decisive victory over hostile Indians and he could point proudly to sundry letters and orders which commended him for his part therein. The valley in the Pronghorn Hills was indelibly stamped in Harrod's mind as the place where gallant young Joe Harris and nineteen men had died miserably while the commander who should have ridden to their rescue was engaged in shooting the terrified ponies of the Cheyennes and in lauding his own marksmanship.

Harrod walked to the forward platform, lit a cigar, and tried to forget the ache that pounded his skull while he considered the immediate problem. He could ignore the royal invitation for a time—at least until his eyes were less betrayingly blood-shot—but before sunset he must repair to the private car and go through the motions of paying his respects to the commander whose regiment he was rejoining. Between them there could be no dissimulation, no polite side-stepping of their personal opinions of one another. He knew, and Tuthill knew that he knew, that he had been transferred away from regimental duties at the first opportunity for detached service for an officer of his rank. The adjutant had notified him of that transfer, and as he cut across the parade ground toward the bachelor quarters he had encountered Tuthill.

"I have just left the adjutant's office, General," he said.

"Yes. I expected the orders, Captain. Department Headquarters requested the assignment of a captain or major some time ago. Only one major is now on duty with the regiment and so——"

"And so you're rid of me." They were quite alone and Harrod had not hesitated to interrupt.

"You may take it that way if you wish," Tuthill had said coldly. "Since you have seen fit to mention it, I do not regret your leaving the Twentieth."

"It is mutual, sir, I assure you."

They had exchanged salutes and parted, outwardly punctilious, inwardly reminiscent, both of them, of the day when they had looked down from their saddles at the hideously mutilated bodies of Harris and his men. Tuthill had saluted the silent forms.

"They died for their country and for the honor of the regiment," he had exclaimed grandiloquently.

"They died"—Harrod's words had reached only Tuthill's ears—"because you let them die, you murdering bastard, and if you want to make anything out of that I'll be happy to oblige you."

Tuthill had completely ignored the defiant insult but Harrod knew that he had heard every word.

And now—Harrod retreated within the car as the thick smoke from the engine swirled around the open platform— and now the wheel had turned a full cycle. He was back with the Twentieth, back to the moment when he had parted from Tuthill in the middle of the parade ground and continued to his quarters. *Years rubbed off the calendar because sherry was on the table instead of lemonade.* He shrugged and continued past his seat and toward the rear of the train. Might as well get it over with.

He squeezed through the narrow aisle which flanked the two bedrooms at the forward end of the private car, then opened a glass-paneled swinging door into the lushly decorated apartment from which the president of the Northern Pacific inspected the line. Something—possibly the reflection of the late-morning sun from the glass of the door—attracted Tuthill's attention. He rose quickly from the overstuffed chair and advanced, hand extended, to meet the junior officer.

"Ah, Harrod, you're with us again. I'm delighted to see you."

Well, I'll be good and goddamned. Wish I had a pat of butter—just to see if it'd melt in his mouth. Harrod gripped the extended hand.

"And I'm glad to get a chance at active service, General. Six years, most of it at a desk, is a long time."

"Yes, yes. I'd die under it, I know, die like a foundered horse. I heard at St. Paul that you'd been reassigned to the regiment. Didn't know you were aboard the train, though, until Corporal Gregory told me."

"He gave me your message. I'll present my orders to the adjutant at Fort Doniphan. However, regard me as reporting for duty, sir, informally."

"Yes, yes. Come back and sit down. You've met Mrs. Tuthill, I know. Martha, my dear, you remember Captain Harrod."

Harrod bowed from the hips; the colonel's lady inclined her head and smiled coolly.

"How do you do, Captain. This is quite a surprise—you have been away from the regiment for a long time."

"Too long, madam. I just remarked to the general that I was glad to get a chance at active service again."

"I am afraid that your wish will be granted, Captain."

Tuthill laughed shrilly.

"There speaks the woman, Harrod. They begin to shiver and shake when the regiment takes the field and their worrying stops only when we return."

"It is natural, I imagine, sir."

"Yes, yes. You've heard the old saying: 'Difficult to live with, impossible to live without.'" He changed the subject abruptly. "You'll find many changes in the regiment, Harrod; many old friends gone, many new faces to get acquainted with. Too many of the men, both rank and file, are new to the frontier and new to fighting. I'm glad that Washington gave me a man with your record of service."

"Thank you, General." *Christ on a crutch, he's smoother than grease on a plate. He's really trying to make me think that the past is forgotten as far as he's concerned. Well, I won't forget and I won't butter him up the way he's buttering me, but I'll be under his command and I'd better be sensible.*

"I mean it. When I took command of the regiment, nearly every officer in it had held brevet rank during the rebellion.

Enlisted men the same; some of them had been captains and even majors. Now—but you'll see for yourself."

"I would be greatly surprised if there were no changes, General. After all——"

"Certainly, certainly. You had F company before and I think I'll give you F again. You'll relieve a lieutenant in command—young fellow named Chance. Good man and seems to shape up well, but no combat experience and as green as grass, only a year or two out of the academy. I'll see Claggett —he's still adjutant, by the way—and tell him you're to have F."

"Thank you, sir."

Tuthill rose. The brief contact with royalty, he implied, was ended.

"Glad you called, Harrod. I have some writing to do and must ask you to excuse me. Tomorrow, after we leave Fargo, I'll pick you up in your car and we'll look over the recruits Corporal Gregory has."

3

The train was an hour out of Fargo when Tuthill walked forward from his private car to inspect the recruits. Captain Harrod, clear-eyed now, accompanied him. Both men were in civilian clothes, but their profession was stamped upon them as clearly as though they wore the plumed helmet and gold-splashed full-dress uniform of the cavalry. Corporal Gregory was playing high-low-jack with Crane and Dugan and was quite oblivious to the approach of his superiors until Gentry leaped to his feet and barked, " 'Shun!" as sharply as a first sergeant. The corporal obeyed instinctively, knocking to the floor the board which served as a table.

"Yes, sir."

Tuthill acknowledged the salute.

"Not gambling, Corporal?"

"No, sir, just passing the time, sir."

"I see. Are these the recruits you picked up in Chicago?"

"Yes, sir."

The colonel's steel-blue eyes flickered impersonally from one man to another. Gregory added unnecessarily, "They'll shape up, sir."

"I'll be the judge of that." Tuthill faced the nearest man. "What's your name?"

"Dugan."

"Dugan what?"

"Dugan Anth— I mean Anthony Dugan."

"I am the commanding officer of the Twentieth Cavalry. You speak to me, or to any officer, only when you are spoken to. Then you say 'sir.' Understand?"

"Yes, sir." Dugan's jaw was set squarely and he looked Tuthill directly in the eye.

"See that you remember it." He turned to the next man. "Your name?"

"Private Martin Hale, sir."

"Your uniform shows your rank and your first name is of interest only to the mustering officer and the paymaster. Now, your name?"

"Hale, sir."

"That's better. Have any of you men had any military service? How about you—you look old enough to have been in the war?"

"No, sir."

"I imagine you mean you've had no service. Your name?"

"Crane, sir."

"Stand at ease, men. By tomorrow you will have reached Fort Doniphan and will have been assigned to companies. I am telling you now what you will learn before you even learn the trumpet calls: the Twentieth is the best regiment in the United States Army! See that you're worthy of it. Corporal!"

"Yes, sir."

"You will have all the rest of the day on this train. Some of the time might be spent in teaching these men how to stand at attention, how to salute, and how to address officers and non-commissioned officers. They might find it more profitable than cards."

"Yes, sir."

Tuthill stepped a half-pace to the right.

"Have you anything to say, Captain Harrod."

"Thank you, General. What is this man's name, Corporal?"

"Gentry, sir."

"Thank you. Gentry, you called 'attention' when the general and I came in. Why?"

"I"—his eyes shifted from one man to another—"it was the general. I'd seen his picture in the papers during the war. There was no mistaking him, sir."

"Then where did you learn to call men to attention when an officer entered?"

A pulse was beating visibly in Gentry's throat.

"At—at home, sir. I've watched soldiers drilling and seen them called to attention for officers. So I did it."

"I see. If it meets the approval of the general, I'd like to have this man assigned to F company."

"No objection whatever, Captain, if you want him," said Tuthill. "He's a bit fat in the rump to make a horseman, though."

"We'll work off any surplus tallow, I'll guarantee. Thank you, sir."

"That will be all, Corporal. Carry on."

"Yes, sir." Gregory's hand snapped to his forehead. He remained at attention until the two officers had left the car. As the door closed behind them, Dugan spat on the floor.

"Son of a bitch!" he snarled. " 'What's your name?' 'Say "sir" when you speak to me.' 'Don't forget it.' 'Too fat in the ass' to suit him. If he'd talked to me like that back on Avenue

A, I'd have smacked his teeth clear through into his back hair. You might think we were the dirt under his feet."

The corporal chuckled.

"You are and don't you forget that, either. You—all of you —are buck-ass John recruits and he wore two stars during the war and he's wearing an eagle now. I'm telling you—and this goes for all of you—don't ever forget your place with any officer from the old man down to the newest and rawest cliptail lootenant fresh out of West Point. Call one of 'em a son of a bitch, like you did just now, Dugan, and you're getting off lucky with five years and a bobtail discharge. Punch an officer in the teeth, like you talked about doin', and the law says they can stand you in front of a firing squad or hang you. They're officers, you're enlisted men—and it's further from their side of the flagpole to yours than it is across the Atlantic Ocean." He paused an instant. "Ain't that right, Gentry?"

"Guess it is, Corporal, since you say so."

Gregory's eyes narrowed.

"You're pretty smart, Gentry, but don't get to thinkin' how smart you are. Captain Harrod's asked for you for F company. Git smart with your company commander and you'll find your hide pegged out to dry on th' corral fence."

The recruit made no reply. He turned his face to the window and the flat Dakota landscape beyond the tracks. The corporal drew a deep breath.

"You fellers heard what th' general said. When we git to South City he'll want you t' know how to stand at attention and how to address an officer. Salutin', too; there's nothin' he hates worse t' see than a sloppy salute, especially from a recruit.

"First thing you got t' git through your skulls is that you ain't nobody. You're just a part of the regiment, like the horses and guns. Only difference is that you don't have US branded on your flank and a number burned into your front foot. If an officer tells you to do something, you do it; that's all. If he tells you to go some place, you don't ask where it is or how to get there—y' salute and do an about-face and then you find somebody else to tell you where you're supposed to go. When you're told to report to the company commander, you don't grin all over your silly face—like one rookie did at Laramie—and say, 'This is me, Capt'n.' Not unless you want your tail chewed off clear to the root. What you say is—Gentry, how would you report to your company commander?"

Gentry replied without turing his head.

"You'd better tell 'em. I haven't any idea."

"I was just wonderin' if maybe you knew—like you knew enough to call ' 'Shun!' when you seen the old man and Harrod comin'. I'll tell you . . ." he rose, stiffened rigidly, and snapped his hand to the visor of his cap.

" 'Sir, Private Jones reporting,' or, 'Sir, Private Jones has the permission of the first sergeant to speak to the company commander.' Maybe you'll say, 'Reporting as ordered,' but you don't say, 'I report,' and you don't call the captain or the first sergeant by name and you don't say 'you' to them. It's, 'Will the captain permit Private Jones to visit South City on Sunday?' That's the army way of doing things and you either do it that way or get a call-down.

" 'Nother thing: in the cavalry we have trumpets. The feller that blows it is a trumpeter. It's the infantry that has bugles and buglers and you'd better keep that straight, too. Always say 'trumpet'—and God help you if you ever call it a horn."

He paused for breath.

"Did you get all that, Dugan?"

"I got it," the recruit muttered. "I can say, 'Sir, Private Dugan requests permission to go to the water closet,' and I'll go along with it until some of them high-and-mighty officers starts telling me that I'm just dirt under his feet. Then I'll tell him! Maybe I'm only a raw-ass rookie like you said, but I'm a man, same as they are, and I've got my rights."

Gentry's lip curled.

4

The name on his enlistment papers, the name under which he had sworn to preserve and defend the Constitution of the United States against all enemies foreign and domestic, was Amos Clark Gentry. The Amos he could not have explained. It was a name, nothing more, which had entered his mind in the shabby hotel room in Chicago where he had planned the statements he would make to the recruiting officer the next day. Clark? The restaurant where he had bought his breakfast was on Clark Street; so was the army recruiting office. The source of the last name was clear. The train had stopped at a station—he had not noticed the name—in Indiana. As it pulled out slowly, he had read the sign on a blacksmith shop which faced the tracks. P. GENTRY, HORSESHOER—and the name had remained in his memory.

Amos Clark Gentry. It was a good name, he decided. It was easy to remember and it had no resemblance whatever to Jervis Samuel Pryor. No man who had known or had heard of Captain Jervis Pryor, 40th Wisconsin Infantry, would be reminded of him by the name Amos Clark Gentry. So far as he was concerned there never had been a Jervis Pryor. He was, and always had been, Amos Clark Gentry, and he stood in front of the mirror, looked himself in the eye, and repeated it over and over.

"Gentry!" he said aloud, then turned quickly to face the imaginary speaker and answered, "Yes, sir." *I should salute, of course, if I recognize an officer. But I'm a recruit. I've never been in the army. I don't know anything about saluting. I'm Amos Clark Gentry and I'm a carpenter by trade and I come from Cleveland, Ohio.*

Amos Clark Gentry, carpenter. Amos Clark Gentry, Cleveland, Ohio. Amos Clark Gentry, next of kin Mrs. Hannah Gentry, mother, 407 Hamilton Street, Cleveland. I wonder if there is a Hamilton Street in Cleveland. Amos Clark Gentry, born in Cleveland on the twenty-second of February, same day as George Washington—1840. That's knocking off a few years but it ought to be all right. Unless I've forgotten something or unless they've put in some new questions, that's all they'll want to know. Write it all down, read it over a dozen times, then burn the paper. Amos Clark Gentry, in all his life, had never been in the state of Wisconsin; he'd never heard of the town of Shelby where the citizens had given a man named Pryor a coat of hot tar and had rolled him in white feathers.

Amos Clark Gentry, private soldier, United States Army.

5

There had been two courts-martial. The first had considered the case of Captain Jervis Pryor, 40th Wisconsin Infantry. The second court had passed sentence on Private Jervis Pryor of the same regiment. The charges in both cases had been the same—cowardice in the face of the enemy.

The trial judge advocate must have been a preacher in civil life; his voice boomed like a bass drum and the words echoed from the walls of the shabby room where the court sat . . . "in that Captain Jervis Pryor, on or about the twenty-fourth day of November, 1863, in the fighting about Missionary Ridge, did desert his command which was engaged in an attack on a rebel position . . . and that, in the course of such desertion, he did shout to the men of his company and did advise them to retreat immediately or they would be killed by the heavy fire from the rebel lines."

There had been more, of course. His lieutenant had been killed in that fighting, but his noncomissioned officers had testified as to his actions and had stated that in Mississippi he had ordered advances but had remained in the rear, that he had fallen to the ground and rolled into a ditch when the company attacked a rebel trench near Vicksburg. "I saw him fall and thought he'd been hit, but he came on after we'd got to the trench and cleaned it out. He wasn't even scratched."

Findings: To the charge, Guilty. To the specifications, Guilty.

Sentence: To be reduced to the ranks.

Within the year Private Jervis Pryor had been tried for the same offense. "The firing wasn't heavy—just snipers in the timber that were trying to delay the advance; but a rebel battery on the crest of the hill flung a shell that hit a cavalry scout who was riding just off our left flank. It killed him and his horse—tore 'em all to pieces—and Private Pryor flung his rifle away and started running and hollering . . ."

Findings: Guilty.

Sentence: To be hanged by the neck until dead.

It had been General Sherman himself—old 'Cump—who had set aside that death sentence and directed that Private Jervis Pryor be dishonorably dismissed from the service. "The accused has been tried twice for the same offense, that of cowardice in the face of the enemy, and the record of both trials has been carefully reviewed. It is the feeling of the reviewing authority that the first trial court was in error in permitting the guilty man to be reduced to the ranks within the same regiment in which he had served as an officer. Service as a private soldier with men who knew of his offense and his demotion could have done nothing to inspire him to live down that record and to make a new and more honorable name for himself.

"That circumstance was not noted by the second court which approved, not without justice, the death sentence. Military justice, though necessarily strict, is not vengeful. . . . The findings of the court are approved; the sentence, however, is set aside. The reviewing authority directs that Private Jervis Pryor be dishonorably dismissed from the service of the United States of America. That sentence will be carried out in the presence of all officers and men of the 40th Wisconsin Infantry and in accordance with established regulations and the customs of the service governing such cases."

He was alive. He would stay alive until he died decently in his bed as a man should. He wouldn't die on some rocky slope in Tennessee or Mississippi or Georgia with his head torn off by a shell and his blood spurting like a crimson fountain two feet in the air. He wouldn't be a mess of bloody guts dangling from the branches; he wouldn't be wiped out into complete nothingness like the men on that artillery caisson which had taken a direct hit from a rebel shell. God damn 'em all. God damn Abe Lincoln and 'Cump Sherman and the cold-eyed colonels who'd presided over the courts-martial. They'd gone by the book; they'd done what courts had done in similar cases ever since Princeton and Brandywine and Yorktown. There was nothing in the book to tell them what happened to a man, to Jervis Pryor, when rifle fire rippled across the front and the lead slugs hummed like angry bees over his head; when artillery shells crashed into the lines and men vanished in geysers of red mud and redder fragments of flesh; when the rebel lines erupted in a charge of gray-clad soldiers who screamed like demons from the deepest pit and whose bayonets ripped and tore into those who faced them. You couldn't tell a court-martial what things like that did to you; that something—God knows what—broke inside of you and screamed at you to run, run like hell, before you were dead like those others. He had said at the first trial, "I couldn't help it," and even the cavalry major who had been appointed to act as his counsel had sneered. You couldn't . . .

The regiment—all twelve companies—was formed about the four sides of a square. The usual guard details had been taken over by another regiment of the brigade and not even the cooks and their helpers had been excused. The only men not present were the sick, and each of these, he was told by the sergeant who guarded him, had been examined by the surgeon to determine if he was too sick to walk or ride to the scene. The colonel and his staff sat their horses in the middle of the square; the adjutant, red-bearded Captain Mulloy from Racine, conducted the ceremony of public disgrace.

"Prisoner and escort, foward—march."

"Step out, Pryor, you ain't bein' shot at so there's no need of runnin'."

Pryor stepped out. Two guards and the sergeant marched in front of him, two guards and a corporal behind. Their long Springfield muskets were sloped on their shoulders, the hammers were cocked and a percussion cap gleamed on the nipple of each piece. A new uniform had been issued him for the occasion. The buttons were polished and on the top of his new kepi was the dark green device of the corps to which the 40th was assigned.

The adjutant stripped off, one by one, all evidences of military service. He cut the buttons from the blue coat, ripped off the embroidered French horn which was the infantry insigne —ten years were to pass before the crossed rifles appeared to designate the foot soldier—and finally jammed a dilapidated soft hat on Pryor's head to replace the smart kepi. Finally, Captain Mulloy stuck a dozen white feathers in the hatband.

"Jervis Pryor," he declaimed, "I now announce that the sentence of the court-martial, as amended by General Sherman, has been carried out. You were a soldier in the United States Army and in this regiment. You were convicted of arrant cowardice in the face of the enemy and sentenced to be dishonorably discharged. This has been done. Sergeant of the guard, drum this man out of camp!"

6

He had gone home to Rossville on the turnpike out of Madison. His wife was there and there was no other place for him to go. He learned within a week that news of his disgrace had already reached the town where he had been born and reared, where his parents were buried, and where he had married Grace Bailey, daughter of Edward Bailey, who owned the largest dairy farm in three counties. Men whom he had known from childhood passed him unseeingly on the street. Nils Berger's son, young Jon, who had lost a leg at Gettysburg, looked him in the eye and spat at his feet. He reopened the woodworking and cabinetmaking shop which he had operated profitably before he had been elected a lieutenant in the infantry company which had been recruited in Rossville, but no business crossed the threshold. From time to time he obtained work for a few days or a week when a new barn was being built or when the county replaced the old bridge over Sugarmill Creek, but he was told pointedly that he was hired only because all able-bodied men were in the army and there were no other carpenters available. He had resumed his attendance at the Lutheran Church where he and Grace had sung in the choir, where they had been married; on the second Sunday the pastor had visited his home and asked that he drop his membership.

"It is not a Christian spirit, Jervis," the Reverend Hochberg had said sadly, "but a committee of members of the church has insisted upon it. I am the pastor, but I must be guided by the wishes of the members of the church. Do I have to say anything more?"

"No, Reverend, that's enough. I know what to do. Tell 'em that they can quit worrying—they've seen me in church for the last time."

It was that which killed Grace, he decided later. She had been active in the church almost since childhood. She taught a Sunday-school class; she served on any committee which might be organized; she was one of those who appeared regularly to sweep and dust the building and to arrange the hymnbooks in their proper places. Withdrawal from church affairs broke the spirit which, for a time, had made her defiant of gossip and slurs.

"It's me they don't want, Gracie," he said. "No call for you to quit going there."

She shook her head.

"You're my husband, Jervis, for better or worse——"

"—and it sure turned out worse for you."

"—and I certainly won't go to the church or the Grange or any other place unless you can go too."

"It's better I should leave town, get out and go some place where I'm not known, where—well, where what happened in the army wouldn't follow me. Then, afterward, you could join me."

"No. It's up to you whether or not we leave Rossville, but wherever you go, I'll go with you."

Once, and only once, had she referred directly to his disgrace. He had entered the house and found her lying across the bed, sobbing.

"Grace, what happened, what's wrong?"

"Nothing, nothing. Oh, Jervis, what made you do it?"

"I don't know," he had answered miserably. "So help me God, Grace, I don't know."

She was, he thought, like a lamp when the oil has become exhausted and the flame flickers in the wick. It will flare strongly for an occasional moment but it fades steadily until at last it vanishes. Grace weakened like that flame. The doctor—her father summoned him—examined her and stated that there was nothing really wrong. He prescribed a tonic, but he spoke bluntly to her father.

"There's no tonic in the world that'll do anything for her, Bailey. You know that as well as I do, and you know what's really wrong with her. Get her away from here, a thousand miles away where none of this—this business will follow her, and she might come around. That's the only medicine I can prescribe."

They moved to Shelby in the extreme northern portion of the state, close to the boundary of the upper peninsula of Michigan. He dropped his given name of Jervis, changed one letter in the spelling of his surname, and identified himself as Samuel Prior. When questioned, he said he was a Pennsylvanian and had been turned down three times for military service. "Something wrong with my kidneys, the doctors say —gravel stones, they call it. Doesn't seem to bother me as long as I can do most of my work in the shop and don't have to walk too much."

None questioned the statement. There were many in Shelby and in the county who had not enlisted, many who had bought the services of a substitute when their names were drawn in the draft. Such men were not held in contempt, and for a time all went well although there was little improvement in his wife's health. She attended church almost every Sunday and he accompanied her, but she declined all invitations or suggestions that they affiliate themselves formally as members of the congregation. The war ended and the men who had fought under the Michigan banners came home. Pryor peered into each bronzed face but he saw none that he recognized. The 40th Infantry, as well as the other regiments of its brigade, had been recruited in the southeastern section of the state and even its replacements had been drawn from that region. His fears slowly subsided and he told himself that Grace, too, had permitted the past to sink into memory. Then, three years after Appomattox, Major Alexander Richardson, brevet colonel, U. S. Volunteers, arrived in Shelby.

Every war that has ever been waged has produced its Richardsons, the professional veterans who carry with them into civil life the bugle and the rolling drum, who live only to refight old battles, to don old uniforms for parades, and to be active in veterans' organizations. With Richardson it was the Grand Army of the Republic, then two years old and barely beginning to realize its political power. He had come to northern

Wisconsin ostensibly to set up his law office, actually to organize a new G.A.R. post in every town between Menominee and Duluth, and he had commanded a battalion in the 40th Wisconsin Infantry.

He and Jervis Pryor met face to face in the Shelby post office and recognition was mutual and instantaneous. The former major was first to speak.

"I remember you very clearly, Mr. Pryor," he said. "I am now living in Shelby and I do not think that I or any other man who fought for his country will want to know you."

"I am working here to support myself and my wife," Pryor answered. "I am trying to live down all that happened in the army and I don't intrude on anyone."

Richardson brushed past him without a word. *He's out to make trouble for me. He'll say it's his duty to tell everyone who I am and what I did. Oh, God, I can't let Grace face it. It'll kill her sure.* He returned to his shop, worked through the afternoon, and went home at his usual time. He gave Grace a letter from her father which had been in their box at the post office.

"Mother's been sick," she remarked. "Father thinks I ought to come home—I'd cheer her up, he says, and he needs me."

Pryor fought to make his voice casual.

"Why don't you go? I can make out all right."

He saw her off on the southbound train the next day. *I'll sell the shop here if I get an offer; if I don't, I'll just pack my tools and leave. Same goes for the house. We rented it furnished and there won't be more than a couple of trunks to pack and put in storage. This time I'll really get away from Wisconsin—Texas, maybe, or California—and I'll write Grace after I'm on my way. If I see that goddam Richardson I'll tell him I'm leaving town. Maybe that will shut him up.*

It was Richardson who organized and led the mob of masked men three nights later. When Pryor opened the door in response to the knock, he was seized and dragged through the quiet streets to the outskirts of town. A fire had been built there and the flames were licking about the base of the tar pot. They stripped him, dipped brooms in the hot tar and daubed it over his naked body from head to foot, then rolled him in the feathers they had dumped from a ripped feather-bed. Few words were spoken—"Stand still, you, or I'll ram this broom in your mouth" . . . "Watch out for his eyes, that's all" . . . "White feathers! Too damn bad if they'd been black" . . . At the end: "This ought t' show you that we don't want your kind in Shelby. We'll give you forty-eight hours—if you're around this town Sunday morning we'll hang you!"

When he wrote Grace from Chicago two weeks later, he said merely that some people in Shelby had made trouble for him and that he had left the town. He had about decided, he wrote, to go to California, but he would first visit Cincinnati and Pittsburgh where there were opportunities for employment and where there would be little chance of encountering a former member of the 40th Wisconsin Infantry. He asked her to write him at the latter city. The letter he received was from her father. It told him that Grace was dead. She had died, Bailey wrote in his sprawling farmer's script, of the disgrace of learning of what the people of Shelby had done to her husband. The news had reached Rossville within a few days and everyone in the town knew it. "And my advice to you is that you don't come back here, ever." Pryor tore the letter into fragments and tossed them into the wastebasket in the post office. Then, for the first time in his life, he got drunk.

He did not enlist until more than five years later. He worked for a time in Pittsburgh, in Cleveland and Akron, then went to Philadelphia. He learned that a carpenter who knew his trade was assured of work anywhere and he became one of many journeymen who drifted from city to city and from job to job. He lived in cheap rooms, ate in restaurants which had already gained the name hash houses, and spent his evenings in the saloon nearest to his room. The saloons were warm in winter and reasonably cool in summer; he could always be sure of meeting other men, wanderers like himself, with whom he could discuss politics or their jobs, or merely talk aimlessly over a five-cent "schuper" of beer. In all his wanderings no one recognized him as the Wisconsin infantry-man who had been sentenced to death for cowardice. His thoughts turned only rarely to the war, the two courts-martial, and Sherman's final mercy. He felt no desire to return to Ross-ville. Grace was dead. She lay in the Bailey family plot in the Lutheran cemetery—surely the Reverend Hochberg and the congregation had forgotten their contempt for Jervis Pryor and had attended the funeral. Rossville and Grace were laid away in a seldom-opened compartment of his mind, but the town of Shelby and Brevet Colonel Alexander Richardson could not be disposed of so simply. Hate dies less readily than love.

He rejected the thought of returning to Shelby and of shooting Richardson—by preference in the presence of the entire membership of the G.A.R. post. If he did that he would hang, and he had already escaped one hanging. It would be far better to make the professional colonel and his followers regret what they had done, to prove to them that the despised Jervis Pryor was not a coward but a man who had proved himself in battle.

Slowly, very slowly, that thought crystallized into the de-cision to re-enlist, under another name, in the army. In all the world there was no fighting except against the Indians in the West. Indians! They weren't like the Johnny Rebs; they were savages. They scalped white men, even when they were alive, and if they took you prisoner it was a thousand times worse than Andersonville or Libby. They tortured, they burned men alive—to hell with the idea of inviting that sort of fate! He'd go back to Philadelphia, get a job as a cabinet-maker, work steady, and maybe get married again if he could find the woman he wanted. A man ought to be married, ought to have somebody to come home to. Nobody could get any real satisfaction by going down to one of those Oak Street houses every week or so and hiring a woman. All a whore was interested in was money. She acted like she was having a good time—at least some of them did—but she wasn't enjoying it and you weren't either, not really. Not like he and Grace had enjoyed all the good times they'd had together before the war. God, that was a long time ago now. The war was over and Grace was dead. He wasn't a boy any more. He was forty years old, and if he married again it would be to a woman somewhere near his own age. That meant a widow. A single woman of thirty-five or so would be a dried-up old maid with some damn good reason why no man had ever wanted her. A widow was different. She knew what it was all about, and if she was the right kind she'd know what mistakes she'd made with her first husband and wouldn't repeat 'em with her second. A widow—and if she had a little money of her own it would be that much the better. Marriage and a home would be better than going out West and fighting Indians.

Indians? Always his thoughts swung to the notion of enlisting in the army and fighting Indians. Maybe they weren't as bad as some people made them out to be. Sure they scalped settlers now and then and they'd killed a good many soldiers, like that captain at that fort on the Bozeman Road in '66. He'd led eighty men slap-bang into an ambush laid for him by God knows how many Sioux Indians, and the whole bunch had been wiped out. The papers had called it a terrible massacre, but he'd asked for it. Any officer who got into that kind of a jackpot hadn't scouted the enemy position or learned how strong it was. Indians were fighters, all right, but all they had to fight with most of the time were bows and arrows. What guns they had were shot out and rusted till they wouldn't hit the side of a barn except from the inside. One thing was dead sure, Indians didn't have any artillery. They couldn't

fire from a mile away and tear a dozen men to bloody fragments. Most of the fighting out there was on horseback and
it was hard as hell to hit a man on a galloping horse. He'd
tried and he knew. A man on a horse had just about everything
in his favor.

In Buffalo he was summarily discharged for the first time
since he had worked as a journeyman carpenter. A minor argument with a foreman over the spacing of some studding developed into a quarrel which ended when the foreman told
him to pack his tools, get his time, and get the hell off the
job. It was a Wednesday afternoon, warm and sunny, and a
pleasant breeze blew off Lake Erie. Suddenly his course
seemed clear to him. He sold his tools in the first pawnshop
he saw and took the train to Chicago. He did not realize the
enormity of the step he had taken until he had put on the
blue uniform. For a moment the muscles of his throat tightened. There was still time to rip off the blue, to resume the
civilian clothes which lay untidily at his feet, and to run, run,
run—then he threw back his shoulders.

"I'll show him," he said aloud. "I'll show the son of a bitch!"

7 THE TOWN AND THE FORT

South City, Dakota Territory, was the western terminus of the Northern Pacific Railway and would remain the end of steel until the hostile Sioux and Cheyennes were defeated and herded on the reservations where many of their brethren who had "touched the pen" in acceptance of one or another of the many treaties were dragging out their remaining days and existing on the rations of scrawny Texas beef issued periodically by the Indian Bureau.

An accurate count of the friendlies and hostiles was impossible. Many of the latter, in small groups, rode inconspicuously to the reservations in the fall and spent the winter months there. In the spring, after the chinook winds had swept the snow from the mountains and the new grass was greening the hills, they rode away again. Buffalo were still quite plentiful in the land drained by the lower Yellowstone and the Missouri, and deer and antelope were abundant. Westward for half a thousand miles from South City and north to the Canadian border was the hunting ground of the Sioux. There they were free and they rejoiced in that freedom. They were free to hunt, to shift their camps from one location to another; free to ride on casual, semisporting, horse-stealing raids against the Absáraka, known to the white man as the Crows, who dwelt west of the Big Horn. Above all, they were free from the supervision and petty tyrannies of the agents of the Indian Bureau and of the missionaries who frowned upon all the "pagan" ceremonials which meant so much to the red man. In the valleys of those streams which white men called the Powder, the Tongue, the Rosebud, and the Big Horn they were free to celebrate the Sun Dance which was anathema to the long-faced missionaries who did not even attempt to understand it.

Fifty years earlier the Fur Brigade—the Mountain Men— had trapped all the streams which drained to the Yellowstone, but as the century entered its eighth decade a man's fingers could list those white men whose presence was even tolerated in the Sioux hunting grounds. There were a few squawmen who had almost forgotten they were white, a few hunters like Sol Rogers who had lived among the Indians, who spoke the Dakota tongue, and who had demonstrated that they hunted only for their own needs and had no desire to strip the streams of beaver and otter, and a few half-breeds or quarter-breeds who seemed able to live with both races without strife. They hunted with the Sioux, many of them had Sioux wives and lived in the camps, and they found employment as guides or hunters with railroad survey parties or the occasional exploring expeditions which crossed the Sioux domain. So long as they avoided the army, so long as they observed the taboo which Sioux and Cheyenne had placed about the Black Hills, so long as they were content to cross the Indian lands by the most direct route, those men were free to come and go.

Perhaps four thousand soldiers, cavalry and infantry for the most part, guarded those millions of square miles of territory and protected the "wards of the nation" from those whose one desire was to obtain entry to the Indian lands and to loot the hills—the Black Hills especially—of the rich store of gold which was thought to lie there. The military were dispersed among the forts along the Platte, the Republican, and the Missouri. There was a detachment of several battalions at Fort Ellis, in faraway Montana; a composite regiment, infantry and cavalry, at Laramie; and a regiment of cavalry at Fort Doniphan.

The fort had been named for Andrew W. Doniphan, a Missouri lawyer who had led a regiment of volunteer cavalry from Fort Leavenworth to Santa Fe in 1846, and from there to victories at El Brazito and Chihuahua which had been of incalculable value to Taylor and Scott. It had been the post of the Twentieth Cavalry almost from the date the regiment was organized.

2

South City, Dakota Territory. New arrivals looked at the name on the weatherbeaten sign on the N. P. depot and asked: "Where's North City? What's this god-forsaken place south of, anyhow?" The reply was always the same. "Take a look out yonder, stranger. You don't see nothin', do you? Well, this here's the first city south of the North Pole!"

A few—for the age of the settlement could still be expressed in a single digit—could supply the historic information that the end-of-rail had originally been called Villasur, but none could say why. There were railroad men who recalled Leonard Hillegas, an engineer on the original survey and who might have remembered that he had been an army lieutenant, Corps of Topographical Engineers, and an associate of Emory and Whipple in the Southwest. None knew that Hillegas had mastered Spanish and had made exhaustive studies of the archives in Mexico City and in Santa Fe.

In time he had focused on the exploits of Don Pedro de Villasur, that *capitán* who, in 1720, had struck out from Santa Fe, journeyed far to the north and east, and had finally —the date had been August 16—died with all his men in a pitched battle with Indians at Grand Island in the Platte River or, said some, at the point where that stream divided into its North and South forks.

Not so, declared Leonard Hillegas and dug into his bulky notes to prove his contention. Villasur had reached the Platte, true, but only to cross it and continue to the northward. The river he had followed had been the Missouri and he had gone on and on, ever north and west, until he had met disaster in an Indian ambush near the mouth of Heart River. How near Hillegas would not guess, but very, very near that spot on the Missouri's banks where the last rail of the Northern Pacific had been spiked to its ties. Hillegas had witnessed the driving of that spike and it had been he who had lettered the name VILLASUR on the final progress map when it became apparent that steel would go no further until certain hostile chieftains, Sioux and Cheyenne, had been conquered.

The name never appealed to the residents of the town. They were far north of the highest point of the Hispanic tide and could not twist their tongues about Hillegas' meticulous "Veel-ya-soor." There were those who asked, "What the hell does it mean?" and South City was born of the translation of Villasur. The new name stuck where the old had not.

The town sprawled north and south along the first bench above the sullen waters of the Missouri, always heavy with silt. It was a frontier town, typical of all those along the outer fringe of an advancing civilization; differing only in that it was a river town rather than a cow town, a mining town, or one that had sprung up about the adventitious crossing of two traveled routes on the Plains. The river effectively barred any expansion to the westward, but in all other directions the limit was the horizon toward which the rutted streets of South City ran out like searching fingers which grew feebler with each rod of their progress until they vanished amid the aimless trails of grazing cattle. One street, and only one, led steadily and unswervingly to the eastward. It closely paralleled the tracks of the Northern Pacific, and its route, like that of the rails, was blazed as far as the eye could see by the telegraph poles which carried a single strand of wire over all the long miles from Fargo to South City. Those poles were the tallest things in all the land save only the yellow bluffs that flanked each curve of the winding Missouri.

There had been a time, a brief time, when the scars of the graders' drags were still raw wounds in the gashed soil, when South City had been a completely lawless town. Then, when the permanence of the settlement seemed assured, rough cabins and "soddies" had replaced the tents and battered wooden cars that had pushed forward with the rails to house the railroad workers. Men learned that this lonely outpost would be their home and they sent back for their wives and families. With the advent of women, wives and mothers, had come respectability and the beginnings of law and order. The West was opened, its trails blazed, its secrets revealed, by the trapper, the hunter, and the prospector; its civilization, the approximation of life as it was lived a thousand miles to the eastward, came with the women.

With South City it was the same as with the towns of the Mother Lode, as with Bannack and Virginia City, as it would be with Leadville and Tombstone. The aimless paths became streets; the scattered buildings drew together and shouldered one another into business blocks. The saloons and gambling houses moved to streets other than those where the stores were built and where the women walked. The keepers of the many brothels and dance halls were told that they could remain in business but only within the limits of the block bounded by the newly named Pacific Street, Missouri Street, Oak, and Strawberry. There the red lights could burn and the pianos jangle with no supervision beyond an occasional visit from the town marshal or the provost from Fort Doniphan.

The town marshal was South City's first municipal official, antedating by some months the mayor, selectmen, and tax assessor. He had been employed by a self-appointed committee which included two merchants, a doctor, the Northern Pacific's representative who was also telegraph operator, freight and ticket agent, and postmaster; and Jasper Fisher, proprietor of the Wickiup Saloon and Restaurant. All were married, all had heard, many times, that "something" would have to be done to curb the rivermen and teamsters and hunters and soldiers who staggered from one never-closed bar to another, who shrieked and whooped and fired pistols when respectable folk were abed and asleep, and who, come morning, lay in drunken slumber in alleyways or sprawled on the board sidewalks which had been built for two blocks on Main Street.

As citizens and as husbands those men agreed. They had hired Thomas Jefferson Baker on the strength of his statement—it was never challenged—that he had been a member of the Vigilante organization which had brought law and order to the Montana mining towns by the effective method of hanging twenty-one outlaws and road agents within the space of five weeks. "After that," said Baker, "you could've put a stack of double eagles on the sidewalk of Wallace Street in Virginia City and come back three days later and picked 'em up."

He was a tall, slightly stooped individual with sad blue eyes and a brown mustache which drooped to his jawline. He wore a tarnished silver-plated star on the lapel of his open frock coat and a Colt .44-caliber revolver—the Civil War model adapted by the Thuer conversion to handle fixed ammunition

—on his left hip, butt to the front. The gun was always there, always in sight of the disorderly, the riotous, or the potential lawbreaker, but Baker had never been known to use it. The actual badge of his authority and the only weapon he ever employed was a stout cane of rawhide braided about a tapered core of steel rod. Three inches of the upper end of the cane were loaded with lead. Baker could attack and counter with the cane as swiftly, and with somewhat greater accuracy, than the eye-blurring strike of a prairie rattler. A thrust of the ferule toward a man's eyes, or a lightning-like slash across the face invariably brought his antagonist's hands up in an involuntary gesture of defense. If a man reached for his gun, Baker shouted "No!" and simultaneously lashed the gun hand with the cane. Drunken men—and the great majority of his arrests were for that offense—rarely knew what had happened to them. Liquor-dulled eyes could not perceive the whirling reversal of the cane before the loaded end cracked under the ear. They fell like poleaxed steers and awoke in the dugout jail which was South City's first municipal building. Drunken soldiers, and in the line of his duty Baker rapped many of them, were turned over to the provost marshal and returned to Fort Doniphan, on the further side of the Missouri and four miles downstream, where Colonel Tuthill had his own method of dealing with alcoholics and recalcitrants. They were first examined by a medical officer to determine if Baker's cane had fractured the skull—no instance of such carelessness was ever discovered—then staked out, face upward, in the broiling sun of the parade ground. In winter they were turned into the bullpen—the yard within the stockade of the guardhouse. No overcoats were permitted and a detail from the guard company, bayonets fixed, kept them trotting back and forth lest they freeze to death. For fighting drunks and other particularly obstinate cases there was the Hole, a dirt-walled pit wherein a man could neither stand nor lie down. When sober, the men faced the summary court officer who fined them one third of their pay of thirteen dollars a month.

The men—the private soldiers—accepted those penalties as the price of a spree and usually got drunk again the next payday, either in the barrooms of South City or on the horrible concoctions sold by the bootleggers who set up their temporary establishments in some coulee or buffalo wallow within a mile of the post. What they called whisky was a compound devised by the fur traders nearly fifty years earlier. Those gentry learned early in the game that a sober Indian was a shrewd trader; a drunken one would trade his furs, his ponies, or his women—if the white man happened to want them—for more whisky. Good whisky was expensive and was not particularly appreciated by the red man who demanded a drink with a kick equivalent to that of a stout club dropped on the skull. "Injun whisky" was composed of raw alcohol, water, caramel or burnt sugar for coloring; sugar, molasses, and plug tobacco for flavoring; a generous addition of red pepper; and a few cloves or other spices if the trader possessed them and wanted his whisky to possess a distinctive taste. A couple of handsful of gunpowder were frequently tossed in the keg—no one knew exactly why.

The troopers of the Twentieth Cavalry, almost without exception, were convinced that the bootleggers paid heavily for the privilege of plying their trade almost within the shadow of Fort Doniphan's flagpole. It was this tribute, they declared, that supported the officers' club, housed in a dilapidated structure which had been abandoned for quartermaster's storage because of a leaky roof, and which paid for the liquor which was consumed there—*and you can bet your last goddam cent that they don't drink this goddam rotgut, either; nothin' but bonded liquor is good enough for them sons of bitches!* The barracks did not know, nor would it ever learn, that every officer of the regiment, save one, was hopelessly in debt and that their lives were a constant struggle to maintain appearances, to dress and to live according to the standards established for officers and gentlemen, and to make it their business that no enlisted man should ever cross the barrier which had been erected between rank and file.

Colonel Tuthill's opinion on that last was emphatic. He expressed it at officers' call when his adjutant, Lieutenant and Brevet Lieutenant Colonel Clagett, brought up the name of Sergeant Tiffany of H company. Clagett was so thoughtless as to remark that Tiffany was a college graduate and a gentleman; he should be an officer.

"Why, then, did he enlist?" the regimental commander demanded. "The mere idea of commissioning a man from the ranks is preposterous. He invariably brings the smell of the barracks with him. I will resign my commission, gentlemen, on the day when men from the ranks—common soldiers—are enabled to enter the academy or to gain commissions by examination."

Private Strickland, of G, detailed that day as orderly to the commanding officer, heard the colonel's remarks from his seat on the bench in the adjutant's office and reported it quite accurately when he reached the barracks. G's newest recruit, Private Dugan, expressed his opinion in five words which he spat like bitter seeds from between his teeth.

"The son of a bitch!"

3

The five recruits had been assigned to different companies. The dour Gentry had been assigned to F, as Captain Harrod had requested. Corporal Gregory had taken the little Italian, Morelli, to his own D; Dugan, Hale, and Crane had gone to G, E, and L. Of the five, only Dugan had—in the words of First Sergeant John McNamara—"started off with a jump on the wrong foot." He had arrived at Doniphan with the conviction that the officers of the regiment, without exception, were sons of bitches (the only derogatory term which ever came to his tongue) and that they and G company's non-commissioned officers were leagued in a conspiracy to belittle Anthony Dugan, to rob him of all semblance of individuality, and to reduce him to a characterless nonentity equivalent to that of the troop horses.

Within two weeks he had visited South City without permission, had been staked out through all of a hot morning for drunkenness, and had been given five days in the guard-house at hard labor as an additional punishment. In the Twentieth Cavalry hard labor meant exactly that. He had cleaned out and filled old latrines and had dug new ones; he had worked on the manure wagon and spread the stable manure on the grounds adjacent to the officers' quarters where Colonel Tuthill was striving to persuade flowers and cottonwood saplings to grow in the hard-baked soil. Returned to duty, he had promptly drawn three days in the Hole, on bread and water, for kicking a horse in the belly.

"They're out to screw me, that's all," he declared to Private Lynch of G. "Well, they by Christ can't do it. I'll show 'em."

The gray-haired Lynch had been a member of the Twentieth since the regiment's organization. He had three times been a corporal and three times had been reduced for drunkenness—"and why the hell you haven't learned to come back to barracks and sleep it off is something I'd like to know," Captain Roger Clements of G had declared. "Johnson and Kennedy and Baumholz were all drunk on payday but they got back to barracks with their load and they kept their stripes. They didn't urinate on the flagpole and they didn't sing 'Lucy Was a Lady' in front of Major Marcus' quarters! What the hell's the matter with you, Lynch?"

The newly made private stood rigidly at attention. Darker triangles on the sleeves of his blue jacket marked the areas from which the chevrons had been cut away.

"I can't answer that, sir. At the moment it—the two of them —seemed a good idea."

His years as an officer and company commander had taught Clements to control his features under any and all circumstances.

"I consider that reduction to private is sufficient punishment, Lynch. You've heard me say that before. Why the hell you get drunk as a noncom and manage to behave yourself and stay fairly sober as a private is something else I'd like to know but never will. The next time you put on a drunken show like you did Friday you'll draw five days in the Hole if I have to put you there and stand guard myself. Is that clear?"

"Yes, sir. Thank you, sir."

"Very well. That'll be all, Lynch."

In his conversation with Private Dugan the former corporal was considerably more vocal.

"So you're out to show 'em, huh, and you're waitin' to hear me say 'more power to you.' Go right ahead, Dugan, and when you git to the end of it all, the man you'll be showin' will be yourself in th' dis'plinary barracks at Fort Leavenworth— and if you think you've bit off some hard labor under Old Eagle-beak, at Leavenworth you'll be findin' out what it really means.

"I've seen your kind in the army before, Dugan, th' kind that's always thinkin' th' army is out to screw 'em, so they're out to buck th' system every time. Sooner or later they learn that th' army's bigger than any man in it and that goes for the generals as much as for the privates. It's th' dumb ones that learn later—maybe at Leavenworth. Now go ahead an' say that I'm just a goddam old rumpot that's only servin' his fourth enlistment and that I don't know what in the hell I'm talkin' about."

Dugan did not make a direct reply.

"I'd like to know why in the hell I enlisted in the goddam army, anyhow," he grumbled.

"And so would I, from what I've seen of you. I'm thinkin' that th' company commander and Sergeant McNamara would like to know it too."

Dugan answered the implied question.

"I musta been crazy. Nobody ever told me it would be like this—working like a goddam dog all day long, saddle-soapin' equipment, shinin' brass, swabbin' out rifles and pistols with boilin' water, curryin' a goddam horse until he's cleaner than you are yourself, even varnishin' his hoofs so they'll shine pretty on parade, salutin' your arm off for every pissant officer that comes along . . ."

"It's a hell of a life," Private Lynch agreed. "Some fellers like it and wouldn't be happy any place else."

Dugan ignored the latter observation.

"I don't have to take it," he muttered darkly. "Three days in the Hole on bread and water because a goddam horse stepped on my foot—my toe's still black and blue—and I gave him my other boot in the belly. I got a goddam good mind to desert."

"That's th' way to talk!" Lynch exclaimed enthusiastically. "Now you're really bein' smart! Desert—from Fort Andrew Doniphan, Dakota Territory. Draw your pay, whatever's comin' to you next payday, and go over th' hill." His voice changed. "And just where in hell do you think you'll go—from here?"

Dugan gestured vaguely to the eastward.

"I c'd go . . ." he began.

"Sure y' could," Lynch agreed. "But where?" He spread his right hand before the other man. "Y' see that blue spot, there at th' heel of the palm? It's powder—blown there when I took the back-blast of a Sharps carbine that chose to fire out th' hind end instead of the front. Well, that blue spot is Fort Doniphan. Me thumb is the Missouri River—packet boats run on it clean down to St. Louis. Me two fingers here are the railroad to Fargo and St. Paul and the road that follows it.

"Now, rookie, which of them ways are you goin'? Every packet-boat captain 'r mate, every conductor on th' trains, every settler at the soddies where y' might ask f'r a bite to eat —they've all of them got their eyes skinned for desertin' soldiers. Do you know what they git f'r catchin' one?"

"No," Dugan blurted.

"Y' do now. It's twenty-five dollars in gold coin, that's what it is. Y' wouldn't git fifty miles down th' river 'r along th' railroad before some feller would figure you as maybe a deserter and he'd hang on t' you till y' proved you weren't. Th' fellers you'd run into w'd sell their mothers f'r ten dollars in gold, let alone twenty-five—and two hours after you'd turned up missin' at one reveille formation every telegraph operator on th' Northern Pacific w'd have your description and be passin' it on. So back y'd come t' Doniphan where you'd sit on your tail in th' guardhouse, in irons, until a gen'ral court-martial sent y' to Leavenworth f'r ten years with a bobtail discharge at th' end of it."

"I—" Dugan glared helplessly. Lynch, more amused than he had been since the day when a new charger threw Major Marcus ass-over-head before the entire regiment, continued:

"So y'd git some sense and y' wouldn't go along th' railroad. Y' wouldn't go up th' river either—th' packet boats are there, too. Feller like you w'd be smart, he wouldn't do what they expected him to. He'd hit out 'cross-country, away from either the river or th' railroad. He—I'm talkin' 'bout a real smart feller like you, Dugan—wouldn't go north. Like they say in South City, there's nothin' in that direction till y' come to the North Pole. West, if y' go far enough, is Montana and th' mines where a feller might make out pretty good. South, a long ways south, is th' Union Pacific which'll take a feller back East if he's got th' price of a ticket. Montana 'r th' U. P.—on'y thing a feller w'd have t' ask himself is what lays in between here and there."

Dugan's expression was that of a trapped coyote. Bit by

bit, Lynch was demolishing the plans he had considered as he squatted for three days in the dark Hole.

"Go ahead," he snarled. "I'm listenin'. You think you know it all, so keep on spillin' it. What's in between?"

"Nothin'," said Lynch blandly, "nothin' at all, exceptin' God knows how many goddam Injuns t' whom a lone white man stumblin' through their country is Christmas Day in th' mornin'. They'd catch y', of course—you couldn't go through Injun country without leavin' a trail that a papoose on a squaw's back c'd foller. They'd kill y'; but what y'd be askin' y'rself is how they'd do it and how long w'd it take y' to die if they staked y' out on your back and built a fire—jest a small fire—on your belly. That's one way—burnin' off one arm at a time and then one leg at a time is another, and they got plenty more. Injuns 're plenty smart when it comes to thinkin' up dif'rent ways, like skinnin' alive, f'r handlin' a white man. That's all, Dugan. Come payday, when y' go over th' hill, f'r God's sake don't tell nobody that it was me, Private Peter Lynch, that helped you."

4

Eli Crane, the gaunt New Englander, adjusted himself to the life of an enlisted man as smoothly as a foot sliding into a well-worn shoe. He memorized his general orders and soon learned that the man who could recite them without hesitation was rarely called upon to repeat them. He learned to salute and was as punctilious as a West Point first classman in rendering that courtesy to his superiors. Unlike Dugan, who would duck around the corner of the nearest building to avoid lifting his hand to the visor of his cap, he saw nothing subservient in the custom.

"Hell, Tony," he drawled, "them officers—they got six hundred men t' salute 'em and they got t' return every one. All we got t' do is keep our eyes peeled for 'bout a couple of dozen officers. We're lucky that way—I'd sure hate t' be th' colonel."

"Y' needn't worry . . . y' won't be."

"I reckon you're right—there's one thing I'll agree with y' on."

In horsemanship he was helplessly, almost hopelessly, awkward. Colonel Tuthill—as magnificent a horseman as there was in the army—believed that a cavalryman's seat could be acquired only through many hours of bareback riding. Since the troop horses understood every one of the trumpet calls and signals and obeyed them instantly, the recruits were allowed reins only to ride from the stables to the drill field. There the reins were unsnapped from the bridles and the men sat with folded arms while the horses, at gallop or trot, executed the commands which changed the formation from line to column of platoons, then to column of fours, then into line once more.

If the pace were faster than a walk, Crane simply fell off when his mount changed direction. He rose, grinning, after every tumble.

"I'm gittin' better, Sergeant; did ye notice I lit on my feet that time? Seems daggone funny that a man that c'n stand up in a dory in a Narragansett squall can't stay aboard a daggone horse. Hold him f'r me, Sergeant, and I'll make another try."

In other matters he was far more efficient. He was a skillful mechanic, with the Yankee's inherent ability to make a poor tool do the work of a better one which was unprocurable. He had worked for the entire period of the war at the Colt plant in New Haven and soon demonstrated that he knew more about rifles and pistols than any man in the regiment. After L company had spent one day on the range in pistol practice, Crane went to First Sergeant Hastings.

"Sergeant, I know more about these here things than old Sam Colt did—and I ain't braggin'. These here"—he touched the holstered revolver which lay on the first sergeant's desk

—" 're army guns. They was made t' pass army inspection and that's all. They're rougher than a cord'roy road and they got a trigger pull like h'istin' a bucket out of a well. I c'n fix 'em up, all of 'em."

"How?"

"I won't need much, but what it is y' can't git out here, that I'll bet on."

"What is it, special files?"

"Nope. Th' action of a gun, any gun, shouldn't ever be touched with a file, 'ceptin' maybe t' take off a real sharp burr. I'll want some ilestones, two 'r three what you'd call real damn fine, two 'r three more that's a damn sight finer—jest a mite coarser than what a barber w'd use t' hone a razor. Slipstones, they're called. They're about so big"—he extended a finger —"an' they'll cost mebbe a quarter apiece. I'll need 'bout three of th' flat ones and say a half-dozen of th' three-cornered kind. A few licks with one of them stones in th' right places will give this here pistol an action smoother than a mouse's ear."

"You seem to know what you're talking about."

"I do." Crane said no more.

"I'll speak to the captain about it."

The conversation brought Crane the next day before his company commander, Captain Lamar Steele. He repeated his specifications regarding the stones and demonstrated his familiarity with weapons by disassembling a revolver and indicating the points at which skillful stoning would smooth the action. Steele nodded understandingly.

"Man who's worked for Colt ought to know how Colt guns are made," he said. "Let me show you something."

He opened a drawer of the desk and laid a new revolver in Crane's hands. It was about the same size and shape as the model the troopers now used, but there the resemblance ended. A glance told Crane that it was designed to handle fixed ammunition instead of the unreliable paper cartridges ignited by a percussion cap, that it loaded through a "gate" in the frame behind the cylinder, and that fired cartridges could be expelled, one at a time, by a spring-returned ejector rod beneath the barrel.

"That's Colt's new gun," the captain said, "one of the first ones. We'll all have 'em before too long—the regiment, I mean. Can you smooth them up like you say you can doctor the cap-and-ball?"

Crane opened the gate and spun the cylinder to satisfy himself that the weapon was not loaded. Then he slowly brought the hammer to full cock, his sensitive mechanic's fingers feeling every motion of the concealed action. He lowered the hammer slowly, then repeated the operation several times. Finally he cocked the weapon, aimed at the floor, and pulled the trigger.

"Open her up," he said, "and you wouldn't find a mite of difference 'tween her and the old percussion. I c'n smooth her up so she'll let down smoother'n grease on a hot skillet."

"Do that," said Steele. Neither man noticed that Crane had omitted the "sir" with which an officer was always addressed. "And I'll write a letter tonight to my father in New York. He can get the stones you need."

"Just tell him slipstones"—Crane remembered in time and added "sir. Any good hardware store will know what he wants."

"One thing more, Crane. Can you do the same sort of work on a rifle? On one of the Springfields?"

"I c'n help 'em, sir, far's trigger-pull's concerned. Th' extractor's another matter. I've watched 'em on th' range. When they git hot, th' ca'tridge swells an' sticks jest tight enough so th' extractor jumps th' rim of th' case an' y're stuck with an empty in th' chamber an' no way t' git it out. 'Tain't right f'r a recruit t' say it, but seems like they ought t' 've figgered that out at Springfield Armory—sir."

"I've noticed the same thing; any sort of rapid fire and

they're not worth a damn. Only God, and the Ordnance De-
partment, knows why they didn't give us repeaters like the
Winchester." He shoved back his chair. "I guess that's all,
Crane—and thank you."

The slipstones reached Fort Doniphan before the month
was out. Within the next month L company, with half of the
men on the firing line raw recruits, won both the pistol and
rifle championships of the regiment. More, Captain Steele had
decisively beaten the regimental commander in a match for a
fifty-dollar side bet. The captain shot a Remington Creed-
moor rifle with an action smoothed and honed by Private
Crane. He called Crane to the orderly room, presented him
with $10, and informed him that he was now classed as a
horseshoer. He would draw $18 monthly instead of the $13 of
a private.

"My God—I mean, excuse me, Captain, but I c'n no more
shoe a horse than I c'n talk Chinese!"

"You won't be asked to. A cavalry company is authorized
to have one farrier, one horseshoer—just what difference
there is between 'em I've never learned, but maybe the army
knows. We've got a farrier—Gillen. He'll take care of the
horseshoeing and you'll be the company—maybe the regimental—gunsmith."

Jealousy over Crane's sudden promotion vanished when
he spent the entire $10 for beer for his fellows in the sutler's
store. As gunsmith for L company and for the Twentieth
Cavalry, Eli Crane was supremely happy.

5

The man who called himself Gentry remained a mystery.
Less, perhaps, to his fellows in F company—there were other
moody men in the ranks who repulsed overtures of friendship
—than to the company officers and to the first sergeant, Henry

Mullins. Captain Harrod often wondered why, on the train from St. Paul, he had impulsively requested that the recruit be assigned to F and had admitted his bewilderment to Burton Chance, his lieutenant, and to the first sergeant.

"He's a good soldier," he remarked in the orderly room. "Isn't much of a horseman, but he seems to catch on quick enough, but——"

"He's just a little bit too damn good, if you're asking me, sir," Mullins interjected. "It's only natural for a man, 'specially a recruit, to grumble about company duties and policin' details and such, and I think just a little bit more of a man, maybe, when he does his share of grumblin'. Shows he's human. That Gentry, though, he never says a word about nothin'. If he was detailed as the colonel's orderly he'd take it just the same as being told to shovel the dung out of the troop stables. He's been in the army before—on that I'll bet."

"He claims different." Harrod's voice was sharp. "What makes you think he's lying, First Sergeant?"

"Just a couple of dozen little things, sir. Th' way he handles his carbine, for one. Not on the range—he's no better than average as a shot—but the way he brings it up to his shoulder when drillin'. Ninety-nine recruits in a hundred, as you well know, sir, can't bring th' piece to their shoulder without jerkin' their heads. Gentry's as steady as a church.

" 'Nother thing: right from the first he's called me 'first sergeant.' Sure, that's what he's supposed to do, but I never saw the recruit yet that didn't have to be reminded of it a dozen times b'fore he got it through his skull. Same with dismounted drill and th' manual of arms, he knows 'em both. I was watching him only today—Corp'ril Langer was drillin' four fours dismounted—and three or four times Gentry took a look back to see if the rear rank was followin' through right. 'Course, there wasn't any rear rank, drillin' by fours, but he was lookin' for one. He's been an infantryman some time, sir, and drilled with a squad rather than by fours."

"Uh-huh. Have you ever noticed anything like that, Mr. Chance?" Harrod's eyes turned to his lieutenant.

"I've got to admit I haven't." The youngster blushed painfully. "I—I guess I just don't know how to look for things like that, not the way old soldiers like you and the first sergeant would."

"Maybe not." Harrod grinned. "But you will by the time you put bars on your shoulders. Have you got any ideas, Mullins; could he be a galvanized rebel maybe?"

"Eight 'r nine years ago, with the war fresh over, I'd 've said 'yes' to that, sir. Now I'm doubtful. We've got half a dozen men in the regiment who were on the other side and admit it. If this Gentry was a reb, why should he keep quiet about it? I'll lay a bet he wore blue—once."

"He seems like a sulky devil," Lieutenant Chance interjected. Harrod's eyes directed the first sergeant to reply.

"I can't go along with that, not entirely," said Mullins. "Begging the lieutenant's pardon and not meaning to contradict, but we're talking man to man, so to speak."

"We are," Harrod nodded. "Go ahead, First Sergeant. I'm sure the lieutenant understands."

"It's what you might mean by sulky. This Gentry, now, he's quiet and he's not one for making friends in a hurry, but I'd never call him sulky. I've seen him in the sutler's store of an evening. He'll buy himself a beer and take it to a table and drink alone. Same in town. I saw him there one night with that E company recruit, Hale. They were in the Elkhorn Saloon. Gentry had a beer and young Hale had what looked like lemonade. They were sittin' there mindin' their own business and sippin' of their drinks. Real cosy like, but not sulky. One thing I do think about him——"

"What's that?" Harrod asked as the sergeant paused.

"I was puzzlin' how to put it. Seems to me as though duty here at the fort sort of bores him. He'd like to see action. He's spoke to me once and again to Corp'ril Gregory of D and asked us if the regiment ever was going into action against the hostiles, like he'd heard they were. I told him I guessed we'd go soon enough, but I couldn't tell him when and neither could anybody else until the orders came."

"Keep an eye on him—one eye is enough—when you get the chance." Harrod rose, lifted his saber from the hook, and snapped it to his belt. The lieutenant and first sergeant rose with him; more than half a century would pass before the punctilious courtesies due to superior rank would be judged unnecessary and even servile.

"That goes for both of you," Harrod continued. "Don't make the opportunity, Mr. Chance, but if an opportunity makes itself, talk to the man. I'll be damned if I know why, but I'm as curious as—as a woman about him."

"Yes, sir." They saluted and Harrod jerked his forefinger to the visor of his cap.

"Do you think"—Chance hesitated a moment—"do you think an opportunity will make itself, First Sergeant?"

"No, sir, I don't. That Gentry just ain't the talkin' kind. Something is bottled up in him, but it's too deep for him to start talkin' about it. Maybe if we were to be in a fight and he'd be hit bad—and know damn well he was goin' out—maybe then he'd talk to whoever was nearest, just by way of un-loadin'. Not here at Doniphan, though, not in a hundred years."

"I'm afraid you're right, First Sergeant," said the junior lieutenant.

6

It never occurred to Amos Clark Gentry that he might be the subject of discussion among his company officers and the first sergeant. So far as he was concerned, the past was buried. More than that; there had never been a past. Jervis Pryor had never existed so there could have been no courts-martial for cowardice in action, no wife to die when her husband was disgraced, no itinerant carpenter who had drifted from job to job and city to city in New York, Pennsylvania, and Ohio. All that had ever been was the now: Amos Clark Gentry, private, Company F, Twentieth Cavalry, Fort Doniphan, Dakota Territory.

Captain Jervis Pryor, Private Jervis Pryor, the 40th Wisconsin Infantry, all were dead. As dead and as buried as a slim girl named Grace, a girl who had sung in the choir of the Lutheran Church, who had walked modestly along the streets of Rossville, and within whom there had lain deep and secret springs of amazing passion. Of her he could never speak nor dare to dream.

What Lieutenant Burton C. Chance, U. S. Military Academy, Class of '73, had called sulkiness was a refusal to associate with his fellows in F company's barracks on the level which they desired. Almost from the moment he had been assigned to the company he had encountered almost womanly curiosity as to who he was, whence he had come, and the trade he had followed before his enlistment. His "Gentry's the name . . . I hail from Cleveland, Ohio . . . been a carpenter all my life" was insufficient. Men with nothing to do nor anything to occupy their thoughts wanted to know more. Their probing questions were born of loneliness and the terrible isolation of existence in a frontier post, but Gentry saw in them only curiosity as to his past life and personal affairs. He talked to none of them nor knew that his fellows in F company speculated as to his secret past as freely as did the company commander and the first sergeant. He was, variously, a former Confederate, a man sought by the police somewhere in the East, or—like Eli Crane who wryly admitted his past—he had abandoned a wife and family.

He had found one man, a boy of less than half his own age, who had asked no prying questions. He had crossed the Missouri on the wheezing sternwheel barge that dodged in and out of the twisting currents, and on the dock at the foot of River Street had found himself walking beside Martin Hale, the Ohio recruit with whom he had ridden from St. Paul.

"Hello, kid," he remarked. "Ain't seen you since we were passed out to our companies. How 're things going?"

"Good enough, I guess. How 're they with you?"

" 'Bout the same. You seen any of the other fellows who came out with us?"

"Yeah. I went to E, you know, and Captain Nason has been using me as a company orderly, so I get around. Morelli, he's with D and he's sort of a company pet. One of the fellows there had an accordion—seems he got drunk in St. Paul and bought it even though he couldn't play a lick. Well, Morelli can get music out of it that the bandleader never even heard of and he plays for the whole company every night."

They walked along the dusty street, talking idly, until they had passed the shabby saloons that hugged the river bank. A number of the soldiers who had been on the ferry turned to the left at Pacific Street. It was not yet dark but already the naphtha torches were flaming smokily in front of the dives that lay beyond Strawberry Street a block to the north.

"Some of the boys are in a hurry," Gentry remarked. Hale merely nodded. The Elkhorn Saloon was at the corner of Pacific and Main. Gentry checked his stride.

"I'll buy a beer, Hale," he said. "Just t' cut the parade-ground dust outa our throats. Then, if you've a mind to, we might scout around for something to eat that don't taste of the barracks."

"That—that would be fine. Thanks, Mister—I mean——"

"Amos is the name, 'r Gentry if you'd rather. We've left that mister stuff a long way behind us, kid."

"That's right. Don't take you long to find it out in the army either." They pushed through the swinging doors and approached the long bar. "If it's all the same to you, Amos, I'll take a lemonade. I know what beer tastes like but I just don't like the stuff."

"If there's a better reason for not drinkin' it, I've never heard it."

They carried their drinks to one of the many small tables and sat there, talking idly and commenting on the heads of wápiti, bear, and bighorn sheep that decorated the walls. They ate at the Ace High Restaurant, recommended to Hale by one of E company's sergeants as a place where soldiers were welcome, the food good, and prices within the means of men who drew $13 monthly. The dinner was fifty cents and included split-pea soup, cooked with a hambone and so thick that it stood above the rim of the spoon, baked hump rib of buffalo with rich brown gravy, potatoes, peas, baked beans, all the coffee desired, and chocolate pudding.

"Enjoy your supper, boys?" The proprietor flicked their half-dollars into the cash drawer.

"Sure did. After a meal like that a feller can put up with mess-hall grub for a while."

"Glad y' liked it. The Ace High ain't the cheapest place in town, but there's plenty where you can pay more and get less and not so good. Don't think I've seen you fellers b'fore."

"Reckon you haven't. We've only been at Doniphan a couple of weeks, him and me."

"There's worse places for a soldier and worse towns than South City. Come again, boys, any time. Here, have a cigar. On the house."

"Thanks."

They left the restaurant and slowly walked the length of Main Street, returning on the other side. At Pacific Street they turned west toward the river and the dock from which the government ferryboat left every hour. The dives a block to the northward were in full blast now. Windows had been opened and they could hear the jangle of the pianos and, occasionally, the shouts of boisterous men and shrill laughter of women. Gentry removed the cigar from his mouth and spat into the gutter.

"I take it, Marty, that you don't go for that sort of stuff."

"No. I guess—well, for one thing I never had a chance. At home, where I come from in Ohio, there just wasn't any wide-open cathouses. Burnsville was just a small town and a place like those down the street would have been run out inside of a week. I—well, maybe I'm a sissy but I can't see how there'd be any fun in paying a woman for—for that."

"Takes some fellers a hell of a long time to find that out, Marty, and there's some that never learn it."

They walked on toward the dock and the clamor from the bagnios died away behind them. At the entrance to E company's barracks they halted. The barracks of F were next in the long line of shabby buildings. Gentry's hand touched the younger man's shoulder.

"G'd night, Marty. I enjoyed that meal—and y'r company. Maybe we can eat together again some time."

"I'd like it, this coming Saturday, maybe."

"F's on guard Saturday."

"Too bad. I'd figured on going over to town Saturday and trying some of those buffalo ribs again. Maybe I'll get a pass Sunday—and maybe go to church."

"Good idea. I'd say I'd go with you but we won't be off guard until retreat. There'll be plenty of other chances, looks like, 'fore we go out chasing Sittin' Bull. Good night, Marty."

"Good night—Amos."

8 MARTIN HALE

On his occasional visits to South City young Hale found himself strictly alone except when his new friend Gentry happened to obtain a pass at the same time. He learned that he
was a private and as such could associate only with other
privates, or rarely, with a corporal who might permit a recruit
to stand at a bar with him and pay for his beer. Sergeants
drank with others of their rank. Noncommissioned officers of
higher rank—the first sergeants, the regimental quartermaster
sergeant, and the sergeant major—were in positions as far
removed and as exalted as the colonel himself. Even within
the ranks there were lines of rigid demarcation between
higher and lower grades and the recruit was at the very foot of
the ladder. So far as his fellow privates were concerned, a
visit across the river meant only drink or women or both.

"Where y' goin', Mart?"

"I dunno. Up to the Ace High, I guess, and have a decent meal. I'm gettin' so damn sick of that rotten pork that I'm ready to try mule."

"Is that all y' crossed th' Missouri for, just eatin'? Stick around with us—me and Shorty and Joe are goin' t' have two 'r three beers and then we're goin' down th' Line."

"Th' Line meanin' Kitty McCoy's place on Strawberry Street, in case y' didn't know, Mart," Joe Flagg interjected.

"If you know any better place than Kitty's, name it and we'll go there. Jesus, there's a little black-haired girl named Minnie—says she's from New Orleans and, boy, is she good! Knows every trick there is in the book and some she made up herself. You comin', Mart?"

"Not now. I might be seeing you later. Like I said, I'm hungry enough to eat raw dog and I'm headin' for the Ace High."

He never kept, nor intended keeping, any of the half-promises to see them later, in Kitty McCoy's or Bessie Rivers' or Number Ten or the Green Front Dance Hall, or anywhere else. He ate slowly and appreciatively at the Ace High, walked the length of Main Street, and now and then, if alone, extended his strolls to the residential streets of the straggling town. He was afforded occasional glimpses into lighted homes where men, women, and children sat at supper tables, where youngsters played and quarreled in their play, where older children sat hunched over schoolbooks and homework. At times he would hear the notes of a piano or parlor organ and would see the straight back of the woman who sat at the instrument. He was homesick in the true sense of yearning for a home and for those to whom he was an individual, Martin Hale, and not number-three man in the third set of fours.

There were churches in South City and twice he attended Sunday services. There were men and women in the congregation, their sons and daughters accompanied them, but none spoke to him. Once he lingered after the services and joined the line which was passing the minister. When Hale reached the pastor he experienced the quick touch of a flabby hand on his own, heard the words, "Glad you joined us, young man," and then was shunted through the door so deftly that he wondered how it had happened. He mentioned the incident to Corporal Gregory who sat beside him on the ferry to the fort.

"What did y' expect . . . t' be asked home f'r Sunday dinner?" the noncom snorted derisively. " 'Come right along, soldier, and we'll kill an extra chicken just so you can have all the white meat you want. And this here is my daughter, Myrtle Lou, who's just crazy to keep company with one of the brave boys from the fort.' Is that what y' thought might happen?"

"I—no, of course not, but they could have been friendly, couldn't they? Just because I'm a soldier doesn't mean——"

His voice trailed off. Gregory rose, spat into the river, and returned to his seat.

"You're findin' things out, Hale," he said calmly. "Just like you found some things out on the train when Old Eagle-beak and Cap'n Harrod came back and looked over the new recruits; like others you found out when y' got assigned to E. You're a soldier now, a goddam yellowleg in th' Twentieth Cavalry. Only time that people like them—townies that call themselves decent people—only time they got any use f'r a soldier is when he's got his pay to spend in their stores or when we pack up and take out after the Injuns. That's all we're good for: to fight Injuns so these here decent people will be nice and safe in their churches. The rest of the time we're dirt. Git that through your skull and you'll be a heap happier!"

They separated on the dock but Hale heard his name called as the troopers circled the parade ground toward the barracks.

"Hey, Hale! I just happened to think of it. If it's church

you're lookin' for—preachin' and singin' and that sort of stuff —there's one place in South City that don't look on a soldier like he had ticks."

"Which one is that?"

"It's called the Bethel Mission, out to the north end of town and three or four blocks off Main Street. No steeple or anything like that, just a little beat-up shack that ain't been painted since it was built. Feller named Poole runs it, th' Rev'rend Poole. He's as loco as they make 'em. Claims that all men are brothers and that this is th' Injuns' country and we ought t' pull out and let 'em have it. There's even been talk of runnin' him out of town, but his is the only church where folks really act like they're glad to see soldiers. Y' might try it if it's churchin' you want."

The picture Gregory painted was not an attractive one, but Hale had little difficulty in obtaining church leave the following Sunday, and in South City he followed the directions the corporal had given. Paint was peeling from the sign which announced BETHEL MISSION. ALL WELCOME. The building, however, was deserted. Weeds were growing about the sagging steps which led to the door. The thought that Gregory's misplaced sense of humor had sent him to a long-abandoned structure prompted Hale to accost an elderly man who was seated on a porch diagonally across the street.

"Maybe you can tell me, mister, if there 're going to be any services at the mission today."

"Reckon not, bub. That there's the Rev'rend Poole's place."

"So I was told."

"You wasn't told much 'bout th' rev'rend," the ancient cackled. "Come cold weather, he'll open up ag'in. This here's his huntin' season."

Hale stared at him.

"What do you mean, hunting season?"

"Jest that, sojer. He's up north, God only knows where, 'long th' Missouri 'r maybe th' Yellerstone, huntin' f'r souls what need savin'. Injun souls—th' rev'rend figgers that Injuns got 'em same as humans. So he closes up th' mission an' goes a-huntin'."

Hale said, "Thanks," and turned away. The old man's quavering voice halted him.

"His wife," he said, "Missis Poole, she lives two blocks down th' first street this side o' Main. Her and her daughter Beth. White house with a white picket fence 'round it. Some of th' pickets 're busted; they git that way while th' rev'rend is huntin'. Missis Poole an' Beth—they're mighty nice folks."

Hale said thanks again but did not seek the white house with the broken picket fence.

2

Elizabeth Poole had just passed her eighteenth birthday. She had been born in Vineland, New Jersey, where her father was pastor of a dilapidated church from the rickety pulpit of which he preached hellfire and brimstone and the wrath that awaited those who had failed to acknowledge Christ as their personal Saviour. His congregation was composed of farmers and of rivermen who netted shad in the Delaware in the spring and with fall dropped downstream to Morris River and other brackish streams for oysters which they sold in Philadelphia and Camden. He gave those men precisely the brand of religion they demanded and enjoyed, nor did any of them dream that he hated Vineland and the flat Jersey countryside or that in his own mind he was a man appointed for greater things and a wider horizon of service to the God he worshiped and feared.

Beth was six years old when Joshua Barnett, skipper of the oyster boat *Lucy H.*, fell down an open hatch on his craft—he was drunk at the time—and split his skull on a stanchion. When Joshua's will was probated, the Reverend John Wesley Poole regretted that he had not spoken more eulogistically of the dead riverman, for the testament bequeathed the sum of $2500 "to my pastor, Reverend John W. Poole."

"It is truly a gift from God," said Poole to his wife. "God spoke to Captain Barnett and inspired that noble and generous act. Now I can answer the call which has always been in my ears."

Doris Poole knew well what that call was. She spoke quickly.

"We must be practical too, John. That is more money than we have ever seen before and more than we probably will ever see again. We must lay some of it aside—invest it, maybe, for our old age or for Beth's education. I don't want her to grow up like some of these farm girls or fishermen's daughters."

"The Lord will provide for thee and me and for our child," the pastor declared. "He called me long ago and I heard Him. Now I can answer Him. I am resigning from this church, wife, and am entering the mission field as I have always prayed that I might do."

John Wesley Poole was bigoted, fanatical, zealous, and completely sincere. He was a Protestant who inveighed against the scarlet woman of Rome and all her works and would have risen in fury had he been told that his dream was identical with those which had illumined the lives of Ignatius Loyola, Francis of Assisi, and Hermenegildo Garcés, a dream of devoted service with the crown of a martyr as a possible reward.

The dream and the ambition were visionary, their realization a far more practical matter. The missionary societies, the directors of the Board of Control for Foreign Missions, asked for something more than a comprehensive knowledge of the Bible and a powerful voice wherewith to shout evangelistic sermons and pleas for repentance. They asked for some knowledge of foreign tongues, for sufficient medical ability to cope with yaws and syphilis and tuberculosis, for skill with tools that might build a mission or a school.

"I have the Word of God," he declaimed. "I do not need to be able to lay shingles!"

"Possibly, brother, possibly," was the reply, "but the greatest Preacher of all was a carpenter."

He could conceive the missionary field only in terms of foreign lands and strange, dark-skinned people, but in the end he accepted assignment to the Indians of the Great West. The assignment carried with it a stipend of $300 a year and the right to use any offerings and collections "for the upbuilding of the mission." He returned to Vineland with new fervor; a zeal which automatically replaced Zulu and Kanaka and Malay with Pawnee and Comanche and Kiowa and Sioux.

Elizabeth—she was Beth to everyone but her father who, even when she was a baby, invariably spoke to her and of her with the four full syllables of her baptismal name—had been entered in school when the Pooles turned their backs upon the East and its comforts. In the twelve years between Vineland and South City she had seen eastern Kansas and a mission to ragged remnants of Kaws and Pottawotamies; Texas and a short-lived attempt to carry the message of the Cross to a small group of surly Comanches; Nebraska and a mission on the Niobrara where the Pawnees of the vicinity seemed genuinely sincere in their welcome to the "Jesus man" and his message; a brief domicile in Minnesota where Indians and whites alike had vivid memories of the bloody Santee uprising of 1862; and, finally, South City and Dakota Territory.

Over the span of twelve years and in nearly as many homes, she and her mother had never once known real comfort or freedom from want and from anxiety. Their clothes, many of them, were diverted from the missionary barrels which Eastern churches forwarded at irregular intervals to the Western evangels—diverted, usually, in defiance of the wrath of John Wesley Poole who regarded the shabby garments as the property of his wards. Other clothes, shoes especially, were the result of frankly begging letters which Doris Poole sent to the congregations which supported, or considered that they supported, the mission.

By the time Beth had reached the third grade she was aware, acutely aware, that other children were far more fortunate than she. Classmates, with the cruelty of which only children are capable, ridiculed the dresses which her mother cut down from the mission offerings; they called her "squaw" and spoke to her in a gibberish of their own which they called "Indian"; and they compared their own fathers' positions and professions most unfavorably with the evangelistic activities of the Reverend John Wesley Poole.

"There's an Indian school out at the agency," said Nancy Baum, the butcher's daughter. "Why don't you go there to school?" She paused a moment, then added: "Seems to me you smell like an Indian anyhow."

It was inevitable that the growing child would compare her own home with those of her contemporaries. She witnessed her mother's struggles to keep household expenditures within the limits of the modest pay allotted to the mission's representative; she heard the fervent expressions of gratitude which welcomed the gift of a chicken, a ham, or a buffalo steak; and she learned that any request which called for the spending of money would be received with: "I'm very sorry, Beth, dear, but we can't possibly afford it."

"We could afford a new black suit for father," she snapped on one occasion, "and a set of almost-new harness for his team. Why can't we afford shoes for me like other girls have? It's just not fair!"

Genuine sincerity was not in Doris Poole's reply.

"You mustn't talk that way, Beth. You must remember he's your father and he's doing God's work."

"That's what I've heard all my life," she snapped. "God's work—God's blessing on this mission and all it is doing—God bless my labors among the red men! I'm sick of it! It's about time he asked God to bless you and what you're doing instead of traipsing off up north somewhere and leaving you and me to get along the best we can!"

The door slammed noisily behind her and she did not hear her mother's gasp of shocked disapproval. The angry tears in Beth's eyes did not blind her to the loose boards in the front steps, the sagging gate, and the broken pickets in the fence which surrounded her home. She turned to the north until the street had run out into a cowpath, then struck westward toward the river. On its bank she was far beyond the town and its clamor; here were only the sunshine, the smell of clean earth, the chatter of small birds, and the unceasing rush of the Missouri.

She sat down close to the water's edge, her arms about her knees, and let her emotions drag her into self-pity so intense that it approached ecstasy. If her father had possessed only one trait that made him lovable, she told herself, she would be able to endure the poverty, the thinly veiled sneers, and the long weeks and months when she and her mother sat alone, in the dark, sometimes, when the kerosene for the lamp represented an extravagance.

He's never told me he loved me . . . I've never even heard him tell that to mother . . . he calls her "wife" most of the time and the only times I can remember seeing him kiss her is when he's leaving on one of those missionary trips of his, and then he just touches her cheek with his lips. . . . If I ever wanted a man to kiss me and he did it like that I—well, the first time would be the last time. . . . If I was a boy I'd get a job on the railroad or on one of the packet boats or I'd join the army—just to get away from everything.

The tears that welled in her eyes blurred the flow of the yellow waters and the sound of those waters against the bank at her feet deadened other sounds. She did not hear the footfalls on the earth behind her nor see the man who made them until his shadow fell across her. She dropped her knees quickly and pushed down her skirts until their hem covered the tops of her shoes. She saw a young man, a boy, in the blue uniform of a trooper from Fort Doniphan. A soldier—and the girls of South City were taught from the cradle to avoid soldiers—but a very young one and quite sober.

"I didn't hear you coming; you frightened me," she said quickly.

"I didn't mean to—I didn't even see you till I came over the bank." His gray eyes stared at her levelly from under the stiff peak of the ridiculous kepi. "You've been crying," he said bluntly.

"What if I have?" she demanded angrily. "Is it any of your business if I want to cry?"

"No." He sat down a foot from her, picked a pebble from between his feet, and snapped it into the river. "It's none of my business," he said at last, "but I'm not saying I'm sorry. I don't like to see a girl cry, that's all. 'Specially when it's the first girl I've even spoken to since——"

"Since the last time you were in South City," she interrupted.

"No." The gray eyes turned to her. "You don't know me and there was no call for you to say that. What I was saying when you cut in was that you were the first girl I'd spoken to since I left home to join the army. That was more than three months ago."

"Where was it—your home?" she asked and then, angered by her betrayal of curiosity, added hastily, "Never mind."

"I don't mind. I come from Ohio, a place called Burnsville. I guess you've never even heard of it. It's not far from Youngstown."

"No," She shook her head.

"My name's Hale," he said. "Martin Hale. Maybe I ought to say 'Private Martin Hale, E company, Twentieth Cavalry.'"

"You don't have to tell me that last. I've been around South City long enough to know a private soldier when I see one and to read the big E and the number twenty and the crossed sabers on your cap."

He nodded.

"I hadn't thought of that. We're branded, sort of, like the horses."

"You don't like the army, do you?"

"I didn't say that!"

"You thought it; at least, it seemed like you were thinking it."

"I wouldn't say I liked it and I wouldn't say I disliked it. I know I don't hate it, like some fellows do." He was thinking of Dugan.

"Why do they join the army if they hate it so bad? Why did you join?"

"It—well, it seemed the best thing for me. I wanted to get away from home and the army seemed the best chance."

"You're a man!" she said furiously. "I wish I was a man. I wish there was something I could do to get away from here, just as far away as I could!"

"I knew something was wrong or you wouldn't be sitting on the river bank by yourself and crying. Can—is there anything I can do to help you?"

"No. You're a man and you'd never understand." She was silent for a long moment. "My name's Poole, Elizabeth Poole —they call me Beth—does that mean anything to you?"

His reply surprised her.

"It doesn't really mean anything but I've heard of you."

"Heard of me? Not at the fort surely."

"No'm. It was a couple of Sundays ago. I went out to the Bethel Mission that your father runs and I found it closed up. An old fellow out there said that the reverend was up the river on a missionary trip but that his wife and daughter lived down the road a piece. He mentioned your name, Beth."

"I guess there isn't anybody in South City who doesn't know what he told you—that my father's away and that he won't be back until snow flies and all the Indians have either gone back to the agencies or holed up in their winter camps.

When that time comes he, he'll remember that he's got a home and a wife and a daughter!"

Nearly a minute passed before he said, "I see," slowly and thoughtfully and from the words and their intonation she knew that he did see, that he understood her anger and her tears.

"And," he continued, "being a girl there's nothing you can do about it, is there?"

"Nothing. Even if I wasn't a girl, I guess I couldn't leave— there's my mother, you know."

"Yes. If you were a man, though, you could do more for her."

"That wouldn't be hard!" Her voice was low, bitter. "A man, well, he could take a buggy whip to the Reverend John Wesley Poole!"

"It's as bad as that, is it?"

"Yes. You'd never understand. Nobody could unless they came to our house and lived there while my father was away carrying God's Word to the red men. That's what he calls it, and that's all he thinks about. One dirty, greasy Sioux who lets Father baptize him is more to him than his family."

"That's tough, Beth. I—I wish there was something I could do."

"There's nothing. Just knowing that there's somebody—like you—who understands a little of it, that helps."

He snapped one pebble after another into the water and watched the expanding ripples race downstream.

"Maybe—I know how it must be around a house when there's nobody there—no man, that is, to take care of things. I —I'm kind of handy with tools and a friend of mine—he's another soldier and a lot older than I am—he's a carpenter by trade and a good one. He'd be glad to help if I asked him to."

Her hand moved quickly until it rested on his.

"You—you're sweet, Martin. Thank you. There's a million things a man could do around our house; things that Father never got around to doing because they might take time from his missionary labors. Every time I walk across the porch I wonder if this is the time I'm going to go through. And there isn't a chair or table in the house that isn't about ready to fall apart.

"Mother's proud, though, Martin. I know that 'way down inside she thinks the same as I do about some things, but she wouldn't say so if she was being burned at the stake. I couldn't bring a strange man, a soldier, to the house and tell her that he'd come to do the things Father hadn't done. Why, if she knew that I'd met you out along the river and talked to you like I've been doing, she'd have a conniption!"

"I guess she would. My mother would be the same if it was my sister."

"You've got a sister?"

"Two of 'em. Molly, she's three years older than I am, and married. Pauline is only fifteen. She's a twin; the other's a boy, Paul. Listen, Beth."

"I'm listening."

"Why don't you tell your mother something that's true or could be? Tell her that you walked past the chapel to—oh, to make sure that it hadn't been broken into or anything—and you met me. I asked you when there would be any services because I'd heard—and this is the truth—that Bethel Chapel was one church in South City where soldiers were welcome. Tell her we got to talking and that I said that next Sunday, if I could get a pass, I was going to stop by your house because I wanted to meet her. She can't throw a conniption over that, can she?"

"No," the girl said thoughtfully. "It's kind of almost lying, I guess, but if I'd been near the chapel when you did go there, it could have happened. I, oh, Martin, I'm awfully lonely. You will come on Sunday, won't you?"

3

That had been the beginning. Doris Poole accepted Beth's account of her meeting the young soldier at the chapel and did not ask more than a dozen questions about the man himself.

"He, well, he's just a private soldier, Mother, but he's a gentleman too. He comes from a good family. I can tell and so can you as soon as you meet him."

"There's no reason he shouldn't be a gentleman. People here in South City act as though the soldiers from the fort were—well, you know how they act, Beth."

"Yes, I've seen——"

"—and there's really no reason for it. They're just boys, lots of them, and I guess they come from the same kind of homes as the people that take on so about them."

"I'm sure that Martin does, and——"

"Martin? Are you first-naming him already, Beth? You've only met him that once."

"No, Mother. Certainly not to his face. I don't know what to call him. He's a private soldier and you just can't call one of them 'mister.' It just doesn't seem right."

"No." Doris Poole considered that point of etiquette, then changed the subject abruptly.

"He'll be here Sunday?"

"He said he would, if he could get a pass. You—I think you'll like him, Mother."

"I don't see why we can't have a chicken. With your father gone it's not often we have company in this house. I've got my mind on one old hen that hasn't given us an egg since goodness knows when. She'll be too old for roasting, though—I hope this young Hale likes stewed chicken."

"He will, I know. He couldn't help but like your stewed chicken and gravy and dumplings, Mother."

"A few dumplings," said the mother thoughtfully. "They're nice in the gravy, but a man wants mashed potatoes. There's plenty left in the sack Mr. Bowers left here. And a Hubbard squash from the root cellar. And I'll see what I can do in the way of a pie."

"That will be lovely, Mother. And if you don't like him—if you don't think he's a gentleman—we'll just never ask him to come again."

It was the mother, not Beth, who urged Martin Hale to come again, any time that his duties permitted. The Sunday dinner was the first of many visits in the course of which the broken boards in the porch were repaired, the loose pickets replaced and whitewashed, and the weaving legs of chairs and tables were tightened. It never occurred to Mrs. Poole to suggest that Hale bring with him any of his friends from the fort, so Amos Gentry never accompanied him. It was Gentry, however, who cleaned and reset the rusty rip and crosscut saws which Hale found in the barn, who sharpened the chisels and replaced a broken hammer handle with a new one. The lock on the Poole front door had been out of order almost from the time they had first occupied the shabby house, one of many things which the missionary had promised to get fixed some time. Mrs. Poole never heard the name of the dour New Englander, Eli Crane, who completely disassembled that lock, made a new spring and two keys, then buffed the accumulated rust from the parts and assembled them. It was Crane, too, who listened to Hale's description of the wheezing water pump in the Poole kitchen, prescribed new washers, and told the boy how to install them.

"I declare," Doris Poole said, "I just never knew how many things were wrong around here until you started in on 'em, Martin. When the Reverend gets home I'm going to take him by the arm and just lead him around from one to another and show him what a little bit of work can do."

His visits were not all work. Doris Poole never thought of the slim lad in blue as a possible suitor for her daughter's hand but he was a boy—the mother could not think of him as a man—and the first boy who had ever indicated the slightest interest in the daughter of the missionary.

"My land," said the mother to herself, "Beth was eighteen last month. Plenty of girls are married by then. It's 'bout time she was beginning to learn something 'bout men."

In her own phrase she kept one eye on them—the mid-Victorian mother might have trusted her daughter out of her sight but she never appeared to. She rocked quietly, her mending in her lap, while Beth pumped the parlor organ and joined her young soprano with Hale's uncertain baritone in the old, old hymns that would never die until mankind forgot Christianity and its God. She played dominoes with them on the scratched table—"you can't play dominoes, Mother, with just two people"—or listened to their amiable bickering over the checkerboard.

"When your father comes home," she remarked, "you must get him to teach you and Martin how to play chess. He hasn't had much chance to play since we came out West, but he used to be considered a fine player."

"We'll ask him," said the girl sulkily. "Maybe he'll have time to do it."

"When do you expect the Reverend will come back?" asked Hale quickly.

Doris' eyes rested for a moment on her daughter.

"It's hard to say. Sometimes, if he's on the river or if he gets into one of the river posts, he can send me a letter by one of the packets; but if he's off in the mountains I'm liable not to hear a word from him until he turns his team into the barn. It won't be very long, though. This is the eighth—or is it the ninth?—of September and the nights are getting frosty already. When snow flies the Indians either come in to the agencies or break up in little bands and find their own winter quarters."

"This is Father's agency, Martin," said Beth. "By first snow he comes in where he can keep warm for the winter."

"Beth! For shame!"

The girl's back was turned to her mother. Only Hale saw her nose wrinkle in contempt and defiance.

4

Company E was on guard the following week end and Hale's name appeared on the company duty roster the week after that. Three weeks passed before he was able to win a belated pass which permitted him to visit South City from suppertime until the last boat crossed the Missouri at eleven o'clock. It was quite dark by the time he reached the Poole home and he stood for a moment beneath the cottonwood at the street's edge and stared into the lighted living room. Mrs. Poole and Beth were seated at the circular table beneath the hanging lamp. The elder woman was sewing, the girl's attention was fixed on a book in her lap. The light touched the girl's fair hair and the matron's flashing fingers—and a voice spoke from the darkness at Hale's elbow.

"You lookin' for anything, soldier?"

Hale whirled quickly; no sound of footsteps had reached his ears.

"What——"

"Nothin' t' git spooked about, soldier. I asked was you looking for anything in there?"

"No. I know them. I was just going in."

"I know 'em, too, Mis' Poole an' Beth. I got somethin' t' tell 'em an' maybe y'd better let me go first, even though I'd a heap sooner walk barefoot through a cactus patch than through that door yonder."

"Why's that?" Hale peered at the man but his features were in the shadow of a broad hat brim pulled low on his forehead. The stranger continued as though he had not noticed the interruption.

"Mis' Poole's husband—th' rev'rend. Job I've got, an' don't want, is t' tell her that she's a widder."

"You mean he's dead!" Hale gasped.

"That's what makes wimmen widders usually. He's dead."

"Good God! What happened to him?"

"That I ain't sayin', leastways not to her 'r Beth. What I'll tell them is that a horse fell an' rolled with him an' th' saddle-horn punched through him an' killed him. Lots of men——

"No, that won't do. They'd want t' know where he was buried an' if he couldn't be brought back an' buried again in a reg'lar graveyard. I reckon I'll tell 'em he was drownded tryin' t' ford th' river. I'll tell 'em I rode both banks of th' river f'r ten mile tryin' t' find him, but I couldn't. That'll cover it."

"But what did happen to him?"

"Maybe I'll tell you that, maybe again I won't. I'm goin' now, 'fore my nerve runs out th' toes of my moccasins. You wait f'r me, bub."

Hale waited until he heard the stranger rap on the door and saw Beth rise. He walked to the end of the block, toward town, and stood there until the man's lean figure loomed out of the darkness nearly an hour later.

"That you, soldier?"

"Yes."

"I looked 'round f'r you outside—was beginnin' t' think maybe you'd run out on me."

"No. I—well, there weren't any shades at the window, you know, and I thought maybe Mrs. Poole and Beth wouldn't like it if somebody was looking through at them when they heard about the rev'rend. How did they take it?"

"They was kinda broke up, 's y' might expect. Let's head f'r town, bub. Only thing I need more'n a drink right now is two of 'em. Just so we'll know who we're talkin' to, what's your name?"

"Hale. Martin Hale. Private, E company, Twentieth Cavalry."

"That'd be Nason—pretty good officer."

"Yes, Captain Nason."

"My name's Rogers, Sol Rogers."

They walked, speaking no more, to the Pacific Hotel where Rogers had a room. Rogers extracted a bottle of whisky from a scratched and battered saddlebag and set it on the washstand. There was but one glass which Rogers gave Hale.

"Pour yourself a drink, bub—there's water in th' pitcher —while I rinse out this mug. You take th' chair too. Don't argue. I'm a damn sight more used t' settin' on th' ground. Gotta break myself t' settin' on a cheer, like breakin' a pup t' scratch on th' door when he wants t' h'ist his leg."

Within the next half-hour he had consumed about half of the quart bottle. Hale had taken one drink, well watered from the pitcher on the washstand. He had heard many times of this man, of his prowess as a hunter, of his exploits among the Indians, and of his knowledge of every foot of the country from South City to the Yellowstone and westward to Montana. He wondered what Corporal Gregory would say if he remarked that he had sat in Sol—for "Solitary," the soldiers maintained —Rogers' room and had drunk with that famous individual, and in the next breath knew that he would not mention the meeting to anyone at the fort. Hale saw before him a tall man —a full inch above six feet—lean, slightly stooped, and clean shaven of lip and chin in an era when youths who had not voted displayed full beards and sweeping mustaches. His black hair was lightly sprinkled with gray at the temples.

"You asked what happened to th' Rev'rend Poole," he said at last—the pint of whisky he had consumed seemed to have no effect whatever. "Reckon I'll tell you. Somebody ought to know 'sides me and old Broken Horn's Minneconjous. I'd thought of tellin' Tuthill over at th' fort—I'll be talkin' to him t'morrow—but he's a soldier! He'd make me set down and tell him all about it and then tell it over again while it was wrote down so's he could make a report on it. Soldiers got t' make a report in writin' t' somebody every time they go to th' privy. Y' said y' didn't know th' rev'rend?"

"No."

"Well, he was a good man. Accordin' t' his lights he was a goddam good man, but his lights didn't always show him th' sensible ways of doin' things. Figger a saint that was considerable of a goddam fool an' you got th' Rev'rend Poole. Every year, soon as th' ice was out of th' river, he packed his possibles an' went a-missionaryin', a-carryin' th' cross of Jesus to th' hosstyles. An' every year, till this'n, he come back. Pass th' bottle, bub."

He drank and resumed as though there had been no interruption.

" 'Bout a month ago—no, it was nearer two months—it was his bad luck t' ride into Broken Horn's camp on Lame Squaw Creek only th' day after some of th' young bucks had come back from raidin'. They had three nice fresh skelps—one of 'em was a woman's—and they was all puffed up with what they'd done and was set f'r a big celebration when th' rev'rend come over th' hill.

"Right there th' damn-fool part of him took a holt. He should've known that wasn't no time to go chargin' in on a bunch of Indians. He'd be alive now if he'd just gone blind t' them fresh skelps, passed th' time of day with old Broken Horn, an' hightailed outa th' camp. 'Stead of that, he laid 'em out! He gave 'em hell an' repeat—he c'd talk Sioux fine, y'know—f'r a bunch of bloodthirsty, murderin', bastards that deserved all th' hate th' whites had f'r 'em. An' then he ripped them fresh skelps down off th' pole an' flung 'em in th' fire.

"That clinched it." His big hand circled the neck of the bottle. He gulped, set the bottle down, and wiped his lips. "Even old Broken Horn turned on him like a stomped-on rattler. He never raised a hand 'r opened his mouth when th' young bucks swarmed over th' rev'rend like wolves on a buf-f'lo calf. They stripped him as naked as a jaybird and staked him out an' let the wimmen—they're a heap wuss than th' men some ways—an' th' boys have a little fun with him while they painted up an' got ready f'r th' main show. He'd cooked his own goose when he grabbed them skelps and flung 'em in th' fire. After that there wasn't an Injun in th' camp that wasn't set on seein' him die, the slower th' better, t' make up f'r it."

"How do you know all that? Were you there?" Hale's voice was hoarse. Stories of Sioux torture, of slow, horribly slow, death by burning, of war shirts made from skin flayed from a man's body while he was still alive, such stories were common in the barracks when old soldiers endeavored to impress the recruits. His stomach turned and the whisky he had drunk rose into his throat. Rogers shook his head.

"I was told about it. I wasn't there, bub, so y' c'n quit lookin' at me like that. I come along later an' th' Injuns—I've known Broken Horn and some of his bucks f'r years—told me about it. They didn't tell me jest what they'd done to th' rev'rend and I didn't ask. One thing they did let slip was that it didn't last long, not very long."

"That's something, I guess."

"Yep. He was a woman, they said, and to an' Injun that's shameful. He started blubberin' an' screamin' 'fore they'd even made a good start on him and one of th' bucks got dis-gusted and beat his brains out with a warhawk—that's a stone-headed club, kinda like an ax."

Hale took a deep breath. *How would I act, I wonder, if they had me staked out naked while they worked on me with flaming splinters driven into my flesh? Could I laugh at 'em and dare 'em to do something worse like they expect a brave man to do? I couldn't. I know I couldn't. They'll never take me alive. I'll save one bullet, always.* Rogers' voice seemed to come from far away.

"I told his wife he'd been drowned, like I said I was going

to. She and the girl was plenty broke up, of course, but it didn't hurt 'em like th' truth might 've."

"What are they going to do?" Hale remembered the question and wondered why he had asked it.

"I dunno, I didn't wait 'round long enough t' find out. There was some sort of church 'r missionary sassiety back of him. Mebbeso they're fixed t' do somethin' f'r widders an' children."

5

Sol Rogers rented a horse at the South City Livery, stood at the animal's head while the flatboat ferry made its pitching crossing of the Missouri, and rode to Fort Doniphan. The sentry at the gate, a recruit from B company, dropped his carbine to the port and commanded, "Halt!" Rogers said, "Hello, bub," and rode on. The recruit's protests were stilled by the corporal of the guard.

"F'rget it, Adams. Take a good look at him so you'll know him the next time. That's Sol Rogers—he comes and goes just as he damn well pleases."

"Sol Rogers, huh?" The recruit was angry. "Just who does he think he is t' go vi'latin' orders like that?"

"He don't think he's anybody. It's just what he *is*—and that's Sol Rogers, th' greatest scout in th' whole West since Jim Bridger!"

"I never heard of him neither," the sentry grumbled and resumed his walk from one gatepost to the other.

At post headquarters Rogers tied his hired mount to the well-gnawed tie rail and strolled into the adjutant's office. The regimental adjutant, Lieutenant Clagett, was at his desk. He was a huge man with drooping side whiskers that swept to his shoulders. Though only a lieutenant in permanent rank, he held a brevet lieutenant colonel's commission for gallantry during the rebellion.

"Hello, Sol; where did you come from?"

"Upriver—I been coverin' ground. Th' old man in?"

"He's busy right now; Major Marcus is with him. Have a seat."

"I don't mind interruptin' him."

Rogers never conveyed the impression of swift movement, but he had crossed the room and passed into Colonel Tuthill's office before Clagett could protest. The regimental commander and his senior major were standing in front of a large map which purported to show the Missouri River from just below the mouth of the Little Missouri, the Yellowstone and its southern tributaries, and— sketchily—the character of the terrain between the many rivers. Both men wheeled as the scout entered.

"Rogers! It's about time you showed up. Where have you been?"

Tuthill got the same answer his adjutant had received.

"Upriver—I been coverin' ground." His gray eyes swept the map. "Where'd you git that there?"

"I had it drawn from all available information. That's the territory where we'll operate if we move against the hostiles next year. Why?"

"Nothin'. I figgered it was kind of homemade. It's all right, I reckon, long 's y' don't take it too serious and try t' travel 'r fight by it. F'r that it ain't wuth a damn."

"What's wrong with it?" Major Marcus asked testily.

"'Tain't right, that's all. Right here, f'r instance. Y' got a dotted line drawed like mebbe y' figgered it as a route through there. It ain't. All of that"—his hand swept through a short arc—"is badlands. There's no water, less grass, and it's rougher than hell's slagheap."

"Red Axe"—Tuthill named an Arikara Indian who had served him as scout on several occasions—"Red Axe says he and his people have hunted buffalo all over that country."

"Mebbe they have. I ain't arguin', but I been through there

right about on th' line you drawed. It'd have been a tight squeak if I hadn't packed a keg of water and walked most of th' way t' save my pony's feet. I didn't happen t' see any buff'lo 'r buff'lo sign.

"Here's another place y'r map's wrong. These rivers ain't where y' got 'em drawed as bein', not by a good many miles. Th' Rosebud goes 'way t' hell-an'-gone south of where y' got it endin', an' this here crick—y' must mean it f'r Tullock's Crick—it empties into th' Big Horn an' not th' Rosebud like y' got it doin'. I just come from up there, Gen'ral."

He spoke quietly, unargumentatively. Tuthill stared at the map, then took a pencil from his desk and changed the course of the creek which Rogers had indicated. Then, almost reluctantly, he erased the dotted line which traversed the area Rogers had called impassable for troops.

"We'll go over the whole thing later," he said. "Now, tell me what you learned? Where are the hostiles camped?"

"Right now, t'day? Mebbe God knows, Gen'ral, but I don't. They might be anywhere west of th' Little Missouri, but they're prob'ly closer t' th' Tongue 'r th' Rosebud. Broken Horn an' his Minneconjous was near Tongue River when I was in their camp. Crazy Horse was 'way south an' west, over toward th' mountains. I was there too."

"And Sitting Bull?"

"I dunno." Rogers shook his head. "Y' know, Gen'ral, some of them hosstyles don't mind seein' me around. With others I'm 'bout as welcome as smallpox 'count of, well, 'count of where I showed up last summer, y' know. Sittin' Bull an' Pizi —that's th' feller you call Gall—they wouldn't throw no parties f'r me so I kinda go 'round 'em."

"Well, you heard the talk in some of the camps anyway. What are they saying?"

" 'Bout what you'd expect. They got a pretty good idea 'bout what you army fellers are figgerin' on doin'."

"Just what do you mean by that?"

"Jest what I said, a big sweep over all th' country 'tween Fort Fetterman an' th' Yellowstone. Next summer, prob'ly."

Major Marcus whistled softly and Tuthill glared his disapproval.

"How in hell," the colonel demanded, "do they learn that? They must have spies around the forts, white squawmen and renegades."

"Don't git up a lather, Gen'ral. Y' ain't got no Injun spies 'round Doniphan. All y' got is the same that's at every other post—seven 'r eight hundred soldiers that talk with their mouths. There's soldiers at every agency an' th' agency Injuns hear 'em talkin' 'bout what's goin' t' happen 'r mebbe goin' t' happen. Same sort of talk goes on in th' sutlers' stores an' th' town saloons. Come summer th' agency Injuns go huntin' buff'lo and meet up with their hosstyle cousins; come winter plenty of hosstyles traipse into th' agencies t' curl up in a warm tepee an' fill up on Uncle Sam's beef. Soon 's th' young grass is up in th' spring, they head f'r th' Yellowstone country again where Sittin' Bull an' Gall an' th' rest of th' big boys git told what's bein' cooked up f'r them."

"All right, all right, all right." Those who knew him could always gauge the degree of Tuthill's irritation by his repetitions. "What are the hostiles saying?—and never mind an oration."

"They're happier than a kiyote with a yard of buff'lo guts, Gen'ral. One 'r two of 'em are worryin' 'bout how maybe th' army will change its mind an' put on a winter campaign—they don't like that—but th' most of 'em are sayin' that there'll be a big fight next year. If that's what you're lookin' for, you're sure goin' to git it, a good one."

"You're not trying to scare me, are you, Sol?"

"Me? Y' know better'n that, Gen'ral."

"All right, all right. When the time comes they'll get their fight. My only hope is that they don't break up and scatter."

"They're doin' that now, f'r th' winter. Come spring, late spring, it'll be Sun Dance time an' they'll git t'gether again. Injuns'd no more miss a Sun Dance than a foot-washin' Baptist'd miss a camp meetin'."

"I hope you're right." He hesitated a moment, stared at the map, then faced Major Marcus. "Have you any questions, Major? No? Then, if you'll pardon me, I have another matter I want to speak to Rogers about."

The dismissal was obvious. Marcus nodded to Rogers and left the room. The latch had scarcely clicked behind him before Tuthill spoke.

"When did you get in, Sol?"

"Yestiddy, 'bout sundown."

"Have you seen her?"

"Her? Oh, sure, *her?* You still worryin' 'bout her—an' me —are you, Gen'ral. No, I ain't seen her but from what you say I take it she's back here in South City."

"She is. She went back East after—after last summer—and I thought she was going to stay there, but she raised a few thousand dollars——"

"Not back East, she didn't." Rogers interrupted.

"How do you know that?"

"Nem'mine. Jest happens I know. Go ahead."

"Well, she raised some money, returned here, and opened up her brother's shop again. Brought an A-one gunsmith with her, a German who had worked for Christian Sharps. The shop is in the same place on Main Street."

He paused. Rogers merely grunted.

"Uh-huh. I might drop 'round t' say howdy, but I'm not figgerin' on hangin' my hat there, Gen'ral."

"Of course not, but, damn it, Rogers, there was talk. Too much talk but it was unavoidable."

"Reckon there was—th' army bein' worse f'r gossip than a quiltin' party. None of it came from me though. I didn't tell nobody that her an' me curled up in th' same hole an' slept in th' same blankets f'r, well, f'r some time. Stick a man an' woman t'gether in the same bed an' it's kinda nach'ral f'r things t' happen. There wasn't no special reason f'r her t' brag 'bout it though."

"I don't think that it's a matter for jest, Rogers. It's enough that there was talk and—damn it, man, her father was an army officer, a colonel. Died of wounds just a week before Appomattox."

"Uh-huh. An' her brother, th' feller that got himself killed in th' Black Hills, he was an officer too, wasn't he? A captain, until he quit th' army an' started in t' sellin' high-grade buff'lo guns? How come he left th' army, Gen'ral?"

"I really don't know," said Tuthill stiffly. "He resigned his commission at Fort Laramie. . . . I was on duty in the South at the time."

"Uh-huh." The scout's voice was bland, disinterested. "Things happened kinda sudden 'round there. There was Major Buzby, th' c'mandin' officer—his wife packed her stuff an' took off f'r th' railroad th' mornin' after th' major an' Cap'n Woodard had a hell of a fight in th' officers' club— one 'r both of 'em got his nose bloodied. An' that afternoon th' captain up an' resigned. Folks said it was accepted by telegraph, faster'n any other resignation in army history, an' him an' his sister left Wyomin' on th' high lope. Next thing we knew they was here an' he was sellin' guns. It was all a mix-up but 'pears like somebody 'r other caught a hell of a cold from jumpin' out of a warm bed on a cold night."

"Barracks and camp gossip!" declared Tuthill hotly. "I wanted you to know she was here, that's all. No use of starting that gossip all over again by calling on her."

"No, reckon not."

"That's good. Now, look at this map for a minute. Do you think we can assume that the hostiles will return to this area, the lower Yellowstone, next spring?"

"It's likely, there 'r thereabouts. Y' can't take too much f'r granted with Injuns."

"Of course not. But if they should be in that area—south of the Yellowstone and north of the Big Horn Mountains—we could . . ."

For twenty minutes he expatiated on the strategy and tactics of a campaign based on converging columns advancing from east, west, and south, which would trap the hostile tribes and force a pitched battle. Rogers listened attentively and puffed a cigar which he took from a box on the colonel's desk. Finally:

"I'm thinkin' it listens good, Gen'ral. It'll be pretty good— if it works."

"It's got to work. Will you go along, Sol, chief of scouts?"

"Reckon so. It'll be a good fight, like I said b'fore. I'd kinda hate t' miss it."

"Good. That's what I wanted to hear. It won't be a winter campaign, Sol, not on that scale. You know that. What do you figure on doing in the meantime?"

"Hadn't given it much thought, Gen'ral. South City ain't a bad place t' hole up in f'r th' winter."

"Damn it, man, we're back where we started. She's here— Miss Woodard."

"So y' said a while ago."

"Somebody is going to kill you someday, Sol, maybe it will be me!" The colonel's grin canceled the implied threat. "Get it through your head, won't you, that your presence would just arouse all the gossip that's died down. Miss Woodard is a lady, the daughter of a very gallant officer. She's a frequent guest at the homes on this post and at the officers' dances. One of my captains, a splendid officer, seems to be very much interested in her. I don't want all that old gossip stirred up again."

Rogers halted with his hand on the doorknob.

"I ain't stirrin' up nothin', Gen'ral. I don't reckon she will either; a scout an' hunter don't stack up extra high 'longside a captain. Still, though . . ."

"What is it?"

"She wasn't no virgin, Gen'ral."

The door closed behind him.

9 THE SCOUT (1)

More than a year earlier the name of Solomon Rogers had been mentioned at a staff meeting at Headquarters, Department of Dakota, in St. Paul. An infantry major who had served at many posts in the Platte and Missouri valleys remarked that if the information cited came from Sol Rogers it must be considered reliable.

"I know him," he added.

Colonel Tuthill snorted.

"If I may correct the major's statement," he remarked. "No one knows Sol Rogers."

2

Sol Rogers had followed the high backbone of the Rockies from Taos in New Mexico to the Bitterroots of Montana.

There was not a field-grade officer on the Plains who had not at some time employed him as scout or hunter or who had not relied implicitly on information that had come from him. He spoke Sioux fluently, could make himself understood in the totally dissimilar tongues of the Blackfoot and Cheyenne, and by virtue of his command of the sign language, that *lingua franca* of the Plains, could "talk" with any Indian from the Kaw to the Green River. He knew better than any living man the whole vast unknown West, the rolling leagues of the buffalo plains of the Arkansas, the Platte and its tributaries, and the Missouri; South Park, Middle Park, Brown's Park, and a score of "holes" which no man had named; he had stood in the shadow of the Three Tetons—the majestic massif which forgotten French Canadian trappers had named the Three Tits—and had drifted slowly and cautiously in the deep canyons of the Green River and the Grand.

In all his wanderings he was alone. No man called Sol Rogers "partner" or could claim former partnership with him, and from that sprang the mystery with which his name was always associated. He had been an army officer, they said, forced to resign after marrying a half-breed Indian girl of unbelievable beauty . . . he was the child of a Yankee ship captain and the daughter of a California grandee . . . he was the son of a wealthy New Yorker who had come West and adopted the life of a roving hunter after his bride had died on their honeymoon, after his fiancée had jilted him and married another on the eve of their wedding, after he had killed a man in a duel. The only thing factual about any of those legends was that none of them was true.

"Sol Rogers? Hell, man he was living in the West when Pike's Peak was a canyon!"

That, too, was legend and tradition and exaggeration. Only Rogers himself knew the truth and of himself he never talked.

His birthplace had been a farm in southern Illinois. The

year was 1842 and he was the eldest child of a German
immigrant farmer named Rausch and his second wife. The
first, who had accompanied her husband and three children
from Oberbayern, had died, quietly and uncomplainingly, of
overwork. Dieter Rausch drove his wives, his daughters, and
his sons somewhat more brutally than he did his horses and
oxen which, after all, represented a considerable financial in-
vestment. An overworked ox could refuse to respond to the
goad, but a son could be beaten to renewed effort and flogged
again when that effort failed to meet his sire's demands.

Young Ludwig, as he was named, had rebelled when he was
fourteen years old. His father had departed at sunrise with a
load of grist for the mill near Shawneetown. The boy had left
his plow in the furrow, mounted the horse, and ridden to the
southeast before the dust of the slow-moving wagon had vanished from the air. Near Cave-in-the-Rock he had forced the
horse into the Ohio River and swum that wide stream. On the
Kentucky shore he had tossed the bridle into a thicket and
turned the animal loose. At dusk, ten miles downstream, he
had swum to the stern of a river packet which had nosed into
the bank to load wood, climbed aboard, and concealed himself among the crates of the deck cargo. He was discovered the
next morning and dragged to the texas deck and the captain,
who did not like stowaways.

"What's your name, boy?"

"Rau—Rogers," he answered, and quickly added his mother's maiden name, "Salmang. Salmang Rogers."

"Sol—was that what you said? Solomon Rogers? That sure
ain't a Dutch name—you talk like a Dutchie."

"I've been workin' for one for—for a long time. I couldn't
help pickin' up a lot of Dutch talk."

"Runaway bound boy, eh?"

"Yes, sir, that's just what I am." The boy faced him boldly.

"What y' run away for, y' git tired lookin' at plow handles?"

"No, sir."

"Well, what was it—a notion t' go West an' hunt buff'lo?"

"No, sir, I'll show you." He pulled his still-damp shirt over his head and turned to exhibit the weals of his most recent flogging, crisscrossed over the unhealed welts of others. That's why . . . I got sick of bein' beat every day."

"Huh. Y' got a back on you like some niggers I've seen in Mississippi an' Loo'siany. Put your shirt back on, boy. Mr. Marks, you reckon the cook can use another boy in the kitchen from here t' St. Louis?"

"I reckon so, Cap'n."

"Turn this boy over to him. Tell him he's workin' his passage, but if he lays a hand to that back of his'n I'll take his own hide off from his neckbone to his black rump."

3

That had been the first chapter in the development of a frontiersman. He lived in St. Louis for nearly three years during which he worked in a livery stable, as a cook's helper, as swamper in a barroom in the quarter known as the Vide Poche, and, for three lurid months, as "night messenger" for one of the town's better bordellos. Throughout those three years, in all those jobs, he ate regularly and well; in 1859 he was four inches taller and fifty pounds heavier than the boy who had bared his scarred back to the Ohio packet captain.

He had gained height and girth and strength and, even at seventeen, a definite maturity. He had lost all trace of the Teutonic accent which had once marked his speech. The necessity for self-support had made him self-reliant; he could fight if a situation required fighting, and when he fought it was with a savage speed that invariably amazed his antagonist. He could read and write, but it had never occurred to him to communicate with his parents or to advise them that he lived. They, his brothers and sisters, the farm and the labor it demanded, were as forgotten as the name he had once borne. He was and would remain Sol Rogers.

In 1859 he found employment as a herder—the word "wrangler" had not appeared in the vocabulary of the West—with a Santa Fe caravan and in the course of the eight hundred miles from Independence to New Mexico learned that he could shoot. John Chain, owner of the wagon train, had employed a very able hunter to keep his teamsters supplied with meat from the inexhaustible herds of buffalo along the Arkansas. Pete Hatch was afflicted, however, with a congenital antipathy to work or exertion in any form and always managed to recruit volunteers who would assume something more than the major share of the labor of obtaining meat. He watched Sol Rogers cutting hump ribs for the mess to which he was attached, learned that the youth had worked as a cook's helper in St. Louis, and promptly went to Chain and obtained his services.

Hatch was talkative too. He chattered incessantly about tracks and how to read them, how to determine their age and the identification of their makers—buffalo, antelope, the occasional deer, wolf, coyote, and wild horse. He talked as he loaded his heavy-barreled Hawken rifle, talked of the merits of certain powders, of shaved buckskin versus linen for bullet patches, of sights and set triggers. When one subject was temporarily exhausted he turned to another and told Rogers of trapping expeditions on the Green and the Gila and the Snake and their tributaries, of peaks and rivers that no man had named, of secret valleys where the wápiti bugled on the threshold of the trapper's cabin, and of Indians and how to get along with them or to circumvent them.

He let Sol shoot the heavy Hawken. The quarry was a cow buffalo—only the cows were considered fit to eat—at a range of two hundred yards.

"Buff'ler's heart is low in th' chest," Hatch muttered. "Jest kneel here an' steady y'r left arm with these shootin' sticks.

When she takes a step y'll see a bare patch where th' hide's rubbed back of her front leg. Hold on that bare patch; that's where th' heart lies."

The boy drew back the hammer and pulled the rear trigger which "set" the front so that it would trip the sear at the lightest touch. He did not kneel as Hatch had suggested, but as the grazing cow took a slow forward step he raised the rifle to his shoulder, dropped the front sight to cover the bare patch, and touched the trigger. The smack of the 400-grain bullet was like striking a side of beef with a fist. The cow stood for a few seconds, then raised her head, slowly lowered it, and collapsed. She was dead when she struck the ground. The boy was quite unaware of Hatch's searching gaze.

"We c'n use a couple more," said the hunter quietly. "Pick another cow, a young one, an' see if y' c'n drop her the same way."

The boy reloaded deliberately nor knew that the hunter watched his hands as he manipulated powder flask and ramrod; watched, more closely, his eyes. It is the eyes, always, which betray nervousness or excitement. Without moving more than a couple of strides from his original position, Sol killed two more cows.

"Thought you said you'd never done any shootin'," the hunter remarked.

"I haven't. Nothing 'cept rabbits and ducks down in the sloughs, with a shotgun. That"—he gestured toward the fallen buffalo—"they're the first things I ever shot bigger than squirrels."

"Hmmmph. Looks like mebbe you got a natchral knack f'r it."

4

He left the train in Santa Fe. John Chain offered him work, either in the wagon yards which sprawled along the *acequia madre* or in Independence, but the boy shook his head. He took the money he had coming, shouldered a rifle—not a Hawken but a serviceable piece—which Pete Hatch gave him, and struck out to the north. His destination was Fernando de Taos, the 'dobe hamlet in the shadow of the Sangre de Cristo peaks which was still a headquarters for the trappers who worked the streams of the southern Rockies.

He remained in the mountains for three years. Beaver, the fur which had earned for the Mountain Men their fame and had made a very few of them rich, was no longer in great demand nor did it command the fantastic prices of thirty years before. Fashion's whim had replaced the beaver hat with the silk tile, and the soft fur was now used for coats and for trimming. There was always a market for furs, however, and money could be made in peltries which the Fur Brigade would have scorned, wolf and bobcat and badger.

Individual proficiency and knowledge of the craft were taken for granted by the men who rode northward from Taos to the headwaters of the San Juan, the Animas, and the Pine. From the beginning they accepted Sol Rogers as one of themselves. They nodded approval of his marksmanship, his stoical acceptance of the discomforts incident to storm and high water, his ability to handle horses. None realized that his skill was imitative, that he remembered everything that he was told or that he saw, and that he never made the same mistake twice.

In his second year in the mountains, 1861, he had a partner for the last time. He had met the man at the settlement still known as the Pueblo on the upper Arkansas and they had joined for "wolving" in South Park of the Rockies. The man called himself Cortez, Joe Cortez, and undoubtedly had some Spanish or Mexican blood. He was swarthy, black-haired and black-eyed, and given to Spanish oaths when things went wrong. Wolves were plentiful and their take of pelts was good, but the partnership ended when Cortez tore the body of an

Indian from a burial scaffold. He laughed when Sol protested.

"*Cristo*, it's only an Injun," he exclaimed as he tore the wrappings from the corpse. "We got here 'fore th' wolves did, that's all." Sol noticed the full skirt of white tanned elkskin, the high moccasins, and did not heed Cortez' statement. "Jees, it's a woman. Well, she ought t' be tenderer than some old buck."

He tore the garments from the body and butchered it as unconcernedly as he might cut up a calf.

"Bait! Plenty bait—an' a sight easier come by than followin' them snares we set f'r rabbits. I'll wrap it in th' skirt; take a holt of th' other corner, Sol."

"No," said Rogers. He turned away and, when the other man reached camp, had divided their equipment and was packing his horses.

"Pullin' out, eh," Cortez jeered. "What's th' matter with you, Sol, stummick weak?"

"Nothing's wrong with my stummick, 'cept f'r th' way you turned it. I'm pullin' out. I b'lieve in gittin' along with Injuns if it's possible—and that ain't no way t' do it. So long, Joe."

5

He spent that winter in an encampment of the Northern Cheyennes on Burnt Moccasin Creek. It was there that he "married" the first of the Indian girls, of various tribes, who were to share his lodge. She taught him much of the Cheyenne speech—an Algonquian dialect—and from her father, Bull Belly, he learned the ABC's of the sign language.

He reached Fort Union, at the mouth of the Yellowstone, after the ice had left the river in the spring of 1862. There he learned of the war in the South, of a nation divided, and of armies sparring with armies in the valleys of Virginia and Tennessee. He reasoned, shrewdly, that his furs would bring a far better price in St. Louis than at Fort Union, so he traded his horses for a flat-bottomed bateau, loaded his furs and equipment, and drifted unconcernedly downstream.

Dealers in St. Louis fought to outbid one another for his packs of fur, and Sol, for the first time in his life, experienced the security incident to a plump wallet. He tossed his grease-blackened buckskin garments into a trash can, bought new clothes, inflicted the discomfort of boots on feet which for years had known only moccasins, and luxuriated in one hot bath after another and in being shaved daily by a deft Negro barber at the Planters' Hotel. There were girls—mestizas from Mexico, brown-eyed and golden-skinned; blonde and brunette French girls who claimed, all of them, New Orleans as their home; an Amazon, five feet ten and one hundred eighty pounds, who called herself Hilde from Heidelberg. Her hair was the color of unripened cornsilk, her unblemished skin as white as milk. She was gentle, affectionate, and passionate—and tried to rob him while he slept. He could choose, it seemed, from among a thousand girls and the novelty palled swiftly.

There were also men. He could look from his window and see more men on the sidewalks of a single block than he had seen in three years in the mountains. Every third man, it seemed, was in uniform—the blue of the Union—and it was inevitable that their number would include many rabid patriots. Some were sincere opponents of secession and haters of slavery; the interest of others lay primarily in the organization of new regiments and companies which they would be appointed to command. Men who had graduated from West Point, who had served in the Indian country for nearly a decade to win promotion to first lieutenant and the right to place a silver bar on their plain shoulder straps or dress epaulets; those men saw horse dealers and planters and third-rate lawyers blossom suddenly into uniform as captains, majors, and even colonels, appointed by the governor of the state. Social as well as military prestige accompanied those ranks, and the competition was bitter. The difference between twin bars and a colonel's eagles might depend on the vigor with which an individual condemned the rebellion, the thunder with which he called for the blood of all who followed the flag of the Confederacy.

It was one of these, a lawyer from Poplar Bluff, who persuaded Sol to enlist in a company identified as the Sedalia Sharpshooters. It would be, he declared, an independent unit, attached to no regiment or brigade and answerable only to a division commander. No man would be accepted for enlistment who could not demonstrate that he could bark a squirrel at a hundred yards.

"That's all I ask—can you shoot?" said Captain Krieger—the governor had not confirmed his appointment but he had given himself the rank. "And if you can shoot, that's all you'll be asked to do—sit in a tree or back of a stump and knock off the Rebs as fast as they stick their heads up. One thing I'll promise you: there'll be no drilling or any of that sort of foolishness; I never heard that knowing how to slope arms and present arms helped a man's shooting."

"What kind of guns 're you gittin'?" Sol interrupted. "These here Springfield rifles with bay'nets like I see 'em carryin'?"

"No, sir! You'll be shooting, not charging. What I'm trying to get are Sharps rifles, sharpshooters' rifles with either tang or telescope sights. What do you say, friend Roberts?"

Sol checked the correction that rose to his lips. If this man misunderstood his name—well, for purposes of soldiering any name would serve. He signed the enlistment papers and took the oath of allegiance as Sam Roberts.

Three months later the Sedalia Sharpshooters saw action. Shiloh had become history and the blue-clad forces under Grant were feeling their way south and west across northern

Mississippi. A skeleton company of weary Confederate infantry had intrenched itself on the slope of a hill and was effectively delaying the advance. Krieger's sharpshooters were called on to pick off those rebels which exposed themselves and to keep the others down behind the parapet until artillery could be brought up to shell the position.

Krieger had obtained six Sharps rifles equipped with set triggers and telescope sights—long tubes which extended almost the full length of the forty-three-inch barrels. Sol Rogers—Sam Roberts to his mates—had one of them. He lay on his belly in a thicket of scrub oak and swung the crosshairs of the telescope along the line of the revetment. Midway of the line a Confederate rifleman thrust the barrel of a Glaze "Palmetto" musket over the parapet and aimed carefully at some target along the road below. Sol touched the trigger and the man—his shoulder almost torn away by the .52-caliber ball—leaped to his feet, fell, and rolled for several yards down the slope.

Sol passed the rifle back to the loader who crouched behind him and was given another rifle. A young man with an officer's sash crossing his gray coat vaulted the parapet and ran to the aid of the wounded soldier. Sol killed him. The breeze whipped the smoke away from the muzzle of the Sharps, and through the telescope Sol saw the youth's features contort with agony as the bullet ripped through his breast. He fell across the body of the other.

Later, in the sharpshooters' bivouac, Captain Krieger complimented his marksmen.

"Thanks to you fellows," he said, "our boys took that hill without losing a man. The rebs pulled out when their captain was killed. It was you that killed him, Sam. Why don't you cut a notch or drive a brass-headed tack into the butt of your gun?"

Sol grunted.

"I don't need to count *coup*," he said soberly. "I been settin' here wonderin' why I killed that feller and hurt the other one pretty bad. They'd never done nothin' to me."

"They were rebels," Krieger snorted, "and that ought to be enough for you or any other loyal American——"

Sol interrupted him. Discipline was not a particular characteristic of a sharpshooter.

"Seems to me them two fellers was Americans too," he commented. "That one feller, th' little officer boy, he didn't look t' be more'n twenty year old."

"Hush that kind of talk, Roberts!" Krieger commanded. "He was an enemy of your country, just like every other rebel between here and the Gulf of Mexico. You're a soldier!"

That night Sol Rogers quietly walked away from the camp and set his face to the northward. The numerous Union patrols, alert for stragglers and deserters, presented no difficulty to one who had stalked the elusive—and rather more intelligent—horned sheep of the Rockies. The patrols never included less than four men, mounted. All he had to do was avoid the roads and the infrequent towns which the Union forces had occupied. He traded his blue uniform to a farmer near Holly Springs for a pair of homespun pants and a linsey-woolsey shirt. He found—a stroke of luck—a cavalry officer's broad-brimmed felt hat and trimmed an inch from the brim. Thus equipped, he walked boldly into Memphis and registered at a hotel a block from the Mississippi and the wharves. He let the clerk see the contents of the well-packed wallet from which he paid for the room.

"Never mind lookin' that way at my clothes, young feller," he remarked. "A feller can't be persnickety about th' cut of his pants when he gits outa Vicksburg at two in th' mornin'."

"You—you got out of Vicksburg!" The man's eyes were wide. "Say, Gen'ral Braymer 'll sure want to talk to you!"

"I've already talked to one gen'ral, a stubby feller name of Grant. I couldn't tell him much. Th' rebs were all ready to throw me in jail and hide th' key. Lissen, I want a room and I want a hot bath, an' then I want to sleep for ten hours. After that you can get a tailor 'round here so I can buy some decent clothes. That clear?"

Some weeks later he watched a cloud on the western horizon slowly lose its nebular appearance and develop into the looming massifs of Watoyah, the Spanish Peaks. Names came unbidden to his tongue—Fernando de Taos, Cochetopa, Rio de los Animas Perditas, Bayou Salade, Jackson's Hole, Pa-sappa —all totally unknown to the men and women of the crowded lands which lay behind him. He grinned and nudged his pony with his heel.

"This here's where I belong," he said aloud.

He had served his country for some four months; he had fought for it for perhaps half an hour.

6

The story of the decade that followed, could it be written, would be a saga comparable only to those of Jedediah Strong Smith, Joseph Reddeford Walker, Jim Bridger, and other giants of the golden years of the Mountain Men. It never entered the simple mind of Sol Rogers that he created the mystery which came to surround him and that from that mystery legend sprang. He journeyed alone because he preferred that independence, he learned the Sioux tongue and made friends with the roving bands for no other reason than that friendship paid dividends and enmity did not. He sold his furs at the most convenient market and in that way became known at Bent's new fort at Big Timbers on the Arkansas, at Laramie, at the young city of Denver on the South Platte, and once—that was after he had spent a season on the upper Green and its tributaries—at Great Salt Lake City.

He saw nothing worthy of comment in the circumstance that during the Cold Moon of 1868 he had ridden into Yellow

Moccasin's winter camp in a snowbound canyon of the Big Horn Mountains, or that he had saved that chief and all his people by trailing a herd of elk to where they had yarded, by killing and dressing an even dozen of the animals, and by packing the frozen meat to the starving Sans Arc. When he was told that the Sioux had named him White Hunter, he laughed.

"I reckon there's just as many call me a son of a bitch if th' truth was known," he grunted.

He was already famous in the land when he first rode into South City with Colonel Tuthill and the Twentieth Cavalry, returning from what was called a "scouting expedition" along the Yellowstone. Actually, the column was escorting surveyors and engineers of the Northern Pacific Railway whose directors in faraway New York were urging impatiently that the rails be pushed on toward the Pacific which, on paper, was their goal.

Sol had been at Fort Union when the troops reached that once-important trading post at the mouth of the Yellowstone. Summer was on the land, there was no trapping, and he had gladly signed on as hunter to keep the six companies supplied with meat.

"Two dollars a day," said Colonel Tuthill. "You'll supply your own horses; draw what ammunition you need from the quartermaster. I'd do the hunting myself—I enjoy it—but I have to stay close to the column. Nearly all the men, and that includes the officers, are greenhorns when it comes to Indians."

In Sol's opinion Tuthill was as ignorant of Indians and their ways as any of the men who rode behind him, but he did not say so.

"I'll take it," he said. "I'll draw th' ca'tridges I need, but I'll pull th' bullets an' run th' lead over f'r my own bullets."

"There's no need for that. There are plenty of rifles in the command."

"Army guns." The two words expressed several volumes of opinion. "I'll use my own, Gen'ral."

That expedition consolidated an opinion Rogers had already formed of military commanders. The Twentieth quite literally stumbled along the Yellowstone from Fort Union and highly amused the Sioux, whose parties paralleled the course of the two battalions. Indian alarms were of almost daily occurrence and were received in an identical manner. The rear guard, or a flanking party, would ride pellmell to rejoin the main column and the officer in command would report that he had seen the Indians in considerable strength or that his small force had been fired upon. Tuthill would detach one company and lead it himself in pursuit of the hostiles who would scream defiance, fire a few shots, and dash into the hills over ground too rough for the heavily burdened cavalry chargers. Tuthill would then lead the weary troopers and their exhausted mounts back to the column. On one such occasion he encountered Sol Rogers. The scout was squatted beside a small fire and was broiling the liver of an antelope he had killed.

"Dammit, man," Tuthill exploded, "are you crazy? These hills are lousy with Indians; we just drove back a band of nearly fifty. You'd better kick that fire out and come along with us."

"I'll be along, soon 's I eat. Them Injuns now, Gen'ral——"

"Yes. What about them?"

"Their chief, 's you call him, is an old feller name of Claw. He's a Minneconjou. Got 'bout fifteen young bucks with him— was figgerin' on takin' 'em over west an' mebbe stirrin' up a little rookus with th' Crows."

"He was, was he? Just how do you know all that, Rogers?" He smiled for the edification of the captain and lieutenant beside him.

"He told me so, Gen'ral. I was talkin' to him 'bout an hour

ago—jest b'fore he threw a scare into Loo'tenant Nace an' th' rear guard. Old Claw's a pretty good Injun—I've knowed him f'r some time."

That story was repeated, with considerable embellishment, in the camp and, later, when the Twentieth returned to its station. So was the story of how Tuthill fired three times at a running deer and missed with each shot from his repeating rifle. Rogers then fired, once, and the deer rolled head over heels and was dead when they reached the carcass.

At Fort Doniphan, Rogers cashed an order for the pay that was due him, turned his horses into the quartermaster's corral, and crossed the river to South City. He wanted a hot bath, a barbershop shave, new clothes to replace his trail-stained garments, and a good meal. After that was time to consider the purchase of powder and other necessities.

"There's a place down th' street a piece," the proprietor of the restaurant told him. "Feller name of Woodard runs it—Cap Woodard—and he won't carry anything but the best in powder and such stuff. He makes rifles, too, f'r them that want a really good gun."

Rogers thanked him, paid for his meal, accepted a cigar, and walked slowly north on Main Street. His feet were already hot and uncomfortable in the Wellington half-boots he had purchased; the woolen coat and trousers seemed shapeless and as stiff as boards.

A wooden gun, gilded from stock to muzzle, hung across the board sidewalk. If that advertisement were not sufficient, ornate blue lettering on the window announced: J. C. WOODARD. TOOLS & HARDWARE. FINE GUNSMITHING. Rogers blinked for a moment in the gloomy interior. As his eyes adjusted themselves to the darkness, he saw a rack of heavy-barreled rifles behind the counter, some revolvers in a case, and, through an archway, a small machine shop wherein he identified a drill press, a rifling head, and a lathe. A man stood between him and the half-finished stock of a rifle in a stocking cradle. Sol waited a few moments, then coughed a little more loudly than was necessary. The workman turned, laid down his gouge, and advanced through the doorway.

"Howdy. I thought my sister was keeping an eye on the shop, but I guess she's stepped out. Woodard's my name—generally known as Cap. What can I do for you?"

"Le's see. I can use 'bout ten pounds of powder, th' three-F-G, in two five-pound cans. Dupont's, if you got it."

"I got it. What else?"

"I'll need lead—better have 'bout twenty pound." He continued with various items he lacked and which he knew he would need through the fall and winter.

"You're stocking up heavy," said Woodard genially. "Where you headin'? Not that it's any of my business but I might be able to advise you. I've outfitted plenty of fellows."

"I don't figger you'd foller me—not far, anyways. I just come in from th' Yellerstone with Colonel Tuthill. Reckon I'll head back up there—beyond th' Big Horn."

"By God!" Woodard exclaimed. "You're Rogers—Solitary Rogers."

"I been called that."

"By God," the gunsmith repeated reverently. "You're the one man in Dakota Territory I've been hoping to meet. Listen, Sol—do you mind if I call you that? It's the only name I've ever heard given you."

"I usually answer to it."

"Fine. Let me shuck this apron and put on a coat and hat. Then I'll shut up the shop and buy you a drink. You're the one man who can answer some questions that 've been botherin' me for a long time."

"Dunno 's I can answer 'em, but a drink is a good idee. Ridin' with Tuthill is dry work."

As they reached the door of the shop, a woman turned from the sidewalk so suddenly that she and Rogers collided. He grasped her arm and steadied her. For a moment they stood breast to breast, then she shrugged lightly and stepped back.

"I'm sorry, ma'am."

"Don't apologize; the fault was mine."

"She's always in a rush, Sol," said Woodard quickly. "Sis, this is Mr. Rogers, the famous scout. He came in with the general yesterday. Sol, my sister, Miss Genevieve Woodard."

"I'm honored, ma'am." Sol tugged at his battered hat. He saw, in one quick glance, a mass of dark, almost blue-black hair brushed low on her forehead and confined in a tightly twisted knot at the back of her neck. She wore no hat. Her dark eyes were almost hidden beneath heavy brows and long lashes. Her skin was clear, creamy, and her full, pouting lips a startling crimson. The snugly fitting basque of the period revealed rather than hid her breasts. Their eyes held for a moment, then she looked away. She nodded lightly.

"I'm happy to make your acquaintance, Mr. Rogers."

"And I too, ma'am." *So that's the girl that Major Buzby's wife left him over. It was f'r her that Cap'n Woodard punched his commandin' officer, th' same Buzby, an' then resigned. Seems like them fellers at Laramie said it wasn't th' first time she'd figgered in husband-an'-wife trouble. Wagh! Lots of woman there, lots f'r any man t' brag about handlin'.* His face was a mask as he turned to follow Woodard.

In the Oriental Saloon the former captain called for whisky and carried bottle and glasses to a table across from the bar.

"My regards, Sol. I'm really happy to meet you."

"Thanks. Here's lookin' at you."

They drank and Woodard refilled the glasses.

"Hope I'm not keeping you from anything else you wanted to do, Sol."

Rogers grinned.

"If there's anything more important than good licker when y've just come off th' trail, I dunno whut it is. I've got nothin' t' do but set till th' next packet comes upriver t' take me t' Fort Union. That'll be Thursday, I'm told."

"Yes," Woodard agreed. "Walsh and the *Prairie Queen* ought to be along Thursday. And then, Sol?"

"What d'you mean?" Sol spun his empty glass but waved the bottle away when Woodard extended it.

"What I said. Which way are you heading from Fort Union? I'm interested in all that country."

"Ain't rightly decided. I'll see what I c'n get at Union in th' way of hosses an' then make up my mind. Up th' Yellerstone, most likely."

"West, eh?"

"Yep."

"Not south?"

"South from Union? Not this coon. There's nothin' t' interest me in that part of th' country—badlands 'long th' Little Missouri after she hooks t' th' south; then y' find yourself runnin' into th' Black Hills."

"Ever been there, Sol, the Black Hills?"

"Nope—an' ain't aimin' t' go. Th' Hills are *wakan, wakan tanka*. That's Sioux f'r what y' might call goddam holy."

"I know." Woodard's thumb and finger dipped into his pocket and withdrew a muslin tobacco sack. It thumped heavily when he dropped it on the table.

"Gold," said Rogers. It was a statement, not a question.

"Yes. How did you know?"

"It clunked down heavy—like gold 'r lead. 'Tain't likely a man 'd be carryin' lead scraps 'round with him."

"You're right. It is gold, Sol, and from all I can gather it comes from the Black Hills."

"It might," Sol shrugged. "How'd y' git it, if it ain't askin' too much? Injun tradin'?"

"Yes." The man's eyes were brilliant. "Sol, somewhere out yonder"—he waved his hand widely—"there's a gold strike that'll beat th' Comstock or Alder Gulch. Gold from the grassroots down! There's got to be."

"Mebbe." Rogers was clearly uninterested. "There's color

t' be found in lots of cricks in th' mountains. I picked up three—four dollars' wuth of nuggets once in a little riffle below where I was settin' a otter trap. Injuns 've learned about gold. Only nach'ral that they pan out a few dollars now an' then. I'll bet y' a new hat that th' buck y' got that stuff from made y' give him just about full value for it in trade."

Woodard nodded ruefully.

"He did—watched the scales like a hawk. Sol, it was the same at Laramie and some of the trading posts along the Platte as it is here. Any trader will tell you that every now and then an Indian brings in a few dollars' worth of dust. Never very much at a time——"

"He's too smart f'r that," Rogers chuckled. "Last thing an Injun, any Injun, wants is to see a gold rush into his country."

"I guess that's right. I've talked to them, though. I've picked up a little information here, a little there. All of it points to one thing—one place, rather. That's the Black Hills."

"It c'd be—and it c'd just as likely be five hundred miles from 'em. I'm just tellin' you I don't know; an' if an Injun wants t' lie t' you, he can tell you with a straight face that he dug gold outa th' pigpen over at th' fort. Nearest I ever been to th' Hills—Pa-sappa, they call 'em—was 'bout two 'r three days' ride, over west of th' Belle Fourche. I c'd see 'em stickin' up against th' sky, that's all."

"And you've never heard of gold there?"

"I've heard plenty fellows guess about it, same as you. No Injuns, though. One thing I never talked t' Injuns about was th' Hills. They're *wakan*—holy—like I said, an' a man that wants t' git along with Injuns never asks 'em a lot of damn-fool questions 'bout their medicine 'r how they come 't git names like Hairy Gut, Noisy Walking, 'r Mouse's Road, 'r what's holy to 'em 'r why. That's why they hate missionaries."

Sol Rogers rarely spoke at such length. He reached for the bottle and filled his glass. Woodard poked the sack of nuggets disconsolately.

"That's kind of bad news," he said at last. "I—I've heard a lot about you, Sol, and I thought that you were the one man who could help me; that getting around among the Indians the way you do you must have heard something."

Rogers shook his head.

"I can't help y'. Sure, there's gold in th' mountains, jest as there was in Californy, but I never got int'rested in huntin' for it."

"And the chances you must have had! My God, man, haven't you ever wanted to be rich?"

"Not 'specially. Tryin' t' breed two dollars into six never struck me as fun."

"We're different, I guess. All I want is money enough so I can afford to tell some people to go to hell and watch 'em start off! My sister feels the same way. I was in the army— no man ever got rich as a line officer. I'm making a good living here with the store and my guns, but I'll never get rich, really rich, at that either."

Sol whittled a small chew of tobacco from his plug and tucked it in his cheek.

"What you call a good livin'," he said slowly. "That'd satisfy most people."

"Not me!" Woodard's clenched fist struck the table lightly. "Someday I'm going to have money, big money. Gen and I'll go back East in a private car, and I'll buy a team of high-stepping, bangtail hackneys and a yellow cutunder with red wheels and a nigger-boy in livery on the box behind. Then, in Washington, we'll put in two weeks just driving around the State, War, and Navy Building until every goddam general officer there has seen me and learned who I am: Woodard the millionaire, the same Woodard they kicked out of the Sixteenth 'for the good of the service'!"

Jesus, he's sure riled. Reckon they had him in a split stick there at Laramie. Must've been more 'bout that business than was talked about. Aloud he said, "Reckon a millionaire c'd have a pretty fancy time—I've never given much thought to it."

Woodard terminated the conversation abruptly. He pushed back his chair and, rather obviously, replaced the cork in the bottle. *Eight drinks at two bits; a couple of dollars thrown away.*

"I've got to be getting back to the shop. Your powder and other stuff will be ready whenever you want to pick them up. I'm glad I met you, Sol."

"Same here." The scout was somewhat more sincere. A little information about the Hills, totally nonproductive, and four drinks of excellent whisky. Good bargain.

10 THE SCOUT (2)

Weeks later and nearly a thousand miles to the westward, that meeting with the former captain was recalled forcibly to Rogers' memory. An old Cheyenne—his name was Wide Feather and his left leg had been crippled and virtually useless since the day, ten years before, when a pony had fallen with him, rolled on the leg, and broken it above and below the knee— had asked him if it was true that he was considering traveling further to the west, beyond the Madison and the Tobacco Roots to the mining towns of Montana.

"It has been in my mind," said Rogers in the Cheyenne tongue. "The white men there are so busy hunting the gold that they have no time to seek food for themselves. They will pay well for the meat of deer and wápiti and antelope."

"I have so heard." Wide Feather accepted the tobacco which the white man offered. "They will pay for other things too— for such as this."

He produced from beneath his blanket a buckskin sack that was inordinately heavy for its size. Sol hefted it, then laid it on the ground beside his knee.

"It is gold; the gold the white men are forever seeking," Rogers remarked.

"Yes. Here in the mountains it is worthless; but I have been told that in the towns of the white men there are places where it can be traded for guns and blankets and tobacco and much that is good."

"That is true." Rogers smoked quietly. *Never try t' rush an Injun.* Wide Feather picked the dottle from his redstone pipe and repacked the bowl. "It is gold from Pa-sappa," Rogers added.

The Cheyenne nodded.

"My brother knows then," he said.

It was Rogers' turn to nod, gravely.

"I have traveled much in the mountains," he said. "I have known few white men but my friends are many among the Sioux, the Cheyenne, and the Absáraka. There has been much talk as we sat about the fires—the gold that lies in the creeks of Pa-sappa was but a part of it."

"It is not talked of among the white men." The Cheyenne's words were a simple statement of fact.

"No. Did they know that this"—he nudged the fat sack of dust and nuggets—"was there, the Hills would no longer be *wakan.* There is no place where the white man will not go for gold, nothing that he will not do."

"That is true. My son's skin is white but his heart is red. He has been to the Holy Hills?"

"No. I have seen them from far off, against the sky, from beyond the great peak that is called Inyan Kara."

"I have been there many times. The Sioux—the Dakotas—have named it Pa-sappa and say that it is theirs. It is the land of my people, the Cut Arms. I am of the Burned Artery clan of the Cut Arms. And before the Cheyenne came into the land, the Hills belonged to the Absáraka, the Sparrowhawk people whom the white man calls the Crows. And before them the Hills belonged to many others who have been here and have gone."

"That is true. My father Wide Feather is old, and the old are wise about many things."

The old man accepted the compliment as his due.

"I am old and wise, but with this"—he touched the twisted limb—"I am poor. In the towns of the white man this gold will buy me many things that I need, but if I or my sons took it there we would be robbed. I can hunt no longer, but this would buy a new rifle with which my sons could hunt for me. It would buy powder and ball for that rifle. It would buy the white man's blankets to keep us warm in the cold moons. It would buy iron pots and knives and many things that my wife and my sons' wives could use."

"It would buy all those things," Rogers agreed. *It looks like the old jasper is getting down to cases.*

"The skin of my son is white. He could take this and another like it and would not be robbed. He could use it to get for me those things that I and my sons need."

Rogers made up his mind swiftly.

"It is good. I am the son of my father. I have sat in his lodge and we have eaten together from the same pot. When I go to the towns of the white men, I will get those things and will bring them to him."

Wide Feather inclined his head.

"My son is of great heart; my heart is on the ground to him."

"It is done for love and for friendship—for that there can be no thanks. When I return from the white man's towns, my father and I will talk more of Pa-sappa. He will tell me of the Hills and of the streams that come down from the Hills and of where in those streams the gold is found."

"I will tell him. My son speaks with the tongue of an Indian and we are of one blood. He will not lead the white men to Pa-sappa."

2

He entered the Hills from the west and on foot, as Wide Feather had advised. His horses were Indian ponies and un-shod and he concealed his saddle and other equipment as shrewdly as he knew how. He carried a single blanket, half a dozen extra pairs of moccasins, a shovel and short-handled pick, and—he grunted at its weight—a back-pack of food and other necessities. He left his rifle with the saddle and debated for some time as to whether or not his revolver—a .44-caliber percussion Colt of Civil War vintage—should not rest in the same place. Finally, however, he buckled the heavy weapon around his waist.

A man on foot is far less conspicuous and can move almost as swiftly over the span of a day's journey as one on horseback. No betraying dust rose from beneath Rogers' moccasins, he remained so far as possible within the shadow of the trees— spruce and pine which grew ever larger as he climbed toward the divide—and he crossed no ridges until after he had scanned every visible foot of the country which lay beyond. When night fell he sat beside the stream, chewed some jerky and pemmican from his pack, then crawled into the brush, rolled in his blanket, and slept. He built no fires, nor would he until he had located a spot where a fire or its odor was not dangerous. Not once did he encounter any tracks or any sign of men, nor did he see the faintest tracery of smoke against the blue sky. The heavily timbered slopes and the deep gorges of Pa-sappa were unoccupied, he decided, and his thoughts went little further than that. He was quite blind to the beauty of virgin pine and spruce against the dark granite cliffs, blind to the beauty of the wild flowers which, in thousands, splashed with color every open meadow.

There was no gold, Wide Feather had told him, in the gorges which came down from the western slope of the Hills; the dust and nuggets so prized by the white man lay in the gravel bars of the deep gulches which ran eastward. The old Cheyenne had traced a map of that terrain in the earth beside his lodge and Rogers had memorized its every detail. There were caves in the Hills, the old man had added; he had seen their black openings as he and his people had ridden along the creek beds. That was true, but Wide Feather had never climbed to the level of the caverns and Rogers searched for several days before he found one that offered adequate shelter. It was as dark as a pocket and stunk abominably of fox and skunk, but he grunted his satisfaction when he observed that the narrow opening was almost invisible from below, that the cave was dry and reasonably level, and that there was a mysterious draft which sucked constantly inward from the entrance and drew any smoke into deep recesses of the cavern which he never explored. Above all else, there was water: a seepage no wider than a man's finger which crawled down the wall and filled a deep hollow in the rock at the base. It held about a pint and was full again within fifteen minutes after he had drained it.

He found gold with considerably less difficulty than had attended his search for suitable shelter. The gulch immediately below his cavern carried water only after a storm and he did not attempt to prospect it. There was another, a third of a mile to the south, where he found color within a foot of the surface of the first bar in which he dug; with each successive shovelful the color became more abundant, the nuggets larger.

These were virgin bars and he was the first prospector who had ever entered the gulch or, so far as he knew, this section of the country. The wealth of the virgin placer deposits of the West would seem fantastic and completely incredible were the figures not thoroughly attested by scores of records. More than four million dollars in gold—assay-office and express-company valuation—came from a single high-level bar in Alder Gulch in Montana in 1864. The clerks and soldiers and mariners who rushed from Yerba Buena to the north fork of California's American River in 1848 knew nothing of mining. If a pebble was yellow and heavy and if it could be cut with a knife, it was gold. Those early prospectors accepted only that which met those requirements and men became millionaires on what they left behind. Confederate Gulch, the Comstock, Yuba and Feather Rivers, Cripple Creek, the list is endless and each name a monument to fabulous wealth.

From his first trench and a smaller one some fifty yards upstream, Sol Rogers took within two weeks more than twelve pounds of pure gold. Its value at the current rate of twenty dollars an ounce was nearly four thousand dollars, and he had barely skimmed the richest cream from the golden store which lay in the crevices and pockets and in the deep stratum of black, auriferous sand which covered the bedrock like a blanket.

His store of dust and nuggets would have been doubled or tripled if he had dared really to strip the bars, to pan the gold-bearing sand, to build a sluice or a "Long Tom" and let the stream do the work of separating the precious metal. This, in his superlative caution, he had not dared to do. Any placer operations would have roiled the water of the stream for miles and would have aroused instantly the suspicions of any wandering Sioux who crossed its course.

Rogers trenched his bar without approaching the water. When he reached the dark sand above the bedrock he could, in many instances, pick out the gleaming nuggets as a man would pick raisins from a pudding. When washing was necessary he carried the gravel, a panful at a time, to the edge of a deep pool below the bar. There the water moved sluggishly and, if he washed his pan slowly and carefully, all the rejected sand and gravel sank to the bottom long before it reached the end of the pool. Rogers never permitted himself to forget, even for a moment, that this gorge lay in Pa-sappa, the Black Hills, which had been sacred to the Sioux and Cheyenne since they had first looked upon the dark, pine-clad peaks. Pa-sappa was the dwelling place of Wakan-tanka, the Great Mystery. Since *tanka* meant great or large, and anything incomprehensible was *wakan*, the missionaries happily interpreted the compound word as Great Spirit, Supreme Being, God, and thus encouraged the fallacy that the red men were monotheists. Since that was what the missionaries devoutly wanted to believe, they ignored the fact that lightning was also *wakan*. So was a meteor, an albino buffalo, or a menstruating woman. An eclipse of the sun or moon, highly incomprehensible and unpredictable, was Wakan-tanka.

At this season, Wide Feather had assured him, no Sioux visited the Hills except small family groups who rode to the eastern slopes to cut lodge poles. He should be watchful at all times, of course, but the Sioux would not come in numbers until early fall when the leaves of the squawbush began to turn red and the aspens to gold. It was then that the men of the Wakan-wacipi fraternity made medicine and danced in Pa-sappa.

All of which was good, but in every act and movement Rogers was as cautious as a hunted animal. He gathered only dead wood for the fire in his cave—an Indian would have noticed even a willow shoot which a knife had severed—and he built his fire only while the sun was still in the sky and no flickering light might reveal the entrance to his cave. He awoke at dawn and from the cavern mouth inspected every inch of the ravine below, then he followed the ledge to the rim and surveyed the eastern slope of the Hills. The family groups who might visit Pa-sappa would have no reason to hide their fires and the smoke would rise high in the still morning air.

Reassured, he returned to the cave, breakfasted, and then went to his diggings. At least twice during the day, he climbed the steep sides of the gulch and took another long survey of the land to the eastward. It was from that vantage point one morning that he heard the shot.

It came from far away. There were no audible echoes and the shot itself was no louder than the *clop* of cupped palms struck suddenly together, but it intruded almost obscenely into the cathedral quiet of the dark Hills. Rogers glanced once over his shoulder into the gulch and the deep scar of the trenches which crossed the bar. There the signs of white man's handiwork were impossible to conceal, but he considered the advisability of returning for the revolver. He rejected the notion even as it formed in his brain—it was his task to learn only the source of that shot, not to carry a fight to the Indian who had fired it.

I'm lucky. They might 've come over the ridge and had me like a sitting duck. How in hell did they get deep enough into the Hills for me to hear that shot? There wasn't a sign of smoke last night or this morning.

It never occurred to him that the shot had been fired by other than an Indian and he was angered by the thought that he had failed to discover the intruder's presence. He crossed a second gulch and a third, then checked himself when the unmistakable sound of hammering struck his ears. There were half a dozen blows in quick succession, a pause, then three or four more.

That's nail-drivin'—Injuns sure don't do that. It's white men and I'll bet my pile they're buildin' a cabin. The pounding continued. *Listen to 'em—not a worry in th' world!*

He advanced boldly and from the rim of the next gulch looked down on two men who were busily establishing a camp. They had cut slender aspens for the frame of a lean-to cabin which was roofed with a square of canvas. Rocks had been rolled into a parallelogram to form a fireplace and the carcass of a deer, gutted but not yet skinned, hung from a tree against which a long-barreled rifle leaned. A deep trench furrowed a bar and the water in the stream was heavily roiled.

Rogers picked up a rock and hurled it down the slope. One of the men dropped his hammer and leaped toward the rifle but halted as Rogers stepped into view and raised his palm in the world-old gesture of peace. The scout's face was grim but he waved his hand and angled down the hill. He was within a few yards of the cabin when he recognized the two who stood there. The man's features were covered with a stubble of new beard, but there was no mistaking the gunsmith from South City, the one-time infantry officer, Cap Woodard. Behind him, half-hidden in the doorway of the cabin and obviously embarrassed by the man's shirt and trousers she was wearing, was his sister. Recognition was mutual. Woodard glared angrily at the scout.

"Surprised to see me, eh? Well, I knew you'd be showin' up, Sol. You must 've counted on having first crack at these creeks for yourself—you and your fine talk about never having been in the Hills, never wanting to go there, never hearing about any gold. It was a good story, Rogers, but just a little too good. Here we are and here we're staying."

"Looks that way." Rogers' voice was mild. "I heard a shot an' figgered I'd find out where it come from. When I heard y' poundin' I knew it was white men—prob'ly sojers."

"Why soldiers?" Woodard's curiosity was too much for him.

"Couldn't be nothin' else; only a sojer w'd be such a da— dumm fool. These here are the Black Hills—Injun country. Only a sojer w'd go stompin' round in boots an' leavin' tracks that a blind man c'd follow, shootin' an' cuttin' timber an' muddyin' up th' creek till an Injun crossin' ten miles below w'd follow upstream t' see what was goin' on. All that—an' bringin' a woman! Looks like y' left y'r brains back in South City."

Woodard stood squarely in front of him, his booted feet spread, his thumbs caught in the waistband of his pants. An angry flush rose slowly from his throat; his eyes narrowed to slits. When he spoke, the words tumbled angrily one over another.

"You've spoke your piece, Sol Rogers," he said thickly, "now I'll speak mine. I had a good hunch you were lying back there in South City—you and all your smooth talk about the Hills. I made it my business to find out a few things and I know what I'm doing. There won't be an Indian in the Hills until six weeks or so from now, not until there's a frost and the leaves begin to change and there's yellow in the aspens. That's the sign—I'm telling it to you for your own good. Until then we're keeping to this gulch of ours and you can keep to wherever you are. You're not wanted 'round here—is that clear?"

"Reckon 'tis." Rogers was as mild as the former captain was furious. *I'd be wastin' breath t' tell him I wasn't lyin' to him. He's mad enough t' pop a blood vessel. Prod him a little an' he'd spit in his own eye.*

He turned on his heel and walked around the lean-to. Genevieve Woodard was leaning against the doorpost. The man's shirt she wore was open at the throat and her breasts rose and fell quickly. Her dark eyes met his but she did not speak. Rogers retraced the zigzag course by which he had descended the hill but did not look back. *I can't blame him much. Seein' me, after what I told him, sure entitled him t' think I'd been throwin' sand in his eyes. One thing's sure: if any Injuns do come in they'll find him 'fore they do me. He won't have no more chance than a horny-toad under a wagon wheel—n'r her either.*

3

Genevieve Woodard's dark eyes followed Rogers until the scout had vanished over the crest; then she turned toward her brother.

"Well, Gen, that ought to hold him," Woodard declared. "I sure told him off."

"Yes," she agreed. "Telling people off is one of the best things you do, Jim. What's the use of my talking—you won't ever learn to hold your tongue. That man, Rogers, we could have given him a cup of coffee and a quarter off the buck and he'd have been friendly. He didn't come here to jump your claim or work this gulch and you know it." Her voice rose. "You just went out of your way to make an enemy . . . again."

The man grinned.

"And you don't like to make enemies, do you, Gen? Not when they're men, anyway. Sol's the first man you've seen for some time—is that it, Gen?"

"No, you know it isn't!"

"I don't know any such thing. What you forget, Gen, is that I've known you a long time. I've seen the different ways you play with different men and sometimes—when I could figure out just what your game was—I knew why you played 'em."

"Oh, shut up!" she snapped. "You're twisting what I said, like you always do, always trying to put me in the wrong."

"George Boltz," Woodard said dreamily. "He owned three Missouri River packet boats and was worth a pile of money. With him you were colder than an iceberg."

"He wants a woman to be like that," she said indifferently. "Always proper, always dressed just so and smelling faintly of rose water." Her slim hands touched lightly the shapeless pants and the rough blue shirt. "I think he'd die if he ever saw me in anything like this."

"I don't. George or any other man would look at you in pants and you know it. Wanting a proper woman never kept George away from Nancy Woller's place in Saint Jo or Bessie Rivers' when he got to South City or a dozen other sporting houses up and down the river."

She shrugged.

"Maybe not. He's not my husband—he's free to go wherever he pleases."

"Huh! Any man you married would lose interest right away in Nancy's place, wouldn't he?"

"Yes." She added nothing to the affirmative but she raised her chin, turned her head slightly, and stared at him from sultry eyes. He was suddenly aware that the top button of the blue shirt was open, that the rough cloth framed a white throat and the swelling curve of her breasts. Her eyes flickered and the man looked quickly away.

"Quit it, Gen, goddam it. I'm not that mining man from Denver—that's the way you looked at him."

"His name was McKean, remember?" she said. "You thought he was rich. You almost gave up the idea of the Black Hills in favor of those diggings in the Rocky Mountains that he talked about. He talked about millions but that was all it was—talk. I found out how much——"

"You sure did. He was talking millions and all he had was a couple of thousand—wasn't worth undoing a button for, was it, Gen?"

She stamped angrily, but he continued speaking.

"And there was the saloon man, Conley, in Omaha. He had cash in every bank in town, but whenever he was around you sat with both feet on the floor and your nose in the air like a preacher's wife. You wouldn't even touch a glass of wine in front of him, but you could have had him—and his money— like that!" He snapped his fingers. "He was crazy to marry you, Gen."

She shook her head, then sat down crosslegged in the doorway of the lean-to.

"I know, but look where his money came from. I'd never marry a chain of saloons, Jim. The smell of the whisky would follow you everywhere and respectable people——"

"My God," he jeered. "All you talk is money, money,

money, and what you could do with it. But you got to be respectable and have a pew right up front in the church, too. I thought——"

"You thought! You want money just the same as I do and for the same reason. We're both as greedy as hogs. Money means travel to me. It means London or Paris if I want to go there. It means a big house and servants and silk next to my skin. Someday I'll have it too!"

Her lips parted, her breast rose and fell in quick, passionate, breaths. Her brother swore softly.

"God, you're something, Gen! If it's money you want, you'll have it! There's gold from down below in those saddlebags and more waiting in this gulch. When we ride away from here you'll be fixed to buy yourself any kind of a husband you want. You can go back to Doniphan and take your pick of the garrison."

She sniffed.

"No, thank you; no army officers for me. Unless, of course, it's some officer in a staff corps with about ten thousand a year private income."

"Come down off your perch, Gen," he jeered. "You've lived on army posts all your life and you've played around with everything from colonels—if they weren't too old for playing —to shavetails. I could 've opened up the shop in St. Paul or Chicago or anywhere else, but, no, you wanted South City."

"It was the end of the railroad," she said quickly. "It was——"

"It was as close as you could get to Fort Doniphan," he interjected. "Fort Doniphan . . . and Captain Hanford. He took on right where Buzby—damn his soul—left off. God, how I laughed when I came home and found him trying to button his blouse and look for a missing spur at the same time. He was cussing his orderly for letting that spur drop off his saddle, where it hadn't ever been. I found it that night while you were getting supper—found it under your bed."

"You didn't any such thing! I looked——"

"You did? Whatever made you think a man's spur might be under your bed, Gen?" He cackled merrily. "You never were a good liar. I gave the captain his spur and told him I'd found it under the edge of the sidewalk and he thanked me kindly and bought me a drink. And I chewed a clove before I stopped by to take you home from the Ladies' Aid at the church. You were playing the piano for them and butter wouldn't have melted in your mouth. You're a humdinger, Gen, a ripsnortin', star-spangled humdinger. You can fool any man in the world, except me, your brother. I can tell what you're thinking about the minute I see you looking at a man. Like you were at Sol Rogers a while ago. You had that light in your eyes, that do-I-or-don't-I-want-to light. Better watch yourself with Sol Rogers, Gen. He's no shavetail fresh out of the Point. He's seen the elephant and heard the owl."

"I'll ask him about them some time," she retorted coolly. "The only reason I don't fool you, Jim, is that I've never tried to—after all, you're my brother and why should I? And I'm not afraid of Sol Rogers or any other man. Do you know what I am afraid of?"

"No, Gen, I don't. What?"

"Two things. Being poor is one and the other is suffering. I mean suffering real pain, like being tortured or something like that. I thought of that while Sol Rogers was talking about the Indians. Suppose they did come in here, Jim, and captured us. We wouldn't have a chance. They'd——"

"Forget it!" he snapped. "Sol Rogers has been dodging Indians all his life and he's as nervous as a whore in church. So long as we're out of here before the leaves turn, we won't see hide nor hair of an Indian."

4

Rogers dismissed—or told himself that he had dismissed—the Woodards from his mind. The ex-officer had had his warning. If he chose to disregard it . . . well, it was his funeral. A damn good chance that it would be a funeral, too.

Each day he added a few nuggets and some store of dust to his hoard. Once he lay all day in his cave while a storm pelted the hills. The lightning leaped from ledge to ledge of the cliffs and the thunder crashed like artillery. There had been storms before, violent while they lasted but soon over. This one was the daddy of them all, a real gully-buster. On the next day the sun shone from a cloudless sky and he reached his gulch to find the stream running bank-full and the two ditches obliterated. The flood had washed them clean, but when the waters fell he found an exposed pocket in the bedrock so packed with gold that he pried it out with his knife.

Two of Woodard's six weeks passed; the third was two days old. Sol made his meager breakfast, buckled on his revolver, and climbed the ledge to the rim. A lightning-blasted cedar lay there and he stepped over it and turned his face to the east. There, clear and dark against the blue sky, were two tall columns of smoke. He stood for perhaps two minutes and tried to calculate their position. It was impossible to locate them precisely, but they were a considerable distance from the ravine he called Woodard's gulch. There'd be plenty of time to warn the man unless the Sioux had left those fires to burn out and were already on their way deeper into the Hills. If they'd already jumped the Woodards . . . well, he'd see them and hear them long before they knew another man was around. He hitched his belt and set out rapidly through the timber.

Woodard received the news as though the Sioux and Rogers had conspired to drive him from his bonanza. The leaves wouldn't even begin to turn for another month—it didn't make sense.

"Not to you, maybe," said Rogers, "but it looks like it makes sense to them. Anyhow, they're here."

"You're sure it was smoke?" The man still did not want to accept the news.

"I'm sure. Two fires close together. Mebbe five 'r six miles east of here and a couple of miles south."

Woodard was silent for a moment.

"Well, I guess we've got to pull out," he said regretfully. "Gen, you'd better roll the blankets and get what stuff you can together while I catch up the horses."

"Hosses!" Rogers exploded. "There's no time f'r that, man!"

"Why not? You're scary, Sol. Them Indians ain't necessarily heading for where we are. Hell, their big camp ground is twenty miles south of here—I scouted it on the way in. That's why we moved north to this gulch. Our horses are only about a mile below. I threw a couple of trees across a narrow place there so they couldn't stray."

He was superbly confident. He lifted a bridle from the horn of one of the saddles and marched off. Genevieve came from the cabin with an armload of bedding. She turned aside as Rogers moved to help her.

"I can manage," she said. She dropped the blankets on the ground and re-entered the lean-to. When she appeared again she carried a pair of saddlebags which hung heavily over her arm. She placed them over the cantle of her brother's saddle.

"Do you think there's any real danger, Mr. Rogers?" she asked. The brim of her wide hat shaded her face, but he could see that she was pale and that a pulse throbbed in the side of her throat.

"Not unless they're really headin' this way," he told her, "but the sooner we're all out of here the better."

He stepped past her into the lean-to. A line had been

stretched from one end to the other and the saddle blankets hung over it as a screen between the two beds of hemlock boughs. Woodard's long rifle and its cartridge belt lay beside his bed. Rogers carried gun and belt out and leaned them against the bedroll which the girl had already lashed.

"That's a lot of rifle," he remarked.

"Yes. My brother——"

The words died on her lips as a shout reached their ears and Woodard appeared, running, around the bend of the creek.

"Reds!" he panted. "A big bunch of them, heading right up this gulch. We got to light out fast."

"The horses, Jim——"

He shook his head.

"The Sioux got 'em by now. I saw them from that rise at the head of the meadow—the Indians, I mean."

"How many?" Rogers asked.

"Plenty . . . I sure didn't stop to count. They didn't see me; I'm pretty sure of that." He was breathing normally now. He buckled the cartridge belt about his waist, then picked up the rifle and fed one of the long cartridges into the breech. "Grab a blanket, Gen, you can't pack more than one. Where's the dust?"

Her finger was shaking as she pointed toward his saddle. She picked up a blanket from the pile at her feet. Her brother threw the heavy bags over his arm.

"You're trailing along with us, I reckon, Sol?"

"Yes." Rogers' mouth was dry and hot. *The damn fool! Now I'll have to dry-nurse the pair of 'em clear to God-knows-where to dodge th' Injuns.* "I've got a cave four miles or so north of here. If we can git there without bein' tracked——"

"Good enough." The former captain assumed leadership. "We'll head straight up the gulch and cut over that bare shoulder. Then we'll follow the ridge north."

He faced the hillside and his sister fell in behind him. Rogers was unburdened except for his revolver and he stripped another blanket from the pile and picked up a two-quart canteen from near the fireplace. He glanced back repeatedly as they angled up the slope and it was he who sighted the Indians. There were two of them, on foot, and they were bent almost double as they climbed up the steep wall of the ravine more than two hundred yards below. He shouldered past the girl.

"Get down, quick. Down!"

They stood at the edge of the huge shoulder of naked rock which Woodard had pointed out. As they stepped behind its shelter they saw that the bare granite fell away into a shallow depression some eight feet wide and half again as long. The projecting shoulder shielded the basin from the view of any observers who might climb the hillside; from the bottom of the gulch it was invisible. Woodard threw himself flat and his sister dropped beside him. Rogers squirmed over her body and put his lips to the man's ear.

"There was two of 'em. They didn't see us. If they had they'd 've yelled."

"Scouts, I reckon." The man was pale beneath his beard but his voice was steady. "They came along a sight faster than I thought they would. It looks like we sit out the party right here. We're hid after a fashion and maybe they'll think we spotted their smokes and pulled out yesterday."

"Leavin' th' hosses?"

"That's right, too. Maybe we're lucky at that. If we'd cut straight up the hill we'd have run smack into those scouts and we'd be fighting now."

Yeah, and if we'd lit out when I first warned you we'd be holed up and safe. He drew his revolver and laid it on the rock beside his hand. The girl's face was buried in her folded arms. He saw her shoulders quiver. *She's scared green, but I can't blame her. You're in a tight, Sol—you and these two.*

"Here they come," Woodard whispered. He was peering between two of the loose rocks which lay along the rim of the basin. Rogers put his eye to another crevice. There were some twenty warriors in the band which appeared around the bend below the cabin but at the moment the gulch seemed packed solidly with Indians. Rogers surveyed them appraisingly.

They weren't painted for war, which meant nothing. They hadn't expected a fight until they'd crossed the muddy stream or seen Woodard's boot tracks or something which warned them of whites in Pa-sappa. Only five or six were mounted and one small corner of his brain recorded surprise. The Sioux were horse Indians; a brave wouldn't walk fifty yards if a pony was handy. Still, the gulch was narrow and horsemen would be handicapped in a fight between the steep walls; most of them must have left their mounts in the meadow which Woodard had barricaded for his own horses.

All but the mounted men dived into the brush like frogs into a pool when they sighted the lean-to. A yell announced the discovery that it was empty and at a word from one of the riders the footmen scattered to right and left to scout for tracks. They didn't stop to loot the cabin or to seize any of the many articles which had been left behind. That showed they were plenty mad—an Injun had to be wild with rage to pass up a new blanket or a chance to rummage for sugar or tobacco. Rogers whispered softly to Woodard.

"That feller on th' black pony looks like he's bossin' th' show. If you hear me shoot or if I holler to you, pour it into him."

Woodard nodded. His face was grave and a little muscle twitched in his cheek. The Indians in the ravine didn't offer any immediate danger, Rogers thought, it was those who might climb the hillside who had to be watched and the rocky buttress which protected the three also blocked any view of the slope which lay beyond it. Then, so suddenly that he seemed to have sprung from the cliff, an Indian stood beside that granite shoulder. He was less than twenty feet away and for a second he stared in amazement at the three whites. His mouth opened but the triumphant yell of discovery never passed his lips. Rogers' Colt barked and the Sioux clutched his throat with both hands and fell. The old cavalry carbine he carried clattered on the rocks. Rogers, stooping so that he would not offer a target to the Indians below, hurried to the buttress in time to get a shot at a second warrior. The man shrieked, dropped his gun, and tumbled out of sight in the brush.

Woodard's big rifle bellowed. Rogers peered beneath the cloud of smoke and saw the black pony racing down the gulch and the chief, his dignity forgotten, scampering for the shelter of the alders. Woodard fired again and missed a second time. Rogers jumped back into the shallow basin. The movement exposed him momentarily and he heard yells and three or four shots.

"You missed him twice! What's the matter with you—buck fever?"

"I don't know, and that's the truth." Woodard's teeth clicked sharply. "I loaded those cartridges myself and I know they're right. I had the bead right on him both times and it's not a foot over two hundred yards."

Rogers snorted.

"Jest where d'you think he was, up on th' Yellerstone? It's just a mite over a hundred yards to where he was standin' on the far side of the cabin. Call it a hundred an' fifteen. No more."

The former captain growled what might have been a contradiction. A rifle barked from the gulch. The bullet whined from the face of the cliff ten feet away and the girl flinched and whimpered. Neither man paid any attention to her.

"There's a chance for you, Cap," Rogers whispered. "Take a sight over the near corner of the cabin—do you see that clump of alder a little this side of a lone pine tree?"

"Yes."

". . . and above it a little patch of red. Looks like red leaves, maybe, or a flower?"

"I see it."

"Hold just a hair over that red spot—it's three hundred an' twenty yards."

"You're crazy! It's better than four hundred."

"Three-twenty," said Rogers severely. "You're in the mountains now, not out 'long th' Missouri. Do what I tell you f'r once."

The other obeyed. He adjusted the vernier sight on the tang of the rifle and thrust the heavy octagonal barrel through the cranny in the rocks. The sears clicked as he set the trigger. The buffalo gun roared and a forty-five-caliber, five-hundred-fifty-grain bullet, driven by a hundred and twenty grains of black powder, smashed through the screen of brush and into the Indian who crouched behind it. The man screamed like a wounded horse as he leaped high into the air. The girl thrust her fingers in her ears at the sound of the death yell.

"Three-twenty," Rogers repeated. "It's a sight further'n any of their guns will shoot. Mebbe it'll slow 'em up a little."

"At three-twenty this rifle's just beginning to reach out," Woodard boasted. "I can put five shots out of six on a barrel-head at six hundred. Think I'm lying, don't you?" He read the unbelief in the scout's eyes. "I'll show you if I get a chance. That's my business, rifle-making. I made this gun myself and chambered her for the Sharps forty-five, one-twenty, five-fifty."

Sol completed the task of reloading the fired chambers of his revolvers. He inspected one cap, flipped it over the rim of the cliff, and pressed another on the nipple.

"I'm goin' over there a ways where I c'n watch th' hill," he said. "If any of 'em climb th' gulch on this side, I'll try t' git 'em out of th' notion. You watch down below and along th' other side. If they ever git above us, we're cooked."

They're respectin' that long-range shot of his an' hangin' back. Injuns 're funny that way. A white man always thinks th' other feller might git killed but not him. An Injun has th' notion that every bullet is marked f'r him, pers'nal, an' he gits outa th' way if he can. That's why a couple of men can break up a charge if they keep their heads an' hold their fire till a bullet's bound t' hit. Sure wish that Woodard wasn't so green when it comes to Injuns.

There was no charge. A few Indians tried to approach the basin from the flank but withdrew quickly when Rogers slammed a couple of shots in their direction. Woodard fired twice; once at an Indian who exposed himself in the gulch, again at one on the opposite side of the ravine. He hit the first, he said.

The sun climbed higher and the bare rocks were like the top of a stove. The Sioux had guns and, apparently, abundant ammunition, and maintained a galling but ineffectual fire, no two shots of which came from the same position. By the time Woodard swung the muzzle of the big rifle on a mushroom of white smoke, the Indian had vanished. They respected the buffalo gun and most of their firing was from long range. All but a few bullets fell far short, but about one in ten reached the cliff and ricocheted with a high-pitched whine. Genevieve Woodard flinched whenever she heard the sound.

"There's no sense in jumpin' like that," Rogers told her. "By the time you hear them bullets they're gone. It's th' one you don't hear that c'n be bad medicine."

She didn't hear the bullet that killed her brother. It was a chance shot, fired by an Indian who merely thrust his carbine through the brush and yanked the trigger, but the blunt .56-caliber ball found the cranny through which Woodard peered, hit him below the left eye, and blew the back out of his skull.

Genevieve didn't scream, for which Rogers was grateful when he happened to think about it. A scream would have told the Sioux that one of their random shots had found a target. When the scout reached the basin, she was crouched beside her brother and was shaking his shoulder.

"Jim! Speak to me, Jim. Open your eyes. Oh, dear God, he's dead—Jim's dead. What will I do?" She whimpered like a sick puppy.

"Nothin', right now." Rogers' voice was harsh. The afternoon was waning and the Sioux had lost three, possibly four, of their warriors. Two or three had probably been wounded, and as far as they knew they hadn't even scratched one of the whites who had invaded Pa-sappa. They were certain to attempt something before darkness offered their enemies an opportunity to escape.

"He's gone and you got to take his place," the scout continued. He extended his revolver to her butt-first. "C'n you shoot?"

"I—I've shot a pistol." She made no attempt to take the gun. "I can't—I can't——"

"You've got——" He was about to tell her that their lives might depend on her vigilance, but checked himself as he heard the throbbing of a drum far down the gulch. He pushed Woodard's body to one side and peered through the crevice. The Sioux fire had died away and the warriors were gathered about a man on horseback in a little clearing some distance downstream.

"He's painted!" Rogers exclaimed.

"Who—why?"

"Th' chief . . . th' feller your brother missed a while ago. As f'r why, well, when an Injun paints up it shows that th' party is goin' t' be formal, like a tailcoat an' silk vest an' patent leather shoes. It ain't what I'd call good news, neither."

The mounted warrior was a long way off. Better'n five hundred yards—call it five-forty—if it was an inch. A long shot for any gun, but the kind of shot for which this rifle of Woodard's had been made: extremely long-range shots at buffalo and antelope on the open plains. He drew the weapon across his knees and made a careful inspection of the rear sight, a sliding disk with a peephole orifice which could be moved up or down a vertical stem and locked into position by a thumbscrew.

That sight was accurate. Woodard had set it on the first line above the three-hundred-yard graduation and he'd made a center shot. Five hundred and forty yards to where the chief sat on his black pony. There was a patch of yellow sand about —he estimated it at four hundred and seventy-five yards, moved the disk to that point, and fired three shots at intervals of about a minute. The smoke drifted away before the heavy bullet reached the end of its arching flight and each time he saw the sand spurt under the impact of the big ball.

The mounted man must have thought himself far out of range. With each report he raised his arms and waved defiantly a small shield he carried. His companions shouted.

"Hoka-hey! Hoka-hey!"

Rogers moved the aperture to the five-hundred-and-fifty-yard mark, then dropped it by the thickness of a hair. He drew a deep breath, exhaled half of it, and held the bead of the front sight squarely on the Indian's chest. His finger touched the sensitive trigger as lightly as a butterfly's footfall. The buffalo gun roared. An instant later the Sioux flung his arms wide and pitched backward over the black pony's rump.

The horse galloped away as Rogers threw out the empty case and closed the breech on a fresh cartridge. By the time he had cocked the gun a second Indian was bending over the chief's body. Rogers killed him in his tracks.

"Take my gun an' git over there by th' rock," he snapped at the girl. "Shoot at anything you see move. We'll know th' whole story in a couple of minutes now. Either they'll rush us or they've got their bellyful of fightin'."

There was no attack. Not an Indian showed himself through the few hours of daylight that remained. *Nickin' them*

*last two was what done it. This here's Pa-sappa and it's plenty
wakan. Somethin' sure went wrong with their medicine—ad-
dled it, like—or I'd never have counted coup on their chief at
close t' six hundred yards. Right now they're skeered. There
ain't a gee-string in th' hull outfit that ain't kinda damp, but
t'morrow things'll look different. If you're aimin' at keepin'
your hair, Sol—an' hers—you'd best be a long ways off by
then.*

Dusk crept up the gulch from the east. Rogers took the
cartridge belt from Woodard's waist and buckled it about his
own. He moved quietly to where the girl stood beside the cliff.

"It'll be dark soon"—he tried to speak gently—"an' we'd
better get out of here before they change their minds about
fightin'."

"Where can we go? We've no horses."

"We'll hole up in that cave I told you 'bout. It's not very
far."

"But Jim . . . we can't leave him here. The Indians——"

"We got t'. He—he's past hurtin', miss. You c'n go down
an' say good-by t' him if you want to."

He took the revolver from her limp hand and returned it
to his holster. He kept his back to the spot where Woodard lay
and did not turn until he heard her boots slip and scrape on
the smooth rock.

"I—I couldn't do a thing for him."

"Nobody could. Now follow right close behind me an' if
you lose sight of me f'r even a second, speak up. Don't holler,
just speak to me. Take your boots off first, though, an' sling
'em 'round your neck."

"Why?"

"They'll leave tracks," he said patiently. "White men's
tracks that Injuns c'n follow on a run. Take 'em off."

She sat down obediently and removed the heavy footgear.
He moved off, angling toward the rim of the gulch, and she
followed a stride behind. Now and then he heard her catch

her breath as a sharp rock bit cruelly into her foot. It was dark now but the sixth sense of a wilderness hunter enabled him to identify landmarks which to the stumbling girl were blacker shadows in the blackness. He was burdened with the rifle and the two blankets and he left her by the dead cedar while he carried them to the cave. The ledge path was narrow and treacherous; he'd want both hands free when he led her along it in the darkness.

He crawled ahead of her through the narrow entrance crevice and told her when she could stand. It was dark outside, but within the cavern the blackness settled upon them like a blanket thrown over their heads. Rogers had become accustomed to it and had developed a blind man's awareness of the proximity of rock walls. He left her standing while he spread her two blankets on the opposite side of the cave from his own. He could hear her hurried breathing.

"Where are you? Sol, have you . . . ?"

"I'm right here. You don't have to whisper any more. Nobody c'd hear you."

"Are you making a fire? It's so awfully dark."

"Not at night. T'morrow, when it's light outside, we'll make a fire and eat somethin' hot. Are you hungry?"

"I don't think so. Can I have a drink?"

"Sure, here's the canteen. We're safe now, so calm down. It was tough about your brother, but when we squatted in that pocket I wouldn't 've given a plugged nickel f'r any of our chances." His fingers touched her arm in the darkness. Her muscles stiffened but she let him lead her to where he had spread the blankets. He continued talking, hoping that the mere sound of his voice would calm her. She was as taut as a fiddlestring, as frightened of the cave and the darkness and of him as she had been of the Sioux.

"These rocks ain't no featherbed, but you'll git used to 'em. I'd 've liked to 've made me a spruce bed, like you folks had, but cuttin' branches was takin' too long a chance.

"Don't sit down right away. Here's some matches—put 'em in th' pocket of your shirt but don't light 'em up here, ever. Now follow behind me an' keep your fingers touchin' th' rock on your right so you'll know where you're goin'. . . . Now, feel that corner where the wall takes a bend? Once you're 'round it, you can light a match. See?"

He struck a match and cupped it in his hands until the flame had taken hold. Her eyes were still wide but some of the terror seemed gone from them and her breath came less rapidly. He touched the match to the wick of a candle which stood in a pool of its own grease on a narrow ledge.

"You c'n light it whenever you come here, but be sure to put it out; there's only one more left when this here is gone. Here's the spring—you can stoop down an' kinda straddle it when you want to drink—and down there 'bout twenty 'r thirty feet you'll find a place where you can"—he gulped—"you'll find a kind of drift of sand. That's th' privy."

"Here!" she exclaimed. "I couldn't——"

God, what damn fools women were!

"That's th' privy, just th' same," he said.

11 THE WOMAN

The Plains Indians were never eager for night fighting or even for activities that might end in combat during the dark hours. A man killed at night was doomed to wander forever in darkness, a prospect far from pleasing to the Indian mind. Rogers was quite certain that the Sioux would not attempt to follow their trail until after sunrise. He rolled in his single blanket and slept soundly, but there was no sign of daylight on the cavern walls when he was awakened by the sudden flare of a match. Genevieve Woodard was holding the match aloft in one hand and with the other was fumbling among her blankets and in the space between them and the rock wall. Rogers was wide awake in an instant. He leaped across the cave and struck the match from her fingers.

"What's the matter with you?" he demanded harshly. "I told you——"

"The gold!" she exclaimed. "I just remembered. Jim's gold. It's mine now—where is it?"

"Dammit, girl, all the gold in the Hills ain't worth takin' the chance of lightin' a match in here. It c'd draw the Sioux——"

"Where is it?" she repeated.

"That gold y'r brother had? It was in the saddlebags. I never even gave it a thought."

"You took it!" she flared angrily.

"I didn't, but we'll settle that point when it's light. We're cooped up too close f'r fightin', you an' me, an' we're gonna have t' stay cooped f'r some time. Right now you listen to me —don't ever light a match in here again, not ever!"

"Jim's gold!" She gulped noisily. "He worked so hard for it; he took so many chances and now he's dead and the gold——"

"It's gone, gone f'r good an' you'd better f'rget it. Did you hear what I said 'bout lightin' matches in here?"

"I heard you," she said sulkily.

He did not sleep again. The stars which hung in the sky beyond the cave entrance told him that dawn was less than an hour away, and he lay there, his chin propped on his arm, and watched the sky pale. There was sunlight in the gulch before he rose and built a small fire.

"It's safe now," he said. "I'll have some grub ready in a couple of shakes and things won't look quite so bad after some coffee." He chuckled at sudden recollection. "I might as well tell you now there's only one cup."

That homely reminder of their enforced intimacy freed her tongue.

"That will be all right. I—I'm sorry I said what I did about the gold. I don't think you took it." He was looking directly at her from the further side of the fire and her eyes shifted quickly. *You're lyin', girl, and you know it. Losin' that gold, to you, is as bad as losin' your brother. You'd take these Hills apart, one rock at a time, if you thought you c'd git it back.*

He patted the dough into a flat cake and placed it in one of his two small pans. The other held a rich stew of jerky and crumbled pemmican which he had set to soak the morning before. He edged it into the coals.

"We'll eat soon," he said. "While you're waitin' y' c'n look on that ledge over my bed. All them little sacks 're full of gold I took out of th' bar I was workin'. There's close t' twenty pound, I reckon, an' it'll make a load t' carry out. Why should I bother 'bout stealin' yours?"

"I said I was sorry." She stood with her back to him as she leaned across his blankets. She had laid aside the broad hat and he saw that her dark hair was tangled and matted. *I'll have to loan her my comb—mebbe a shirt, too. She ain't got a damn thing but what she's standin' in.* She took one of the buckskin sacks in her hand and hefted it.

"Goodness, it's heavy. You—you're rich, Mr. Rogers."

"Not exactly rich, but it's a good stake. It ought t' cash in f'r around six thousand dollars. C'm on over an' set down. Grub's 'bout ready."

In the gloom he did not notice the movement of her lips as she repeated his words—*six thousand dollars.*

He gave her the one plate and for himself used the pan in which he had heated the stew. He placed the single cup between them and they drank from it in turn. Save for a small spot directly within the entrance, the interior of the cave was never brilliantly lighted. He could not see her features clearly but it was evident that the tension had eased with the coming of day. He mopped the last of the gravy from the pan and pushed it aside. She was eating more slowly, but the generous helping he had given her was nearly gone. He moved to the entrance and stretched out there, his face close to the opening but not so close that a motion would be visible to a hidden watcher on the further side of the gulch. He saw nothing, but the vigil occupied his mind and made talk unnecessary. He could hear the girl moving about the cavern. She had pulled on her heavy boots and the hobnails scraped and clattered on the rocky floor. She heated water and scraped and washed the few utensils of their breakfast. Once she came close to where he lay and asked him where she should throw the coffee grounds and the few scraps of biscuit which remained.

"Take 'em down th' other side of th' spring—you remember where I showed you."

The hobnails scraped in diminuendo. Some minutes passed before he heard them again and he grinned. The coffee grounds had given her an excuse—not that she wouldn't have gone down there anyway, sooner or later. Nature would have taken care of any simple ideas about modesty.

"Mr. Rogers——"

"Y' better git used t' callin' me Sol. I answer to it a heap quicker. What is it?"

"I filled the canteen you brought from our camp. I'd like to heat some water and wash my face and hands. Is it all right to build up the fire again?"

There was enough wood stacked in the cave to last them a week and he told her to go ahead.

" 'Longside th' head of my bed," he said, "is my possible sack. You'll find a brush an' comb there an' a mirror. Soap, too."

"Thanks very much. I hate to be so much trouble to you, but——"

"That's all right. It can't be helped an' it wasn't your fault."

"It was mostly Jim's fault, I guess. He was sure, absolutely positive, that there'd be no Indians until after the leaves turned. When he was convinced of a thing, nothing could change him."

He did not reply. A pair of grouse rocketed out of the timber across the gulch and flew swiftly beyond his vision. He fixed his eyes on the spot from which they had broken cover and watched it for a long time, but there was no movement beneath the trees nor any sign that aroused his suspicions. A couple of birds in sudden flight didn't necessarily mean Injuns. Coyotes hunted in the daytime. So did foxes, although not so often. Maybe those fool-hens just decided they wanted a drink and headed for the creek.

"I wish——"

He turned his head at the sound of Gen's voice.

"Did you say somethin'?"

"No. I mean, I was just thinking out loud."

"Wishing you'd had time t' bring some other clothes along, I'll bet."

"You're a good guesser, but all I was really wishing—out loud—was that I could wash this shirt."

"There'd be no way of dryin' it. I'd as soon build me a smoke-fire on the bare point yonder an' sit 'longside of it as I would spread a shirt out in the sun."

"I know. And I'd have nothing to wear while it was drying. I just never dreamed of having to wear the same clothes day and night."

"It's no dream right now," he said grimly. "Still, if you're wishin' f'r somethin' else t' wear, there's a couple of shirts in that pack of mine. There's some moccasins there too, new ones. They'll be big f'r you but more comfortable than boots . . . an' won't make so much noise on the rocks."

A minute later he heard a quick exclamation of pleasure.

"Oh, that will be wonderful, Mr. Rogers—Sol, I mean. You're sure you don't mind?"

" 'Course not." *Goddam it, what's the matter with me? I ain't scared of her, but I don't feel easy with her around like this. If she was Injun, 'stead of white, there wouldn't be any lallygaggin'. We'd know where we stood, both of us.*

"If it's all right," he said at last, "I'm comin' back and take a smoke. I can't smoke out here."

"Yes, I'm dressed." She giggled. "Your shirt fits me kind of quick."

He drew back from the entrance, filled and lit his pipe, and, as always, watched the course of the first few puffs of smoke. They were carried away on the never-failing draft into the depths of the cave and he relaxed. Genevieve moved into the patch of sunlight which lay at the mouth of the cave. She had combed and brushed her hair and the heavy braids were wound tightly about her head. She had found a black-and-white checked shirt in his possible sack and discarded the blue garment. The top button of the new shirt was open and the collar points lay back across her shoulders. Her throat and the deep V of her bosom were a soft golden tan. The scout knew suddenly that she was fully aware, and not unappreciative, of his inspection. He puffed sharply on his pipe.

"You look like you're feelin' better," he said.

"A little more like a woman, you mean, and less like a scarecrow."

"More like a woman, yes. You c'n skip th' scarecrow part—what you went through yesterday w'd make anybody look pretty rough."

She raised her hands and patted into position the braids which were looped over her ears. The movement stretched the shirt tightly over her breasts. *There's no call f'r her t' do that. She ought t' know that we'll be t'gether f'r a couple of weeks and that it's been a hell of a long time since I've even seen a woman. If she was only a squaw, now——*

She moved suddenly close to his side. There was no ungraceful stooping or scrambling over the rocky floor, but at one instant she was eight feet away in the triangular patch of sunlight, the next she was alongside of him, the light in her face.

"Let's sit down, Sol," she said quickly. "There's so much I want to know."

"Sit over here then—where I c'n kinda keep one eye on th' gulch."

He moved to the entrance and she followed him.

"You—you think they're still looking for us?" she whispered.

"They're Injuns. They took a lickin' yesterday—me killin' their chief an' all—an' it's Injun nature t' try t' trail us, jest t' even things up."

"If they did find us, Sol——"

"I don't reckon they're likely to. If any of them knew 'bout this cave an' how deep it was, they'd 've been here long b'fore now."

"I hope you're right, but if they should find us, what would they do?"

"Dif'rent things—whatever might come into their mind. None of 'em w'd be what you'd call comfortable."

"They'd kill you, wouldn't they?"

"Reckon so . . . it'd be surprisin' if they didn't."

"And me—would they kill me, Sol?"

"Mebbe so, an' again mebbe not. It'd depend on jest how they were feelin'. Y' can't tell with Injuns."

Her breast rose and fell. She was so close that he could hear the panting intake and exhalation of each breath.

"Tell me," she commanded. "You don't have to beat around the bush like that. I—I'm not ignorant. They'd—they'd do things to me, wouldn't they?"

"Likely they would. Mebbe th' first one t' lay hands on you w'd claim you as his'n; mebbe they'd figger you was c'mmunity property, common t' th' whole bunch, an' they'd take turns with you, one after another. I've heard of 'em doin' both." His eyes rested on her for a moment.

"That—" she began, but he interrupted her.

"Stir up the fire a little, will you," he said quickly, "and put some water on to boil. Just a little—enough to clean that rifle of your brother's. I should 've taken care of it last night."

"You—" he heard her teeth click sharply, then she was gone from beside him. *Ain't she somethin'. Goddam if she didn't want t' talk 'bout a couple of dozen reds takin' turns with her.*

Sol, y' sure got a heap t' learn 'bout white wimmen. Some minutes passed before she spoke, sulkily.

"The water's boiling."

He lifted the rifle from the ledge above his bed, drew the hickory ramrod from the brass ferrules underneath the barrel, and carefully swabbed the bore clean of the black powder residue. He did the same for his revolver and oiled both weapons.

"That rifle's yours now," he said at last. "If you're of any mind t' sell it, I'd like t' buy it."

"I don't think I'd want to sell it. It was Jim's. He made it for Captain McKeown, Mike McKeown, of D company. He sent word over to the fort that it was finished, but Mike was drunk—that's his failing—and when he came off his drunk he didn't have money to pay for the gun. Then Jim took it out and shot some antelope and buffalo with it. He said it was the best gun he'd ever made and that he was going to keep it for himself. He made another for McKeown."

"I don't blame him. It's a mighty fine gun—I found that out yesterday." *We're talking now, just talking. Keep it that way.*

"It's yours, Sol. I want to give it to you."

"I'd a lot sooner buy it." He made the slightest gesture toward his store of gold.

"No. You saved my life after Jim was killed. I want you to have it."

"Well, if you feel that way, thanks." *This 'll make it easier for her. She'll remember about givin' me the gun when she has to take some money from me t' get back East on. She'll need some clothes, too, wimmen's fixin's.* He closed the breech and leaned the rifle carefully against the wall, then returned to his vigil at the mouth of the cave. She sat down crosslegged, facing him.

"You never stop watching, do you, Sol?"

"Not while there's any light. It's a sure bet they haven't

picked up our trail, if that's what's worryin' you. I tried t' make it hard f'r 'em last night. That's why I made you take off them boots and why I walked you over bare rock wherever I c'd find it. Y' don't leave much in th' way of tracks there."

"You thought of everything, didn't you?"

"I didn't go out of my way t' be foolish—like a dozen 'r so things your brother did. Another day 'r so an' I c'n make a scout t' see if they 're still in th' Hills. If they ain't we c'n pull out."

"For where?"

A movement in the timber on the further side of the gulch caught his eye. The quick "Sh-h-h" had scarcely left his lips when a doe stepped boldly into a little clearing and, head raised, cropped daintily at the browse. A fawn trotted at her heels.

"Is it the Indians, Sol?" she whispered hoarsely.

"Nope. See th' deer—there comes another. That's a pretty doggone good sign there ain't a Injun within a mile."

"I'm glad, awfully glad. Now that they're gone, how long will we have to stay here—in the cave, I mean?"

"I ain't guessin'. We'll lay close f'r another day 'r so, like I said. Not takin' fool chances when y're dealin'. with Injuns is th' best way there is of keepin' y'r hair. Come day after t'morrow, 'long 'bout sundown, I'll scout around a little."

Her eyes narrowed but she expressed no dissatisfaction with the restriction. Rogers puffed slowly on his pipe, savoring the tobacco to the utmost, and watched the smoke curl slowly away into the lower passages. He did not notice the girl's movement toward the mouth of the cave, but he turned quickly when she spoke.

"They're gone."

"Huh?"

"The deer. They've gone away. Everything's quiet."

"I figgered they'd move off. I'd quit thinkin' about them."

"What were you thinking about? I've been watching you for a long time—except for the smoke puffing out now and then you might have been a stone man."

"Reckon I was thinkin' 'bout gettin' away from here an' whether 'r not I'd come back next year for another crack at the gold."

"You think you could, Sol?" She moved quickly across the cave until she was close to him. "The Indians——"

"I know. It'd have t' be planned right. One 'r two men wouldn't stand a chance, but a larger party ought t' be able t' handle things. Say a dozen 'r twenty men, used t' this country an' used t' takin' care of themselves. A couple of 'em c'd ride th' Hills, scoutin', while th' other worked th' bars. Two scouts that knew what t' look for c'd spot Injuns long b'fore they was close enough t' make any trouble. Then th' whole outfit w'd just fort up. Injuns ain't got much stummick f'r tacklin' fifteen 'r twenty good shots forted up in th' right sort of place. That's been proved plenty of times."

"The army—" Genevieve began. The scout spat into the ashes of the fire.

"The army!" he snorted. "Last man in th' world I'd pick w'd be an army man. Army has its rules an' it's got to foller 'em—that was what Grant did at Shiloh Church 'r somebody else did at Gettysburg, so that's what we got t' do here. Put an army man in th' fix we was in yesterday an' them Sioux w'd have been dancin' his scalp 'fore sundown. I'd pick hunters an' trappers an' fellers like that. Nobody c'n say f'r sure that it'd work, but they'd stand a good chance. One thing's certain, there'd be gold enough f'r everybody."

"You think so?"

"I know it. Look what I've taken. Look what your brother got in a few weeks. Figure from that what twenty men c'd take out of some of these gulches if they really tore into it. They'd come out rich, really rich."

"Rich," she repeated, her voice little more than a whisper. "In one summer—really rich. Oh, Sol, do you think you could do it?"

"Reckon so. Only trouble might be in roundin' up th' kind of men I'd want. If word of what I got there"— he jerked his thumb toward his store of gold—"if word of that got 'round every barroom bum from Saint Louis to San Francisco w'd volunteer."

He prepared their supper—the jerky, pemmican, and unleavened biscuits on which he had existed for weeks—while the sun was still an hour above the western peaks; then scattered the coals of the tiny fire so that they would die quickly into cold ash. She scrubbed the few utensils clean in the sand that lay deeper in the cave. The sky beyond the cavern mouth was rosy with sunset when she returned and sat down at his side.

"I took a look around while you were gone," he said. "If there was any Injuns in th' Hills, 'bout this time y'd be liable t' see smoke. There weren't a sign of it."

"I'm glad, so glad. There's nothing for us to worry about, then."

"We'll lie close t'morrow, just the same."

She nodded.

"Until then, though, we'll just forget them." Her shoulder touched his. She half turned and increased the pressure. "Let's —let's forget Indians, Sol. Shall we?"

Her hand touched his thigh. *God Almighty, f'r all she knows th' Sioux are dancin' her brother's skelp right this minute. That's what a squaw would be thinkin' about—th' man she'd lost.* Aloud he said:

"Reckon we might 's well—with a woman like you there wouldn't be much use in my objectin', w'd there?"

He rose and spread their few blankets. She moved to them and laughed as her fingers sought the buttons of her woolen shirt.

"Not a bit! You are human, aren't you, Sol? There's something else to do than lie like a snake on a stump and stare into the gulch. Now, come closer, Sol, . . . closer."

2

He did not leave the cave until late in the afternoon of the second day following; then scouted cautiously to the south from the cover of the thick timber along the crest of the ridge. From the head of what he called Woodard's Gulch he could see that the cabin had been burned to the ground. Woodard's body was gone from the ledge and only the heap of gray ashes and the trench which had been dug across the bar showed that the gulch had ever known a white visitor. Within a year, or two years at the longest, even those signs would be gone. The spring floods would level the disturbed bar, alder scrub would quickly erase all signs of the cabin.

Dusk was falling when he returned. He paused at the head of the trail and whistled the first bars of "My Old Kentucky Home." Indians, he had told the girl, did not whistle.

"Stack some more wood on th' fire, if you want to," he said, "or light up th' last candle. We don't have to save it now."

"They're gone then; we're safe! Oh, Sol——"

"Nary a sign of 'em. I scouted clear to th' head of the gulch where you were camped. It looks like they gave up an' pulled out."

"My brother——"

He shook his head.

"Th' ledge was empty an' there wasn't a sign of his—of him." He stirred the stew on the fire and added, "They burned the cabin an' everything they didn't carry off."

"You mean . . ." her inflection completed the sentence.

"Mebbe. I didn't go down there an' poke around. It's likely they put him in th' cabin when they thought of burning it."

"And when they found him they found the gold, too."

He nodded again.

"Injuns know what gold is, all right, an' what it's worth. They'd never leave it. Even them wild Sioux can get rid of gold."

"Yes." She brushed her fingertips together as though to signify that she was resigned to the loss. "Will we leave the Hills now, Sol?"

"Sure, first crack of light t'morrow mornin'. It's a long walk t' where I left my hosses."

3

The vengeful deities who guarded the Hills had deserted their posts on the dark peaks. The two saw no Indians nor any sign that Sioux or Cheyenne had ever set foot in the pass by which they crossed to the western slope. More than thirty miles lay between the cave and the canyon where Rogers had left his horses, a distance too great to be covered swiftly by heavily burdened marchers.

Early in the afternoon a covey of grouse crossed their path and Rogers killed two of the foolish birds with a stick. They fried them that night and devoured the last morsel, doubly delicious after the unvaried diet of jerky and pemmican. They slept on soft pine needles beneath the trees and the stars and in the morning bathed in a mountain stream and splashed the water in reckless wastefulness. The bottom of the pool was tawny sand and their shadows followed them across it as they dived. The icy water tingled against their bodies.

"Some fellers," Rogers drawled, "w'd say that this sort of stuff was takin' long chances with our skelps, but I've got a feelin' we've seen our last Injun. Don't ask me why—I just know it." He rose and turned his back to the sun. "Damn, it's good t' be kinda clean again—even cold-water clean. First

thing I aim t' do is t' trade in enough of this dust t' pay f'r five
dollars' wuth of hot baths."

". . . and another five dollars' worth of haircuts and
shaves," she laughed. "And when you do see a barber, Sol,
have him shave you so that there's just about an inch of side-
burn in front of your ears, and to leave you a narrow goatee
and mustache. You'd look really distinguished."

"Like a faro dealer!"

"No. You'd be handsome. I mean it. The handsomest man
I ever saw in my life was Wild Bill Hickok, the scout. He had a
mustache and goatee like that. You'd look just like him."

"Mebbe I wouldn't want to. All I want t' do is get rid of
this hair mattress I'm wearin' on my face."

He smoked patiently while she combed and braided her
long hair, and they resumed their journey. It was nearly noon
of the third day when they mounted a ridge and descended
into the gulch where he had left his two ponies. The animals
had not strayed from the lush grass and cool water. They
raised their heads, snorted, and circled away. Rogers grinned.

"Our luck's holdin'. There they are, fat as pigs an' sassy
as dance-hall girls. They'll take some catchin'—an' some
ridin', too."

They made camp where he had cached his saddle and the
packhorse's sawbuck. A doe followed by a half-grown fawn
moved from where they had bedded and Sol all but tore the
head from the smaller animal with a ball from the big rifle.
He caught the horses and staked them out for the night as a
reminder that their holiday was over. Genevieve ransacked the
packs for additional food and prepared dinner. Her face was
bright in the firelight as the scout returned from watering
the horses.

She's tried to do her part, more ways than one. I wonder if
she'll ever tell anybody the whole story of how her brother got
killed and what happened after. 'Tain't likely. A woman c'n
bury things down inside her and never let 'em come to th' top.

They don't f'rget 'em, they just rub 'em out like they'd rub out
a pencil mark on a piece of paper. That's the way she wants it
t' be; that's why she's never asked me nothin' about myself 'r
told me anything 'bout herself. I wonder if—by God, of course
she is! She's married, has a husband somewhere. That explains
it.

4

He laid their course steadily to the southward but turned west
when the square summits of the Rawhide Buttes cut the horizon. The girl noticed the change of course within a mile.

"Fort Laramie," said Rogers shortly. "I ain't aimin' t' tangle
with no newsy officers who'd want to know where I'd been—
we'd been—an' what doin'. You don't p'ticularly want t' go t'
Laramie, do you?"

"No." She spoke through taut lips but the scout's expression did not change.

"Nope," he agreed. "They might even want to know where
this extry horse come from. He's branded."

The horse was a dark bay which had joined them on Beaver
Creek. There were healed saddle galls on both withers and the
off front hoof still carried a broken shoe. The beast had been
pathetically glad to find human beings. Rogers had accepted
him gratefully.

"Which way will we go, Sol?" she asked. "Maybe you'll
laugh at me, but I'm thinking about clothes. I don't want to
ride into some town looking like this unless I absolutely
have to."

"Reckon not. What looks best t' me is to cross th' North
Platte twenty miles 'r so west of Laramie, then head south an'
east toward Cheyenne. There's a few ranches round there but
we c'd ride jest about into town 'fore you, 'r y'r clothes, was
noticed."

"Cheyenne!" she exclaimed delightedly. "That's a city—

there'll be stores. You'll let me have some money to buy some clothes, won't you, Sol?"

"Shore. I'd kinda like t' see you again in women's fixin's."

"You won't be ashamed of me, Sol." Her laughter was as clear as the note of a silver bell. "Why, in Cheyenne—if we stayed there a day or two—we could find a preacher. Then when you went back to the Hills——"

The word struck him like a blow in the belly. *Preacher! All a preacher was good for was christenin's or buryin's or marriages!* He checked his horse sharply and turned on her.

"Preacher!" he repeated. "What're you thinkin' about, Gen —marryin'?"

"Of course, Sol. Haven't you been thinking about it too?"

"No," he said bluntly, "I ain't. Goddam it, girl, all this time I've been thinkin' you was already married."

"What?" Her voice was shrill now. "What did you say?"

"You heard me. Back there in th' cave an' every night since we pulled out of th' Hills. You knew what you was doin', all right, th' way any woman—any married woman—knows what she's doin' when she asks a man under her blankets. I figgered you had a husband somewhere, that's all."

"I haven't. What's more, I never have had one. Take anything out of that you want to." A smile tempered the biting words. "I—I'd make you a good wife, Sol. Maybe you don't think so, but you'd learn. I'd go back to the Hills with you next year. I'd help you get rich, really rich, like you said, and then——"

"You c'n quit talkin' 'bout it, Gen. Maybe we've both of us misunderstood th' other one. I ain't th' marryin' kind, that's all. There ain't a woman in th' world c'd crowd me into a house 'r my feet into shoes. Let's f'rgit it, both of us."

"Of course." She laughed again. "That's the only thing to do, isn't it, Sol Rogers? Sleep with a woman, get everything you want from her, then tell her 'forget it, both of us.' That's easy, isn't it—easy for the man?"

"I—" He stammered uneasily. *Goddam it, if she cussed me out 'r if she squawked an' carried on, I'd know what t' do, even if it meant takin' a quirt to her. But she don't. She's like a kid that's got a bug on a pin, watchin' it squirm.*

"I ain't figgerin' on marryin', not anybody," he blurted. "You talk 'bout th' Hills next year. I don't know for sure if I'll go there—I know I won't unless I c'n find the right men."

"I see." Long afterward he seemed to recall hearing the sharp intake of her breath. "We've both of us misunderstood the other, Sol, so let's forget it, and no hard feelings."

"Jesus!" He sighed his relief. "You—you're shootin' pretty square, Gen. I—I—" He struggled for words.

"Never mind, Sol. Forget it."

When they camped that night it was she who spread the saddle blankets and covered them to form the bed they had shared since leaving the Hills. She laughed at his surprise.

"I said to forget it, didn't I, Sol? I didn't mean to forget everything—just the misunderstanding. It'd be silly to make two beds now, wouldn't it? What was that you said?"

"I said"— he gulped—"what I said was 'I'll be God damned.'"

5

They forded the North Platte just above the ruins of the old Warm Springs stage station and, at the Laramie River, picked up Chugwater Creek and followed it to the south and west until the line of the Laramie Hills stood high upon the right hand. West of the Red Buttes they met the tracks of the Union Pacific and the horses set their feet stubbornly and had to be beaten into crossing the steel rails.

There they swung eastward, paralleling the railroad and with their goal the embryo capital of Wyoming Territory. They left the ashes of their campfires beside Nitowan Creek, Four Women Creek, and other watercourses which often were mere trickles from one alkaline pool to another. As they neared Cheyenne they encountered occasional cattle and twice saw, far on the horizon, mounted men. From the ridge behind their last camp they watched the lights of the territorial capital winking into existence as darkness fell.

"We c'd wait till it's full dark," Rogers remarked, "an' then ride into town an' find a hotel. By keepin' to th' alleys we wouldn't run into many people."

"No, and we wouldn't find any stores open either. Stores where I could buy a dress."

"Nope. Neither would we have any money t' pay f'r it, not till I got a chance to cash in some of this dust. Assay office— I reckon they got one here—won't be open till morning."

He filled his pipe and smoked thoughtfully for nearly a minute. Genevieve Woodard said nothing.

"What we could do," he said at last, "w'd be to camp here tonight. Then, t'morrow mornin' after we figgered th' assay office 'r banks w'd be open, I c'd cash in a couple of hundred dollars' worth of dust an' see if I c'd find a woman clerk at one of the stores who'd come out here—I c'd hire a team—an' bring you some dresses."

"What would you tell her?" Genevieve chuckled. "I don't imagine they're called on very often to deliver dresses out here in the sagebrush."

"Tell her the truth," said Rogers bluntly. "Part of it, anyways. Tell her we just come down from up north, campin' all th' way, an' that you've got to have some female fixin's 'fore y' come into town. So long as th' dresses are paid for——"

"And a chemise and drawers and a petticoat and stockings and shoes, size six. There's more to what you call female fixings than a dress, Sol."

"Reckon there is," he grinned. "Reckon I hadn't given much thought to how much more, either. If we git you outfitted with one dress, though—an' what goes with it—then you could go in an' get what other stuff you need."

He took two of the buckskin sacks of dust with him the next morning and, as a last thought, left with Genevieve his Colt .44-caliber revolver. It was after noon when he returned, driving a rented team and accompanied by a highly curious woman from a Cheyenne store. Genevieve was nowhere in sight but his pistol and belt rested on the neatly folded blankets. Each night since leaving the Hills he had scraped beneath their bed a shallow depression in which he had hidden the gold—not because of any distrust of Genevieve Woodard but to safeguard it against the most clever thieves in all the West, the young bucks from the bands of "friendly" Sioux. He threw back the blankets and stared for a moment into the empty hole where he had placed the sacks.

"I reckon, ma'am," he said at last, "that th' lady I mentioned hasn't waited f'r th' dress. When we git back t' town y' c'n tell me what I owe you."

"I couldn't think of charging you anything; after all, there was nothing bought. But—but——"

"Never mind 'bout that, ma'am," said Sol Rogers. "I don't know an' even if I did I wouldn't tell you."

6

To trainmen and travelers on the Pacific Railway in the '70s, the unusual was the commonplace. Buffalo were still to be found on the Plains and occasionally trains were halted or forced to reduce speed to a crawl when the great beasts disputed possession of the right of way with the puffing, diamond-stacked locomotive. Indians delighted in taking long-range shots at engine or cars. Antelope raced the trains and drew shots from the passengers, who also wasted much lead on the countless prairie dogs and jackrabbits. Any halt other than at one of the infrequent stations might mean a holdup.

Such things were taken for granted, but the crew and passengers of Number Two, eastbound, on September 23, gossiped mightily of an event unparalleled since the Golden Spike had linked East and West on Promontory Point in 1869. A woman had flagged the train to a stop when it was about an hour out of Cheyenne. She had climbed aboard and paid her fare through to the eastern terminus at Omaha. What's more, she'd paid it in gold dust! Told the conductor that was all she had and that he'd have to take it. She was a young woman, mighty fine-looking, and she was dressed in man's clothes—pants, by God, pants no different from those you're wearing yourself, and a man's shirt and hat and hobnailed boots like you'd see on a hunter or a prospector. She'd been wearing those clothes for a long time. The boots were scratched and battered from hard usage and there was mud and grime on the rest of her clothes. She was afoot, standing right out in the flat where there wasn't enough cover to hide a jackrabbit, let alone a horse—but she'd been riding. You could tell by the wrinkles around the knees of her pants and the shiny glaze that only saddle leather can impart.

She didn't say a word to anybody. Not a word as to who she was or what she was doing out there all alone on the Plains. When the train stopped at mealtime, she got out along with the other passengers and piled into the eating house and took what was offered. The conductor had cashed enough dust for her to pay for her meals—bet he made a plenty on the deal, too. After eating she just came back to her seat. When anybody tried to talk to her, she turned her back and looked out the window. And when the train got to Omaha, she walked through the depot with everybody staring at her like she was Sitting Bull himself in all his warpaint, and she climbed into a hack. That was the last anybody saw of her. Whatever her game was, she played a lone hand.

12 THE COLONEL

October was young when Sol Rogers returned from his scouting trip in the Yellowstone basin with the news—quickly circulated throughout South City—that the Reverend John Wesley Poole had lost his life in an attempt to ford the Missouri near Little Muddy Creek, a few miles below Fort Union. At the time, he reported, the river was carrying the runoff of storms which had raised the Yellowstone and upper Missouri to flood stage.

"If'n th' rev'rend had only waited two 'r three days," he added regretfully, "he could 've made it—but you know how he was."

All agreed that the Reverend Poole was impetuous at all times and especially so when driven by evangelistic zeal.

"I wonder what his wife, his widder, I mean, will do now."

There was no immediate answer to that question. The

group that supported the mission expressed its deep sympathy for the widowed Doris and the fatherless Beth in their hour of sorrow, and stated that the stipend of four hundred dollars yearly would be continued until December, and closed with the information that there was no thought at present of assigning another missionary to the Sioux. The present state of unrest in the Indian country would seem to make the idea impracticable. Since nothing was said about the house, Mrs. Poole and Beth continued to occupy it.

"I declare," Doris Poole told her daughter, "I don't know which way to turn. For twenty years now I've done just what your father thought was right or what the Board told him to do. Now, well, I've got to learn to do things for myself and it's not easy."

"Have we got any money?" asked the practical Beth.

"Some. There'll be a hundred dollars coming from the Board—the last quarter's salary—and sooner or later the insurance company ought to pay your father's insurance. That will be two thousand dollars more."

"Two thousand . . . how on earth did Father ever keep up the payments on two thousand dollars' worth of insurance?"

"He didn't." There was the slightest curl in Doris Poole's lip. "It was a wedding present from his father when we were married: a fully paid-up policy with a provision that it couldn't be borrowed against under any circumstances. Your father didn't like that."

"I guess not. Have you any idea when we—I mean you—will get the money, mother?"

"No. Mr. Tustin, the undertaker, told me that they'd demand what they call proof of death. Sol Rogers—he's been very good to us, Beth—went to a notary and swore to a statement that he'd seen your father and his team carried away by the flood when he tried to ford the river, and that there wasn't any doubt whatever that he'd been drowned. He said that he and a couple of Indians were the only witnesses and that it would be impossible to get an affidavit from them. I hope the company will accept it."

"I do too. We could live for a long time on two thousand dollars, certainly for long enough until we knew what we wanted to do."

"Yes," Doris Poole agreed. "We—I wish we knew just what it would be."

It was Amos Gentry who supplied an answer to the immediate problems of Doris Poole and her daughter. Martin Hale had told him of the missionary's death—by drowning—and he sought the youth in the E company barracks.

"I was over to South City last night," he said, "and got my supper at the Ace High. Tucker, the fellow that runs it, was in a hell of a stew. He's got a Chinaman cooking for him and the Chink gave him notice that he was quitting—no likee wintel, he said, and he's pulling out for warmer climate. Tucker don't know where to turn for a cook. Nobody wants to come here in cold weather. I was thinkin'—them folks you know in town, that Mrs. Poole. Haven't I heard you brag on the meals you've et there?"

"Yeah. She's an awful good cook, 'specially when you think she never has much to put on the table."

"Why don't you tell her to go down and talk to Tucker? He pays good—he said something about paying the Chink six dollars a week, his grub, and a place to sleep—and it's a respectable place. No bar and Tucker won't stand for drunks."

The suggestion was relayed by Hale to Mrs. Poole and was settled in a single interview with the owner of the restaurant.

"If you can cook, you're hired," he said decisively, "and if you can't—well, I was going to say it wouldn't take half a day to find that out, but I won't say it. I know who you are, ma'am, and I know you'd never come here with false claims. Your daughter now, Mrs. Poole? I haven't lived in South City for eleven months without knowing of her."

"My daughter—I'm afraid I don't know what you mean, Mr. Tucker."

"I open early at the Ace High and I close late. When the Chinaman goes, the yellow boy that's been helping him around the kitchen will go with him. If you wouldn't want to be leaving your daughter alone all day, she'd certainly earn her meals and a couple of dollars a week helping you here."

"It seems too good to be true," said Doris Poole some two weeks later. "Think, between us we're making eight dollars each week, Beth. Eight dollars and our meals. That's more money than I ever dreamed of."

"And we're not feeding any begging Indians out of it either! Mother, I'm going to buy that dark blue coat I saw at Schwarz's Emporium. It's fourteen dollars but I want it—the first coat I've ever had that didn't come out of a missionary barrel."

"Well," her mother considered. "Really, I don't see why not. What with winter coming, you'll have to have something."

2

With October, winter moved in upon the land. The level of water in the Missouri dropped visibly from day to day, each inch of fall marking the freezing of the headwaters of tributary streams far to the northwest. The quartermaster at Fort Doniphan, Captain Bellew, ordered a thousand bales of hay for winter feeding of the regiment's horses and another thousand bales of straw which would be stacked like building blocks against the outer walls of the stables as insulation against the subzero weather and lashing winds that could be expected from December to March. Horses had been known to freeze to death on the unsheltered picket lines before the stables had been built. Buffalo coats, fur caps and mittens, arctic overshoes, and felt boots half an inch thick were taken from summer storage and laid out for issue to the troops.

"An' ye can thank God," said First Sergeant McNamara, "that it's Colonel Tuthill ye're servin' under an' not Gen'ral Crook. Th' Gray Fox, th' Injuns call him, an' he's a wild man f'r winter campaigns. They're as rough on the troops as they are on th' Injuns. I'm gettin' old, I guess. I've lost me taste f'r horse an' mule that have starved to death and to makin' a camp when it's forty below.

"Th' Old Man is different now. Thank God, as I said before. He got his bellyful of winter campaignin', I'm thinkin', in 'sixty-eight when we fought Black Eagle. Since then, come cold weather he takes a leave and goes back East with his wife. He's done it before and he'll do it again, if I know him."

3

First Sergeant McNamara had spoken somewhat figuratively of his knowledge of the regimental commander. Even as Tuthill had said that no one knew the scout, Sol Rogers, it could be said that no one knew Frederic Chase Tuthill, Colonel, USA, Brevet Major General of Volunteers, save possibly his wife, Martha. In this year of grace 1875 he was thirty-six years old, the youngest full colonel in the army and as proud of that fact as he was that at twenty-four he had been the youngest of the army's brigadier generals, brevetted to that rank from first lieutenant. There had been much debate concerning that meteoric promotion of a man who had graduated from West Point scarcely two years before and been commissioned a second lieutenant of cavalry. A rank example of preference, some declared, or political influence shrewdly exerted, and there were some who stated, sneeringly, that the error of an overworked clerk in the War Department had placed the name of Tuthill on a commission intended for another man. None found evidence to prove any of those things; all ignored the fact that two other men, captains of cavalry, had won similar promotions to brigadier on the same day. They ignored the fact that the Cavalry Corps of the Union forces had been created only a month before, that many of its units were militia organizations accustomed only to full-dress parades, to escort duty as an honor to governors and senators, and that many of the cavalry officers were hopelessly unfit, physically or by training, for combat command. Men quoted, with delight, the query of General Hooker, when commander of the Army of the Potomac: "Who ever saw a dead cavalryman?"

Now, with the stroke of a pen, those coffee-coolers and Fancy Dans had been made fighting troops. Since many of their own officers were incompetent, others must be found to lead them. Two things, closely related, the gaunt, bearded chief of Union cavalry demanded in the men would lead his brigades and regiments against the gray-clad troopers who rode behind the matchless J. E. B. Stuart and "Rooney" Lee. These two were youth and the fiery audacity which is youth's concomitant. In Tuthill he found them both.

Jealousy was inevitable. There were captains, majors, and even colonels who had known the red-haired stripling as a lieutenant and now saw him skyrocket past them to head a brigade of three regiments.

"By God," marveled one, "I was cadet captain of his company at the Point and if there was ever a sloppier man in the academy, I wouldn't know where to start looking for him. His room looked like a hogpen and he—most of the time—as though he'd just come out of one. Five demerits for a dirty room, five for late at formation, ten for slovenly dress and dirty equipment—that was Red Tuthill's record all the way through.

"If there hadn't been a war, he'd never have graduated. When I saw his name on the list—second lieutenant of cavalry —I thought, well, they've got to have somebody to drill the new volunteers and that's where he'll land, sure."

"He fooled you," his companion remarked. "He fooled plenty of people—he turned out to be a soldier."

"Yes, but what in God's name turned him?"

The one man who could have answered that question had taken a rebel bullet through his breast at Second Manassas; the man who, had he lived, would have commanded the Army of the Potomac: one-armed, hawk-faced Phil Kearney, commanding the New Jersey brigade. He had served with the Chasseurs d'Afrique in Algeria, he had charged at the head of a dragoon company into Mexico City and had paid for that admission with his left arm, he had won the cross of the Legion of Honor at Solferino. A month after the debacle of First Manassas Tuthill had been transferred to his staff as an aide.

"Your name, young man?" Kearney had asked icily.

"Tuthill, sir. Second Lieutenant, G company, Second Cavalry."

"Yes. G, I believe, had three officers."

"Yes, sir. I——"

"Three officers," Kearney had repeated. "One more than regulations call for in a cavalry company. So"—his eyes, blacker than obsidian, swept the youngster from head to foot.

"You ride well, Mr. Tuthill," he said quietly.

"Thank you, sir."

"How long"—there was a distant crack in the brigadier's voice—"how long, Mr. Tuthill, since you have shaved?"

"I . . ." he met Kearney's eye and his voice rose a half-octave—"it's been two or three days, I guess, sir."

Kearney was silent for a moment.

"Mr. Tuthill," he said at last, "for your information I do not repeat orders. You will report to my adjutant, Captain Jerome, and request assignment to quarters. You will shave, you will clean your uniform and equipment, you will polish your boots, and will then report for duty. Should I ever see you again looking as you are now, you will be transferred within twenty-four hours to a wagon train of the Quartermaster Corps."

"Yes, sir." Tuthill saluted.

"Within a mile of where we are now," Kearney continued, "there are hundreds of Negroes, former slaves, who are following the Union Army. They are hungry, they are pathetically eager for work of any kind which will assure them food and a dollar now and then for tobacco, and they are faithful and loyal. Find one, Mr. Tuthill, and make him your orderly. And each day, Mr. Tuthill, look at yourself in the mirror as you shave and say, 'By God, I'm an officer in the Union Army; I'll look like one.' That is all, Mr. Tuthill."

One may speculate endlessly upon the forces which change the lives of men. In the meticulously clad and imperious Kearney, young Tuthill saw the *beau sabreur*, the true cavalier, the apotheosis of all that a cavalryman should be. He told no one of his reception by the brigadier, of the biting rebuke he had received, but the slovenly cadet and junior officer vanished at that moment and never returned.

Kearney, throughout his military service, was notorious as a martinet. This, too, Tuthill copied as he rose to command. He drove his men relentlessly, but always he led them. Stars may have been on his shoulder straps, but he was never in the rear. There was, he maintained, but one tactic for which cavalry was fitted; that was the charge, mounted, and he resented with poorly concealed bitterness when orders came to fight on foot.

What Kearney did not, could not, give him were those qualities which were inherent in him: fearlessness, an utter disregard of opposing strength, and a constitution which did not know the meaning of fatigue. He could ride from dawn to sunset, satisfy his hunger with cold coffee and hardtack, sleep for three hours under a tree, and ride again. There were men who cursed his steel and whalebone stamina, for he could not conceive that others might be weary when he was still strong.

Less commendable, perhaps, was the circumstance that his displays of personal courage, of the hell-for-leather fearlessness of the true cavalryman, were most brilliant when the eyes of others were upon him. At Patsega Creek a New York rifle regiment moved cautiously toward a ford which was well protected by Confederate marksmen. Tuthill had been ordered to accompany the infantrymen and to report immediately to Kearney when the enemy strength on the further bank was determined.

The Confederate commander interpreted the cautious sortie as an attack in force and hastily withdrew his regiment. When the New Yorkers penetrated the woods beyond the stream they saw, less than two hundred yards away, a train of eight cars and an engine on a siding. Tuthill's high-pitched voice rattled commands. He formed three platoons and led them in a pellmell charge that resulted in the capture of the train and the release of more than a hundred Union prisoners who had been loaded into two of the cars for transport to Richmond.

Kearney promptly brevetted him to captain and ignored the protests of the infantry colonel who demanded that the aide be reprimanded for assuming command of troops he was supposed to accompany only as an observer.

"No one could avoid seeing that train," he declared. "I had already sent orders to Major Barnett to take his battalion and advance. And then—well, before Barnett could move, that wild young lieutenant had taken matters into his own hands, awed a captain—a captain, sir—into relinquishing command of his company, and had taken the train."

"Exactly," said Kearney. He made no further comment and the New York colonel withdrew.

Tuthill retained his captaincy until Kearney's death, then

reverted to first lieutenant and was assigned to a cavalry regiment. He hated the routine duties: inspection of quarters and stables, standing reveille formation while his captain slept, the constant drilling of heavy-handed, awkward recruits who had never ridden anything more spirited than plow horses. The regiment was split into squadrons—battalions at that time— and the only duties were those of guarding temporary camps of Confederate prisoners, of acting as mounted errand-boys for the regimental commander; or of riding as escort, arms reversed and colors draped, for the bodies of officers who had been killed in action or had died of wounds or disease.

Tuthill seethed inwardly. What chance of fame was there for a man imprisoned in such a rut? Then, suddenly, opportunity struck at his door and he threw the portal wide.

He had ridden to division headquarters on a routine errand and was returning by a road which followed the crest of a long ridge. Guns muttered in the south and the blue sky was sullied from time to time with the smoke of exploding shells. Those in the valley were oblivious to the war so close at hand. A group of staff officers, mounted, seemed to be waiting for something to occur within an area some three hundred feet on a side which was kept clear by a long file of infantrymen.

Within that living fence a shapeless, bulbous, object bulked hugely. Soldiers worked busily around several large fires over which canvas pipes, kept open by hoops, led to the central object. Tuthill rode slowly behind the mounted group until he noticed the single bar of a lieutenant on one officer's shoulder straps.

"What's all the excitement, Lieutenant?" he asked. The other turned in his saddle.

"B'loon," he said briefly. "Hot-air b'loon. They figure on sendin' her up on the end of a rope so somebody can spy out the rebels' positions."

"Who's going up?"

"That's what the old man—General Pleasanton—would

like to know. Some engineer captain, name of Wynkoop or something like that, was supposed to go. 'Bout fifteen minutes ago, though, just when they were really beginning to get air into the thing, an orderly came up with the word that Captain Wynkoop had been took sick, very suddenly."

"They're still pumping her up though." Tuthill gestured toward the bulging shape.

"Uh-huh. The old man told 'em to go ahead, regardless. He sent the orderly back with word to the engineers to send up another officer." He snickered. "See that cloud of dust over yonder—that's a whole regiment of engineers deserting to the rebs!"

"What—" Tuthill checked himself suddenly. "Which one is General Pleasanton?"

"The only two-star gen'ral in the bunch. Big fellow with a square beard. Bay horse, two stars on the saddle cloth."

Tuthill did not hear the last words. He swung his horse around the group and checked the animal squarely in front of the major general. His hand remained at his hat brim until Pleasanton had acknowledged the salute.

"Well, young man?"

"Sir, Lieutenant Tuthill, Fourth Cavalry. I heard, sir, that Captain Wynkoop would not be able to make—to go up in the balloon. I wish to volunteer if the general has not assigned another officer."

The lips beneath the black beard parted in a smile.

"You are the first volunteer, Mr.——, what did you say your name was?"

"Tuthill, sir."

". . . Mr. Tuthill. And I have not had any requests for the assignment. Have you ever made a balloon ascension, Mr. Tuthill?"

"No, sir."

"But the idea of going up six or seven hundred feet in a basket at the end of a rope doesn't frighten you?"

"No, sir."

"Hrrmph." Pleasanton's eyes swept the lean figure of the young officer from head to foot. "I must admit that it is not an assignment that I would seek. However . . . you see that ridge yonder, across the valley?"

"Yes, sir."

"That is Pender's Ridge. The rebels hold it and their lines —give me that map, Captain Biddle—now, Mr. Tuthill, you will see . . ."

Within the week Tuthill had made three ascensions in the captive balloon. The wicker basket pitched and plunged like a demented creature at the end of its long restraining rope. At times it spun like a top under the impact of sudden gusts which seemed to come from every quarter of the compass. Tuthill was violently nauseated on each occasion, a circumstance which had been anticipated by the superintendent of the balloon crew and provided for by a galvanized bucket as part of the equipment.

Between retchings, however, he was able to trace the Confederate lines with considerable accuracy, to locate the position of several batteries which were quite invisible to ground observers, and to report that sappers appeared to be working on the site of another battery which would command both the crest of the ridge and the valley road. Pleasanton was highly pleased, so pleased that he transferred Tuthill from company duty to his personal staff. Visions of completing his service as a balloon observer haunted Tuthill's dreams—a man was meant to ride a horse, not a gas bag—but he managed to express an outwardly sincere disappointment when the flimsy balloon was torn to fragments by a violent wind and hailstorm. Three or four hours of pitching at the end of a rope five hundred feet above the ground was a small price to pay for transfer from company duty to the infinitely greater opportunities to be found in a staff assignment.

He hoped for promotion to the temporary captaincy which

Kearney had given him, but it was not forthcoming. Then, less than a year later, he received his commission as a brigadier. He donned the insigne of his new rank—General Pleasanton contributed a pair of brigadier's stars, a Negro woman who cooked for one of the officers' messes embroidered others on the collars of his shirts and the shoulder straps of his mess jacket—and rode northward to Jethro Chapel and the headquarters of his new command, the Ohio Cavalry Brigade.

Two weeks later—two weeks of day-and-night drill and of discipline as demanding as Kearney's—he led the three regiments north and west across the rolling hills of southern Pennsylvania to a little hamlet called Gettysburg. A fortnight before he had been a cavalry subaltern, entitled by rank to the command of a platoon. Now a brigadier's star was on his shoulder and on the flag which a sergeant carried two horse-lengths behind him. The hoofs of nearly three thousand horses drummed a hollow thunder; three thousand troopers, led by colonels, majors, and captains, looked to him for orders. A word from him could send them to death and glory. And he—Freddie Tuthill, farmer Abner Tuthill's red-headed son, Red Tuthill of West Point—he commanded them! His blue eyes glittered with an unholy light which regiments and brigades were to learn to recognize. His nostrils twitched and his gauntleted hand dropped to the hilt of the long, straight sword which he had snatched from the body of a Confederate officer long before. Red Tuthill—"Old Eagle-beak"—was sniffing battle.

He was assigned to hold the Hanover Road lest J. E. B. Stuart, darling of the Confederacy, break through upon the Union flank. From his position on the crest of one of the many low hills of the Pennsylvania countryside, he saw a gray division—it turned out to be Wade Hampton's of Stuart's corps—appear on the road in the valley below. Tuthill wheeled his horse in front of B company of the Third, screamed a command, and himself led the single company in a hell-for-leather charge on the division. Long before the charge reached its goal, Hampton's hard-bitten troopers had poured a volley into the blue ranks and had blasted half of the meager force from the face of the earth. Tuthill's horse was killed under him and he escaped capture by a hair's-breadth. A sergeant who survived the volley saw the unhorsed officer and checked his own frantic mount for sufficient time for Tuthill to swing up behind him.

The reckless gesture served only to inform the Ohio brigade that their new commander was not a coward. On the next day —it was July 3—he encountered Hampton again. Two brigades, Hampton's and Fitzhugh Lee's, advanced in column of squadrons on the Union lines. Tuthill charged them, at the head of a regiment this time, and smashed them with an impact that could be heard above the thunder of the artillery's guns. Saber strokes flickered like lightning in the dust, trooper pistoled trooper as their knees touched, and Tuthill's red hair was an oriflamme in the advance. The gray wave broke before his charge and those of two infantry regiments on the flank and Tuthill led what was left of the regiment—two hundred men were dead on the field—back to the Union lines.

On July 4 his brigade with another of the Union cavalry pressed hard on the heels of Lee as the Army of Northern Virginia, licking its wounds, withdrew from the high-water mark of the Rebellion. Tuthill sent five riders back with messages imploring Meade to hasten an advance and trap Lee before he reached the Rappahannock, but the Pennsylvanian ignored the suggestion.

The fighting through the late summer and fall of 1863 firmly established Tuthill's fame as a cavalry leader. He met Stuart once and trounced the bonny "Jeb" right soundly; he met him again at Brandy Station and was trounced in his turn; he sparred with "Fitz" Lee and Hampton; and he became the darling of every correspondent of Northern newspapers. When all else failed, Eagle-beak Tuthill, the Boy General, could always be depended upon to furnish material for a colorful story of fighting men and their intrepid leader. The blue forces of the Civil War produced very few popular or colorful heroes; of those few, Tuthill was easily first. None was more aware of that fame than Tuthill himself; none could have preened himself more assiduously to attract and to hold the public eye when he strutted in the gloomy corridors of the State, War, and Navy Building in Washington or sought the admiring glances of feminine worshipers in Willard's Hotel.

During the winter of 1863-64 he obtained a month's leave of absence. Accompanied by his aide, Lieutenant Northrup, and a Negro orderly, he tarried briefly in Washington and Philadelphia, then continued to New York which Lieutenant Northrup called home.

"With your permission, sir," young Northrup remarked, "I will telegraph my parents that we are leaving for New York tomorrow and will arrive at the Desbrosses Street ferry at about four o'clock. I know very well what they will do."

"What is that, Mr. Northrup?"

"They will insist—I know my father and mother, sir—that you make our home your headquarters while you are in New York. They would be more than honored to entertain you."

"You may telegraph them, of course, Mr. Northrup. As to the other—well, we will see when we get there."

The aide smiled and fingered the gold aiguillettes which draped his shoulder.

"You will find, General, that a frontal assault on a rebel fortification is easier than refusing my mother if she has decided on something. You . . . well, she has written me many times about how honored she and father are to have their son serving as aide to General Tuthill. You and the brigade are famous, sir."

"Shall I tell them that I selected you as aide because of your flattery?" Tuthill smiled in his turn. There were moments when he wondered if young Northrup was aware that his appointment was due in no small measure to Tuthill's knowledge of the senior Northrup's wealth and position; other moments when he wondered if his aide ever pondered over the circumstance that he, a first lieutenant, was nearly two years older than the brigadier for whom he fetched and carried.

"It's not flattery, sir," the lieutenant protested. "I'll leave that for my sister. There'll be no holding her, I know, when she meets you."

The brigadier, his thoughts at the moment far away, scarcely heard.

4

One of Mrs. Northrup's ancestors—she was always a bit uncertain of the relationship—had been a Ball of Virginia and she had named her daughter, born in 1846, Martha Washington Northrup in honor of the most distinguished scion of the Ball family. The girl—she was three months short of her eighteenth birthday when Tuthill visited the Northrup mansion on West Nineteenth Street—did not meet the requirements of staid dignity and deportment which her name implied. She was dark—jet-black hair and olive skin—but with the high coloring which appears occasionally with some Italians, very rarely in those brunettes who are not of Italian extraction. In her stocking feet she could walk beneath a string held five feet from the ground. She weighed exactly ninety-nine pounds, evenly distributed over a slim, sylphlike body which she, in private conversations with those friends with whom she occasionally spent the night, declared she hated. The era in which she lived was one in which the feminine body was supposed to be truly feminine, full-bosomed, wasp-waisted with the assistance of tightly laced corsets, and, below, decidedly steatopygous.

Martha Washington Northrup, standing wide-eyed on the brink of womanhood, told herself bitterly that her figure resembled only a plucked jaybird, that her chest was as flat—well, almost as flat—as when she had been nine years old, and that behind—a gesture indicated the location referred to —she was positively scrawny. No man, she declared, would ever look twice at a girl with so unattractive a figure; she was doomed to spinsterhood. She quite ignored such attributes as eyes that were as dark and deep as woodland pools, a straight, pert nose, and a rosebud mouth with a deep dimple at its right corner. Her body was slim, but it was as lithe and graceful as a white birch, as joyously alive as a fawn's.

Lieutenant Northrup's telegram to his parents was considerably longer than his remarks to Tuthill had indicated. He urged that the family carriage meet him and his chief at the Desbrosses Street ferry and that his father be there to deliver to Tuthill the invitation to make the Northrup house his own during his stay in New York.

"The war is a long way from being over," he said with a lordly disregard of expense possible only in a collect telegram. "To have General Tuthill as our guest will be of tremendous advantage to me in my military career and certainly should please Mother. There is no more famous man in the Union Army. Everyone in New York will want to meet him socially."

Brigadier General Frederic Chase Tuthill and Martha Washington Northrup met in the parlor of the Northrup home a few minutes before the butler announced dinner. Tuthill had bathed and shaved and had donned the resplendent uniform which he had himself designed. The black velveteen jacket, buttoned to the throat, was fastened by two rows of gold bellbuttons, arranged in pairs. Each shoulder strap carried a large gold star, and on the sleeves, from the cuff to above the elbow, was an intricate series of interlocking loops in gold braid. His trousers, also of black velveteen, bore twin stripes of

gold down the outer seams. In the field those trousers would
have been stuffed into high boots with long-shanked golden
spurs, but for formal evening wear he had adopted half-boots
or Wellingtons on which he wore much shorter spurs with
shielded rowels which would not catch in the sweeping skirts
of his dinner or dancing partner. His red-gold curls hung to
his collar and a brigand's mustache, flaming red, swept across
his upper lip. His chin and cheeks were shaven.

The door from the hall was open and Martha's tiny feet
made no sound on the deep-piled carpet. Her brother was
seated with her mother on a chesterfield sofa which flanked
the fireplace, her father and another man—*yes, that must be
he; that's General Tuthill*—stood facing the fire. The aide was
first to notice her and rose quickly. He presented his arm and
advanced to the other men.

"Martha," he said formally, "it is my honor to present my
chief, General Tuthill of the Ohio brigade. General, my sister, Miss Martha Northrup."

Piercing blue eyes met Martha's dark ones, then vanished as
their owner bowed low over her hand.

"It is an honor—" she began.

"It is indeed," Tuthill interrupted, "but the honor is mine,
all mine." A hint of the drill-ground rasp crept into his voice.
"Mr. Northrup, you have been remiss in your duties. Why did
you not tell me, long ago, that you had such a charming sister?"

5

On the battlefield Tuthill knew but one tactic—a headlong
charge without thought of opposing strength. In love he was
the same. He stormed the battlements of Martha Northrup's
heart with the fiery recklessness, the single purposefulness,
with which he might have led his brigade against the fortifica-

tions of Richmond. He had fallen in love with her at the moment of their first meeting and before the week was out had confessed that fact proudly to her brother and had asked that young man's advice as to whether or not he should immediately request Northrup, senior, for his blessing. Young Northrup gulped.

"My God, sir," he exclaimed. "It—isn't it pretty sudden?"

"Yes, I imagine it is. I'm quite certain in my own mind, but it would be better, I think, to wait a little, perhaps another week. I have thought of visiting the Academy at West Point during my leave—I've not been back there since I graduated. Please ask your mother and sister if they would accompany you and me to West Point over the coming week end. If they accept, will you telegraph for the necessary reservations."

"Yes, sir. And—" the aide hesitated. "And do you wish me to say anything about your . . . your sentiments toward Martha?"

"As to that, Mr. Northrup, you may use your own judgment. Should you mention my sentiments, as you call them, you have my permission to inform your parents that I have asked you to be my best man when your sister and I are married."

Tuthill's goal might have been more difficult to attain had Martha Tuthill been flirtatious or inclined to keep dangling so persistent a suitor. In truth, however, the girl fell as violently in love as did Tuthill himself. Between them, the pair by sheer weight of words overcame all parental objection to an immediate—or almost immediate—marriage.

"But, Martha darling," Mrs. Northrup fluttered. "You have known him only three weeks! It's quite out of the question to think of marriage on such short acquaintance. It would be indecorous! What would people say?"

"If you're finished, Mother, I don't care a snap of my fingers what anybody might say or think. Fred and I love one another. We want to get married. What's wrong about that?"

"There's nothing *wrong*, daughter, of course. It's just the idea of so short an engagement. Your father and I were engaged for two years before we were married."

"There wasn't a war then, and Father wasn't a soldier—that makes all the difference in the world. You're not deaf, Mother; you've heard all that Ned has told us about how General Tuthill just doesn't know what it is to be afraid—how he charges at the head of his men right into the rebel lines." She caught her breath quickly. "Why, Mother, anything could happen in war. He might be captured or wounded or even— I won't say it, I won't! We want some happiness, Mother, and we want it together!"

Tuthill spoke in somewhat the same vein to Martha's father. It never entered the brigadier's mind that Northrup might or—since Martha was a minor—that he could forbid the marriage.

"It was very sudden, sir. I know, and I think I understand how you and Mrs. Northrup must feel."

"Perhaps you do . . . if you have a daughter eighteen, no, seventeen years old." The banker's eyes swept over the eager youth in the picaresque uniform. *My God, when all's said and done, what do we know about him?*

"I haven't, sir, of course. I mean—I'm trying to put myself in your place and understand how you must feel."

"You must admit then, General, that you and Martha have known one another a very short time. I think"—he spoke judiciously—"I think that you, coming here almost directly from the battlefields in Virginia, have been greatly impressed by her youth and beauty and that she, in her turn, has been quite carried away by your brilliant record. Such mutual attraction might develop into love—but not in three weeks' time."

"But it has, Mr. Northrup. I—we are sure of it."

"You are young, General Tuthill, if you will let a much older man remind you of that fact. Martha is even younger. I do not think either of you really know your own minds as yet. After another year, perhaps——"

"Do you recognize such a thing as fate, Mr. Northrup?" Tuthill did not wait for a reply. "I do. I am convinced that fate led me to appoint your son as my aide and that the same fate brought me to New York and to your daughter. I have never even looked at another woman with thoughts of marriage."

"Granted. Fate brought you here and fate made the two of you fall in love or think that you did. A year is not long to wait, General."

"But it is. In another week my leave will be up and I will have to return to my command. Then, as soon as weather permits in the spring—April, possibly, certainly by May—we will take the field against the rebels. Martha and I want to be married before then."

Northrup shook his head in sharp negation.

"I will report all that you have said to her mother, but I think I can tell you now what her reply—and mine—will be. We cannot approve so . . . so precipitous a marriage."

"I—I'll be wearing two stars inside of a year," Tuthill blurted.

"That will be splendid, General, but the number of stars on your shoulders would not affect our opinion. Of that I am sure."

The parental verdict amounted to an ultimatum. They would permit an engagement to be announced in the spring. Six months later, in October or November of 1864, the two could be married.

". . . and I think," said Northrup, "that if you think the matter over, both of you, you will agree that we are being very considerate."

That was said on December 2, 1863. Frederic Chase

Tuthill, Brigadier General, U. S. Volunteers, and Martha Washington Northrup were married on February 14, 1864, in St. Christopher's Episcopal Church in New York City. The bride advanced to the altar on her father's arm, her mother combined audible sniffles with beaming pride from a front pew, Lieutenant Edward Northrup was best man, and the couple walked from the church beneath the arched sabers of the entire staff of the Ohio brigade. Somewhat to the surprise of his fellow officers, Tuthill did not appear in the gaudy uniform he had designed but wore the more sedate full dress of a brigadier.

The wedding and reception were the outstanding event of the winter's social season. The reception and the dancing which followed were, for the men, a dreamy farewell to things they had known before the shells crashed on Fort Sumter, a chance to hear again the gentle voices of women and to touch soft white shoulders with saber-toughened hands. Tonight was tonight, but just beyond tomorrow lay northern Virginia and the campaign of 1864 when, men said, the backbone of the rebel snake would be broken and the war would end. Of the cost, in death and wounds, of that breaking they said nothing nor did they hear in the soft melancholy of the waltzes an admission that many of these strong young men in brilliant uniforms would not live to another fall.

Tuthill and his bride danced together only once. They stood with her parents and her brother—Tuthill had not notified his own father and mother of his marriage—and bowed and smiled to hundreds who were as eager to meet "the Murat of the American Army" as to extend their wishes for happiness to Martha Northrup Tuthill.

"They make a really striking couple, don't you think," Mrs. Tryon of Philadelphia remarked to another dowager. "Martha is so tiny and he's so tall, she's dark and he's so fair——"

"Yes," the other agreed. "I wonder, oh, I do hope he'll make her happy!"

"Why, the very idea, Estelle! What on earth makes you think——"

"Nothing, Edna, nothing at all . . . but have you looked closely at his face? His eyes—they 're so cold and cruel. His mouth is cruel-looking too."

"You're imagining things. General Tuthill is a soldier. He was just a lieutenant at Bull Run and now he's a brigadier. What you call cruelty is just the firmness that a commander must have."

"I hope you're right—for Martha's sake."

Naturally, Tuthill heard neither criticism nor praise. He concealed his impatience successfully through the long evening and finally escaped, with his bride, shortly before midnight. He changed to civilian clothes, Martha to a plum-colored silk, a pert beaded bonnet and sealskin sacque, and drove to a hotel where a suite had been reserved—and to the discovery of a maenadic passion which neither had dreamed they possessed and which they were never to lose. Two days of their brief honeymoon were spent in Washington and until his brigade took the field she occupied a tent pitched close to his headquarters. It was a foretaste of what their life was to be for twelve years.

She adored her husband with a singleness of purpose that was blind to all faults and could tolerate no one who did not share that worship; he was truly happy only when she was at his side. Both were destined to make enemies. Men were to hate Tuthill, and hate him devoutly, for his bombast and vanity, his cruelty, his ambition, and his selfishness, and for his self-inspired conviction that history was to know him as one of the greatest of military leaders. A few men and many women were to dislike Martha Tuthill intensely because of her superior manner and for the flaming rage of which she was capable at a chance remark which she interpreted as critical of her husband. None of those who hated them ever questioned the love they bore for one another.

She learned within a few days that the three hundred miles' travel from New York to Tuthill's field headquarters had transported her to a new and vastly different world from that she had known. She learned that she might nod her acknowledgement to the sentry who presented arms when she entered or left her tent over which he stood guard, but that she must never speak to him. He was an enlisted man; her husband was an officer, nay, a general officer, and the gulf between the man who carried the carbine and him who wore a star was unbridgeable. On the third morning of her stay in camp Tuthill entered the tent to find her white-lipped and on the verge of tears.

"Oh, Fred, I'm so glad you came," she gasped. "I was going to send for you. Those poor men—Fred, you must do something!"

"What poor men, Mattie? What are you talking about?"

She gestured toward the rear of the tent.

"Back there, just a little way. I stepped out for a walk, just to get the air, and I saw them."

"Wait a minute, Mattie."

Tuthill left the tent and returned almost within the minute he had mentioned. He was laughing.

"You'll get used to things like that, little girl. A couple of men who get bucked and gagged are nothing for you to get excited about."

"Bucked?" she asked, bewildered.

"That's all." He squatted on the floor and illustrated. "A man is ordered to sit down and they—the sergeant of his platoon usually—tie his ankles and wrists. Then, while he's sitting, they pass a stout stick—a pick handle if one's handy —over his forearms and under his knees. He's about as helpless as a man can be. If he argues or if he curses the sergeant, he's gagged in addition."

"But they were suffering. I could tell."

"It's not comfortable. It's not meant to be, Mattie. At

that, they're better off than if they had been spread-eagled."

"What's that?"

"Well . . ."

"Tell me. If you don't I'll find out from somebody else."

"There's a spare wheel on the back of every artillery limber. A man stands on the felly—that's the rim of the wheel—and his ankles are tied to two spokes and his wrists to two others so that he's spread out like the letter X—spread-eagled."

"That"—she hesitated—"that doesn't sound as bad as the other."

"I didn't finish. Then the wheel is given a quarter-turn. He's hanging—his whole weight—from one wrist and ankle. It——"

"It's barbarous. Even a savage——"

"This is the army, Mattie. Men—soldiers—are absolutely worthless unless they're disciplined—disciplined to obey instantly even though they know that they are going to their deaths. If a man hides out somewhere so he won't have to drill, if he curses a noncommissioned officer, if he commits a nuisance behind his tent because he's too lazy to go to the latrine—that man isn't disciplined. He must be taught to obey, taught discipline. What you just saw is one way to teach him that orders must be obeyed."

"And"—she bit her lips—"and we're fighting the South because of what they do to the slaves, the whipping that Mrs. Stowe told about in *Uncle Tom's Cabin*. You might as well flog the men as do things like you've told me!"

"We don't," her husband said curtly. "It isn't permitted. It was abolished, by army order, two years ago and you won't have to go far to find officers who doubt the wisdom of that order. A taste of the cat would make soldiers out of some of these unwilling draftees or bounty-jumpers."

"I . . ." She did not finish the remark, nor did she ever comment again on military punishments.

6

On March 10, 1864, a horseman dismounted at the headquarters tent of George Gordon Meade, commanding general of the Army of the Potomac. He wore the full dress of his rank, lieutenant general—first officer of the regular army to wear three stars since George Washington.

"Grant," he said as he acknowledged Meade's salute.

He had come from the West, this stocky man with the stub of a cigar always half-buried in his bushy red-brown beard, come from Shiloh Church and Vicksburg and Chattanooga. He had graduated from West Point and had fought in the Mexican War but had never wanted to be a professional soldier—his desire was to teach mathematics—and for a time had resigned from the army. He was virtually unknown when he again took up arms in 1862, but in him Lincoln found the general for whom he had sought through two long years of stalemate, of inconclusive victories, and of defeat.

He brought others with him from the West and among them was a bullet-headed major general named Sheridan, Philip H. Sheridan. He had commanded an infantry division, but Grant made him chief of cavalry and sent his predecessor, Pleasanton, to the western armies.

Sheridan's ardor, his tirelessness, his insistence on drill, drill, drill until every man and horse was letter-perfect in each maneuver; these were Tuthill's delight. This man, this black-eyed, hard-riding leader who was less than five years older than himself, this was Kearney redivivus, and Tuthill drove himself and his brigade as he never had before. He rode personally with the cavalry units, regiment, squadron, and company, and his shrill voice lashed like a whip at any commander or noncom who showed error or hesitancy. He who had neglected shamefully his studies in gunnery now found himself in command of the artillery units of his brigade. No newly assigned lieutenant could have worked harder to gain complete knowledge of artillery tactics, of emplacement, of movement under fire, of targets and ranges and the cutting of fuses. When he felt he had mastered the abstruse subject—and confidence came quickly—it was the gunners' and the caisson drivers' turn to hear that cutting voice and the rare bursts of blistering profanity which accompanied a reprimand.

Slowly, far too slowly to suit the impatient Tuthill, spring dried the Virginia roads. On May 4 the Army of the Potomac moved, cavalry in the lead, to the Rapidan crossings and the narrow roads that led into the Wilderness, a tangle of second-growth timber twelve miles wide and half as deep. Within that tangle, a year earlier, Stonewall Jackson had been mortally wounded.

Fifteen thousand men died in two days' fighting in the Wilderness but the Army of the Potomac went on. Grant was leading that army now and its days of retreat were over. The army went on, south and a little east, to an insignificant village called Spotsylvania Courthouse where more thousands were to die at the Bloody Angle. It was there that Sheridan—fiery Phil Sheridan who could outride a centaur and outcurse a mule-skinner and a tugboat captain in concert—it was there that Sheridan clashed with his commander, George Gordon Meade.

The Union generals, Sheridan declared sulfurously, lacked even rudimentary knowledge of cavalry and its tactical employment; they regarded mounted troops merely as errand-boys, escorts, and scouts; had they learned nothing from "Jeb" Stuart and the rebel horse? . . . if they hadn't, it was about time they started studying. He, Phil Sheridan, was goddam sick of the whole business, sick of being at the beck and call of any staff officer with enough rank to give orders. Cavalry was a fighting arm, and if they gave him a chance he'd by-God show them it could fight. Turn him loose and he'd by-God lick "Jeb" Stuart on his own ground and at his own game.

Meade, furious, reported the outburst to Grant, who briefly removed his cigar.

"Thinks he can lick Stuart, does he? Well, give him a chance."

The few words carried authority and Sheridan detached the cavalry, ten thousand strong, and flanked the Confederate right. Within the next few days there were half a dozen actions of the sort which Tuthill loved; with attack, retreat, rally, and counterattack following one upon another like the swift play of saber on saber. At Yellow Tavern, only six miles from Richmond, the gray cavalry made a determined stand. Tuthill led a charge against a battery, captured two guns, and broke the Confederate line. Stuart countercharged and in the hurly-burly a dismounted Union soldier snapped his Colt at a rebel officer and put a ball through the liver of "Jeb" Stuart. He was dying when his men got him into an ambulance and headed for Richmond. Later, much later, Private John A. Huff of Company E, Fifth Michigan Cavalry, asserted that he fired the shot which killed the Confederate leader.

The sparring—the swift lunge, riposte, and lunge once more —at Beaver Dam Station, Yellow Tavern, and at the crossing of the North Anna River, established Tuthill as a cavalryman. Here was no strategist, Sheridan learned, but a leader to whom the shock of combat was sheer delight, and he sent Tuthill into a daylong scramble of wild fighting at Trevilian Station where the redheaded youth reformed his own shattered troops and led them to recapture a gun which the Confederates had taken. The rebel horse fell back and Sheridan withdrew to Lighthouse Point on the York River to refit his command. On June 7 the cavalry moved toward Charlottesville and in August Sheridan received the orders which created the Army of the Shenandoah and his appointment to its command.

Those orders were simple—and as cruel as war is cruel. The Shenandoah Valley was, and is, a long narrow trough which runs from northeast to southwest beyond the Blue Ridge and from Harpers Ferry to Staunton and Lynchburg. It was called, rightly, the granary of the Confederacy. Sheridan was ordered to lay it waste. He was ordered to follow the rebels south and "eat out Virginia clear and clean as far as they go, so that crows flying over the valley for the balance of season will have to carry their provender with them. . . . He should make all the valley south of the Baltimore and Ohio Railroad [Harpers Ferry] a desert . . . all provisions and stock should be removed and the people notified to get out." There was little necessity for the orders which Sheridan issued: ". . . you will seize all mules, horses, and cattle which may be useful to our army . . . The object is to make this Valley untenable for the raiding parties of the rebel army."

Tuthill's eulogists, of whom none was more vocal than himself, were to speak of the Shenandoah campaign of 1864 as though it were entirely a series of cavalry actions with the Boy General as their most brilliant leader. Actually, in addition to the three divisions of cavalry, Sheridan had under his command three infantry corps: the VIII under George Crook, the XIX of two slim divisions under William H. Emory, and the superb VI under Horatio Wright. A total of some thirty-six thousand men wore the blue. Tuthill saw his share, a generous share, of fighting, but always he was under the command and direction of a superior.

The grim orders to make the beautiful valley a desert were carried out. The standing crops fed the cavalry and artillery horses, the flames of burning barns and houses painted the skies from Harpers Ferry to Waynesboro; thousands were homeless and destitute and the richest portion of the Confederacy was a band of ruin sixty miles wide. The Union Army wintered near Winchester and in February of 1865 the last vestige of rebel resistance fell when Devin, who had replaced Torbert as chief of cavalry, and Tuthill led their two divisions, eight thousand strong, against two thousand weary and hungry Confederates under Jubal Early who had taken position on a ridge west of Waynesboro. Tuthill's division led and the gray front wilted before the direct attack. Sixteen hundred of Early's men were captured and the beaten general narrowly escaped. Sheridan, the dynamic, led his army eastward through the mud to the remount station at White House, where the cavalry refitted. Winter was over, spring and the spring campaign were at hand, and the hopes of the Union for victory had never been brighter.

On March 29, Sheridan's cavalry led the Union movement around the defenses of Petersburg; on April 9, Robert E. Lee and Ulysses S. Grant met in the parlor of the McLean house in Appomattox Courthouse, seventy miles west of Richmond, and the Civil War was ended. Between those dates were twelve days of scrambled fighting, with Sheridan, who knew that his opponent was knocked out but still on his feet, everywhere along the shifting front and everywhere shouting for speed and more speed. Twelve days with men sleeping on their feet, eating where they could snatch some hardtack and lukewarm coffee; twelve days of stumbling through the mud and tangled woodland; twelve days to victory.

At Five Forks, Tuthill led a brigade in a charge which broke ingloriously and ignominiously in a quagmire; he led his regiments more brilliantly on the Deatonville Road where —with infantry help—he cut off and captured a wagon train. Always the cavalry was the slashing blade with which Sheridan hacked and pierced and hacked again at Lee's exhausted legions; always, when the cavalry struck, Tuthill—a division commander now—was in the van. Dashing, impetuous, utterly fearless, heedless of odds; there were unquestionably more able leaders against the Confederacy's last stand, there was none more conspicuous.

Lee surrendered. The gray veterans laid down their arms; the blue, equally weary but triumphant, retraced their steps eastward to Alexandria where worn equipment was polished and faded uniforms brushed for the final review of the Army of the Potomac in Washington. Tuthill, two stars on his shoulders now, rode at the head of his division in that march past the new President, the inconspicuous, unknown Carolinian who had succeeded Lincoln. The war was over, he had led his shouting troopers in their last charge, glory and the opportunity for ever greater glory seemed far away. That night, in a shabby boardinghouse which was the only place where he could find accommodations in the crowded city, he buried his face in his pillow and wept. Only Martha Tuthill heard his sobs and she attributed them to joy because four years of slaughter had ended at last.

Circumstances permitted him to hold his brevet rank for ten months after Appomattox. The Rebellion—Tuthill and his contemporaries never referred to the Civil War by any other term—was over, but there was trouble far to the Southwest along the Mexican border. There was imminent danger, said rumor, that Texas and its irreconcilables would secede again and that secession would be welcomed by Maximilian, Emperor of Mexico. Cavalry was rushed to Louisiana and Texas. Sheridan was in command; Tuthill would head the Third Division.

Texas did not secede; the ambitious Maximilian was already on the path which would end at Querétaro and a firing squad, but one incident of Tuthill's leadership of the Third Division is worthy of mention.

The men he commanded were resentful of the enforced continuation of their military service. Their plaint was that the war for which they had enlisted was over; they wanted to go home. In protest, some eighty men of a Michigan regiment appeared for inspection in the most ridiculous uniforms they could contrive. Some had their right trousers' leg rolled to the knee, some the left. Shirts were torn and dirty, jackets worn inside out; one side of the face would be shaved, the other might display a luxuriant beard.

Tuthill was furious. He ordered all of the clowning recalcitrants thrown in the guardhouse and preferred court-martial charges against a sergeant who, an investigation revealed, appeared to be the instigator of the travesty. The court sentenced the man to death by shooting and Tuthill announced that the sentence would be carried out in the presence of the entire command. A second soldier was to be shot at the same time; his conviction was for desertion.

It was now the turn of the enlisted men of the Third Division to be enraged and a delegation was selected to present a protest to the commanding general. The soldiers admitted that they had been thoughtless, but to sentence a man to death for a prank was a gross injustice. Tuthill refused to meet the committee. Through an aide he informed the men that the sergeant would be shot. The muttering became a clamor and various trustworthy noncommissioned officers carried to headquarters the word that Tuthill himself would be shot if he attempted to execute the sentence.

The day dawned. The division, regiment by regiment, was drawn up on three sides of a square. Adjutant's call, then the general, was blown. Tuthill and his staff rode to the center of the square, then—attended only by a single orderly who carried the headquarters flag with its twin stars—Tuthill reviewed the massed troops. He was entirely unarmed, and he rode slowly within six feet of the men from the extreme left of the hollow square to the right. There he paused long enough to dismiss the orderly, then retraced his route—this time at a walk. Occasionally he halted and turned his back on the ranks while he spoke briefly to a brigade or regimental commander. Finally he reached the left flank once more and halted. He had shoved his chips to the center of the table and none had called his hand. His voice was as shrill as a trumpet blast.

"Provost marshal, execute your orders."

An escort wagon, top removed, advanced slowly through the open end of the square. The condemned men, the deserter and the sergeant who was to die with him, sat within the wagon, each man on a rude coffin. Two squads of picked marksmen marched behind the wagon and four men, unarmed, walked on either side. These aided the two men to the ground and lifted out the coffins. The provost marshal, a major, showed the men where to stand, each at the foot of his coffin, and tied a bandage about their eyes. Tuthill rode slowly across the square to where his staff waited.

"Proceed, provost marshal!" he snapped.

The firing squad moved into position and dropped their carbines to the order. There was a moment's hush. If the men of the Third Division had been bluffing, their commander had called that bluff. The provost marshal stepped swiftly behind the sergeant, pulled the blindfold from his eyes, and led him away. At the command, *Fire,* a volley from the carbines of one of the squads ripped through the deserter's body and left the man dead across his coffin. The sergeant fainted.

In later years Martha Tuthill spoke of the incident as a demonstration of her husband's mercy.

13 WINTER

The winter of 1875-76 at Fort Andrew Doniphan and at South City was like all the winters that had passed since the post and the town were established. There were frigid days followed by nights so cold and clear that the stars of Orion and the Bear blazed like torches in the purple sky, so low that they brushed the crests of the Missouri bluffs. There were days of wind and of wind-driven snow screaming out of the north, snow so thick that the merchants of South City stretched ropes along the curb line that the townsfolk might find their way from home to store and back to their homes again.

Ice locked the waters of the Missouri from bank to bank and transportation between post and town was by sleigh. Drill was possible only when weather permitted and military duties were limited to a skeleton guard maintained far more for protection against fire than against possible marauders. Sentries walked post for only an hour, then were relieved to hasten to the shelter of the guardhouse and its red-hot stove.

Naturally, there was no abatement in military routine. Reveille was at five o'clock, a full hour before the first paling of dawn, and taps were sounded at nine. Passes to leave the post and visit South City were granted only when weather permitted and were canceled at the slightest hint that a blizzard was on the way. It was history that in one blizzard, two years before, an officer and six troopers had been trapped in South City for three days and part of a fourth. The officer, at his own expense, had taken a room at the Pacific Hotel; when credit there for quarters and meals was denied the troopers, they had found shelter, good food, and highly satisfactory entertainment at Bessie Rivers' establishment on Strawberry Street. Rumor stated that Bessie was still endeavoring to collect from the government for housing and feeding the men.

Restaurant proprietors found their business excellent in spite of the difficulty in obtaining supplies over the highly uncertain rail connections with the East. Businessmen who waded to their stores or offices through crotch-deep drifts got their noon meals at a restaurant rather than buck the drifts or the cutting snow to return to their homes. The town's scanty hotel and rooming-house facilities were crowded with men who, like Sol Rogers, had holed up until spring permitted their return to the river packets or to their summer vocations of hunting, trapping, prospecting, or Indian trading.

Sol Rogers had taken a room at a shabby rooming house on River Street beyond the Northern Pacific depot. He was holing up, he declared, until the ice left the river and a decision was reached as to the 1876 campaign against the hostile bands. If he felt like it, he added, he could sleep for eighteen hours of the day, but twelve hours was usually sufficient. He ate all his meals at the Ace High, a patronage which Mrs. Poole believed was due to her presence and to the circumstance that Beth waited on table. The scout sat always in the same place, close to the window, and none noticed that the pane was always rubbed clear of the moisture which had condensed there in the steamy atmosphere of the restaurant. From that window he could see the front of the gun shop where Cap Woodard's name was still displayed, but there was none to observe that his departure from the restaurant frequently corresponded with the entrance of a customer to the shop or with some activity on the part of the woman who owned and managed it, Genevieve Woodard.

It was a casual, outwardly innocent surveillance; so casual that in all of South City only one person realized its closeness. Cattlemen gravitated naturally to a saddlery, farmers and homesteaders to the stores where they bought their supplies; what was more natural than for a scout and hunter, a man who had lived for years by his skill with his rifle, to frequent a shop where firearms were made and sold? Only Genevieve Woodard recognized that there was some calculated reason for Rogers' visits; only she sensed the irony in his drawled remarks to the shop's customers.

"It's a mighty good gun," he'd say. "Some 'd say that it's a shade on th' heavy side f'r a man t' carry afoot, but weight in th' barrel is what makes Woodard's guns shoot th' way they do.

"I know what I'm talkin' about. My own rifle's a Woodard, one that Cap made f'r himself. It got me out of one mighty tight squeeze that's too long a story t' tell here—but y' can't go wrong on that gun. Ain't that so, Miss Woodard?"

Again he might volunteer to help Adolf Hoffmeier, the German-born gunsmith, with some task.

"Shucks, Adolf, I ain't got a doggone thing t' do. Lemme run them bullets for yuh—it'll take my mind off th' wimmen an' all my other troubles." While the lead was heating he would chatter aimlessly. "Seen a feller f'rgit where he was aimin' one time an' spit into a pot of hot lead—he like t' blowed th' whole blame place up; hot lead was flyin' in every direction. That was in Cheyenne. Last time I was there was 'bout a year ago. I went broke, real sudden-like, and had t' hang 'round f'r a spell. Couple fellers name of Freund, brothers, have a gun shop there. Th' oldest one—I f'rgit his name —he's sure got some ideas of his own when it comes t' makin' actions. Y' ought t' git Miss Woodard t' send y' out there some time t' look over his work—it'd take some time but it wouldn't cost no fortune."

All of which would be delivered expressionlessly and with no side glances at Genevieve Woodard, but always in her hearing. Only Sol himself could have told how he achieved it, but he seemed always to be in the shop or loitering near the window when Captain Hanford, in command of B company of the Twentieth, entered. There was nothing subtle about Jerome Hanford. His interest was not in the rifles and revolvers on display but in the dark-haired proprietress of the establishment, and he usually walked directly to the door which led to the living quarters in the rear.

"Genevieve!"

"Oh, it's you, Jerry. I was just about to make some coffee. It'll be ready in a jiffy. Sit down. No, leave the door open."

"All right, if you insist—but why?"

"People talk, Jerry, you know they do, and Adolf isn't a chaperone." She peered over his shoulder. "Is Sol Rogers out there, with Adolf?"

"No. I passed him a few doors down the street, outside Bedell's grocery."

She turned and busied herself at the stove, then stepped to the cupboard and lifted down cups and saucers.

"Gen."

"Yes, Jerry?"

"Sol Rogers, what's he to you, Gen?"

"Nothing, of course. What on earth made you ask such a thing?"

"Plenty. Every time I come here I see him. I——"

"He's wintering here, in South City. It's only natural, I guess, that a hunter should hang around a gun shop."

"Maybe." The captain stared glumly at the toes of his heavy boots. "He knows you, Gen."

"Of course he does—do I have to account to you, Jerry Hanford, for every man who happens to know who I am?"

"The other day"—Hanford ignored her question—"Monday, I think it was, he was in the shop, talking to Adolf, when I left. We walked down the street together and he started talking about you."

"Talking . . . Sol Rogers . . . about me?" Her voice rose.

"Not really talking about you. He mentioned Jim's death and then he said—it sounded odd coming from an ignorant scout and hunter—that you were a remarkable woman. He repeated it. A truly remarkable woman, he said."

"I guess I should be flattered—or should I?" she laughed.

"He was there, in the Hills, when Jim was killed," Hanford persisted. "Everybody knows that—you told it yourself."

And I should have had sense enough to cut my tongue out first! Aloud she said quickly. "Of course I did! I had nothing to lie about. Jim—it's not right to say it, but Jim was a fool. He didn't keep a lookout and when the Indians jumped our camp he got killed. Sol Rogers saved my life—and I'm grateful! There!"

She stepped around his chair and pushed shut the door into the shop. Then she leaned over his chair. The curving swell of breast was against his shoulder; her lips touched his cheek.

"You're jealous, Jerry. You shouldn't be, really you shouldn't, but I'm glad you are, even if it's of a hunter who smells like a bear's den."

He turned quickly and pulled her to him.

"Gen!" His lips sought hers. "If I didn't love you so much, Gen, you couldn't devil me the way you do."

"You devil yourself, Jerry, thinking the things you do about Sol Rogers. Kiss me again, then I must open the door."

When he had gone she sat at the table for a long time, but the only sound from the shop was the clink of steel on steel as Hoffmeier worked at his vise. It was not until the next day that she saw Rogers as he passed his shop after a late breakfast at the Ace High. When she called to him he turned, unhurried.

"Come in, Sol, please, I want to talk to you. No, not here in the shop, back here. Sit down, please."

She closed the door behind them until the latch snapped, then faced him across the table. His eyes roamed about the room, the clean stove, the painted china on the shelves, the burnished copper utensils . . .

"Nice place yuh got here, Gen. Real cozy-like."

"Never mind my place or how cozy it is. What are you trying to do, Sol?"

"Me? Whatever give you th' notion I was tryin' t' do anything—anything special, that is?"

Scarcely twenty words had been spoken, but she was already angry.

"You know what I mean. Don't talk like a child kept after school. Why do you hang around this shop all the time? Why do you talk to my friends about me? What are you after?"

"Ain't you kinda excited, Gen? Ain't you makin' somethin' outa nothin'? Man's got t' go somewhere an' I'd ruther hang 'round this shop than 'round a saloon. An' as f'r talkin' 'bout you——"

"Damn you, Sol Rogers! I had plenty of chances to cut your throat and I should have done it. I——"

"Reckon it would've been better all 'round—f'r you especial."

"Shut up!" She was furious now. "Listen to me. You're taking this way of getting even with me because of that money, that gold. Go tell the truth about it—tell it everywhere —and I'll do the same. Then we'll know which one will be believed."

"Uh-huh," Rogers was enjoying himself hugely. "I been wonderin' now an' then why you didn't tell it long ago, when yuh first showed up here at South City an' told how th' Sioux had wiped out Cap Woodard in th' Hills. It w'd have been a mite stronger then."

"I—what do you mean by that?"

"Y' should've told th' truth, Gen, 'bout how you an' Cap took all sorts of gold outa that bar an' how—after Cap was killed an' you an' I got outa th' Hills with our hair—how I just nach'rally latched on to th' gold f'r myself. Soon 's we got loose—where was it yuh told folks we parted company, Gen? —you watched your chance an' grabbed th' gold back an' took off. Mebbe it ain't too late now, Gen. There's no way in God's world I c'd prove which one of us dug that gold."

"You—you——" Genevieve Woodard stammered but her shrewd brain was racing.

"'Course," Rogers continued blandly, "there'd be some folks that'd remember that you an' Cap had told a hell of a lot of stories, one time an' another, 'bout dif'rent things. Same folks might remember that Sol Rogers never was known t' talk with a split tongue—that's Injun talk f'r lyin', Gen— an' they might jest kinda wonder. Even when I told 'em I couldn't prove a thing, they might wonder just th' same."

"They'd believe me!" Genevieve was emphatic but she was on the defensive.

"Shouldn't wonder. Th' ladies out to th' fort—Mrs. Tuthill an' Mrs. Bellew an' th' rest of 'em—shouldn't wonder but what they'd take your word f'r anything, Gen. So'd th' gen'ral an' Major Marcus . . . did yuh know that Marcus and Major Buzby served t'gether in th' South after th' war? Marcus came to th' Twentieth an' Buzby, bein' infantry, went to Fort Laramie. You might've run into him when yore brother was there. They'd believe you. So'd Cap'n Han——"

"Get out!" Her voice rose almost to a scream. "I know what you're trying to do now. Get out of here, Sol Rogers, before I kill you!"

Rogers rose slowly.

"I'm gittin', Gen, but you ain't th' killin' kind. Killin' takes a dif'rent sort of nerve from what you've got."

His leathery features cracked in a grin as he walked out of the shop. *She's crazier mad than a locoed kiyote. Mebbe I was a little rough on her—or was I? She had it comin' to her, pullin' a whore's trick like she did on me.*

How desperate she was in her anger he did not realize for nearly a week during which he avoided the gun shop. Then— he was on his way to the restaurant through a gentle snow that promised a heavier fall—she halted him and thrust a paper into his gloved hand.

"Take that. Don't open it now, but you'll see what it is. Take it and stay away from here and from me. Keep your nose out of my business. If you don't, so help me God I'll kill you! I mean it!"

The paper—he unfolded it in the restaurant—was a certificate of deposit with Wells Fargo, South City, for thirty-five hundred dollars. Sol regarded it almost owlishly.

"I'll be good and Goddamned!" he said slowly. Beth Poole, at his elbow with a cup of coffee, heard him.

"Why, Mr. Rogers!"

"Sorry, honey, I was talkin' out loud to myself—but I meant every word of it."

2

Beth and her mother thoroughly enjoyed their employment as waitress and cook at the Ace High. The work was hard at times, the hours long, but for the first time in their lives they were in daily contact with people, average men and women, who did not think or talk in terms of the church, the missionary society, or the need for bearing God's word to the heathen in his blindness. The eight dollars of their combined weekly wage—Mrs. Poole was paid six dollars, Beth two— was more actual money than either of them had ever handled before. It was augmented by the tips which Beth found from time to time on the tables which she served—sometimes as much as a quarter. She bought a wool dress and a pair of stout shoes, the first really new clothes she had owned since childhood.

Tucker, proprietor of the restaurant, soon learned that Mrs. Poole's cooking was far more pleasing to his customers than that of the Chinaman she had succeeded, and that Beth's shy smile and eagerness to please made her extremely popular. He was in luck, he told himself, and was quick to enter the kitchen and help in every way possible. He scrubbed and repainted the cubbyhole off the kitchen which the Chinaman had occupied, burned the soiled bedding, and told the pair that it was theirs for use whenever the weather made it impossible or inadvisable for them to walk to their home. During one severe blizzard the two did not leave the restaurant for four days.

The only person who was not satisfied with the arrangement was Private Martin Hale of E company.

"I never get a chance to really see you any more, Beth," he complained. "By the time this place closes and you go home, it's too late for us to—to play checkers like we used to or talk or anything like that."

"No," she agreed, "but it can't be helped. You'll just have to come here when you want to see me. There's always a slack time in the morning——"

"I can't get here in the morning. You know that."

". . . and in the afternoon before people begin to come in

for supper. I—I'm just as sorry as you are, Marty. I've missed you."

"Not half as much as I've missed you, I'll bet. I think I can get a pass next Sunday, Beth. Maybe we can take a walk if it isn't too cold. I want to talk to you."

Sunday was clear and windless but bitterly cold. The two walked the length of Main Street and then—noses and ears tingling, toes numb—ran back to the warmth of the Ace High. There were no customers and they seated themselves at a table in a corner of the room. Doris Poole brought them coffee.

"That'll warm you up. You're crazy, both of you, to go out when it's as cold as this unless you have to."

Martin waited until Mrs. Poole had returned to the kitchen.

"She's pretty near right," he said. "I tried to tell you while we were out, but I was afraid my mouth would freeze open."

"It was the same with me." Beth curled her fingers around the hot cup. "My, that feels good—what was it you wanted to tell me, Marty?"

"I heard from home, from my father."

"I'm glad—I told you to write him, remember? Was he mad about your enlisting?"

"He already knew that. I wrote him and Mother from Cincinnati when I first enlisted, but I didn't know where I'd be sent. He didn't blame me for enlisting——"

"Why did you, Marty? You've never told me."

"I—I guess I just got tired of things around home and wanted to get away from them." He plunged on to a less dangerous subject. "What he said in the letter was that he wants me to come home, to go back to college—I'd had a year at Denison at Granville—and finish my education."

"But you're enlisted, Marty. You can't get out until your time's up . . . I know that much about the army."

"So do I. Father thinks it might be arranged though. What they call release by purchase. I've heard talk of it in the barracks, but none of the soldiers has the two hundred and some dollars it costs, so that's all it is, talk. It'll take some time but Father is going to write to Washington, to our congressman, and see if it can be arranged."

"I guess you'll like that," the girl said slowly. "To be out of the army and back in college. Won't you, Marty?"

"Some ways I will. It all depends."

"Depends on what?"

"On you, Beth."

"Me? How could——?"

"On you. That's what I wanted to tell—to ask you. We haven't known each other very long, Beth, but I've come to like you an awful lot."

"Have you? I'm glad, Marty, because—because I like you too."

"How much?" he sparred. He reached across the table and took her hand in his.

"A lot. You're not like most of the soldiers, Marty. Maybe that's why."

"I—Beth, if I get out of the army and go back to college . . . will you wait for me, Beth?"

"Wait for——?"

"You know what I mean, you know you do. I mean wait for me, wait until I'm out of college and have a job. I want to be a teacher, maybe a college professor, and then we'll be married."

"Marty! You really——"

"Of course I do." His hand tightened on hers. "I—I love you, Beth. You're the sweetest girl I've ever known."

"Say that again, Marty, all of it. Because——"

"Because why?"

"Because I love you, too, Marty."

"Beth!" He moved his chair closer to hers. Their shoulders touched. "You mean——"

"Of course I mean—whatever it was you wanted to know if I meant. I've loved you for a long time, long before you ever loved me."

"You haven't any such thing!"

"I have too." Her head was on his shoulder. "I love you, Marty Hale. Now kiss me—that's what you're supposed to do."

Lew Tucker was dozing in a corner of the kitchen, his head tipped against the wall. Doris Poole was seated near the stove, happy in the opportunity to get off her feet for a short time. The two in the outer room were unaware of Sol Rogers' entry until the cold air from the opening door struck their faces.

"Thought I'd git a—what's wrong with you two? Yore eyes are shinin' like a brush fire in th' dark of th' moon?"

"I—we—" Beth stammered. Martin Hale found words.

"We're going to get married, Sol. I just asked Beth and she said she would."

The scout snorted.

"Y're f'rgittin' y're wearin' Uncle Sam's brand, son. Cap'n Nason wouldn't ever let no private, and a recruit at that, git married. S'pose he did—w'd you want t' take Beth out to th' fort, out t' one of them shacks on Suds Row?"

"Of course I wouldn't. My father's going to get me out of the army, Sol, buy my discharge. Then I'm going back to college in Ohio and when I finish college we're going to get married."

"I should've knowed yuh better, both of yuh, than to think yuh'd do anything hasty. That—that shines, boy. Shake on it."

3

First Lieutenant Walter Blake had ridden behind Tuthill when the Twentieth's commander had been a brigade and division leader. Blake had been a captain then, commanding a company in a Pennsylvania cavalry regiment, and his major's brevet had been confirmed just three days before the meeting of Lee and Grant at Appomattox Courthouse. Like Tuthill, Blake regarded the end of the conflict as the death of dreams. War, the shock of combat, the thunder of hoofs in a charge, the barking of revolvers as enemy met enemy, the acrid odor of mingled powder smoke and dust—those were sublime, glorious. Now they were ended.

Unlike Tuthill, he was a volunteer officer, serving only for the period of the emergency. He was discharged with his regiment after a final review in Harrisburg, but he shared none of the jubilance of the men in the ranks or the other officers. Reluctantly, sullenly, he returned to the family home on Pine Street in Philadelphia and to a desk in the wholesale grocery and import business which had made his father wealthy.

"You take your time, Valter," said the elder Blake whose speech still carried the accent of the Germany of his birth. "Joost hang around the office—talk to the salesmen and the bookkeepers, go into the varehouses and the shipping rooms, go down on the docks ven a cargo is being unloaded. Learn the business, all of it. It vill be a big job, but there is plenty of time. Then ve change that sign over the door. Should it be BLAKE AND SON, or BLAKE AND BLAKE?"

Yes, thank God, the name on the sign would be Blake, the ex-captain said to himself. Blake and not Blaustein. Martin Blake was his father's name and Martin Blake was as far removed from Mendel Blaustein as was the Blake carriage with its team of matched chestnuts from the pushcart from which a German-Jewish immigrant had peddled his wares along Carpenter and Tasker and Christian Streets in South Philadelphia. Thank God he'd changed that name when he'd been naturalized and that his son, Walter, had been born Blake. And should God or old Mendel himself be thanked that he'd prospered in every undertaking; that he'd made himself a rich man long before the war and that national disaster had enabled him to double and redouble that fortune? *It'll be mine some day and I ought to learn the business, but, God, how I hate it!*

He stuck it out for three years of growing discontent, then spoke to his father in the first of many long discussions of his future. He hated the grocery business; the war had ruined him as a possible business executive; he had been happy in the army and he wanted to return to it. There were competitive examinations for regular army commissions; he planned to take them.

"Do so if you really vant to," the older man said at last, "but it vill not be necessary. There are still plenty of men in Washington—senators, cabinet members, generals—I have done business vith. I vill get you a commission fast and you vill learn, I hope, that being in the army ven there is no var is more dull than the grocery business ever vas."

The senior Blake was in Washington for only three days. He returned to Philadelphia with the information that Walter could be appointed a captain in the Quartermaster Corps, a captain of infantry with assignment to one of the new Negro regiments, or a first lieutenant of cavalry. He chose the last and was assigned to the Twentieth.

He was the only officer in the regiment with independent means. His father hoped sincerely that his return to the army was a manifestation of boyishness which Walter would outgrow in a few years; then he would resign and approach the grocery business with genuine interest. In the meantime there was no need for him to restrict himself to the meager salary of a cavalry lieutenant and the merchant established a trust fund which assured the young man five thousand dollars yearly, a sum which was considerably more than the base pay of a major general.

He was assigned to G company under Captain Roger Clements and was quite content—or told himself that he was content—as a junior officer. In a line regiment he had ample opportunity to observe the inconsistencies and apparent in-

justices of the ponderous machine that was the army. He saw
gray-haired captains who had been regimental commanders
during the war; other captains—Harrod was one—who were
little older than himself but were West Point graduates with
assured positions on the seniority lists. In time, if they lived
long enough, they would be majors and colonels. He saw
many officers, captains and senior lieutenants, who owed their
appointments to political or personal influence. Some were
able in their profession; others were utterly unqualified to lead
men into battle. All were somehow passed over for promotion
when vacancies occurred. In general, Blake considered himself
fortunate, but that satisfaction waned with the rumor, repeatedly confirmed, that an all-out campaign was planned against
the hostile Sioux and Cheyennes. Early in December he called
on Tuthill at headquarters.

"I told Captain Clements that I was coming to see you, sir,
but said nothing about the nature of my business. It's—well,
I regard it as personal."

"I'll be glad to help you in any way I can, Mr. Blake."

"Thank you, General. It's pretty generally known, sir, that
we're going out against the hostiles next year. I—sir, I want to
go into that campaign as a company commander, not as a
subordinate!"

Tuthill's eyebrows rose.

"That's rather ambitious under the circumstances, Blake.
You know the regiment: ten captains heading companies and
two—A and K—with first lieutenants in command. Both
Hanna and Richards are senior to you."

"Yes, sir."

"Then why did you come to see me? What do you think I
could do about it?"

"I wanted your advice—what you thought. You see, General, my father knows a good many people on a pretty high
level in Washington. Some of them are greatly indebted to
him, not only financially but in other ways——"

"Politically, so to speak," Tuthill interrupted. "Political appointments and promotions are not regarded very highly, Blake."

"I know they're not, sir, but a captain's a captain no matter how he's appointed. If I wrote my father and asked him to see what he could do about a captaincy for me, would you approve it if your approval was asked? That's what I want to know."

Tuthill was silent for a long minute. His expression was completely inscrutable and betrayed nothing of whatever thoughts were racing through the shrewd brain behind the steel-blue eyes.

"That is not easy to answer, Blake, without reservations. I can tell you frankly that I would approve your promotion if my opinion were asked. I'd do that for any man unless I knew that he was quite unfit for higher rank. But could I approve your promotion to captain and request your continued service with the Twentieth? It would be quite unjust to Hanna and Richards and others who are senior to you. A promotion with immediate transfer to another organization would be another matter."

Blake shook his head.

"I wouldn't want that. I'd refuse the promotion if it meant leaving the Twentieth."

"I take that as a personal compliment, Mr. Blake," Tuthill smiled. "I regard you as a highly efficient and promising young officer and I want you with me in the coming campaign. It's coming next year, Blake, as sure as a gun's iron!"

"And I'd like to lead a company of the Twentieth—any company—in it. You can understand that, can't you, General?"

"Of course I can, but I can't slap half a dozen men, senior to you, in the face by approving in writing a promotion which would give you a company. You can understand that, I trust."

"Yes, sir. It—it seems to close the gate, doesn't it?" He rose, then seated himself at Tuthill's command.

"Sit down, Blake, sit down. I'm thinking—thinking if there might be a way for you to get your second bar, and a company, without my approving the promotion in writing, as I'd have to do if the papers came through official channels. Let me think . . ." He slumped low in his chair, his chin in his hands. "St. Paul—please don't interrupt me—St. Paul's out of the question. Anything done there would have to be relayed to Washington, then back to St. Paul and out here. It would have to be in Washington . . . If your father should go to Washington and talk to those friends you mentioned, and if I should just happen to be there at the same time it might be possible for me to drop a word here and there, to speak to those officers who pass on such things and—possibly—see to it that the promotion does not include a transfer."

"Would you, sir, would you? I—I wouldn't know how to thank you!"

Tuthill shook his head slowly.

"I was thinking out loud, Blake, with a great many 'ifs.' I could add another—if you will consider it in strict confidence. If I were able at this time to afford the very considerable financial outlay of such a trip for Mrs. Tuthill and myself. Let me tell you very frankly, Blake, that I can't afford it."

"I—I—" Blake gulped. "If my father will do what he can at his end and if you'd go to Washington at the same time and—and do what you said you would—if you'd do that, sir, I'd be more than glad to assume all the expenses of the journey for you and Mrs. Tuthill."

He paused expectantly.

"That is very generous of you, Blake, very generous indeed. However, it is scarcely becoming for a regimental commander to be indebted so greatly to one of his junior officers."

"No one would ever know it, sir," said Blake bluntly.

"I trust not. Nevertheless, I would insist on giving you my note."

"I'd tear it up!"

"That would be your privilege." Tuthill rose and Blake was instantly on his feet. "Write your father if you wish, Mr. Blake. If he will go to Washington in your behalf you can telegraph him the date of my arrival. It would be better, I imagine, if he reached Washington several days before I did."

"I'll write him tonight, sir . . . and thank you a thousand times."

"Save your thanks, Mr. Blake, until you're wearing a captain's bars. It will be up to your father to make the snowball; all I'll be able to do will be to push it in the right direction."

Tuthill returned to his desk and sat there for some minutes after the lieutenant left. Then he shrugged, drew a basket toward him, and placed his sprawling signature on sundry documents. In the outer office he spoke to the heavily bearded adjutant, Clagett, who had been a first lieutenant since a month after Appomattox when he had reluctantly stripped the silver leaves of a lieutenant colonel from his shoulder straps.

"I signed those returns and the requisition forms, Clagett. I'll be at my quarters if you should need me."

The sentry at the door presented arms; the two orderlies leaped to attention. Tuthill saluted absently and buckled his heavy buffalo coat before leaving the building. His pace quickened as he crossed the parade ground; he mounted the steps to his quarters in a single bound.

"Matt! Hi, Mattie!"

"In here, Fred. You're early."

She met him at the parlor door and he swung her into his arms, then deposited her on top of the square piano. She squealed ecstatically but he held her firmly, his hands about her tiny waist, her knees under his arms.

"What happened, Fred? Something did, I know. Tell Mama."

"Good news, Mattie! It looks as though we'll get away from here for a month or six weeks. Washington, New York, your folks, the theaters! Yippeeee!"

"How, Fred? Did you hear from Father? I didn't write him —you told me not to."

"I know I did. We've asked him for loans too often. No, it's not your father. It's, well, it's another source. I'll tell you about it when the time comes. It's not absolutely dead-for-sure certain yet, but it's about ninety per cent sure."

"Can I tell people we're going? Mrs. Marcus—Mrs. Bellew?"

"Not a word to a soul. If you do, I'll paddle you pink— right there!"

He pinched her plump rear and she squealed again.

"Stop it! Fred, I cried, I really did, when you told me not to write Father. He doesn't mind lending us money . . . he knows how terrible it is out here in the winter. But how, how on earth did you manage it, darling?"

"It, well, it just came to me like that manna from heaven that took care of Elijah—or was it Elisha?—I always get those old fellows mixed up. Manna from heaven, that was it."

4

The bottle had been wrapped carefully in many thicknesses of soft paper, then boxed and addressed to Captain Demas Harrod, 20th Cavalry, USA, Fort Andrew Doniphan, Dakota Territory, via Wells Fargo Express. There was no card, but Harrod, as he stripped the final wrappings, knew the gift's source. There was only one person in the world who would have sent him a quart of Monongahela whisky, a bottle which had once rested on the shelves of Long Cy Pierce's cellar in

St. Louis. *Damn it, I should have written her. That note saying I'd reached the fort and was commanding F—that doesn't count. She hasn't forgotten and she picked the best way there was of showing me she hadn't. Lulu . . .*

Such whisky, he decided selfishly, was entirely too good to be made community property. Take it to the officers' club on Saturday night and it would last about as long as a June snowflake. He'd keep it in his room, locked in his trunk, and ration himself to one drink a day, a nightcap, after taps had sounded and he'd dismissed his striker and taken off his boots. A nightcap toast to Lulu, bless her heart. *Here's to it and to it again.* If he shared that whisky, if he let even one man know that he had so precious a possession, he'd pick someone who would appreciate it, someone who knew the difference between old Monongahela and the sutler's forty-rod, someone like Mike McKeown.

McKeown, like himself, was a bachelor, a tall Irishman as lean as a rapier and endowed with what he described as a periodic unholy thirst. About twice a year he drank himself into oblivion. It might be in the seclusion of his quarters, where he tippled alone, one drink following another, until he collapsed; or it might be in a boozing den in South City from which fellow officers would bear him in a closed hack to a hotel room. The chief surgeon, Dr. Thad Venner, straight-faced, would report him sick in quarters, then turn to the unpleasant task of sobering up the unconscious man and restoring him to duty.

When sober, as he was for six or seven months after a debauch, there was no better line officer in the army. Irish by birth, he had been educated—and very well educated—in France and for a time had considered preparing for the priesthood. *There's no cleaner nor easier job in the world than that of bein' a bishop, but me habits and me weaknesses w'd be against me, as I well knew. Since the church wouldn't have me, the army remained.*

He had been commissioned a *sous-lieutenant* of hussars and while in that service had cultivated the sweeping mustache and imperial affected by Napoleon III; but he had left the French Army, and France, rather abruptly after a duel with his battalion commander. *Over the worthless wife of a lawyer in Dijon, it was. He was jealous—the major, I mean—and when I told him the woman was regimental property he laid his hand across my face and there was nothing to do but challenge him. He fancied himself as a swordsman and chose rapiers. I laid open his arm to the bone from the elbow to the shoulder. It could have been his heart or his throat as easy, and he knew it. 'Twas that made me an Italian for a time.*

He had been a lieutenant in the Papal Guard when the shells fell on Sumter. Six weeks later he was in New York where he encountered Alfred Napoleon Duffié—*'twas Duffy to me, always. A County Clare mick he was, but, God, what a soldier!*—and had accompanied that former hussar to Rhode Island and a commission, under Duffié, in that state's First Cavalry. He had fought through the entire conflict and had been a lieutenant colonel when Lee surrendered. His record was magnificent and a regular army commission was his for the asking.

He lounged by the table in Harrod's quarters. A tall glass, nearly empty now, was close to his hand; a kettle of hot water steamed on the stove; on the table were sugar, cloves, and a bottle of lemon extract.

"It was the best I could do, Mike." Harrod indicated the lemon extract. "This weather calls for toddies, but there's not a real lemon to be had in the territory, let alone South City. I trooped the line."

"With whisky like that," observed McKeown, "no apologies are called for. 'Tis smoother than a widow's kiss and twice as tasty."

"Experience speaking, Mike?" Harrod busied himself with another drink.

"Perhaps, perhaps. Ask me no more lest I use a lady's name when in my cups . . . go easy with the water, Demas! God's Holy Name, do you want to poison me?"

"God forbid! There!" Harrod tilted the bottle of Monongahela. "I'll dilute it a bit—the water, I mean."

"That's better." McKeown's long fingers curled around the glass. Harrod moved to his own chair.

"Speaking of widows, Mike, we have one to thank for this whisky. A friend of mine in Saint"—he coughed—"St. Louis."

"My regards to her as a lady of rare discrimination." The Irishman sipped appreciatively. "There's widows—and widows," he added judicially. "Each Christmas, without fail, I get a gift from a widow in Providence. Knitted gloves, a muffler, wool socks—all the work of her own hands. She thinks the world of me, and I of her. She'll be"—his fingers tapped the table in swift calculation—"she'll be sixty-two come March."

Harrod laughed.

"My friend isn't half that. She was married young and soon widowed. I—somehow I've been thinking a lot of her lately."

McKeown set down the scalding toddy.

" 'Tis bitter cold outside," he remarked. "There's nothing like an icy bed to send a soldier's thoughts back to the past. An icy bed—or army cookin'. C'd you stomach the meal we had tonight?"

"I wasn't at mess. I was in town, hunting lemons, and I ate there."

"You were lucky. That pistol scabbard yonder, with a bit of gravy, w'd be more tasty than the beef they served. So we'll charge your dreams to the icy bed, Demas. Drink hearty."

"Regards, Mike." Harrod stared unseeing at his glass. *Why in God's name did you send that whisky, Lulu—the one gift that would bring everything back to me? Your father's Monongahela, brandy from New Orleans, Ruinart '58, the king's peg. Did you want to bring it all back? I should have written you differently. I should have told you . . . but, damn it all, Lulu, I did tell you. Army life is hell for women.*

McKeown's fingers touched his hand.

"Drink, man." The Irishman's deep voice was as tender as a woman's. "Drink. Sure, the Black Dog is riding your shoulder—none knows the sign of it better than I. The whisky will drive him off. Drink."

Harrod drank.

"Thanks, Mike. I guess——"

"Give me no words. You and you alone know where your thoughts were. Keep it so."

"You're right at that. I'll fix another drink. Say, Mike——"

"Yes?"

"I was thinking, as you said. Thinking about myself. In some ways I'm considerable of a son of a bitch."

"And aren't we all? Go easy with the water, Demas."

5

He sat in a room of the Metropolitan Hotel in St. Paul and scowled at a blank piece of paper on the desk in front of him. His coat was tossed on a chair, his shirt was unfastened, and from time to time he mopped his forehead. A dozen sheets of paper littered the floor. He swore softly and crumpled another.

"Christ on a crutch," he growled. "I'm attacking like a damned infantryman with a dozen feints on the flanks to hide the main advance. Charge, Demas. Mass your companies and charge!"

He pulled the pad closer and began again.

Lulu, my darling. I will have to write what I hoped to tell you face to face, but your return here is uncertain and I must go back to Fort Doniphan on tomorrow's train. I was able to obtain only fifteen days' leave for urgent personal business, but when I reached St. Paul your house was closed and your relatives, whom I had some difficulty in locating, would say only that you had gone back East. I think you were right when you said they did not like you, Lulu—certainly they did not welcome me when I said I was an old friend of yours.

"Damn it, man, get to the point!" He extended his cramped fingers and took up the pen.

So I will have to write what I wanted to say to you last summer. I want you to marry me, Lulu. I want you to be my wife.

That is what I came from Doniphan to say to you. Before you answer, though, you should know that the army is a hell of a life for a woman. I told you that before and I will repeat it. Even a captain's quarters, while better than some, are still a long way from what you're used to and I will be a captain for a long time. Promotions are slow. And I will be on the frontier for a long time too. We have the hostile Sioux and Cheyennes to lick next summer—a campaign against them is very certain—and after that, who knows? Maybe the Apaches in Arizona where there is a great deal of trouble.

And I haven't a dime, Lulu, outside of my army pay, which is ninety-five dollars a month, not counting the increase which I get for length of service. A captain gets thirty-two dollars a month for quarters—four rooms—and the government makes a small allowance for my personal horse too, but it's impossible to perform a company commander's duties without two chargers, especially when on active service in the field. Also, an officer can't get along without a striker, which is what we call the personal servant—a man from the company—who cleans his equipment, polishes his boots, and such jobs. I pay mine three dollars per month.

I feel I must tell you such things, Lulu, because you should know before, and not after, you marry a cavalry officer that you will have to count every penny. The dimes you will have to count twice.

If you should say Yes—and I am praying that you will—we will have to wait until after next summer's expedition to get married. I am not one of Colonel Tuthill's favorites and even if I were he could not give me leave before we take the field.

Your relatives here did not know, or would not tell me, when you would return. I may be doing them an injustice, Lulu, but I do not want to trust delivery of this letter to them. That is why you will receive it from the president of your bank whose name was given me by Mr. Holmes at your factory.

I want you to marry me, Lulu. When you get this please write and tell me that you will. You will make me very happy, as I will try all my life to make you.

He laid down the pen and read what he had written.

"Sounds like a schoolboy, but damned if I know any other way to put it. She can't ever say I didn't tell her the truth— it's a hell of a life for a woman."

He signed his full name: DEMAS K. HARROD.

14 THE DICE OF GOD

The Twentieth did not take the field until May. There were many delays. Tuthill had left for Washington early in January but his thirty days' leave had been twice extended by orders telegraphed from department headquarters at St. Paul. Units of other regiments—five companies of infantry and a battery of Gatling guns manned by an infantry platoon—had been designated to accompany the expedition, but their arrival was delayed; and even after they reached Fort Doniphan, it was learned that additional equipment had to be drawn to fit them for the campaign. Ten thousand rounds of ammunition for the forty-five-caliber Springfield carbines were condemned as unfit for use; there was further delay until new issues were obtained.

Each blade of new grass springing from the gray-brown earth seemed rooted in rumor. Tuthill had been relieved; they were

waiting for a new colonel, an infantryman who had never led
a cavalry regiment. That was all wrong; Tuthill was slated to
command the expedition against the hostiles; he would be
promoted to brigadier and all they were waiting for was Senate
confirmation . . . Nothing of the sort. The Indians themselves had caused the delay. Nobody knew where they were.
Scouts were out now to track down the encampments of Sitting Bull, Crazy Horse, and the rest of them. When the scouts
get back they'd move, and fast.

Tuthill reached the post early in April. He was not a
brigadier, that was sure, but he was accompanied by a general
officer whose presence answered many questions and quashed
many rumors. The expedition against the Sioux would be
headed by the commander of the Department of Dakota. Tuthill would be under him, in command of the Twentieth.

Only his wife knew of his disappointment.

"It would have meant my star," he whispered to her. "I'd
have been a brigadier again. It was as close as that"—his thumb
and finger almost touched. "Sheridan wanted me—he knows
what I can do in a campaign like this—but Grant said No.
Grant and Sherman."

Her lips parted but he rattled on.

"Jealousy, Mattie, rank jealousy. Coffee-coolers in Washington, colonels, who don't want to see me go over their heads
again. I'll show them, the whole crew. I'll cut loose on my
own."

"You must be careful, Boy." The pet name was one reserved
for their most intimate moments. "You mustn't be impetuous.
The general could——"

"But he won't." Tuthill's teeth snapped. "He'll be a little
lost sheep in the Indian country—he'll have to turn to me for
everything. You'll see."

She clutched him tightly. Her body strained against his.

"I won't see, I won't. That's the trouble. You'll be out there
fighting those terrible Indians and I'll be here waiting. I've

had so much of that, Boy. Waiting . . . waiting. Thinking every time I hear footsteps on the porch that it might be—oh, Boy, hold me close. Hold me and tell me that nothing is going to happen to you."

"Now, Mattie, little girl . . ."

Later, much later, he continued: "Those coffee-coolers in Washington, Mattie, just don't realize how important this campaign is, but they're the ones who have the ear of the President. One of them—that fathead Leggett—told me that we should avoid a fight and try only to persuade the hostiles to return to the reservations. Can you imagine Rain-in-the-Face listening to persuasion?"

"No-o-o. When we were in New York, Father said——"

"Exactly. Your father and those men he invited to dinner, to meet me. One of them was an editor of the *Herald*. He said that this was war, and that he and his associates regarded it as a real crisis for the nation. Mr. Sturgill of the Northern Pacific agreed with him."

"He wants to see the railroad built further," said the less visionary Martha Tuthill.

"Of course he does. It's men like him that really decide things. They're the ones I want to show. If I go in on my own and whip the hostiles, there's nothing I can't be, darling, nowhere I can't go!"

"Just so you come back to me, that's all I ask. I pray——"

"Don't worry your dear head about it, Mattie. A thousand or two Indians—they're not Lee and the Army of Northern Virginia."

2

The regiment marched on May 17. The wagon train was loaded the day before and departed at dawn, two hours before the stuttering trumpets ordered the cavalrymen to stand to horse.

One hundred and fifty wagons, the greater number drawn by six mules which in time would be distributed among the companies as a pack train. The infantry was marched to the fort's landing and there embarked on a river packet for the voyage up to the Missouri to the Yellowstone; the Gatling platoon, its weapons drawn by condemned cavalry horses, accompanied the wagon train. Tuthill would have no outsiders to detract from the glory of the Twentieth's farewell. He galloped to where his wife stood and swung to the ground at her side.

"Bye-bye, Mattie."

"Good-by, Boy," she answered between sobs. "Good-by." They were silent for a moment and she added: "They—the regiment looks fine, Fred."

"They're glorious! Look at them . . . if all the Indians on the Plains got together in one place, we'd whip 'em!"

Other men left the command for last farewells, then galloped toward their companies. The brigadier halted beside the Tuthills.

"We'll march whenever you give the word, Colonel. Good-by, Mrs. Tuthill, and thanks once more for your many courtesies."

"Good-by, General, and good luck." She caught her breath. "You'll bring him back to me, won't you, General?"

"Of course."

He touched his hat brim in salute and, Tuthill on his left, rode to the head of the long column. The men were already mounted. Tuthill raised his arm.

"Forward——"

From each of the twelve companies came the deep-toned response.

"Forward——"

Tuthill's arm fell.

"Ho!"

At the command the mounted musicians raised their instruments to their lips and the snare- and kettledrummers poised their sticks. The spring air quivered with the melody of the soldiers' farewell.

> *Oh, that girl, that pretty little girl,*
> *The girl I left behind me!*

The Twentieth Cavalry was marching on to war.

If there was cursing in the ranks, no sound of it reached the ears of the regimental commander. The paymaster had arrived at Doniphan the night before, but Tuthill had directed him and his escort to follow the regiment and to pay the troops— two months' pay was coming to each man—two days later when the column had advanced beyond South City and its temptations.

The route lay steadily to the northwest. Rumor—and no man knew its source—had reached Tuthill that the hostile bands were encamped on the lower reaches of the Little Missouri River. Sol Rogers shook his head.

" 'Tain't hardly likely, Gen'ral. A few Injuns, yes, mebbe, but no big bunch like you're lookin' for."

"You seem very certain, Sol. What have you heard?"

"Ain't heard nothin'. Lots of badlands country in there, Gen'ral. Water ain't good f'r much an' there's no grass f'r ponies, not f'r any such bunch of ponies as they'd have. Stands t' reason——"

"Where, then?"

The scout waved his arm to the westward.

"Out yonder someplace. South of th' Yellerstone, prob'ly."

There were no Indians in the valley of the Little Missouri, although the regiment camped for a day while Harrod took F company down the stream almost to its mouth. Arikara scouts flanked the company by five miles on either side.

The column wound on toward the Yellowstone. The recruits —and nearly forty per cent of the men were in that category— learned that military discipline tightened rather than relaxed when the Twentieth was in the field. The regiment was divided into two wings and the wings into two battalions, each of three companies. Each day one battalion was assigned as advance guard, one as rear guard, and one marched on either flank of the ponderous wagon train. Tuthill, with a company of the advance guard, ranged far in the lead. It was he who selected the route and designated the camping place to be occupied at the end of the day. It was then that the troopers' work really began. Horses were unsaddled, their backs were rubbed dry, and they were grazed, sidelined and on pickets, under guard of a noncommissioned officer and several privates. A detail from each company dug a straddle-trench latrine. A second latrine, somewhat removed from that for the enlisted men, was dug for the officers. Officers' tents were pitched and their baggage was carried from the wagon train. Lines were established for the shelter tents of the soldiers and those lines were dressed as precisely as were the ranks of the men at formal inspection. Other details were sent ranging about the campsite for fuel for the cooks: wood if it could be obtained, otherwise the omnipresent buffalo chips. The guard was posted. The officers' strikers scurried to make the beds and arrange the scanty furniture in the tents. Steers were driven up from the herd which followed the wagon train, slaughtered, butchered on the spot, and the still-hot meat was distributed to the company cooks. A detail of privates buried the steaming entrails.

As the weary men straightened their backs, the trumpet called them to other toil:

> *Oh, come to the stable,*
> *As soon as you're able,*
> *And water your horses*
> *And give them some corrrrn!*

The men fell in and were marched to the grazing ground by the company first sergeants. The animals were ridden to water, then returned to the area immediately behind each company's tents, fed their ration of oats in a nose bag, and groomed while they ate. Similar care was taken of the officers' chargers. A company officer and the first sergeant examined each animal after the grooming, with especial attention to the beast's back and feet.

"Watch that place close, Dugan; it looks as though there'd been a wrinkle in your saddle blanket. Remember, if your horse gets a sore back you walk—and lead him—until it's healed."

Dugan's lips moved but he said nothing.

Then, and not until then, the trumpets sounded mess call.

> *Soupie, soupie, soupie,*
> *Without a single bean;*
> *Porkie, porkie, porkie,*
> *Without a streak of lean;*
> *Coffee, coffee, coffee,*
> *Th' weakest ever seen.*

The food was usually good, although monotonous, and hungry men are not critical. First Sergeant Mullins set down his cup and wiped his mustache.

"Any of you fellows that aren't on camp guard or stable guard," he remarked, "you're free to go to town, if you want to. Be back by tattoo—sober."

It was considered humorous.

3

The column pushed on through a lonely land. No smoke columns save their own sullied the skies; the Crow and Arikara scouts, ranging far on the flanks, reported no sign of campsites or the furrows of dragging travois poles which would indicate that Indians had passed. Tuthill's curiosity relative to the Little Missouri was satisfied and the route swung directly west and a little south toward the distant Yellowstone. They crossed O'Fallon's Creek and climbed the divide between that stream and Powder River, easternmost of the main tributaries of the Yellowstone. Beyond, to the west and quite evenly spaced one from the other, were the Tongue and the Rosebud. A little further lay the Big Horn and its branches, Tullock's Creek and the Little Big Horn.

It was Tuthill, riding with his orderly beyond the advance guard, who met the messengers sent with the first news which the regiment had heard since the departure from Fort Doniphan. The steamer on which the infantry detachment had made the journey was now tied up at the mouth of the Powder and the soldiers had gone into camp on the south bank of the Yellowstone. No Indians had been sighted during the voyage, but contact had been established with the Montana column which had been patrolling the north bank of the Yellowstone since April to prevent, or at least to detect, any crossing of that stream by the hostiles.

The Indians, plenty of them, were still south of the Yellowstone. If they were aware of the three columns converging upon them, they were supremely indifferent. Scouts had seen smoke hanging low over the valley of the Tongue; smoke clouds and the dust of a large pony herd had been sighted in the valley of the Big Horn, west of the Rosebud and last of the Yellowstone's tributaries for many miles. The brigadier smiled his satisfaction.

"It looks like we've got them. The column from Fort Fetterman—I wish we'd heard from them—should be in position to prevent any escape to the south. The Montana troops will guard the line of the river to block them on the north. I'll send a strong cavalry command to scout the Tongue and its forks. They'll meet us—all of us—at the Tongue."

He directed Major Marcus to lead that scouting column. So far the wagon train had kept pace with the slow progress of the Twentieth, but it was left at the mouth of the Powder and the mules were distributed among the companies as pack animals. Soldiers who were as ignorant of the intricacies of the diamond hitch as they were of integral calculus took over the handling. The sabers—as useless in Indian warfare as any weapon could be—were packed in the wagons with other nonessential equipment. The regimental standard was left behind; only Tuthill's headquarters flag—a scarlet and white swallowtailed burgee bearing crossed sabers in silver—accompanied the regiment. The Twentieth's band remained to guard the wagons and stored equipment.

Tuthill, with half of the regiment, marched to the Tongue and on to the Rosebud, still further to the west, where Marcus joined them. There were no Indians, he said, on the upper Powder or in the valley of the Tongue. Satisfied of that, he had extended his scout to the next valley, that of the Rosebud. Again no Indians—but they had been there. Plenty of them. He had found where several large bands had been camped and had followed for some distance a trail which led to the west, a trail stamped by the hoofs of thousands of ponies, furrowed by many hundreds of dragging lodgepoles.

Tuthill was furious and tongue-lashed Marcus as he might a raw second lieutenant who had bumbled an assignment. That Marcus had actually exceeded his orders by advancing beyond the Tongue had nothing to do with the fact. He should have gone further, Tuthill shouted, should have followed the trail, and—with six companies—tangled with the Indians. A golden opportunity had been in his grasp and he had botched it. When Marcus protested, Tuthill dismissed him curtly and, alone, walked beyond the limits of the camp. Hands clasped behind him, he paced up and down the bank of the muddy Yellowstone. It was there that Lieutenant Walter

Blake found him. The young man's eyes were sparkling and he thrust an official envelope into Tuthill's hands.

"It came through, sir," he exclaimed. "I'd about given up hope but it came through. I'm a captain, thanks to you!"

Tuthill merely glanced at the paper. In official language it notified First Lieutenant Walter N. Blake, Twentieth Cavalry, of his appointment as Captain, Cavalry, United States Army.

"Where—how did you receive this, Mr.—I beg your pardon, Captain Blake?" *A captain! And there are four men, at least, senior to him in the regiment. God Almighty, his father must have all the political pull there is in Washington. I certainly did nothing about it.*

Blake pointed across the river.

"There, sir. The packet steamer *Josephine* brought up supplies and mail a couple of hours ago. Our mail, the Twentieth's, was brought over in a rowboat. The adjutant distributed it."

"I—" Tuthill's fingers closed but he restrained in time to avoid crumpling the notification. "Coming at this time, this makes matters difficult. For the present, Captain, please say nothing of this—this promotion."

"It's too late, sir. I opened it in the adjutant's tent and when I saw what it was I let out a yell that Sitting Bull would envy. I guess all the officers know it by now." He was quite oblivious to Tuthill's anger. "It means I get my company, sir."

"Don't be hasty, Blake," snapped Tuthill. "You will get a company when and if I assign you to command one. You are in the field now, not in garrison. Kindly remember. That will be all, Blake."

4

Captain Harrod was one of several company commanders who worried over placing completely inexperienced men in charge of the pack train for his unit. He spent the entire day working with one group after another from F company in an attempt to find a few men who showed some slight proficiency in the handling of mules and in packing them so that the loads would not be lost within the first few miles of travel. It was nearly dark when he returned to the company campsite with the last group. First Sergeant Mullins was waiting for him.

"I'll take care of your horse, sir. You're wanted at regimental headquarters immediately."

"No chance for even a cup of coffee?"

"I'm afraid not, sir. The last orderly that was looking for you reported that the colonel was fit to be tied."

"Thanks, First Sergeant. Maybe if I look hungry enough——"

Tuthill was pacing nervously in front of his tent. A faint halo of light was shed by the kerosene lantern on the table beside his bed. Harrod halted and saluted.

"My apologies for my delay, General. I received your message only——"

"That's quite all right, Captain. I was anxious to see you and was a little impatient. Have you had your supper?"

"No, sir. I sent word to the cooks to save something for me——"

"No, indeed. Orderly!" The figure of a trooper materialized out of the darkness. "My compliments to Captain Bellew. Ask him if his kitchen can send some supper to my tent for Captain Harrod."

"Yes, sir." The man disappeared.

"Sit down, Harrod. Take the chair by the table—you'll have some food in a few minutes—I'll sit on the bed."

"Thank you, General." *Christ on a crutch, what's he leading up to? I never saw him so considerate in my life. You'd think I was a senator, at least.*

"I've been out all day with the company, General, trying to find a few men who knew something—or could learn something—about packing."

"We'll take care of that," Tuthill dismissed the subject airily.

"There are plenty of civilian packers with the wagon train. I'll hire a few of them to go along with us."

Harrod shrugged.

"I don't think much of civilians when we're in the field. I wonder how many of them would stick if there was a fight."

"They'll be all right," said Tuthill confidently. "Ah, here's some supper for you, Captain, some good old slum and coffee! I'll talk while you're eating."

"It smells good. Thank you, General."

"Not at all."

God above, what's wrong with the man! Well, I won't have to wait much longer. He dug generously into the stew, quite aware that Tuthill was watching him.

"Have you heard, Harrod, that we've got a new captain? Lieutenant Blake received notice today of his promotion."

"Blake! There are several senior to him! How did he——?"

"I don't know . . . I wish I did. If you didn't hear of Blake's promotion I doubt if you heard about McKeown."

"No—did he get his major's leaves, sir? That would be fine!"

"No such luck. Mike won't be with us on the expedition . . . one of his recruits shot him today."

"My God, General! Don't tell me——"

"No, nothing like that. Mike took a few men out for pistol practice, dismounted. One of the recruits was reloading his revolver and let the hammer snap down from the half-cock position—at least that seems to be what happened. The ball hit Mike above the ankle and broke the smaller bone of his lower leg. Dr. Venner has him in bed on the steamer—the maddest Irishman west of the Mississippi."

"That I can well imagine, sir."

"Which brings me," said Tuthill quickly, "to why I called you. I want you to take McKeown's D company, Harrod, and turn F over to the new captain, Blake."

"I take—General, you don't mean——?" Harrod stammered ineffectually.

"I think you heard me, Harrod. Are you trying to suggest that I give D to Captain Blake and permit you to retain your present command?"

"Yes, sir. I've worked hard with F. I know the men and they know me. I'm asking you to reconsider——"

Tuthill's lifted hand silenced him.

"Captain, if there was one thing I learned from Phil Sheridan it was never—never, I said—to reconsider a decision. This was not made without careful thought. McKeown's injury relieves me of the unpleasant duty of giving Blake either A or K in place of Hanna or Richards. There's no lieutenant with McKeown's company——"

"He has Hardy, sir," Harrod interrupted.

"Only nominally. Hardy's actually serving as adjutant to Major Marcus."

"That's true, sir. I didn't think of that. I gather, then, that you don't want Blake to take a company without a junior officer."

"Exactly. As I told you a moment ago, I considered this decision very carefully. You are the only captain in the regiment, Harrod, to whom I'd entrust McKeown's company with no junior officer."

"I—thank you, sir. I don't mind telling you that I hate the thought of losing F——"

"I know, I know. Of course you do. Let's consider the matter settled, Harrod. I'll tell Blake that he will take F—I wanted to speak to you first, of course—and will then send him down to see you. Talk to McKeown and his first sergeant—his name is Osmer—as soon as you can."

"Yes, sir."

Harrod saluted and withdrew. Some two hours later he was seated in the cabin of the stern-wheeler *Josephine*. Mike McKeown, his left leg in splints, lighted a fresh cheroot and pushed the box toward the new commander of D company.

"And pour yourself a drink, Demas. It's Medical Corps

whisky—compliments of Doc Venner—but it's better than Yellowstone water. Luck to you and to D. If I had to be knocked out, I'm glad it's you that took over."

"Thanks, Mike. Since they moved the *Josephine* over to this side of the river, I may get a chance to see you in the morning. First Sergeant Osmer and some of the other noncoms will be here to see you for sure!"

"They're good men, all of them. You think you'll be pulling out tomorrow then?"

Harrod shrugged.

"Maybe. The old man and the general are chewing things over right now. We'll know in the morning."

"Yes." McKeown tried to shift the position of his leg and grunted at a sharp twinge of pain. "And by morning I'll have thought up some new cursewords for that goddamned butterfingered recruit. Acklin is his name, Demas, Thomas Acklin. When there are latrines to be dug or a dead horse to be buried, remember it."

"He gave me a message to deliver to you, Mike. I went down to the company with Bill Clagett to notify Osmer that I was taking over and Acklin asked permission to speak to me. He said to tell you that he'd shoot himself if it would bring you back to the company. He's really broken up, Mike."

"Tell him I said it was over and done." The Irishman was instantly forgiving when he learned of the recruit's remorse. "It was fate, Demas, fate that the hammer slipped from under his thumb and my big foot was in the way.

"Think of it for a minute, man. Four years of the war—more battles, engagements, and skirmishes than I can count; four horses shot under me, men killed in front of me and behind me and on either side; and I never got a scratch. Not a scratch! How many men can say that, Demas? It was fate, just as stopping that slug today was fate. The dice fell against me. God's dice—and they're always loaded."

"I never heard it put that way," Harrod observed.

"Give the credit to a broader education than they gave you at West Point, Demas. I had to read philosophy and it was Emerson who wrote the words I gave you. Ralph W. Emerson, thirty years and more ago. 'The dice of God are always loaded,' he said, and I'm thinkin' he was right."

He moved restlessly and Harrod rose to settle the pillows beneath his shoulders. McKeown clutched his wrist.

"Don't go, Demas, not yet."

"I was just straightening your pillows, Mike."

"Ah, I thought you were leavin', leavin' me to dark thoughts of myself lyin' here on me back and the rest of you takin' the field for the last crack at the hostiles. They say that the Irish are fey, you know, that we see a little further into tomorrow than others do. Maybe they're right. Demas, pour another drink of the medic's whisky and then tell me—have you talked with Tuthill?"

"No." Harrod placed the glass close to McKeown's hand. "Just a few words when he told me about taking over D company."

"He said nothing about his plans?"

"Not a word."

"Marcus and Lamar Steele were in just after supper. There's but one thought in Tuthill's mind, to break loose and lick the hostiles all by himself . . . him and the Twentieth."

"The hero of Wishbone Creek," commented Harrod bitterly.

"You were there, weren't you, Demas?"

"I was there. So were Harry Bellew and Jerry Hanford. So was Bill Clagett. Talk to them about it."

"I've heard the talk. What I'm wonderin' about is if today, with the Sioux just a couple of jumps over the hill, if Eagle-beak isn't biting off more than he can chew."

"God knows." Harrod shrugged. "The estimates—you remember when the old man gave us the figures—run from fifteen hundred to maybe two thousand warriors."

"Yes, I know. The Twentieth should be able to take care of them. Why, then, are men makin' their wills?"

"Are they? I'd heard nothing of it, Mike."

"There's been four brought to me tonight. Since I'm going back to the States, they say, I'm the logical man to take care of them. One is me little shavetail, Pete Hardy, that's actin' as Marcus' adjutant. Another—figure this if you can, Demas—is Sol Rogers'."

"Rogers! I never thought of him having anything more to leave than—than I have."

"You're wrong. He's got three or four thousand on deposit with Wells Fargo in South City. If he doesn't come out of this scrap, the money goes to a private named Hale in E company or, if Hale is knocked off, too, it goes to Miss Elizabeth Poole of South City. Who the devil is she, Demas?"

"Poole? She must be the daughter of that missionary who was drowned last summer."

"Sure. I knew I'd heard the name. Well, old Sol got Pete Hardy to draw it up for him and he signed it before witnesses and in the presence of Tom Marcus, summary court officer. It's as legal as hell."

"Sol's the kind who will live forever, then dry up and blow away," Harrod commented. "He's been in and out of Indian fights since God knows when. Hardy or somebody probably gave him the idea. You remember how it was during the war, Mike; the night before a battle everybody who was going into action for the first time wrote his will."

"Yes, but facin' a battle with Lee or Jackson was a dif'rent matter from a bunch of Injuns. That was why I asked you if Tuthill had said anything to you about the campaign. I was wonderin' if——"

"If what, Mike?"

"If—" the Irishman drew a deep breath. "Forget it, Demas, forget it. You're going on the expedition and you're leaving behind a crippled mick with the Black Dog riding his shoulder. Forget it, I said, but take this with you———"

His fingers moved to the back of his neck and unfastened a silver chain from which was suspended a medal slightly larger than a dime. He dropped chain and medal in Harrod's hand.

"You're not a Cath'lic, Demas, and it'll mean nothing to you; but wear it for luck and because Mike McKeown asked you to. I've never had it off my neck since it was hung there by a cardinal of the Church after the Holy Father himself had blessed it. It carries the image or the picture or whatever you'd call it of Saint Sebastian, patron saint of soldiers. He died a martyr—shot to death with arrows. The heathen you'll be fightin' will be usin' arrows, too. Will you wear it, Demas?"

"I will, Mike, and thank you."

5

Four days later, at dawn on Sunday morning, the weary troopers struggled to wakefulness in a bivouac in the pass which led from the drainage of the Rosebud to that of the Big Horn. For the past two days, Friday and Saturday, the regiment had followed a trail blazed by successive Indian camps, furrowed by dragging lodgepoles, churned by the hoofs of countless ponies.

Tuthill was like a hound confined on a short leash but with the scent of a hot trail in his nostrils. He was impatient of every delay as the scouts halted to study the week-old spoor of the hostiles; and when the regiment halted at sundown on Saturday, he passed the word to all troop commanders that the advance would be resumed at eleven o'clock.

"A night march, gentlemen," he snapped. "I want to get as close as possible to the divide before daylight. We can hide there during the day while the scouts study the Little Big Horn valley. Then, if the hostiles are camped there, we'll attack. A dawn attack, probably, on Monday morning. I hope that's clear to all of you."

Many weeks later, in attempting to recall the events of that June Sunday, Harrod marked three which—insignificant in themselves—had combined to affect all of Tuthill's planning. The men of D company were struggling to prepare breakfast when Tuthill approached.

"Carry on, men. Harrod, have the company ready to advance at eight o'clock. We're still five or six miles from the divide. The scouts were up there at sunup. They sighted a big village, they say, on the Little Big Horn. I'm going on to the divide to see for myself."

That was the first. The scouts had sighted that village at dawn, with the rising sun behind them. When Tuthill reached the divide, the sun was much higher. He could see nothing and told Sol Rogers he didn't believe there was any village there. Then he came back to where the regiment waited and summoned the officers. He told them he could see no village.

"I've been on the Plains a long time," he said confidently, "and my eyes, I think, are as good as most men's. There's no village there, gentlemen. Even with my field glasses I couldn't see a sign of one."

It was then that Blake, the new captain, raised his hand.

"Yes, Captain?" Tuthill was never patient when interrupted.

"I beg your pardon, General, but after we halted I sent Sergeant Kurtz and two men back to recover a couple of boxes of hardtack which had been lost from the packs during the night. An Indian had found them first. He was trying to open one of the boxes with a tomahawk and when he saw Kurtz and the soldiers he jumped on his pony and loped off out of range. They know there are soldiers in the country, all right."

That was the second and combined with the first it made the third: Tuthill's fear that the hostiles would break up into small groups and scatter. Some might get around his left flank, others would break to the north and cross the Yellowstone, others would head west toward the mountains. Tuthill wanted to catch them bunched up. He wanted a fight and the glory of winning it. And then . . .

Tuthill's left hand tugged at his mustache, his right balled into a fist, then relaxed. He rose quickly.

"Gentlemen, since we've been discovered, we must move forward immediately to locate the village and attack. Company commanders will detail immediately a corporal and six men to accompany the pack train. Inspect your companies and report as soon as you are ready to march. The last company to report will escort the pack train. That's all."

The first sergeants rattled off the names of those who would ride with the pack train. Among those called by First Sergeant Barron, of E, was Private Martin Hale. The man who had enlisted under the name of Gentry spoke quickly to the first sergeant, Mullins, of F.

"First Sergeant, will you keep me with the company, please? If there's to be a fight I want to be in it, with the company. I told you so at the fort, remember?"

Mullins gave no indication that he had heard the request, but he did not call Gentry's name.

"I heard you, Gentry," he grunted as F company fell in. "You should know better, by now, than to speak up at a time like that, with the captain in hearing. It would have served you right if I'd sent you to the pack train to learn you manners."

Bellew, senior captain of the regiment, was first to report his command ready. At a nod from Tuthill he led out toward the crest of the divide. Lieutenant Hanna followed with Company A, and Harrod was third with D. Tuthill called to him as he passed.

"Can you send me a man as my personal orderly, Captain?"

Harrod nodded and saluted.

"I don't know the men, First Sergeant," he said quietly, "who's best for that job?"

"The little dark-complected fellow, Captain. Morelli is his name. He's a trumpeter but since the order is no calls, we can spare him."

"Thanks, First Sergeant. Morelli!"

"Yes, sir."

"Report to Colonel Tuthill as orderly. Stay within call always, understand?"

"Sure, Captain, I onnerstan'. Yes, sir."

He pulled out of line and trotted to where Tuthill was standing.

Hanford, commanding B company, was last to report. Tuthill nodded and jerked a thumb in the direction of the pack train.

"Try to keep 'em up, Jerry. Chances are we'll be moving fast."

He touched his charger with the spur and galloped toward the head of the column. It was shortly before noon when the weary horses mounted the last slope and the distant valley of the Little Big Horn was revealed. Within a mile Sol Rogers trotted down from the hills on the right. Several of the 'Ree scouts were visible against the crestline behind him. Tuthill swung away from the column and rode to meet him. His adjutant, the sergeant major, and the orderly followed.

"Have you seen anything, Sol? Any Indians?"

"Nope. Some of th' 'Rees claim they seen three 'r four Injuns soon after we started down this side of the divide. They——"

"The village—have you located it?"

"Ain't seen it, but I'm still stickin' to th' bet I made you this mornin', Gen'ral—it's 'long th' river. Th' 'Rees——"

"What about them? Damn it, Sol, the hostiles could be pulling out while we're talking!"

"Mebbe so. Whut I was sayin'—th' 'Rees 've jest about got their bellyful. They're dodgin' any fightin', looks like. Thought y'd better know, Gen'ral."

"Are you sure, Sol? Why, last night Red Axe assured me——"

"That was last night, Gen'ral, an' Red Axe is all right. I think he'll stick. Th' others——" Sol shook his head. "I don't savvy much 'Ree, Gen'ral, but their sign talk makes it pretty plain. They saw that camp this mornin'—th' one you couldn't see—an' they're sayin' there's enough Sioux there t' keep you fightin' f'r th' next two days."

"Tell 'em to locate that village," snapped Tuthill angrily, "and I'll guarantee it won't take two days to clean it out! Have any of them been down to the Little Horn, Sol?"

"Nope, and they ain't goin'. Not alone, that is."

"To hell with them!"

Tuthill rode swiftly back to his command.

"Captain Bellew, take command of D and K with your own H. Strike out toward that first line of bluffs"—Tuthill waved his arm to the south and west—"and pitch into anything you find. If there's nothing between here and the first line of bluffs, go on to the second."

"Right, sir!" Bellew saluted and ordered his lieutenant, Myron, to take command of the company. He signaled Harrod, with D, then Lieutenant Richards, Company K commander, to follow the leading troop, then rode to the lead.

"And if you know what I'm really expected to do, I wish you'd let me know, Demas," he remarked as he passed the leading file of D.

"Will do—and I don't like this splitting up," Harrod replied.

"Nor do I." Bellew pulled his watch from his pocket and snapped open the case. "I make it ten after twelve, Demas. Is that your time?"

"Yes, within a minute or two." Harrod glanced at the sun. "It's not that late, you know, Harry. That's Fort Doniphan time, you know, and we're a long way west of there."

"Right. But so long as we agree, what difference does it make? Forward, ho, to the first line of bluffs!"

He laughed and touched his mount with his spur.

Bellew and his battalion were still in sight when Tuthill ordered a second division of the regiment. Major Marcus was assigned command of companies A, G, and M. No orders were given him, but the companies fell in behind the major on the left bank of the dry watercourse that followed the ravine. Tuthill, with C, E, F, I, and L companies, was on the right; the pack train and B company were far in the rear.

The regiment was still far—how far no one knew—from the river, nor was there any sign of Indians. Sol Rogers tried repeatedly to force the scouts to range ahead of the troops, but the frightened Arikaras refused or, after advancing a few hundred yards, circled and returned to the cavalry. When a solitary tepee was sighted, it was Tuthill who was first to investigate it. The lodge held the body of a Sioux warrior who had died two or three days before, at least. Tuthill, thumb and finger pinching his nostrils, backed out of the teepee just as Sol Rogers shouted to him. The scout had ridden to a knoll some fifty yards away which commanded a wider vista of the ravine.

"Look yonder, Gen'ral! Thar's y'r Injuns runnin' like devils."

Tuthill leaped to the saddle and galloped to the knoll in time to see the last of a group of Indians racing toward the river. He shouted angry commands to the Arikaras.

"Take after them! Plenty ponies!"

Red Axe, leader of the 'Rees, shook his head sullenly.

"No do," he muttered. "Too much Sioux."

Tuthill dashed back and spoke briefly to his adjutant, Clagett.

"And tell him," the colonel shouted as Clagett spurred toward Marcus' battalion, "tell him to take those damn scouts with him. I don't want 'em if they won't fight!"

Sol Rogers swung his pony toward the further side of the dry creek but Tuthill halted him.

"That don't go for you, Sol, only those damn 'Rees. Come along if you want to get in the show!"

"Might as well, Gen'ral," the scout agreed.

He checked his pony as the companies, C, E, F, I, and L in order, swung to the right to follow Tuthill. The adjutant crossed the ravine and rode swiftly to Marcus' side.

"Go ahead, Major," he said. "The general's orders are that you take as fast a gait as you think prudent, charge the Indians, and the whole outfit will support you."

Marcus nodded understanding and Clagett turned to the right toward Tuthill's battalion. The time was two-fifteen. Two-fifteen by Fort Doniphan time, as Harrod had remarked, which meant actually that it was Chicago time. By the sun it was not quite one o'clock—a discrepancy which was to confuse military historians for more than half a century.

6

Captain Bellew kept his three companies—about one hundred twenty-five men—at a steady trot whenever the rough terrain permitted. After some six or seven miles he signaled a halt and called his officers to join him.

"Damn it," he said irritably, "we're getting noplace. I'm going to quit this valley-hunting and go back. There's only one thought in the general's mind: that the Indians are going to get away from him and he won't find his fight. What do you fellows think?"

"You won't find any Indians in this kind of country, that's sure," exclaimed Richards of K company.

Harrod nodded agreement.

"If you'd been given any definite orders, Harry," he began.

"That's the damn trouble!" snapped Bellew. He turned to his lieutenant. "Myron, take a couple of men and go on to that next ridge. Signal if you see any Indians or any sign of 'em. If not, come back and we'll try to catch up to the regiment. If Tuthill's run into anything, he might be glad to have us."

Myron's report was negative and the three companies turned

back to the north along the course of a shallow valley between the sage-covered hills. Travel was less difficult there and in an open space they encountered a marshy area which was the source of a small stream of clear water, uncontaminated by alkali, where the thirsty horses got their first drink since the night before. They cut the trail of the other companies and Bellew stepped up the pace and maintained a fast trot over the five miles to the Little Big Horn where the valley of the dry creek widened to meet the river. The hills fell away on either hand and, with the sudden shock of a plunge into icy water, they were on the rim of battle.

Beyond the river a thin line of troopers was racing toward the stream through a gantlet of Indians so closely grouped that they seemed like massed formations. Other soldiers had reached the water; some were still crossing through a deep ford, others were struggling toward the summit of a steep hill on the right bank. A few had already reached the crest and had opened fire in an effort to cover their comrades' retreat. Yellow dust eddied and swirled and rifle fire laced the clouds with crimson spears.

"Jesus God!" The oath was torn from Bellew's lips before he could frame his commands to his battalion.

"To the rear, ho!" he roared. "Harrod! Take the lead! Reinforce 'em on the bluffs. Charge!"

There was a half-minute of wild confusion as the files reversed their direction. Horses collided, reared, and kicked; men cursed as a comrade's carbine slammed them across the shin; hats were lost, and then, as the experienced noncoms quickly took charge, the three companies had reversed position and direction and were charging toward the hilltop. The Indians fell back as the reinforcements advanced. At the summit Harrod swung from his saddle almost into the arms of Captain Wyatt of M company. Instinctively they clasped hands.

"God Almighty, Demas, am I glad to see you!" Wyatt exclaimed.

"It looks like we got here just in time, Bill. What happened?"

"Tuthill sent us across the river. We got jumped by God knows how many hostiles and we got the hell kicked out of us. That's what happened."

The officers and first sergeants hastily placed the men—the six companies numbered slightly more than two hundred—in position for the defense of the hilltop. Bellew shouted an order to his lieutenant, Myron.

"Get back there"—he waved his hand to the south and east—"as fast as you can before they've got us surrounded. Get Jerry Hanford and the pack train up here on the high lope."

"My horse is pooped, Captain. He won't——"

"Take mine," Harrod exclaimed. "I won't be going anywhere!"

He stooped to grasp the dangling reins nor noticed the bullet that buzzed past his head and splashed into the hard-baked soil. Myron vaulted to the saddle and raked the big chestnut's flanks with his spurs. Harrod scarcely heard Bellew's words.

"God Almighty, Demas, that was close!"

"What was close? Myron's all right."

"Not him; you! You grabbed for those reins and the stooping saved you." His toe touched a furrow in the dirt. "That missed you by about two inches."

"Just as good as two miles!" Harrod shrugged. The upper buttons of his shirt were open and he thrust the Saint Sebastian medal back within the V as he hurried along the line and instructed the men to share their cartridges with Marcus' troopers who had shot away nearly their entire supply. Two officers and twenty-five men had been killed when Marcus' advance was checked and he turned in headlong retreat to the river. Harrod found the major with two troopers stripping the saddles from the horses and dumping the reserve ammunition from the saddlebags. Marcus straightened his back and stared downstream.

"Things aren't quite as hot, Harrod. A lot of the reds are heading down the river, to the north."

"How many were you up against over there?" Harrod shook the boxed carbine ammunition from a pair of saddlebags and tossed them aside.

"God knows." Marcus shook his head. "Five hundred, maybe six hundred, and more coming up every minute. One thing sure, we were hopelessly outnumbered. I had a hundred and twelve men, Demas, a hundred and twelve. 'Charge 'em,' Tuthill said, 'and the whole outfit will support you.' There wasn't any support, then or now. Where the hell is Tuthill anyhow?"

That question was asked many times by the harried men on that hilltop. The troop horses and the mules of the pack train were picketed in a more or less level area between two of the ridges. There was little or no protection for them and more than sixty animals were killed by the fire of the hostiles from the surrounding hills. Hardtack boxes were stacked one upon another and covered with shelter tents as some protection for the wounded, of which there were nearly fifty. There was only one surgeon—barrel-chested Dr. Heinkel with a voice like a drum major's and a hand as gentle as a woman's—to care for them. Hanford's company and the men of the pack train—six men and a corporal from each of the twelve companies—had increased the defending force to more than four hundred. These were extended in a pathetically thin line around the higher points. There, as long as there was light, they were exposed to the fire of hundreds of Sioux and Cheyennes.

The hostiles were well supplied with rifles and ammunition and made up in volume of fire for what they may have lacked in accuracy. Return fire was almost impossible. The Indian method was to rise suddenly from behind a clump of sage or other protection, fire one shot, and instantly to drop out of sight. Nor did any man among the besieged troopers attempt to guess the number of hostiles who faced them, although a few remarked that there were many, many more than had op-posed them when they first gained the hilltop.

The firing did not cease until it was too dark for a marksman, red or white, to see the muzzle of his rifle, but there was little rest for the weary men. Darkness brought some relief for the wounded, and more was afforded when four or five men cautiously descended the hill and filled canteens at the river. It was after one of those expeditions that First Sergeant McNamara, of G, sought his company commander, Captain Clements.

"I have a bit of news that may interest you, sir."

"I'll listen if it's good," Clements growled.

"That recruit, Dugan——"

"The troublemaker! Don't tell me he's deserted to the Sioux, First Sergeant?"

"No. It's the last thing you'd expect, sir. He volunteered to go after water and made two trips up from the river luggin' canteens. Then he went down again, but came back to me and said he couldn't make it alone, that he'd need help. 'Help with what?' I says, and you could have knocked me over with a feather when he said, 'With Lieutenant Hardy's body.'

"He—Lieutenant Hardy, I mean—was killed just this side of the river. Dugan had seen him fall, he'd knocked off two 'r three Injuns that had sneaked up to take the scalp, and as soon as it was dark he'd gone down and had carried him, all alone, a third of the way up the hill."

"Dugan did that! God Almighty, why?" exclaimed Clements.

"Exactly what I asked him, sir. Will y' forgive me, Captain, if I give you his answer exactly as he gave it to me?"

"Go ahead, First Sergeant."

"He said"—McNamara drew a deep breath—"sir, what he said was, 'The son of a bitch was one of my officers, wasn't he? Did you expect me to let one of those sons of bitches scalp the son of a bitch?'"

A full minute passed before Clements could speak. Then: "Get the names of all those men who went after water for the wounded, First Sergeant. Including Dugan, of course. If we get out of this mess I'm going to recommend all of them for the Medal of Honor."

7

To the north, beyond the girdling hills and the river, the lights of many fires were reflected against the sky; the night wind carried the cadenced throb of Indian drums and the faraway sound of chanting voices.

"Scalp-dancing," said Major Marcus bitterly. "Dancing the scalps of my poor devils who got killed in the valley. It will be light in three or four hours—light enough for a man to point a gun—and they'll be back after us. Goddam it, gentlemen, why haven't we heard from Tuthill?"

"I wish I could tell you," Bellew answered. "If you want my opinion, as a soldier of some experience, Tuthill made the mistake of his career when he split the regiment up the way he did. What do you think, Roger?"

Clements nodded.

"It was just luck that brought you back in time to save our skins, Harry. My opinion is that Tuthill ran into the Indians further down the valley. There was heavy firing down there just as we pulled back and reformed to head for this side of the river."

"I heard it too," said Major Marcus.

"You got up here almost as soon as we did, Harrod. Did you hear it?" Clements asked.

"No, or if I did I paid no particular attention. The Indians were firing and our men were shooting back."

Bellew bit the tip from a cheroot and placed the unlighted cigar in his mouth.

"You were at Wishbone Creek, weren't you, Demas?" he asked. The pause was more suggestive than any question.

"I know what you're thinking about, but there were only nineteen men left behind there, you know."

"Nineteen men or seven companies, the idea's the same. I'll bet that Tuthill ran into the Indians below here, got licked, and started running for the Yellowstone and the Montana column. We'll have to fight our own way out of this jam tomorrow—Tuthill won't come for us. Am I right?"

"If I'm being asked," said Demas Harrod slowly, "you're right."

15 *DIES IRAE*

Colonel Tuthill waved cheerily to Major Marcus and, with the same motion, signaled the company commanders in his battalion to follow him. Twelve officers and some two hundred men were with the five companies which turned to the north along the slope of the sage-grown hills. Chance of position placed the companies in alphabetical order as they would form in regimental parade. In the lead, behind Tuthill and his adjutant, was Company C under Captain Arnold Wisenant and Lieutenant Parvin. Then came E, Captain Nason and Lieutenant Freeman; F with Walter Blake, acutely aware of his new captain's bars, and Lieutenant Burton Chance. Behind F was Company I, Captain Chase and Lieutenant Berthold, and finally L, Captain Lamar Steele and Lieutenant Travers.

Tuthill increased his lead until he was nearly a hundred yards in advance of the leading files of C company. Beside him was his adjutant, Clagett, and a horse length behind the two were the regimental sergeant major, the orderly Morelli, and a sergeant who bore Tuthill's headquarters flag, the swallowtailed guidon with crossed sabers. Sol Rogers, astride a skewbald appaloosa with a white, rolling eye, rode a dozen paces to Clagett's left. He studied the ground closely.

"Any tracks, Sol?" Tuthill shouted.

"Some, but nothin' that's less'n a week 'r so old. We seen some of them Injuns back at th' gulch, Gen'ral. Th' rest of 'em ain't far away."

"I hope not." The commander grinned. "Let's keep moving."

He turned in the saddle, raised his fist above his head, and pumped it up and down swiftly as a sign to the company commanders to step up the pace. Little of Tuthill's fear that the hostiles might escape and that the Twentieth would be denied a fight had been communicated to the men in the ranks. They rode at ease, talking occasionally as the pace permitted or speculating as to the possibilities of a battle. A very few puffed at their pipes or rolled a chew of tobacco in their cheeks. The day was intensely hot and the canteens which had been filled the night before at the Rosebud were empty now. A thirsty man finds little comfort in tobacco.

Sergeant 'Dolph Kenton, riding beside the leading file of C company, pushed aside the bandanna which covered his face and shifted his bridle reins until they hung from his little finger. He spat, not without difficulty, in the palm of his left hand, gathered the spittle on his right forefinger, and rubbed it in his nostrils.

"That goddam sagebrush," he said aloud, "on'y stinks after a rain or when it's baked dry, like today. Some folks claim they like the smell of it—I say it stinks all times."

The trooper grunted. His horse had a rough trot; he had ridden without rest since early that morning; and he had little interest in the sergeant's olfactory dislikes.

"What the hell time is it? 'Way past noon, I'll bet—and I'm hungry as hell."

"Take a pull at your belt," the noncom advised. "You'll be a sight hungrier than you are now 'fore we eat. Look at Old Eagle-beak—he smells a fight."

He gestured toward Tuthill who, at the moment, pulled off his broad-brimmed white hat and mopped his forehead with a filthy handkerchief. The colonel checked his charger until the companies caught up with him, then spoke to the captains.

"The river's over the next rise, gentlemen, and we ought to see the whole village from there and know what we're up against. Marcus must be on the other side by now and he'll give them something to think about."

He jingled the spur on his heel and the charger moved forward. The company commanders followed and were closely grouped as they reached the rounded crest and looked down upon the winding channel of the Little Big Horn, here some fifteen or twenty yards wide. The hillside pitched away swiftly from where they stood, but the opposite shore was level benchland which seemed to sweep without noticeable break to the distant mountains. From north to south along the bench were scores, hundreds, and still more hundreds of conical tepees. Clagett whistled between his teeth.

"By God, Sol, you were right!" he exclaimed. "It's the biggest village that was ever brought together."

There was a note of wholesome respect, if not of anxiety, in his words, but Tuthill smacked his saddle pommel with his palm.

"We've caught 'em! Not a warrior in sight, by God. Marcus must be attacking down below and they're going after him. We'll hit 'em from this side and it'll be Wishbone Creek all over again!"

The adjutant whispered swiftly to the scout.

"What do you think, Sol?"

The other's jaws worked slowly. He spat cottony saliva before he spoke.

" 'Bout th' same 's I thought at sunup this mornin'. There's a God's plenty of Injuns down there an' 'bout two hundred of us, mebbe a little more'n three hundred countin' Marcus' bunch. There's due to be one hell of a fight this afternoon, Bill. There's got to be."

Tuthill stood in his stirrups and let his eyes follow half a dozen mounted warriors who were racing to the north, downstream, through the heavy growth of cottonwoods that fringed the river. He watched until they and the remainder of the village were hidden by the hills that rose in his right; then turned and surveyed the terrain over which he would make his fight.

Before him, the hillside fell away in a gulch that deepened and widened as it approached the river. This, Sol Rogers remarked to Clagett, was known to the Sioux as Medicine Tail Coulee; the area on the western bank of the Little Big Horn, where the tepees stood, was called Chedi Asdaya—the Greasy Grass—no man knew why. Tuthill stared to the rear over the bay rump of his charger, Danny. Behind him was a shallow depression which rose gradually to the next crest on the east, and within that almost imperceptible hollow were the five companies. The colonel nodded decisively. He pointed toward the river and the village on the further bank. His voice rattled like a Gatling gun.

"We'll hit 'em there—straight down the gulch and across the river. Nason with E company will take the advance. Command will follow, then C and F. Chase, Steele, hold your companies where they are now as a reserve and move forward to this point when you hear us open the ball down below. Is that clear?"

There were no questions and he continued, swiftly, confidently.

"Very well, very well. C and F companies will deploy right

and left at the river. Maintain formation. Give the horses a chance to drink but don't let them break. After we're across the river, I'll give C and F one minute, no more, to form on E. Guide will be center on the headquarters guidon. All clear? Are there any questions? Rejoin your companies, gentlemen. C and F close on E and we'll advance immediately. There are plenty of Indians, gentlemen, but we'll handle 'em, all right."

He watched the captains rejoin their companies, then gathered his reins. His right arm rose high above his head, then dropped to the horizontal.

"Forwarrd—ho!" he barked.

Nason of E repeated the command.

"E company. Forwarrd—ho!"

Tuthill with his staff fell in behind E and were followed by the men of C and F. A cheer rose from those who remained behind. Rogers drove his heel into the appaloosa's ribs and loped across the valley toward L company. Scarcely five minutes had passed since the adjutant had commented on the size of the hostile camp.

2

Steele cantered easily across the swale toward L company and dismounted beside his lieutenant, Travers, and First Sergeant Hastings.

"We're in reserve," he said, "along with I. We'll move forward to the ridge as soon as we hear firing——"

"That'll be now, then." Young Travers' smile apologized for the interruption. "Haven't you heard it?"

Steele's head rose sharply. From the south came the faraway rattle of musketry.

"Guess my ears are sand-packed," he grinned. "That's Marcus. How long——"

"Close to ten minutes, I'd say, sir," the first sergeant answered. We heard it first just as you went forward."

"Rifle fire," said Steele slowly, "and plenty of it. They're afoot already."

"That's how I figured it," the noncom agreed. He and his captain were veterans of the Civil War. Travers, a year out of West Point, was on his first campaign. "It's close to five miles. We wouldn't even hear a pistol."

"No." Steele's face was grave. "There's one hell of a big village down there along the river, Hastings; wait till you see it. I hope to God that Marcus hasn't run into more than he can handle."

"He'll be counting on the general to support him," said young Travers quickly. "That was the last thing he said when Major Marcus left—'the whole outfit will support you.'"

The captain and his first sergeant exchanged glances. They had ridden knee-to-knee at Wishbone Creek eight years before.

"Yes, so he did," Steele remarked. "Remind me some time, Travers, to tell you about another major of this regiment—a fellow named Harris."

The boy gulped.

"I've heard of him, sir. He was killed at Wishbone Creek. I —I think I know what you mean."

"Maybe you do. When you're sure you know, and profit accordingly"—Steele's jaws snapped like a trap beneath the roan stubble of his whiskers—"then you'll be pretty damn close to being a soldier, young fellow."

Hastings hawked noisily and spat. The saliva was speckled with the yellow dust that clung to his lips. His hand touched the canteen on his hip, then withdrew.

"I can go a little longer. I'll be a sight dryer 'fore this day's over. There'll be a fight, Captain?"

Steele's eyes swept the ridge line. C company's files had entered the ravine and the gray horses of F were crowding on their heels. Rogers rode up and dismounted. He pulled a rag from his pocket and wiped the dust from about the breech of his heavy rifle.

"Sergeant Hastings just asked me if there'd be a fight, Rogers," the captain said dryly. "What's your opinion?"

"Old Eagle-beak is takin' it to 'em," he said softly. "Sarge, there's more Injuns 'crost that river than I ever saw or heard of. There's due to be one hell of a fight, if you're askin' me, but th' gen'ral's sure he's gonna lick 'em."

"He's always sure," snapped Steele. "There's such a thing as being too damn sure in a fight." A vagrant breeze bore to their ears an increased tempo in the firing to the south. "Sounds like Marcus is getting his share of it."

"Yeah. I heard it as I was ridin' over here." The scout's face was expressionless. "He's bunched up—sounds like he's makin' a stand."

"Maybe he's got the right idea," said Steele. "Tuthill has seen his Injuns. He's forgotten Marcus and any notion he ever had of supporting him. It shouldn't be long now. There goes F, which means we'll be moving forward in a couple of minutes. Turn loose that locomotive whistle of yours, Hastings, and I'll signal Captain Chase."

Hastings grinned, stuck two fingers in his mouth, and blew a piercing note. Chase, I's commander, turned to face them. Steele whirled his hand above his head in the "Assembly" signal, then pointed toward the ridge and held up five fingers, widespread. Chase waved acknowledgment and Steele turned to his first sergeant just as young Travers screamed.

"Jesus! Oh, Jesus Christ!"

3

E company had passed from sight in its descent of the coulee which Rogers had called Medicine Tail. C followed and the last files of F were at the head of the ravine. Two bands of mounted Sioux and Cheyennes, each counting several hundred warriors, swept over the northern rim like a gaudily painted avalanche. The first struck E and the leading files of C, crashed through the column, wheeled on the opposite slope, and returned to strike again. The second band smashed squarely into F.

The red tide struck and rolled over some one hundred twenty-five men and seven officers in the three companies and headquarters detachment under Tuthill's immediate command. Not one of them was prepared for the attack. The revolvers were holstered, the rifles were in the boots on the left side of the saddles. A number of the Indians had rifles, but few attempted to use them in those first moments of charge and counter-charge. The ideal weapon under those conditions was the bow, the short, heavy, sinew-backed bow of the Plains tribes, and the broad-pointed arrows which any one of the warriors could drive halfway through a running buffalo. Cavalry chargers reared, squealed, and plunged madly in sudden terror. Men were thrown from the rearing horses and as a man scrambled to regain his feet the nearest mounted Indian swooped upon him and split his skull with a stone-headed warhawk.

For the first time in the long history of the Indian Wars, the blue-clad soldiers found the allied Sioux and Cheyennes eager to fight, to meet the white men face to face in smashing attack and not in the hit-and-run, feint-and-withdraw, charge-and-sweep-aside maneuvers which Indians usually followed. True, the red men had employed the only tactic—the ambush—which they understood; true, they outnumbered their white enemies five or six to one and their force was constantly augmented by new arrivals who raced madly across the river at one of the several fords and flung themselves gleefully into the fight; but they attacked as Indians never had attacked before and they drove home that attack in cavalry maneuvers which would have done credit to a Stuart or a Sheridan.

Fully half of the cavalrymen were thrown or leaped from

their saddles within a matter of seconds after the first charge struck. The cavalry mounts, many of them ripped by arrows, reared in frenzy, "cold-jawed," and ran. Men swung to the ground rather than be carried into the midst of the massed Indians by a frantic, uncontrollable horse. The troopers fired the single cartridge which their carbines held, reloaded if possible, or clubbed the weapons and swung ineffectively at the nearest mounted warrior or squealing pony. Others dropped the empty Springfields and drew their revolvers. These were weapons far more suitable for a hurly-burly fight, but few of the troopers had fired more than a dozen rounds or so in practice on the ranges at Fort Doniphan. They learned that a cardboard silhouette is one target; a painted, grimacing warrior, dimly seen through whirling dust or striving to ride down the man with the gun, is another.

Tuthill's big charger was not hit nor was the colonel dismounted. He swung the horse about and spurred madly toward the rear of the shattered column. His shrill voice rose above the screams of the Indians like the blast of a cavalry trumpet.

"Dismount! Dismount and fight on foot! Keep together, men. Bunch up, back to back, and we'll break these red devils and get out of this!"

Two men of C company, obedient to command even in the heat of conflict, strove to link their horses as regulations required for dismounted action, the bridle of one to the cantle of the other's saddle.

"Let 'em go, goddam it!" Tuthill roared. "Grab the ammunition and let the horses go!"

He swung far to the side and avoided the sweeping blow of a warhawk in the hand of a Cheyenne whose face from brow to chin was painted a brilliant yellow, then shot the man through the belly with one of the short-barreled English revolvers he carried. He snapped a second shot at another Indian and had the satisfaction of seeing the man stagger and pitch forward. The warhawk dropped from his lifeless hand a few inches from the skull of the little Italian, Morelli, who had been assigned that morning as Tuthill's orderly. *Funny how one's mind recognized faces and recorded action even when the fighting was hottest. That rebel captain at Yellow Tavern. I shot him full in the face. I saw his nose split, half of it to either side, in a rush of blood. His hands dropped to his side and he fell, first from the saddle and then to the ground, just as slowly as a big tree would fall. Why should I remember that now?* He shouted encouragement to Morelli but did not hear the soldier's reply.

" 'Merican, me! Goddam Injuns!"

A second Sioux leaned over his pony's withers and brained the little man as Tuthill guided the racing charger along the line of what was left of F company. He recognized Blake and his first sergeant, Mullins, and holstered his revolver and swung to the ground. As he left the saddle, he swept his Remington sporting rifle from its scabbard. He smacked the big bay charger on the rump.

"Run like hell, Danny." Again his voice rose. "Close on me, men. Fall back slowly and keep together."

The charger trotted away for a few strides, then turned and whinnied shrilly. There was no swifter horse in the regiment than Tuthill's bay Danny, and a soldier in the little group around Blake leaped to his feet and snatched for the horse's bridle. The bay threw his head back and the man's hands missed the reins by inches.

"Whoa, boy, whoa!" he screamed, but the charger broke into a trot.

"Whoa!"

The man ran toward the horse. He did not notice that every stride took him further from the little band of soldiers and closer to the Indians. Then, suddenly, he realized that he was alone. He checked his flight so swiftly that he fell to his knees, then rose and started back toward his fellows. A Sioux rose from behind a clump of sage and leveled a rifle. He had risen to his full height, however, and before he could press the trigger a ball from Tuthill's Remington crashed through his chest. The trooper gained a few steps, then fell as another Indian, well hidden in the brush and scarcely three yards distant, shot him through the knee. The man dragged himself on, whimpering, his shattered leg trailing behind him, then sprawled again as a second bullet tore through his body. He died slowly, but none of the fighters, white or red, paid heed to him or to the name he called, over and over.

"Grace! Grace!"

Tuthill dropped beside Blake who was crouching behind a dead horse.

"Did you see that—the man who tried to catch Danny and get away? Who was he?"

The new captain put a ball from a Springfield carbine through the brain of a troop horse that had either been hamstrung or had taken a bullet through the spine. Its hind legs were flat on the ground, it was supporting itself on rigidly braced forelegs. The 500-grain ball cut off the indescribable scream of a horse in agony. Blake deliberately extracted the empty shell and thrust another into the chamber. Two men crawled quickly to the protection of the still-twitching charger.

"I don't know, General," Blake replied at last. "Yes, I do too. Gentry—he didn't want to go to the pack train this morning."

Time had ceased on that hillside. None of the men who crouched there knew how many seconds or minutes had passed since the screeching hostiles had swept over the crest or out of the brush-shielded coulees and ravines where they had been hiding. The first fury of the Indian attack had abated for the moment. Many of the red men were engaged in killing the wounded troopers who lay in Medicine Tail Coulee or on its slopes. The dead, and the wounded who were killed, were stripped mother-naked. Their pockets were rifled and articles such as rings and watches were transferred to the medicine pouches of Sioux and Cheyenne. Money, especially greenbacks, was tossed on the ground. Revolvers and carbines which had fallen from the dead troopers' hands were collected and turned against those who still lived. Other Indians rounded up the unwounded or slightly wounded troop horses and drove them toward the village.

Some thirty men, as well as Tuthill could count those who lay behind the hastily contrived barricade of dead horses, remained of the three troops. Thirty men and two officers, himself and Blake. No, by God, there was another, a man with a lieutenant's bar on his shoulder straps. He was crawling toward them, crawling and dragging a couple of carbines and a pair of saddlebags. Only one man in the United States Army possessed whiskers like that, whiskers which drooped from either cheekbone to below the point of his shoulders.

"Clagett!" Tuthill shouted, and the other raised his head and grimaced horribly. A hideous raw wound scarred his right cheek.

"Reporting, sir!" he said and snapped a quick shot at an Indian who rose from a clump of sage. Blood dripped steadily from the wound on his cheek.

"Clagett! My God, what happened to you?"

The adjutant managed to grin. He had been thrown and stunned, he said, when his horse had been killed, but had been restored to consciousness when an Indian "scalped" one side of his luxuriant whiskers.

"He was stooping right over me," he said, "and I got my pistol out and shot him smack in the mouth!"

The men in that little group knew that they could do no more than sell their lives as dearly as possible. There was none to rescue them and retreat was impossible. Wisenant, C's commander, lay dead some fifteen feet beyond the dead horse behind which Tuthill crouched. A broad-pointed hunting arrow had driven through his thigh and pinned him to his saddle. As he wrenched loose he had fallen from his horse. Two troopers had grasped him about the shoulders and had attempted to carry him a few yards. When Wisenant died in their arms, they were crimson from waist to ankle with the blood which gushed from the severed femoral artery.

Tuthill edged to where Clagett squatted. The adjutant now had four carbines and was firing them methodically one after another whenever an Indian showed himself for an instant.

"Chase and Steele," Tuthill panted. "I'd been hoping they might——"

"No chance. They're pinned on that other ridge just as we are here. There's a thousand Indians between us and them. You'd see if this goddam dust would settle."

"Yes." Tuthill gulped a couple of swallows from his canteen and passed it to his adjutant. "This is it, Clagett. We've got ten minutes more—maybe."

"Maybe," Clagett repeated. He lowered his rifle, pulled a fat gold watch from his pocket, and snapped open the case. "Jesus!" he exclaimed. "The whole business—from the time you rode up and looked down at the village—has been less than an hour!"

"An hour!" Tuthill repeated bitterly. "An hour to wipe out the best damn regiment in the army! Always before, whenever I went into a fight, I knew that I was coming out all right. I didn't get that feeling today. I should have——"

The sentence was unfinished. A bullet struck him over the left eye and he fell.

"They got him!" The whisper ran from one man to another of the few who were still alive. "They got Old Eagle-beak!"

Clagett lowered Tuthill's body as Blake rallied the men.

"Keep firing, men, keep firing. If they're going to rub us out, make 'em pay for it!"

The troopers tried to obey, but they died one by one as the Indians swept the little group with gunfire and arrows. The Springfield carbines overheated and a hasty stroke of the lever permitted the extractor to jump the rim of the case and leave it in the chamber. Soon the men had only their revolvers to depend upon and the Indians became bolder as the troopers missed shot after shot with those weapons. Horsemen drew closer, eager to count coup on a white man. They dashed in and out and exposed themselves recklessly to the fire of their fellow tribesmen. The rifles—many of them snatched from the hands of the soldier dead—boomed, the gut bowstrings twanged, the terrible, silent warhawks rose and fell.

4

The officers and men of L and I stood in frozen silence for a few seconds. It was as though they watched a distant stage on which the scene changed instantly from light drama to stark tragedy. At one moment the gray-green slopes lay bare in the sunlight; the only movement was that of the horses of C and F companies as the riders wheeled into the column. Then, while a watch might tick thrice, the bare hills exploded in a flood of naked, screaming horsemen. The Indians held no formation; if there was order or direction to guide their charge it was imperceptible to Steele and Chase and their men. Even the impression that the attackers were in two bands was due to the circumstance that some rode to the right of a low knoll, others passed to the left.

The hostiles who swept over Tuthill and his three companies were reinforced every moment by other arrivals who scrambled up the steep slope from the river or raced around the hills to the north of the battleground. Every gulch and coulee, every sagebrush-screened hollow, was a hiding place of Indians who now rushed to the attack. Within seconds the new arrivals were massed between the detached companies under Chase and Steele and their oppressed companions less than half a mile away.

Chase's lips parted in the order to mount, but he realized

instantly that it would be suicidal for his thirty-six men to charge five or six hundred Indians, and he shouted the command to fight on foot. Steele, a hundred yards to his left, interpreted the situation in the same manner and gave identical orders. Both men, however, obeyed automatically the army regulations for the conduct of cavalry in dismounted action— the horses must be turned over to horse-holders, one for every four animals. Nine or ten men were thus taken from the firing line of each of the companies.

Sol Rogers, the scout, glanced quickly to right and left. *Jesus John God, there were Injuns everywhere! Man couldn't run—there wasn't no place to run to!* Over his shoulder he heard Steele's voice, as steady as though he was drilling his men on the parade ground at Fort Doniphan.

"That's right, men. Bunch up. Keep down and shoot low. Take your time."

The scout stripped saddle and bridle from his appaloosa and slapped the animal on the rump with his big hat. He flung himself prone behind the inadequate shelter of the saddle and pulled the saddlebags into a position convenient to his hand. In those bags were seventy-odd rounds of ammunition for the heavy-barreled buffalo gun which he had taken from the dead hands of Jim Woodard in the Black Hills. *Goddam, looks like there's twice as many Injuns as when I smacked th' appaloosa over th' tail. Over yonder they're givin' Old Eagle-beak hell an' repeat, but right here they're hangin' back. They want th' hosses; they're waitin' till some of 'em get 'round th' flank an' stampede 'em—afterward they'll take on th' men. Wish Chase w'd pull up closer.*

He drew back the hammer of his rifle and set the trigger. One sighting shot—he drew a bead on a warrior, touched the trigger, and peered through the pall of white smoke which belched from the muzzle. The ball kicked up the dust five yards short of the target. He'd never seen Indians fight like this, bunching up and charging like cavalry. They were sure of themselves, just as sure as old Red Cloud and his boys had been when they wiped out Fetterman in '66.

They were charging down on the close-packed ranks of I company now and he recognized the warrior in the lead—Tall Elk, a Minneconjou of Running Bear's band. Rogers had holed up one winter with them and had dipped stew from the same pot with Tall Elk many times. His first shot sent the pony sprawling and the second killed the Indian. He had time to slide in a shell and fire again as the racing ponies smashed into and over the little group of troopers. One moment there had been twenty-six or-seven men and their officers, Captain Chase and Lieutenant Berthold, who stood bravely against the charge —then there were perhaps ten scattered troopers who smashed at the yelling Indians with their clubbed rifles. Chase was ridden down by a Sioux on a claybank pony, then brained by a second rider.

All this Rogers saw between his carefully placed shots. He saw the horses—I's first, then L's—race madly over the hill. With them, white-faced, were the horse-holders who jerked vainly at the reins to turn their frantic mounts. He glanced over his shoulder and saw that he was almost alone between I—or what had been I—and L company. Steele, holding his men well under control, had withdrawn further to the west and north toward the crest of the ridge. A few dead men marked the path of the cautious retreat, men killed by long-range, plunging fire. One lay with his face squarely toward Rogers, who recognized Eli Crane, the New Englander who'd cooked up such a tasty stew out of that antelope on Powder River. Good man—too bad.

"They'll be rushin' me, an' Steele's boys, in a couple of seconds," he said aloud as he got off another shot and re-loaded. He did not see the Cheyenne who raised a battered Starr carbine and fired at him. The ball struck the receiver of the buffalo gun, smashed the hammer, and tore the thumb and forefinger from the scout's hand as it ricocheted. He clutched his right hand with his left in a futile effort to check the hemorrhage.

"Ain't much use," he told himself. "Here they come! Reckon I'd best take it standin' up."

He rose to his feet as a lone warrior circled his pony in front of the mounted braves. Rogers listened to the screaming challenge.

"*Hoka-hey!*" shouted Crazy Horse of the Oglalas. "It's a good day today, a good day to die! Come with me and ride them down—all of them!"

Crazy Horse, the darling of the Sioux, laid the thong of his quirt across his pony's flank. The wild-eyed beast dashed toward Rogers and the troopers behind him. The other warriors —how many no man knew—followed, their ponies belly-to-earth.

That was the last.

5

All through that Sunday night the drums throbbed in the great village beyond the river. All through the night blood-sated Sioux and Cheyenne warriors danced about the fires and proclaimed their feats of prowess. The naked dead, stripped and scalped, lay where they had fallen. On the battlefield there was only one living thing, a cavalry charger so badly wounded that he was worthless even to an Indian.

On Monday a few Indians renewed the battle about the hill where Marcus and his seven companies were besieged but the Sioux had had their fill of fighting. Besides, their scouts told them that other white soldiers were advancing up the river from the north. Late that afternoon the women struck the lodges, loaded them on the travois, and the entire camp withdrew toward the tall peaks of the Big Horn Mountains.

The beleaguered troopers watched the long column march away into the southwest but they made no attempt to change their position beyond moving themselves and the wounded a few yards to where the stench of dead horses and of dead men—many of the latter still unburied—was less offensive. They clung tightly to the hilltop until Tuesday when the advance guard of the Yellowstone column was sighted. Harrod and two sergeants were sent forward as soon as the distant horsemen were identified as white, not red. They were first to learn that Tuthill, his officers, and every man of the five companies were dead.

The next day, Wednesday, the seven remaining companies of the once-proud regiment moved the few miles to the north and undertook the almost impossible task of identifying the dead who had lain naked in the June sun since Sunday. All but a few officers were identified, but not more than a dozen of the graves of enlisted men were marked. One of these was First Sergeant Barron of E company. Martin Hale found him nearly half a mile from the lower reaches of Medicine Tail Coulee in which his fellows of E company had died. Barron lay across his dead horse and around him were fifteen empty .45-70 cartridge cases, mute evidence that the Sioux had paid heavily for Barron's scalp. Neither of E's officers, Nason and Freeman, was found, although Hale and the other survivors of the company inspected one bloated and blackened corpse after another. Their bodies may have been two of the four which, naked and headless, were found in the abandoned village.

Of the dead, only Tuthill and his adjutant Clagett were truly buried. With the others, officers and men alike, a few shovelsful of earth were thrown over the stripped and mutilated bodies and they were left to the wolves and the buzzards. The burial party marked the graves of those whom it was possible to identify and the entire command hastily retraced its way to the north.

They were badly frightened men. They too had anticipated an easy victory; like Tuthill, their only fear had been that the hostiles would escape the trap which had been laid for them. Instead, "the Murat of the American Army" had been overwhelmingly defeated in a trap which the Indians themselves had set and sprung. The men who worked at the task of burial glanced ever to the horizon for signs of Sioux and Cheyenne who might return for another battle.

They withdrew to the Yellowstone, but they took with them the wounded charger.

Author's Note:

It is scarcely necessary to say that all the characters in this novel, save one, are wholly fictional and not based upon any individual, living or dead. The exception is Colonel Frederick C. Tuthill whose character, personality, and military career are largely those of Lieutenant Colonel George Armstrong Custer, Brevet Major General of Volunteers. The Twentieth Cavalry is the factual Seventh with fictional officers and men; Fort Andrew Doniphan is Fort Abraham Lincoln; South City thus becomes Bismarck, Dakota Territory; the final chapter tells of the Battle of the Little Big Horn as many years of study have made it appear to me.

The fate of Custer-Tuthill and his five companies can be rationalized only as the result of an overwhelming attack, delivered by surprise and in force vastly superior to the twelve officers and some two hundred men who were its victims. This attack shattered the companies and broke them into scattered groups which were quickly overcome.

The decision was deliberate to create a fictional regiment with fictional officers and to place them in a historical frame. The first draft of this novel named Custer, and his brothers,

Captain Tom of C company and young Boston Custer who accompanied the expedition as a foragemaster. Frederick Benteen of H company was named, as were Fort Lincoln, Bismarck, and other actual individuals and places. I soon learned that this necessitated far too many liberties with fact. Not all of the companies of the Seventh were together at Fort Lincoln in 1875; I did not wish to touch on Custer's testimony in the Belknap impeachment proceedings or the resultant feuding with President Grant which almost cost him his command. Nor did it seem logical or permissible to have some units of the regiment under fictional commanders while others were led by factual Tom Custer and Frederick Benteen. Other novels have followed that practice and I have never liked it.

The original manuscript of THE DICE OF GOD *has been deposited in the library of the University of Wyoming.*

HOFFMAN BIRNEY

Western fiction
Black Hills (pre Custer prospecting pp – 191 – 240).